The Piper's Story

Wendy Bergin's novel *The Piper's Story* offers readers a well-crafted, satisfying story featuring rounded and believable characters—including a Nova Scotia Duck Tolling Retriever named Mazie—who become involved in an increasingly bizarre and frightening set of circumstances. This is a story that might be read over a weekend, but the next week would be spent pondering the implications; more than a novel of character driven action, this tale raises some interesting speculations regarding the relationship between creative and destructive energies. I urge you to read it and enjoy for yourself the work of a sóphisticated and mature craftswoman.

Robert R Ward
Editor
Bellowing Ark Press

In my memory I hear the bagpipes, feel the foreboding fog surrounding everything and remember the deep emotions elicited by intense relationships. The compelling juxtaposition between the very current and real events, and the mysterious, surreal happenings, will keep you wishing you could read faster!

Sally Webb
Television writer/producer, retired

Moving, engrossing and as spirited and stirring as the pipes themselves.

William Gilbert
Associate Professor of English
University of Houston-Downtown

The Piper's Story

The Piper's Story

A Tale of War, Music, and the Supernatural

Wendy Isaac Bergin

In memory of my mother, my father, and Layne,

for Neal, who has broken free,

for Nicholas,

and for musicians everywhere

Contents

Wer reitet so spät durch Nacht und Wind?
Es ist der Vater mit seinem Kind;
Er hat den Knaben wohl in dem Arm.
Er fasst ihn sicher, er hält ihn warm.

— Johann Wolfgang von Goethe, *Erlkönig*

Who rides so late through night and wind?
It is a father with his child.
He holds the boy close in his arm,
Grasps him securely, keeps him warm.

Thou art my King, O God; send help unto Jacob.

Through thee will we overthrow our enemies, and in thy Name will we tread them under, that rise up against us.

For I will not trust in my bow, it is not my sword that shall help me;

But it is thou that savest us from our enemies, and puttest them to confusion that hate us.

We make our boast of God all day long, and will praise thy Name for ever.

— Psalm 44, 5-9.

Dunkirk, 1940

I

W hen Ian MacGregor left his young wife Barbara to go to war, he was proud, self-assured, and filled more with eager anticipation than fear. He had never been to France or Belgium, or anywhere outside his native Scotland. In his strength and his youth—he was only twenty-two—he was sure that war was going to be a great adventure. It was, of course, but not the kind he expected.

Nature provided a splendid spring as backdrop for the carnage and destruction. On the bright morning of May 10, 1940, the Germans attacked Holland and Belgium, taking the Dutch, Belgian, and French armies, and the British Expeditionary Force by surprise. Less than two weeks later, Ian MacGregor stumbled alone in a waking nightmare through the beautiful days and the clear, tracer-riddled nights. He was a piper with the 6th Black Watch, but they had left him for dead.

Flanders' fields were for him the plains of hell. Death came by air in the nerve shattering scream of the Stukas, dive-bombing and strafing the ground with machine gun fire. Death came from the German artillery shells exploding left and right, behind and before him. Death came from the Panzers that closed in on the Allies from two sides, leaving them only a narrow corridor open to the sea.

Separated from his division, Ian walked and sometimes crawled through a countryside laced with barbed wire, trenches, dead men and animals, blasted tanks, and smoldering farm buildings. He wandered through deserted villages where meals sat molding on tables, drinks were left half-drunk in bars, and forgotten cigarettes had burned themselves out. Panicked farmers, fleeing the Germans, left their animals to fend for themselves. Cows were unmilked, pigs unfed, and starving dogs roamed the countryside. Ian himself had not eaten for two days, and the only water he had found was in the reservoir of a toilet in an abandoned house. Like many other soldiers, he was dirty, unshaven, and he stank, but unlike them, his staring, bloodshot eyes were not fixed on the outer world, but on an inner hell that he alone could see.

He saw it, but he could not speak of it, because the last thing he had seen had bereft him of his voice and flung him into a state near death, where he had lain so apparently lifeless, that his company, retreating from the Germans in the heat of battle, had thought him dead and left him sprawled in a field with the other slain from their Scottish division.

In the early days of May, when the British Expeditionary Force passed near the sites of battles from other times, Ian began to see visions. He had always had the "sight" as his mother called it. He had had glimpses of the future in dreams. He had had countless reprimands in school for "daydreaming" when the window of time opened for him and he, oblivious of his surroundings, saw past and future events. He had always been sensitive to atmosphere and people: the feel of a room or a place, the character of men, and knowledge of their unspoken thoughts. But the sight had never afflicted him to this degree. In fact, he thought he'd lost his ability, outgrown it, when he'd left his teens. Nothing had come to him for years, until now. Now his visions had force and duration that he had never experienced.

The earth where the BEF marched had been fought over time and again, most recently during the Great War. There were reminders everywhere. There were few trees more than twelve feet high, because the original forest had been blasted to earth. Even the trenches and pillboxes of the Great War remained. And somehow as Ian walked in the present, he saw and heard the past. He saw the army of British, Hanoverians, and Hessians under King George II, fighting the French at the Battle of

Fontenoy where the Black Watch first saw action in another springtime, May of 1745. He heard the deafening roar of the cannons at Waterloo, the screams of wounded men and horses in the charges; he saw the mounds of British and French corpses covered with black flies, and he smelled their stench. As the BEF passed through the trenches and pillboxes of the Great War, Ian saw those battles, too. He heard the pounding of the artillery, the rattle of machine guns, and the music of the proud pipers who had led charges armed only with their pipes and their courage. He was consumed by the sights and sounds and smell of the battles that were for him waking visions, so real that they blocked out the present.

He was helpless under the spell of his visions, blind, deaf and unresponsive. His comrades thought he was mad or shell-shocked, but he was neither. At first he tried to explain what he saw when he entered into a trance-like state, but they thought he was lying or trying to get out of his duties. "Get a grip on yourself, man—Napoleon, the Great War—what in God's name are you talking about? This is May twenty-second, 1940." His lieutenant shook him by the shoulders and shouted, "Get your bloody arse in gear and play us a tune or I'll do the Jerries a favor and shoot you myself!"

So, as the Black Watch and the BEF made a slow retreat north from the pincer grip of the advancing Germans, Ian played his pipes to boost the men's morale.

The last visions he'd had were the worst, because he realized they were glimpses of the future. The men he saw this time wore the uniforms of the present. The time was early evening, and he saw a group of about eighty exhausted British soldiers and one officer who were forced to surrender. The Germans wore the double lightning bolt insignia of the SS. The Jerries herded them into an open-ended barn, a kind of cowshed, outside a village. The space was small, and not all of the men could stand. The British captain protested that there was not enough space to lay the wounded. One of the SS guards retorted, "Yellow Englishman, there will be plenty of room where you're all going to!" Then he hurled a stick grenade into the midst of them. Blood spattered the wall of the cowshed. The German soldiers began firing at will, slaughtering the British with rifles, tommy guns, pistols, and more grenades. Some prisoners were brought outside, lined up and executed at pointblank range. Ian saw terror and tears on the face of one young soldier who could not have been more than eighteen. The massacre went on for fifteen minutes. When the vision suddenly ended, Ian was covered in sweat.

That same evening, taking advantage of a lull in the tremendous barrage of shellfire, even as the Panzers advanced from the south, the men rested momentarily in a cornfield. As Ian sat, resting his aching feet, he was seized with another vision. He suddenly saw a farmyard in a different village where there were more men of the BEF, perhaps a hundred this time, trapped in a flaming barn. As they ran out to escape the fire, they were surrounded by German troops who wore the death's head badge of the SS Totenkopf Division. The Jerries marched the men to the barnyard where they mowed them down with machine guns. The SS walked among the fallen bodies, kicking and prodding them, shooting or bayoneting the survivors. Some of the Jerries were laughing.

The officer in charge, a tall blonde with icy blue eyes, stood off to the left, his pistol drawn. In Ian's vision, there was a murkiness around the man, a dimming of the light. As the shooting went on, the dimness shadowing the officer deepened and coalesced, taking on shape. Ian realized with a start that there was an immense black shrouded figure towering over the German. It must have been ten feet tall. The officer seemed completely unaware that the being stood at his shoulder. While the Germans slaughtered the British soldiers, the being slowly turned and smiled at Ian. It was a terrible smile, pitiless and cruel, and Ian realized that the being took deep pleasure in the murders.

Because the creature was aware of him, Ian suddenly felt spotlighted and completely vulnerable; he had been recognized by something manifestly evil. The creature's eyes projected so much malice and hate that Ian was stunned, for this malignance was not the general enmity of war, it was a direct, personal attack on Ian himself, and it shook him to the core of his being. He was shot through with fear so potent it paralyzed him. The figure lifted an arm and pointed a finger at him. It was the last thing Ian saw.

He collapsed into darkness, and hours later, he awoke in darkness. He opened his eyes, and it was night, and there were no stars or moon. He lay flat on his back, and when he quietly shifted position, everything hurt; he ached all over. His eyes burned and his throat felt raw. He smelled damp earth, and remembered he had fallen in a cornfield. Then he recalled what he had seen, and the fear came back. He was overwhelmed with panic at first, but this time he had no more visions, and after a few bad minutes, he relaxed a bit. He was still tense, but not panicked.

He heard machine gun and artillery fire at a distance, but all was quiet in his immediate area. The fighting had apparently moved on. He heard no voices or movement nearby, just the rustle of the long leaves of the corn as they stirred in the faint breeze. The breeze brought him the smell of smoke from the burning farm buildings. All Flanders seemed to be aflame. The Germans dropped tons of incendiary bombs, and the British burned whatever they could to hinder the approaching enemy troops. Ian thought it strange that he could not see any light or flames from the fires. Nor could he see any tracers, although overhead he could hear the drone of planes.

He sat up and fumbled in his pockets for matches. The night was eerie. The blackness was so intense, he imagined it was like the primeval dark. He finally found the matches and struck a light. The acrid smell of sulfur burned his nostrils, and he felt heat as the match flared. He gasped. The match was lit, but he could not see it. He was blind. When the flame burned his fingers, he tried to cry out, but he had no voice. Though he strained to make a sound, there were stones in his throat; no sound issued from it. He had been struck dumb. The being out of hell had taken his sight and his voice with one stroke of its arm. He felt a surge of nausea.

Christ in heaven, Ian thought, you have given me a load. It'd be easier to be dead. His unit was gone, he was probably behind enemy lines, he was bloody blind, and mute as a fish, sitting in a cornfield somewhere in the blasted heart of Flanders. And to top it all off, he had incurred the wrath of a demon from hell. An uncontrollable spasm seized him and he vomited. The bile in his throat was less bitter than his predicament. What should he do?

He spat and wiped his mouth with his sleeve. Sweat stung his eyes and he blinked. He couldn't stay where he was. The Jerries were routing the British and the French, and his division had been ordered to dig in, then fall back, over and over, in a slow retreat northward. His only chance to escape death or capture was to make his way north. His heart sank. How could he do that, blind, mute, and alone?

It was then that he heard the sound of the pipes. He didn't recognize the tune, but the playing was magnificent. What was a piper doing abroad in the middle of the night? Ian guessed it was the middle of the night, because of the chill and the relative quiet. Well, he thought, whoever it is, it's one of my own. It's got to be a Scottish lad. The damn Jerries don't play the pipes—the pipes put the fear of death in 'em.

He listened with all his concentration. The music had a curious effect on him; there was a kind of duality about it. It calmed his fears and roused his blood at the same time. It seemed close, as though he heard it in his own mind, but distant, too; he knew the source was outside himself, and as he listened, it moved away. It was at the same time wild and strange, and yet it made him think of home.

He thought about his wife, his own brown-haired Barbara. He could see her small, impish face, with dimples and cleft chin. He smiled as he thought about her sauciness and her simple goodness, how she trusted him completely, and he was seized by so fierce a longing to be back in her arms, that he decided then and there that he would make it back. *Don't worry lass, I'm comin' home. There's nothin' can keep me from it. Not war, nor a demon from hell.*

The piper's music grew more distant. Ian felt a real urgency to keep the pipes in earshot, so he hurriedly felt around him for the canvas bag that held his own pipes, found it, and hoisted it over his shoulder. He stood up unsteadily, listening carefully, then struck out in the direction of the sound.

II

On the first day, Ian kept trying to catch up to the source of the wild, strange music, but he never could. It was always a little ahead of him, leading him on, but providing him no human companionship. The piper never spoke to him, and Ian, of course, could neither see nor speak to the piper.

As the hours became days, Ian followed the sound through the hazards of war and the haze of his extreme hunger, thirst, and fatigue. He trudged on through fields and hedges, and over dirt roads that were little more than tracks. He fell repeatedly, stepping into potholes, tripping over ruts and fallen branches, and once over the body of a dead cow. He finally broke off a branch of a tree, stripped it of its leaves, and used it to tap the ground in front of him. The stick helped, but he still stumbled over the uneven ground of fields, and once he fell into a trench from the 1914 war. Another day he slid down an embankment, landing in shallow water. From the push of the current he thought it might be the edge of a canal. Grateful for water of any kind, he knelt down, doused his head and then drank his fill. As he struggled in a direction that he hoped was north, he heard sometimes at a distance, sometimes nerve-shatteringly close, the infernal screams of the dive-bombing Stukas, followed by the explosions of bombs, and the barking anti-aircraft guns of the Allies.

He trusted that the piper was leading him safely past enemy encampments and back to the north toward rescue. On his long, lonely walk he encountered no one; no one called out to him and he heard no voices. It was as if the piper's music enclosed him and sealed him apart from all human contact. Somehow he knew that the source of the music could not and would not bring him harm—only help. So he trudged on doggedly until the sound stopped, and then he dropped in his tracks, immediately asleep until the pipes woke him again.

He knew finally, that the piper was not of this world. As time went on, he began to "see" the piper with his second sight. At first he perceived only a pillar of light. As time passed, the image became a tall being whose face and hair, like burnished copper, blazed with light. His flowing white robe, belted at the waist and his mantle, billowing out behind him, red-gold as the rising sun burned and pulsed like no earthly colors Ian had ever seen. The shining figure of the piper seemed more real in Ian's mind than any piper of the so-called "real world" had ever seemed to his eyes.

The tunes the piper played were melodies of a great beauty and power that Ian had never heard before. The music made him feel small and large at the same time, the way he'd felt once when he visited Culzean Castle, perched on its cliff in Ayrshire. He'd stood on the high rampart looking out over the immensity and impersonality of the vast sea and sky. He'd felt insignificant, and yet another part of him knew that his mind and spirit were even more vast, and could contain the sea and sky. He guessed the tunes were from long ago, when giants walked the earth, and men had powers of mind or expression that were dormant in the present time. Or else the tunes were what music sounds like when it is unfettered by the restrictions of this earth, and mortal ears hear tones of immortality.

The music was irresistible. When the piper played, Ian knew he'd follow him anywhere. He felt he could do anything, overcome any obstacle for pure joy. His spirit grew large and soared, while his inconsequential body, subject to hunger, thirst, and bone-deep fatigue, stumbled behind. The piper became for him a symbol of all that was good in the world, and his love of that goodness grew ever more fierce as he struggled to survive in the hellish conditions of war.

Later, when he tried to tell the story, words failed him. It was like trying to describe the colors of a sunset to one who has been blind from birth. Following the piper and hearing his music was something extraordinary, as elusive as it was powerful, that Ian never experienced again.

As he followed the shining piper across the plains of Flanders, Ian's thoughts returned unwillingly to the ominous black-shrouded being that had shadowed the SS officer. The vision of the cruel murders he had seen was a constant, sad companion on his journey. He knew he had witnessed a future event, but when and where would it take place? Whom could he tell and how could he tell them? He couldn't speak and he couldn't see to write. And who would believe him if he managed to get the message across that two different SS divisions were going to murder almost two hundred British soldiers in two separate incidents in times and places he could not pinpoint or identify?

He shivered when he recalled the intense malice and the near-deadly power that had rendered him blind and dumb—a power that delighted in hurt, destruction, and carnage. Now that the creature was aware of him, and had lashed out and injured him, would it leave him alone? Or would it come for him when the shining piper left him?

Why had he been given the sight of evil and now of light? He had no answers. It was a mystery whose purpose he hoped would stand revealed at a later time. Why he had been chosen for a role in it, he had no idea. His goal at the present was simple, to plod on until he was reunited with the BEF, and somehow to return alive to Scotland. As he thought this, the piper ceased, and Ian stepped off the dirt road and curled up next to a tree, asleep before his head came to rest on the mossy surface of the ground between its roots.

"God in heaven! Look at that enormous tower of smoke! Looks like the whole world is on fire."

"Not the world—just Dunkirk."

"Dunkirk—thank God," said the first voice, a baritone, "Maybe we can find food and water there. I'm hungry enough to eat a dead bloody dog."

Yorkshiremen, Ian guessed by their accents. Why was he dreaming of Yorkshiremen? And why were their voices so loud and rough? In the dream, they were just on the other side of the tree, on the road. He sniffed the air. The salt breeze, overlaid with the acrid stench of smoke from burning oil, made him sneeze three times in quick succession, jarring him awake. He stood up, turned his back to the road and relieved himself, surprised, considering how thirsty he was and how little he'd had to drink, that there was any surplus water in his body.

"Hey, Carrot Top! Got any matches? We've got cigarettes, but no matches. How 'bout a smoke?" It was the baritone again, the lighter of the two voices.

Ian stiffened. The voice was real—he wasn't dreaming. It *was* a Yorkshireman. He had finally met up with the British troops.

He slapped his pockets, feeling for the matches, hoping he hadn't left them back in the cornfield or lost them on the way. He trembled with relief for finding human company, and with frustration that he could not talk to them. He located the matches, took them out of his pocket, turned toward the voice and proffered them, trying to control his shaking arm.

"Well, come on then, man. Come up here and have a smoke." The growling bass voice this time.

Ian started out in the direction of the voices, then remembered his bagpipes and stick. He turned back, dropped to his knees, and began to move his hands side-to-side in the area at the base of the tree. He found his canvas bag and the long, thin branch he'd been using to tap and wave in front of himself to avoid falling and tripping over obstacles.

As he carefully walked back in the direction of the voices, he heard the bass in a harsh whisper, "He's bloody blind! Forget the smokes, Jack. Let's go. He'll only slow us down."

There was a pause before Jack answered quietly, "No. I can't do that, man. What if it was me there blind? I'd want somebody to help me. And by the look of him, I'd say he's come a long way all on his own."

"Right, and he can make it the rest of the way, I say. Let's go."

But Jack reached out and took Ian's arm, saying, "Here's a hand." He guided Ian up the slight incline to the road's surface. Jack took the matches, and Ian heard the scratch-flare sound of the match being struck. He smelled the cigarette and then Jack said, "Hold out your hand and take it. I've lit it for you."

Ian took the cigarette and brought it to his mouth. He inhaled deeply.

"What happened to you?" Jack asked.

Ian blew out the smoke. He pointed to his throat and shook his head. He mouthed the words, *No voice—can't speak.*

The other man said, "Blind and dumb. Well, at least the poor bugger can walk."

"He's blind, not deaf, Ed," Jack retorted in a sharp tone of voice.

Ian heard two more matches struck, and realized the men were smoking, too. They smoked in silence for a few minutes.

"Well," said Jack, "we should make it to Dunkirk by nightfall. The whole damn BEF is being evacuated across the Channel."

They finished their cigarettes in silence. He heard someone flick a cigarette to earth and stamp it out. Then Jack said, "I'm going to take you by the arm, mate. Time to go. We'll never get back to Blighty this way."

The simple human touch of Jack's arm through his almost brought Ian to tears. He wanted to thank Jack, but he couldn't. His emotions pushed against his muteness like tons of deep water against a dam until he thought he would burst. But burst he didn't. He just kept walking toward Dunkirk, grateful for his newfound companions. On the way, Ian learned from Jack that he and Ed had also been separated from their unit, the East Yorkshires. But mostly, they walked in silence, conserving their dwindling energy for putting one foot in front of the other, save when Jack described the scene for Ian or Ed complained.

It was hours later when Ian realized he hadn't heard the piper at all that day.

III

As they neared Dunkirk, the dirt track they followed converged on a main thoroughfare. The larger road was choked with civilians, transports, and troops, practically the whole BEF. In fact, all the roads leading to Dunkirk were jammed with long lines of vehicles and men stretching for miles, like columns of ants converging on an anthill.

"Damn lorries," grumbled Ed. "Down into the bloody ditch again." They had been forced off the road and in and out of ditches all day because of the abandoned vehicles left blocking the road at frequent intervals.

"Can't you look on the bright side?" asked Jack.

"What the hell's bright about bein' forced off the road every two minutes?" Ed retorted. "Instead of walkin' fifteen miles on a flat road through this ugly, featureless country, we're walkin' thirty miles up and down through the bloody ditches. My feet are swollen, my stomach is gnawin' my backbone, and my tongue is coated with dust. No, I can't think of one thing that's bright about the bloody abandoned lorries!"

The next time Ed said "Another damn abandoned lorry," Ian inhaled sharply. He yanked furiously on Jack's arm.

"What is it?" asked Jack.

Ian opened his mouth and tilted his head back, pouring an imaginary drink into his gaping mouth. Then he pointed at the lorry.

"Drinking? Drinks?" guessed Jack.

Ed's voice, pitched in falsetto, was rife with sarcasm, "Oh yes, ladies, time for fuckin' charades."

"Water?" Jack tried, ignoring Ed.

"Bloody bugger's lost his mind," said Ed. "There's no water left in that lorry."

Ian nodded hard enough to scramble his brains, and mouthed, *Ra-di-a-tor! Ra-di-a-tor!*

Jack's face lit up, and he shouted, "Aye, man—he's right! There's water in the bloody radiator!"

Even grudging Ed said, "Well done, you blind bugger!" Ian felt a shocking slap on his back. "You're not a complete waste. With all the radiators between here and Dunkirk, we'll have a bath before it's over!"

The water was warm, brackish, with a metallic aftertaste, but it was water. It eased their raging thirst and filled their empty stomachs; it made them think of the relief to come when they got to Dunkirk.

"Only a little to go before we're there," Jack said, speaking what was on all their minds. They were coming to the limit of their endurance. None of them had eaten a meal in four days, and their fatigue was such that they were almost sleepwalking. They were all silently praying for their ordeal to be over. They were thus all the more appalled when they reached the town at dusk on Monday, May 27, 1940.

Dunkirk was a picture of hell come to life. The streets were paved with broken glass and rubble from the bombings. Burning vehicles littered the roadway. Dazed soldiers, British, French, and Belgian stood in shocked groups, while others roamed drunkenly through the town in gangs. At one end of the town, two million gallons of oil burning in an unquenchable fire sent up a huge column of black smoke that cast a pall over the coastline.

The sandy beaches were scattered with the corpses of men and horses killed there by the constant bombardment of German artillery and the dreaded dive-bombers. No one bothered to bury the dead. Corpses floated in the sea. Far out in the harbor was a motley fleet of destroyers, transports, minesweepers, and launches. "Christ," shouted Ed over the noise of artillery shell explosions, rifle and machine gun fire, "How are we goin' to get to the ships? I can't bloody swim!"

Jack screamed back, pointing to an abandoned house, "Let's go in there and take shelter. We can at least sleep for a while, and maybe there'll be food and water." So they ran, faltering and stumbling in fatigue through the gaping doorway of the half-destroyed brick house, and found stairs that led down to the cellar.

They soon found out that the bombing had destroyed all the water mains, so there was no water in the house or the town. After a search of the kitchen and pantry turned up nothing edible, Ed declared, "I'd trade me own mam for a bite of bully beef." But later, when they cleared a little of the fallen rubble in the cellar to make a space to lie in, Jack uncovered a tin of beets. "There you are." he said, "a bit of good luck."

"Sod it all," said Ed, "I hate beets!"

He ate some, nonetheless, and they all drank some of the beet juice. Afterwards, their sleep was almost as profound as that of the dead who lay scattered in the fields, on the beaches, and in the cold arms of the sea.

The next day, Jack and Ed led Ian to the beach, threading their way around piles of debris, dead horses, dead men, and burning hulks of vehicles. Although the sleep had helped, they were weaving with exhaustion and weakness.

On that day, the sea was as smooth and gray as a polished agate. There were a vast number of ships of all kinds in the harbor, and the large ships were loading men quickly from a long, narrow pier that jutted far out into the sea. In contrast, the loading from the beaches was much slower. Hundreds of exhausted, dirty, disheveled soldiers, some asleep on their feet, stood in queues that snaked from the dunes into water that was shoulder-deep. They had to wait patiently for hours while the small boats ferried a few men at a time from the shallows to the deep water where the destroyers, cross-Channel ferries, and minesweepers lay.

"Thank God for the navy," said Jack.

Ed's reply was drowned out in the scream of a dive-bomber. The sound was deafening. They flung themselves face down into the sand, Jack pushing Ian so that he fell on his face. Close by, they heard the dull thud of bombs muffled by the loose sand. Then the Stuka strafed the beach with machine gun fire. The bullets kicked up spurts of sand all around them.

"Where the hell is the RAF?" said Ed, spitting sand out of his mouth after the plane had made its pass. "We're sittin' ducks on this beach. Only a hundred yards of sea between us and rescue, and God only knows if we'll make it. Tell me what the bright side of this is, Jack."

Jack's mouth was open, but what issued from it was his heart's blood, a red river that flowed into the sea of sand.

"He's dead! The bastards killed him!" Ian head Ed's voice crack. "He's dead, poor sod." Then he added in a low voice, "And he was always thankful."

After a moment's silence, Ian heard Ed pound the sand with his fist "Goddamn them Jerries. If I make it back to England, I'm comin' back soon's I'm able and killin' every last Jerry bastard I can!"

Ian pressed his face into the sand and dredged it from left to right and back with such force that the sharp, tiny grains scraped his forehead. He held his breath and no matter how hard he squeezed his eyes shut, the tears burned their way out. Jack had shown him only kindness and consideration, and now Jack was dead. Ed blamed the Germans, but Ian knew the blame lay with war itself, the infernal slaughter of men by men.

His mind filled with the image of the black-shrouded being he had seen. You, he thought, you delight in hatred and bloodshed. It pleases you that a good man like Jack should be slaughtered on the very beach where he looked for rescue. Ian's anger choked him; his breathing grew fast and labored. He, Ian, had to do something to combat this evil, this darkness, this damnable war. Blind he might be, and voiceless, but he could still defy the black shadow of death that seemed to hold sway over them all.

He reached over and found Jack's body. His hand touched the warm, sticky wetness on Jack's back, then traveled up to his head. Ian rested his palm for a moment on Jack's springy hair. *Thank You, O Lord, for this good man's example. Let his soul rest forever with Thee. In Christ's name, Amen.*

That done, Ian sat up in the sand, and wiped his face with his sleeve. He opened his canvas bag, and took out his pipes. He put them together, stood up, and blew up the bag.

"What the hell d'you think you're doing, you daft, blind Scot?" Ed yelled.

Ian began to march slowly down the beach, playing "Scotland the Brave." He'd only gone fifteen paces when he heard the familiar deep, raucous voice.

"Bloody hell, you fool!" Ed shouted, "You're going the wrong damn way!"

He felt Ed's hand on his elbow, turning him in the direction of the East Mole, the long pier. Ian felt a surge of affection for the gruff, grumbling man whose grief for Jack seemed equal to his own.

Over the powerful sound of the pipes, he heard Ed's harsh voice, close to his ear, "There's no instrument on earth as annoyin' as the pipes. And don't they gall the hell out of the Jerries, too. It's as good as spittle in their damn faces. Play 'em strong, lad."

And Ian did. He set his mind on the vision of the shining piper, and the strength he needed came to him. The pipes were his voice, his challenge to the spirit of war.

His challenge did not go unnoticed.

He heard a ragged cheer go up. "The men are fallin' in behind you, lad. Play! Keep playin'!" Ed told him. Ian was elated. The men began humming the tune, and as more soldiers fell in, the song grew in power.

But suddenly in the midst of his high spirits, Ian felt a chill. The dark presence was near; he knew that the creature was observing him. So it's not over, he thought. Fear, like a huge wave, submerged him. His knees felt rubbery; his heart pounded. But as he strove to keep playing, he thought about Jack, and his anger and defiance overwhelmed his fear. In his mind, he addressed the being: *I know you're there, and I oppose you forever with the only voice I have. I'll not quit playing while I have life and breath.*

For answer, the very air around him closed in and took on weight and chill. Ian felt a cold heaviness and a pressure that almost made him stumble. His flesh seemed to compact itself—his legs were turning to stone, and he feared he could not take another step. He would be frozen in place; he could barely breathe. But then, above and all around him, for just an instant, he heard a phrase of music, wild and strange, and he knew the shining piper was with him.

The pressure lifted and the dark spirit was gone.

Ed gripped his arm fiercely. "What the hell was that?" he roared. "Damn gust of wind nearly knocked me on my arse!"

Ian's playing never faltered, and the soldiers followed him. They marched toward the pier at Dunkirk, their courage roused, their flagging energy spurred by the defiant music of Ian MacGregor's pipes.

CHAPTER 1

The House: Darrow Island, 1994

I t was a brilliant, burnished day in late October, the day they saw the house for the first time. It was the kind of Indian summer day for which pale-skinned northerners pray. Neal and Vicky left their small apartment and drove through Stone Harbor to deliver Owen to his school friend's birthday party. People thronged the streets and basked bare-armed in the sun at sidewalk cafés. The beaches were crowded, and the harbor was a festival of sailboats, speedboats, canoes, and kayaks, navigating in intricate patterns on the bright blue bay.

Vicky's mood, rare and infectious, was as buoyant and expansive as the bride Neal remembered. It surprised the hell out of him. After they dropped off Owen, she declared, "It's too beautiful to stay inside, Neal. Let's go for a drive along the coast." He obeyed, grateful for her spell of good humor.

As they traveled west of Coveland on one of the narrow back roads of the island, Vicky spotted the tall, wood frame house, secluded behind its small, overgrown orchard. "Stop!" she commanded, pointing into the distance with a gesture worthy of an Amazon queen, "I've got to see that house."

Neal parked their old red Mustang at the end of the long, obviously little used driveway. The approach to the house was on one side of the small, neglected orchard with its rows of pear trees, apple, cherry and plum. They passed the tilted *For Sale* sign left by a local realtor and walked all the way around the house.

The three-storey Victorian, painted light blue with white trim, sat on a bluff overlooking the sea. It was built on piers, and there was a broad wooden staircase that led from the yard to a generous wraparound porch. The porch stood four feet above the ground with a lattice skirt of white-painted wood. There were two grand old curved glass bay windows facing the sea in the front, and one on each side, facing the forest, but best of all was the irregular line of the roof, a whimsical mix of chimneys and gables, crowned by a square tower.

The house seemed to Neal like a great actress in the twilight of her life. The vestiges of beauty were there, but age had taken its toll, and over all there was a forlorn, neglected, and somewhat lonely air. The forest of Douglas firs and cedars encroached on two sides, the blue paint was peeling, and the porch had broken and missing boards. The grass was ankle-deep, and blackberry brambles threatened to take over on one side. But the front lawn was open to the sea, and there was a magnificent view of the Strait of Juan de Fuca. The deep blue water threw off sparkles in the sunlight, the air shimmered, and the sky, a paler blue than the sea, arched over it all like a bridge from earth to heaven and back. The property ended at the edge of the bluff, where someone had constructed a narrow wooden staircase to the rocky beach below. Neal knew the house could be a stunner, once someone fixed it up and took care of the yard.

That someone was going to need a lot of money.

When Vicky took off her sunglasses, Neal recognized her I've-got-to-have-it look. "This could be a showplace, Neal," she said. Her eyes crinkled as she smiled in glee. "Our neighbors in Stone Harbor would be so jealous."

"I like the house, too, Vicky, but we can't bankrupt ourselves to buy it."

"Oh, you can figure out a way to swing it," she remarked with a casual air, then climbed the stairs to the porch and peered in a window.

"Maybe I can," Neal cautioned her, although he had already begun his calculations. He would have to go over their finances, seriously and thoroughly, but he gave silent thanks that he had paid off the Mustang and his student loan, and they only had a small amount of credit card

debt. He could use the "tidy sum" his grandfather had bequeathed him for the down payment, but then there were other expenses, like taxes and repairs to consider. Plumbing, wiring, furnace, roof—who knew how much it would all cost? No, buying the house wouldn't be easy on his history teacher's salary, even with Vicky's income as Assistant Manager of Ferraday's Hardware. Nonetheless, he had a strong sense—almost a premonition—that everything would work out and the house would soon be theirs.

As he gazed thoughtfully at the fine old Victorian structure, he was swept with a powerful desire to set the house to rights. He couldn't afford to hire it done; he'd have to do it himself. But he was good with his hands and even though it would take backbreaking work to restore the house, he looked forward to it. He could almost smell the sharp scent of new lumber and fresh paint that would bring the house back into its own.

"Get the camera, honey," Vicky said, back from her inspection. "Let's take pictures of it. Don't forget the view. It's fabulous!" When he returned from the car, she was jotting down the number of the real estate agent.

According to Peggy Williams, the plump, cheerful agent who showed them the house the following weekend, it was built in 1899 by a German, Gunter Fritzinger, who had emigrated to the Pacific Northwest, made a fortune in logging, and constructed the house on Darrow Island. He and his wife Maria had two children, Emily and Heinrich. After Maria died in 1940, Gunter lived in the house with his spinster daughter. When Gunter died in the mid-fifties, Emily lived there alone until her death in December of 1993, when the house was put up for sale. The house had kept its owner company, as Peggy described it, "declining at the same pace as poor old Emily."

They lingered on the porch looking out at the white-capped strait, before entering the house. "This place has such a marvelous setting and view, I'm tempted to buy it myself," said Peggy. "Ocean, forest, and orchard, all in a very private location."

Vicky turned her back to the sea and leaned against the porch railing. Strands of her long blonde hair danced in the wind. "Did Emily really live all alone in this huge house?" she asked.

"That she did," Peggy said. "She was a bit of a hermit; she rarely left the house to go into town or anywhere else, for that matter. She called in an order for groceries every week, and Hollander's delivered it."

"Was she some kind of weirdo?" Vicky asked.

Peggy frowned and shook her head, "No, I don't think so. My cousin Vivian is a nurse with Home Health, and she looked in on her." Peggy smiled, "You know how it is in a village like this—everyone knows everyone else's business. Emily was ninety-two when she died last year, and Vivian saw her regularly for the last seven years of her life," Peggy said. "Emily had some problems with arthritis, but her mind was clear and she was physically active. Vivian thought that Emily was just a shy, nervous introvert who felt uncomfortable around most people. She really seemed to want her solitude."

"Didn't she have any relatives to inherit the house?" Neal asked.

"Not that I know of. Her brother Heinrich moved back to Germany in the late twenties, and I believe he was killed, fighting for the Nazis in World War II. No relatives have come forward in the ten months since she died, and even if they did, Emily left a will that authorizes my real estate company to sell the house, and targets the money left over after our fee and taxes to a children's foundation in Seattle."

"Did she have children?" Vicky asked.

"No, she never married."

"It's strange that she'd leave the money to a children's foundation, isn't it?"

Peggy shrugged, "Emily was an odd bird, but I guess she had her reasons."

"Well, did she have any friends?" Vicky persisted.

"I know she had a succession of cats," Peggy laughed, "but I guess you mean human companions. Aside from Vivian, there was one person, and that came about because Vivian noticed how much Emily loved music. Emily had a grand piano that she played occasionally, even at the end of her life. She also had a large collection of records, and she kept her radio tuned to that classical station in Seattle. Vivian tried to get her to go out to concerts, but Emily refused. So Vivian had a young pianist, a Japanese woman, come out to the house occasionally to play for her, and Emily seemed to get along well with her."

"Was it Yoshiko Katagiri?" Neal asked.

"Yes, that's right, her name was Yoshiko."

"She's such a calm, gentle person; she'd be a good companion for someone as nervous as Emily," Neal said. "She's our son's piano teacher."

"Well, there you go!" Peggy grinned, "You've already got a connection to the house. Now let's take a tour." She extracted a ring of keys from her jacket pocket. "The house was designed by a well-known Seattle architect named Auguste Van Dusen. As you probably know by its tower, gables, and the wraparound porch, it's Queen Anne style. Although its condition has deteriorated, you're in for a treat."

The heavy oak door had a beveled glass window in the upper half, with a single Douglas fir tree design in the center. "The lumber baron gave tribute to the trees that made his fortune," Peggy remarked, as she unlocked the door and they entered into a wide vestibule. *"Voilà!"* she exclaimed, with a one-armed flourish. "Twelve-foot ceilings, fine old wood floors. Good material, good workmanship."

Neal gazed at the wide staircase with its curving balustrade. "Oh, my," he murmured, "she's a real *grande dame,* isn't she?"

"Elegant and dignified," said Peggy. "The front and back parlors are on the left; the dining room is on the right, and the hall past the staircase leads to the kitchen."

Stepping into the large front parlor, Neal remarked, "It's very bright in here."

"Two bay windows will do that," Peggy laughed. "We're on the north side of the house. The front window faces west with a view of the sea, and through the other window you see the side lawn and forest."

"The fireplace is Italian marble," Peggy told them.

"The cream color makes a nice contrast with the dark wainscot," Vicky said. "The wallpaper, though," she grimaced, "is hideous. Is that a scallop shell pattern? It's so faded, I can't tell."

"Its heyday must have been nineteen thirty-nine," said Peggy.

Neal leaned forward, examining the scarred, discolored floor. "That lighter patch in the center of the room must have been covered by a rug. Once it's sanded and refinished, I think it could look great."

Peggy opened the sliding oak doors that separated the two parlors. "This smaller room is the back parlor, Emily's music room, where she kept her grand piano."

"Our entire apartment could fit into these two rooms," remarked Vicky, marveling at the generous space. She told Peggy, "Our place near the naval base in Stone Harbor is a glorified shoebox." She put her hands on her hips and addressed her husband, "If we buy this house, you'd better brace yourself, Neal."

"I know," he said, anticipating her, "we'll have to buy a truckload of new furniture."

Peggy smiled and beckoned, "Onward." She opened the back parlor door, which led into the hall by the staircase. "The bathroom is here under the stairs." Peggy opened the door and showed them a classic claw-foot bathtub.

She led them through the open doorway at the end of the hall. "The best feature of the kitchen, in my opinion, is the breakfast alcove," Peggy said, gesturing to her right. "It has a southern exposure, and the three windows make it airy and bright. Take a look; you can even get a glimpse of the sea."

"I like it. I get a good feeling about this room," said Neal.

"The appliances are old," Peggy said, "but they are all good quality and they work. Emily added an oil furnace in the seventies and she also had the wiring brought up to code."

"Well, that's good news," Neal said. "Does the furnace work?"

"Yes. Emily heated the house with it last fall, but of course it hasn't been used since she died."

After Vicky and Neal peeked into the spacious pantry, Peggy showed them the dining room, which also had bay windows and a fireplace. "This was Emily's bedroom for the last years of her life. She closed off the top floors entirely and lived here on the parlor floor."

"Did she have trouble climbing the stairs?" Vicky asked.

"No, she was mobile enough, according to Vivian. I think it was simply too much house for one person; she didn't need all those rooms upstairs. But," she said with a sly grin, "the house is perfect for a growing family. Let's take a look at the upper floors."

There were three bedrooms on the second floor, all with hardwood floors. "See what I mean?" said Peggy. "Plenty of room for expansion." The master bedroom had a fireplace and an adjoining bathroom. "There are only two rooms on the third floor," Peggy told them, "a fourth bedroom and the tower room. The section above the master bedroom is attic space."

Peggy's color was high and she was puffing a little as they climbed the stairs to the third floor. "Oh, God," she gasped, stopping to catch her breath on the landing, "no wonder Emily closed off this part of the house! And with the dampness, I'm afraid it smells a bit musty and moldy. Take a peek into the bedroom and then I'll show you Gunter's study."

After they viewed the bedroom, which had the same dimensions as the one below it on the second floor, they followed Peggy into the tower room. "You see this could be quite nice with that large window facing the sea," she said, "but unfortunately, Gunter's choice of color makes the room a little dreary."

"That's an understatement," said Vicky.

The walls were painted a deep maroon that had darkened with the years and was now a murky red-brown, mottled in places.

"How awful," chirped Vicky with a laugh as she tapped one wall with a long, red fingernail. "What do you think, Neal?"

He couldn't answer; he couldn't breathe. From the moment he crossed the threshold he felt the muscles of his throat constrict and a tensing in his solar plexus. His pulse quickened and he felt a touch of panic.

"Neal?"

He gasped noisily for air. "I think we need to open the window—the air is too thick in here." The window at first refused to budge, but Neal wouldn't be denied. He smacked it with the butt of his hand and pulled on it until it finally gave way with a shriek. He opened it wide. "There," he said. He leaned out and took in deep draughts of fresh air. "Whew," he said, "that's better." He sat on the windowsill, breathing hard, and looked back into the room.

To his left, in the north wall, there were waist-high cabinets with built-in bookshelves rising to the ceiling above them. A brick fireplace stood on the opposite wall. "Obviously, the architect designed this room to be a study," Neal said. "It's perfect for that, but the atmosphere is oppressive. There's something very—"

"Oh lighten up, Neal!" Vicky interrupted, with an edge in her voice. "Don't go all sensitive on us. The study just needs airing out and new paint. A bright color would transform this room."

"I agree," said Peggy. "Maybe a pale yellow? What do you think?"

As the two women traded redecorating ideas, Neal held his peace. He sensed something out of kilter about the room, something very discordant, which he suspected had little to do with interior décor. But he kept his thoughts to himself as they finished their tour of the house.

Vicky and Peggy chattered like sparrows as they descended the stairs ahead of Neal. He knew that Vicky was ready to move in. His own decision had been made the moment he entered the vestibule—he'd felt it in his gut: he wanted the house. It seemed to him, to his great relief, that the house was only dingy inside, needing paint and wallpaper, and some surface refinishing, but no major structural repairs. The walls and the magnificent old hardwood floors were sound and the furnace worked, although he was a little concerned about heating a house with twelve-foot ceilings.

His only other reservation was the disconcerting moment in the study. His reaction to the room bothered him—it set off alarm bells that he tried to quell. It was only one room out of nine, he told himself; it was distant, away at the top of the house. They didn't even have to use it if they didn't want to, and it would be the last room he would have to renovate anyway. It would be months before he got to it. He wouldn't be spending much time there at all, so how much trouble could it be? And Vicky had it right. A couple of coats of paint would cure the atmosphere.

By the time they reached the parlor floor, Neal was whistling a rollicking reel, tapping one hand against his thigh in rhythm. He was in a hurry to drive home and work out his offer for the grand old house.

CHAPTER 2

A Sea Fog: March, 1995

Neal played the bagpipes just once in the Stone Harbor apartment. He should have known better. By the time he played the third tune, the banging began. He opened the door to find his neighbor's frowning ten-year-old son, baseball cap pulled low, arms crossed on his chest. "Mamma is tryin' to sleep, and she says quit playin' that damn saxophone."

Laying down his paintbrush, Neal laughed at the memory. He opened a beer and sat on the porch. As he later told Vicky, "They're not called the Great War Pipes for nothing. At Dunkirk, Grandfather said the men could hear them over the sound of gunfire and artillery." Playing the pipes, like setting off fireworks, was definitely an outdoor activity. But here in this isolated spot, on his own property, he would bother no one. He could play for himself—when and how long he wanted—with only the sea, the sky, the gulls, an occasional seal, and the blue air for company.

After he and Vicky closed with the realtor the week after Thanksgiving, Neal began restoring the house in his free time, evenings and weekends. Between teaching history at Coveland High School by day and working with his hands by night, he stayed tired. But he was glad of the hard work; the days before Christmas were difficult. December twenty-first was the one-year anniversary of his father's death, and he had lost his grandfather in September. He had endured the first Christmas of his life without either of them, but it was Grandfather's passing that had torn a hole in his heart. He wasn't sure if mending the porch, stripping the faded wallpaper, and refinishing the floors was more therapeutic for the house or its owner. It was slow going, but he made steady progress. He loved the smell of new wood, and there was something very satisfying in restoring the house bit by bit to what he hoped would be its former stately condition.

Vicky, as Assistant Manager at Ferraday's Hardware, bought his supplies at a discount, and brought them home to the apartment or delivered them to the house when she could. She and Owen kept Neal company on occasion, but mostly he worked in solitude at the old house. Winter passed into spring and it was all peace.

Neal had finally finished prepping the exterior, and because the weather was unexpectedly warm, he had begun painting. The late afternoon was fine, clear and cloudless. Sitting cross-legged on the porch in T-shirt and shorts, he sipped his beer and watched the ocean, suspended in the sense of peace that great spaces create. As he watched the breakers rolling in over and over, striking the rocky shore, a wave of sadness washed over him. Without Grandfather's "tidy sum," Neal knew he wouldn't have been able to buy the house. Without Grandfather's teaching, he would never have played the pipes, and without the love of both his grandparents, he would never have had a safe haven or a normal childhood. He blinked back a threatening tide of tears.

Finishing the beer, he rose and went into the parlor to get his bagpipes. Returning to the porch, he tuned the drones. He walked out toward the sea, playing as he went, and paced back and forth parallel to the ocean, near the edge of the bluff. He played the tunes he had learned in Edinburgh, the tunes his grandfather had taught him long since. Pacing and playing, he broke into a sweat and he felt his spirits lift. As he played "Scotland the Brave," long tentacles of fog snaked over the top of the bluff and began to slither around his feet. Sudden fogs were common enough, so at first, Neal thought nothing of it. But the advancing white cloud was soon knee-deep, and it made him uneasy, because it obscured the edge of the bluff. He could no longer see where the cliff ended and the open air began. He stopped playing and walked back toward the house. Somewhere in the distance he heard a dog barking.

He watched the mist flow ahead of him across the yard like an incoming tide. It reached the house and rose up around the latticework below the porch. The chill white cloud, now waist-deep, flowed around the sides of the house toward the orchard. Neal saw the surge run along the edges of the forest. He stopped for a moment, looked down and could not even see his feet.

The eerie thing was that the fog had somehow muted all sound—he could not hear the ocean, and no birds sang. He took a few steps forward, feeling like a sleepwalker, or one who walked in a dream. The silent sea of mist created its own atmosphere; it was otherworldly. He would not have been surprised to see a creature out of antiquity, a centaur, emerging from the forest, or a griffin swooping down over the tower.

When movement below the parlor bay window caught his eye, he thought it was the motion of an animal. Something stirred just below the fog's surface—something dark and large. He thought he saw the outline of a black dog. Maybe it was the dog he'd heard barking. No, whatever it was, it was too large to be a dog.

The fog there seemed to swirl in on itself and as it did so it began to rise up, in a continuous motion, folding in on itself and rising higher and higher, undulating and churning in a hypnotic motion, but never totally obscuring the darkness shrouded at its center. Neal had never seen anything like it. When the pillar of fog had risen up past the second storey bay window, the mist thinned to the transparency of a veil. It was as though the central darkness grew stronger, while the veil tore itself to tatters, weaving and dancing on the edges of the darkness. Whatever the darkness was, it obscured the bay windows on the parlor side of the house, and what is more, thought Neal, it seemed to swallow the light, as though it were a living thing. It was like looking into a narrow, vertical black hole: a crack in the universe, an opening into the void. Neal was transfixed—but suddenly afraid, and appalled to find himself drawn toward it.

He took a few steps forward and then stopped. Something emerged out of the column of darkness and slowly took shape in front of the tower window. He blinked and rubbed his eyes in disbelief. He saw, no, he imagined it—it couldn't be real—a still, dark, hooded figure in the midst of the swirling cloud. And stranger still, something called his name in a slow, eerie whisper, "Mac-Greg-or." The dog barked again, far away now. Neal felt the hair rise on the back of his neck, and then the fog on the ground rose like a sea monster and closed over him, completely obscuring his view.

He bolted blindly in the direction of his car. He was so unnerved that when he found his way to the Mustang, he hurled the bagpipes into the back, leaped into the driver's seat, and started the engine. The roar of the motor was the most comforting sound he'd ever heard; it broke that god-awful silence and put him in touch with the world he knew. He realized he had left the paint, the trays, and the paintbrushes on the lawn, but he wasn't going back to store them away. "The hell with that," he said. All he wanted to do was get out of there at a speed that would break the sound barrier and propel him into another dimension, or at least back into the one he knew. His impulse was to rip through three gears and then jam the accelerator to the floor, but he dared not, blinded as he was by the fog. Breaking into a sweat, he peered ahead for the dirt tracks of the driveway, inching the car forward, driving more by memory than sight.

Curiously enough, although the driveway seemed to go on forever like a gray tunnel in purgatory, the road, when he reached it, was clear. The light of day was fading, but he had driven out of that infernal mist. Neal ignored the speed limit and accelerated into fifth gear.

As he drove home, he reran the episode in the mist over and over in his mind, wondering if he had hallucinated or if the single beer he drank could have induced such strange visions. Could it have been a psychic vision, a type of clairvoyance? Abilities like that ran in his family. His grandfather had been a "seer," and he himself had some ability that way. But he'd never experienced anything of that intensity or duration before.

And if it was a true vision, what the hell did it mean? Was it a warning of some kind? A threat, maybe? He didn't know, but he decided in that moment to keep the experience to himself; he'd tell Vicky if he needed to tell Vicky. She'd never believe him anyway; she was as skeptical as a scientist where any kind of psychic sensitivity was concerned.

He temporarily agreed with her. "Whew," he said aloud, "ghoulies and ghosties. Who needs 'em?" He shook his head and laughed, trying to lighten his mood. But he was halfway to Stone Harbor before he relaxed his white-knuckled grip on the steering wheel.

When he arrived at the apartment, Owen came running to greet him. "Daddy, you've got speckles all over you."

"I know it." He swept the boy up in a bear hug. I'm your polka-dotted papa." He gave his son a big smack on the cheek.

"It tickles," Owen laughed. "Your mustache tickles."

"Neal, you're home early. You look washed out. What's up?" Vicky laid her paperback novel face down on her stomach. She was lying on the sofa with her feet propped on a cushion.

"Well, a sea fog moved in as I was painting the exterior. It got so cold and damp that I quit and came home. I'm bushed."

"You think you're tired? Try working at Ferraday's." She sniffed and picked up her book again. "By the way, on Sunday, when Owen and I come out, I'm going to bring the camera and take some photos of the house before it's finished, so we'll have before-and-after pictures." Then as an afterthought, she added, "If you're hungry, there's pizza. I was too exhausted to cook."

In the kitchen, Neal got a beer out of the refrigerator, then thought the better of it and put it back. He wanted all his wits about him later in the evening when he reexamined what he had just experienced at the old house. Best to keep a clear head, he thought, even if a foaming brew seemed at the moment like the elixir of life. He poured himself a tall glass of water and ate three slices of pizza while Owen kept him company. Neal was so drained that he hardly heard what his son said. He simply grunted at appropriate moments while Owen prattled. As soon as he swallowed the last bite, Neal said, "Time for you to be in bed, little man."

Owen accepted his fate with only minimal protestations. In the bedroom, though, he asked his daddy to stay for a while. So Neal lay down beside his son. Then Sparker the calico cat came in and parked herself on Neal's chest.

"Her motor's on," said Owen, petting her. "I hear it."

Neal smiled in the dark. "Yep, she's revving her engine."

They were quiet after that, and in no time, both Neal and Owen fell asleep.

Two hours later, Neal woke up cramped and realized he was still lying on Owen's bed. The cat was curled in a ball next to Owen's feet. When he got up and left the bedroom, the apartment was dark. Vicky had gone to bed.

Neal turned on a lamp in the tiny living room and sat in his old blue recliner. Before he went to bed, he had to think about the events of the afternoon. He took a deep breath and laid his head back against the chair. God, he wished he could talk to Grandfather about it! Vicky would simply laugh at him.

His grandfather—of course! Neal sat straight up in the chair. He suddenly remembered an incident from a summer—good Lord, almost twenty years ago—when he was in Edinburgh with his grandparents, Ian and Barbara. He and Grandfather had taken a walk in the evening. At thirteen, he was proud and eager to describe the city scenes to his grandfather, whose shrapnel wounds from the war had left him blind and mute. "I'll be your eyes, Grandfather," he always said. On the way home they stopped at a shop for tea. They were sitting outside when Neal had a sudden vision of his mother clutching her side and grimacing in pain. It frightened him badly and he told Ian. Once home, they called the States and discovered that Neal's mother Sally had had an emergency appendectomy that very day.

Later that evening, Ian sat him down and questioned him about his vision. Ian communicated by signing, which was second nature to Neal. He spent almost every summer with his grandparents, so he had learned to sign before he was Owen's age, when learning comes as easily as breathing.

Neal confided to his grandfather that it wasn't the first time he had such a vision. To Neal's great surprise, his grandfather explained to him that psychic ability ran in the MacGregor line. "I have it, too, Neal," Ian told him, hands flying.

"It's a natural ability, lad," Ian continued, "and since I've lived with it for a long time, there are a few things I learned that I want you to think about. The first thing is, and this may seem daft, coming from a blind man: don't be afraid of what you see. And secondly, don't believe everything you see. Not all visions are true; many are just constructs of the subconscious mind—like dreams, although you see them when you're awake. Sometimes the visions you'll have are valuable; they may be sent to help you, and other times not—they may simply be misleading. Respected psychics make pronouncements and predictions that are often completely or partially wrong. You don't want to deceive yourself and others, so be skeptical and use your intelligence to discern the true from the false.

"Above all, don't puff up and prance about like a bantam cockerel. You're no better than the next man because you have this ability. It is best to keep your visions to yourself and not trumpet them to the four winds to impress others. Time and experience will tell you if what you have seen is genuine or not.

"But all that aside, lad, the goal of life has naught to do with visions. The goal is to be the best man you can and find out who you really are. You're thirteen now—at the brink of manhood. The best advice I can give you is to live an upright life, Neal. Be honest and treat yourself and others with respect. When you do that, your gifts will improve, for they'll issue from a center within you of balance and calm." Then his grandfather, smelling of wool and pipe tobacco, gave him a gruff hug. "Remember it, laddie," he signed, "Always remember."

Don't be afraid of what you see. Neal burned with chagrin that he had fled through the fog like a panicked Henny Penny, sure that the sky was falling. Damn! The vision had taken him by surprise, and the fact that the figure had called him by name unnerved him. But there again, he didn't know if the voice was external, or if he'd heard it within his own mind. He didn't know if the whole thing was real or if he himself had projected the vision from his own subconscious. All right, then. He'd keep it to himself and he would not dwell on it, unless future events proved to him that he should give it any significance. He'd just let it rest for the time being.

Neal clapped his hands together in relief. "Thanks, Grandfather," he said, "And now it's time for that beer."

CHAPTER 3

A Walk on the Beach

At five-thirty on a splendid Friday afternoon, Sarah Friedkin locked her travel shop, shouldered her backpack, and biked home. The days were growing longer and there were still two hours before dusk—time for a long walk on the beach. She lived in a neat, two-bedroom bungalow about three miles northwest of the village of Coveland. The late March weather was so unexpectedly sunny and fine that she'd ridden her bike into work every day that week.

The day, as far as Sarah was concerned, was perfect: brilliant sun, cloudless sky, cool air. Riding free of jacket and cap for the first time in months, she relished the warmth of the sun on her arms, face, and the ruffling of her short, curly hair in the wind. Somehow she had bypassed the flaming sword of the Cherubim and biked her way back into the Garden of Eden, Eve without her Adam.

The exercise felt wonderful after a sedentary day. She gathered speed as she passed Hollander's, the village grocery store, hardware store, and filling station. The only competitors were ten miles away in Stone Harbor, a town of nine thousand or so whose main employer was the naval air base. The grocery store was a commercial magnet, just two blocks away from Waterfront Street, the heart of the village and a postcard photographer's dream. Waterfront Street, which overlooked Kelly's Cove, was lined by narrow-fronted Victorian row houses painted in bright, contrasting colors, now home to restaurants, taverns, an ice cream shop, a bakery, antique stores, and Sarah's travel shop.

After she passed Hollander's, there were a few houses close together, and then the houses gave way to fields of wheat, berry farms, and pastures dotted with grazing cattle. As she neared Beach Road, the land rose, and the forest closed in on either side. Sarah accelerated and she felt a delicious pull on all her muscles as she fought to maintain her speed up the hill. She was young, healthy and strong, and gravity provided just the resistance she needed. As she approached the crest of the hill, she could feel the flush of heat rise to her face, and she cried out with the effort, striving with all her might. She imagined that every triumphant turn of the pedals signified resistance to all the pain and grief she had endured.

Gasping for air at the top of the hill, she turned right onto Beach Road, descending in a slow glide. The wheels of the bike hummed over the black asphalt, and the wind sang in her ears. At first, there was a narrow swath of trees and underbrush on her left, veiling the sea, but as the road canted gently downhill, it angled to the left until there was only a narrow, grassy verge on Sarah's left, and she rode along the edge of the bluff, relaxed as an eagle soaring above the sea. The strong wind off the strait spanked the deep blue water into whitecaps and swirled Sarah's glossy hair.

The high tide line at the base of the bluff was lined with white driftwood, ranging in size from sticks the size of Sarah's little finger to massive logs five feet in diameter and fifty feet long. Bleached and worn soft and smooth by the touch of the salt sea, the logs lay eight deep here and there, while in other places there were only one or two, or sometimes none. From the logs, a band of white sand sloped down to the rocky seabed where boulders of varying sizes dotted the water. They, too, were scoured smooth by the icy, turbulent sea.

Inland, to her right, waved a golden sea of wheat, part of a farm owned by a family who had lived on the island since the mid-nineteenth century. Where the wheat fields ended, there was forest for a half-mile. At last she turned right onto Harlech Road and then right again into her driveway, fifty yards back from the bluff. The modest wood-frame cottage, white with green shutters was framed by forest. As she turned her bike into the yard, her dog Mazie rocketed off the front porch, a long-haired, fifty-pound dynamo of enthusiastic loyalty, innocence, and joy, whose qualities could only be matched by very young children or very old, enlightened Tibetan monks.

Sarah hopped off the bike, knelt down and embraced the shaggy, grinning dog. "Hello, my Mazie! Faithful and true, you are, just like Uncle Murr—the two pillars of my existence. What would I do without you?" She scratched the dog behind the ears. "Let's eat, and then we'll take a walk on the beach. C'mon."

Mazie barked again, wagged her tail furiously, and bounded around the yard in a series of stiff-legged, cockamamie leaps that would have made a pronghorn antelope jealous.

She was no ordinary dog. Sarah had bought the black and silver pup from a man who claimed she was a German Shepherd. "Well, I got no papers, but the parents," he told her, "they're big, black and silver shepherds, good guard dogs, like this here pup."

A bald-faced lie.

Mazie was no German Shepherd. Her transformation from puppy to mature dog was a metamorphosis unlike anything Sarah had ever seen. Mazie developed a thick, fuzzy clump of fur that stretched from mid-ear to mid-ear over the top of her head, creating a remarkable resemblance to a musk ox. Her ears refused to stand up. Instead, when she wanted to she could make them stand out horizontally, like a B-52 ready for take-off. Mazie's black coat, which fell out in clumps, was replaced by a crop of long, curly strawberry blonde fur. For months her coat looked as appealing as a castoff sofa with its springs and stuffing showing. Her tail kept its over-the-back curl, but it became a thick, flamboyant plume of long, white hair that looked like the crest of a Roman centurion's helmet. She had feathered forelegs with tufts of blonde fur between her toes. At eighteen months, Mazie was a beautiful strawberry blonde, bearing as much resemblance to a German Shepherd as flying squirrel does to a Boeing 747. It was impossible to believe that she had once been a short-haired black and silver pup.

Although she was not a tall dog, she had a deep chest, and a deeper, ferocious bark. "Good dog," said Sarah. "You sound like a cross between a grizzly bear and a two-hundred pound man-eating Alsatian."

Knowing that Mazie was probably *part* German Shepherd plus Breed X, Sarah tried to discover what Breed X might be. At last she found a picture of a dog that looked similar, but with more red-orange in the coat. "The Nova Scotia Duck Tolling Retriever?" Sarah looked back at the title page in disbelief. *North American Dogs*, by Elgin Palmton. "Elgin, you must be kidding." She read the caption underneath the picture: the dogs were intelligent, enthusiastic, friendly, playful, and good family dogs. "Check," said Sarah. They were hunting dogs, used to toll ducks. Trained to run up and down the lakeshore, the dogs attracted ducks that would fly in close to inspect the flamboyant tail. While the ducks' attention was focused on the dog, the hunters would shoot them. Then the dog retrieved the birds from the water.

"Sounds like science fiction," Sarah had said, putting the book down. But it wasn't, as she later discovered on her walks beside the sea with Mazie.

After she had eaten and changed clothes, Sarah and Mazie scrambled down the bluff at the point where Harlech Road met Beach Road, and clambered over some of the big driftwood logs that lay at the base of the bluff. Mazie—the halfbreed Nova Scotia Duck Tolling Retriever— attracted seabirds as inevitably as the presence of royalty draws paparazzi. The birds flew overhead, spinning around the dog like pinwheels, and zooming in for close-up views of the startling plume. Mazie barked, and ran after them, muzzle lifted into the air. She chased them until she splashed in the cold blue water.

Sarah walked north at an easy pace along the band of white sand, while Mazie bounded here and there in a series of ellipses, keeping Sarah at the center of each orbit. Sarah wore beach sandals, cutoff jeans, and an old, faded long-sleeved denim shirt that was softer than Mazie's fur from many washings. She had covered her hair with a red bandanna.

For Sarah, the beach was many things. She had moved to the Pacific Northwest two years ago, drawn by its beauty and peace, in full flight from her native New York and all memories of Danny Levinson, who had shattered her trust and broken her heart. Well, here on the brink of North America was as far west as she could go.

The beach was her place of healing. But the beach was also a place of discovery; the very air was exhilarating. She loved the wind, and she was stirred by the clean, wild salt scent of the sea. She stopped occasionally to poke among the rocks and pebbles at the edge of the water. She never knew what the sea might yield. Sarah had found agates, a gold ring with a large amethyst, a fully stocked tackle box, and once, she saw strips of mottled green paper floating in the sea, which turned out to be three hundred-fifty dollars in twenties and tens. Sometimes she sat and watched the gulls, and she had seen orcas, humpback whales, and barking seals.

As she and Mazie rounded the point, above the sound of the surf and the wind, Sarah heard a faint music. At first, she couldn't identify the reedy sound, but the farther she walked, the better she could hear the music, and she realized at last that she heard bagpipes.

Out of curiosity, she quickened her pace, and looked up at the bluff, because no one else was on the beach. Above her, near the edge of the bluff, there was only forest, but perhaps two hundred yards down the beach was a cleared space, at the back of the old Fritzinger house.

As she neared the Fritzinger property, she saw the piper. He was a young man, perhaps her own age, probably in his early thirties, dressed in a navy blue T-shirt and khaki shorts. As he paced and played near the edge of the bluff, the stiff wind swirled his longish red hair about his head like a corona. He wasn't particularly tall, but he carried his compact, muscular frame in a way that suggested height.

Sarah was moved by the proud music and the upright figure of the piper. Who is he, she wondered. She stopped while she was still about one hundred yards from him and sat on a log, facing the bluff. She hoped he would not notice her, and that he would continue playing.

Mazie came over and sat on her haunches, leaning against Sarah's left leg. As she listened, Sarah draped an arm around her dog. Mazie was perfectly quiet, dividing her attention between Sarah and the piper.

The music of the pipes blended with the sound of the surf, the occasional cry of a gull, and the susurration of the wind. Like the sea, the music had a power and a call in it that drew the heart. Sarah listened with all her attention. She never knew if it was the effect of the music, the sound of the instrument, or the piper himself, but she found herself sitting straight-backed on the log, thinking about honor and courage. I know why they play the pipes in war, she thought, listening to the tunes. They make me want to follow—to go anywhere.

A sudden low growl from Mazie erupted into a ferocious fit of barking, making Sarah jump. They were suddenly enveloped by a cold, white mist, and Sarah could no longer see the piper. A fogbank had rolled in off the sea, but that did not explain the dog's agitation. Mazie's reaction frightened Sarah. The dog barked furiously, with hackles raised, and she bared her teeth.

"What's wrong, girl?"

The dog wheeled in several directions, barking at the mist. Then she whined and took Sarah's hand in her mouth and gently tugged, pulling Sarah back in the direction they had come.

"Okay, Mazie, let's go back."

Mazie released Sarah's hand and trotted ahead of her toward the point. Sarah, feeling frightened and vulnerable, followed the dog, trusting Mazie to lead her out of the mist. Sarah could not see any landmarks at all, nor could she hear the sound of the pipes any longer. Even the sound of the sea was muffled. She walked in a chill white cloud where natural laws seemed suspended. She kept putting one foot in front of the other, but seemed to go nowhere. It was as though some property of the mist made space expand, swallowing up all her forward progress, while her own fear magnified time, trapping her in a hellish continuum from which she would never escape.

After what seemed like a lifetime, Mazie and Sarah suddenly emerged out of the fog. Sarah almost cried with relief to see the sun and the blue sky again. They were just past the point. They hadn't really walked any great distance, although it had seemed like the crossing of a continent. Sarah glanced back at the fogbank and shivered. Her knees felt weak, as though she had just escaped an awful danger. What was it? What had frightened the dog?

Sarah wasn't going to investigate—her immediate instinct was to flee. She strode quickly down the beach, toward the safety of home. Mazie trotted at her side. Clouds were moving in from the west, hastening the evening. Almost dusk, thought Sarah, when day meets night, a time intersected by other dimensions. "C'mon, Mazie," she called, and broke into a sprint, racing the darkness for home.

CHAPTER 4

Nightmares

When Owen insisted Neal show him the attic, they opened the narrow door and startled a mouse family. Frantic mice of varying sizes squeaked and scattered in a wild scramble to the dimmest recesses of the space. Their only other discovery, besides dust and spiders, was a large cardboard box containing about twenty-five LP records and a stack of dilapidated books with German titles. The records, mostly music by Mozart, Brahms, Schubert and other German composers, appeared to be in fairly good condition. The books were another matter. The yellowing pages were coming loose from the bindings, and the books gave off a musty smell that made Neal sneeze when he handled them. Opening one book, Neal found a faded inscription written on the flyleaf, *Für Maria, von Günter*. Neal smiled; the book had been a gift from Gunter Fritzinger, the house's original owner, to his wife. Relying on his college German, Neal thumbed through that volume and a few others, discovering in the process that they were nineteenth-century novels that also apparently served as the mouse family's favorite snack.

"Do these belong to the lady who used to live here?" Owen asked, running his fingers over the edges of the record jackets.

"Well, they did. But when she died, all her things were given away or sold, except for a few odds and ends like the contents of this box. Whatever was left in the house is ours to keep."

"Then let's go listen to these, Daddy."

If Owen were a compass, Neal thought, then music was his true north. It drew him steadily, inexorably; it was his direction. "All of them at once?" Neal asked, placing the books back in the box.

"No, but all of them by tomorrow."

"Well, the only way to accomplish that is not to sleep, since there's close to twenty-four hours of music here. Should we stay up all night?"

"Yes," Owen grinned. "Tomorrow's Saturday and we don't have school."

"Well, you're out of luck, me bonnie boy, because in addition to painting the tower room tomorrow, I'm playing a bagpipe concert, and I'll need a good night's sleep. But we can listen a little tonight after dinner. Just don't be disappointed if the records are warped. They're old and the music might not sound true."

Later that evening, even though he guessed she would decline, Neal asked Vicky to join him and Owen when they listened to the records they had found. No, she told him, she wanted to watch a television movie in the den.

"Fine," he said.

"Isn't this great?" she said.

Both parties were pleased. It was a luxury; it was the first time the MacGregors could pursue their separate interests simultaneously without disturbing each other. Neal's dislike of television equaled Vicky's distaste for classical music. In their former apartment, the only way either could escape the sound of the other's entertainment was to leave.

After Neal shut the double sliding doors to the back parlor, he let his son call the shots and they listened to records Owen chose for two hours. Like Emily, Neal had made the back parlor his music room. The upright mahogany piano he had bought for Owen stood against the back wall. He kept his bagpipes there and he had set up his phonograph, CD player, and speakers, and his own collection of records and CDs. At present, the only other furnishing was an oval rag rug and Neal's blue recliner, both of which were occupied: Neal relaxed in the chair and Owen sprawled on the rug while they listened.

The record jackets were worn, but the records themselves were in good condition. They listened to Beethoven's *Emperor Concerto*, an entire album of short piano pieces by Brahms, and a recording of Mozart opera overtures. After the third time through the overture to *The Marriage of Figaro*, Owen's favorite find, Neal finally laid down the law and made Owen go to bed.

That done, Neal helped himself to a scotch on the rocks and then decided to listen to some of the vocal music from Emily's collection. He picked a recording of Schubert's *lieder*, sung by a famous German baritone. Sipping scotch, and sitting with his stocking feet propped up in the recliner, he followed the translations on the record insert. He entered the world of nineteenth-century German poetry and song, an emotional world rich in all the aspects of love, from bitterness and sorrow to joy, from tragic love to love transfigured by death. There were songs about the wonders of nature, and those describing another fascination of the period—the supernatural. By the time he finished listening to the entire album, it was late, and Vicky had gone to bed. He turned out all the lights and joined her.

Six hours later, he woke up disoriented and rigid with fear. His pulse was a frantic drumbeat in his ears, and his chest heaved as his breath kept ragged time. When he realized he was still in bed, he moved from paralysis to action; he threw off the covers and ran for the bedroom door, jarring the bed and waking Vicky.

"What's the matter?" she asked. But Neal had already raced out of the room.

Five minutes later, he was back. "It's okay, Vicky, he's asleep in his room. He's fine."

"Why wouldn't he be?" Vicky's tone was irritated. She sat up and squinted at the bedside clock. "It's six-fifteen in the morning, Neal. What the hell's wrong with you?"

He sat on the edge of the bed facing her and said, "I had a nightmare. It was about Owen, and I . . . I was afraid for him."

"Oh, for God's sake, you and your nightmares. You have them all the time now. Last week it was the blonde boy crying in the tower room." Vicky lowered her voice and intoned theatrically, "He was wrapped in shadow, and then the shadow absorbed itself into the child. He looked at me with eyes that were not the eyes of a child, they were white and so full of malice and hatred that it took my breath away. And then you realized it was—Owen!" She glared at him, "What's wrong with you, Neal?"

"Nothing's wrong with me. It's something about this house." He rubbed his eyes. "But I know what brought on this dream. Last night after Owen went to bed, I listened to a recording of some songs by Schubert. The last one was a very famous song called *Erlkönig*, Erlking. Goethe wrote the poem."

"Who?"

"Goethe. He was one of Germany's greatest writers in the nineteenth century."

"Never heard of him."

"Well," continued Neal, "The song tells the story of a father riding on horseback through the night, carrying his young son in his arms. The Erlking, according to German folklore, is a supernatural being whose touch means death."

"The German version of the bogeyman," Vicky said.

"Something like that—a kind of forest troll, really." Neal rubbed the sleep out of his eyes. "Anyway, as they ride, the boy sees the Erlking, so he tells his father, but the father only says, 'Now son, that's a wisp of fog you see.' But the boy gets more and more frightened. When the Erlking speaks directly to the boy in a sweet voice, trying to lure him, the boy tells his father, and the father says, 'It's only the rustle of the leaves you hear.' The Erlking promises the boy that they will play games. His daughters will dance with him and sing him to sleep, and so on."

"But the boy doesn't believe him. So the Erlking reveals his true self. His tone hardens, and he says, 'If you won't come willingly, I'll take you by force!' The boy screams, 'Father, Father, he's hurting me!'"

"Doesn't the father see or hear the Erlking?" Vicky asked, more interested now.

"No, but by this time, the father realizes that something is very, very wrong, so he spurs the horse and rides like the wind. When they reach the courtyard, in his arms, the child is dead."

"Sounds like *The Twilight Zone.*"

"It's a damn grim story is what it is," Neal replied.

"But what did you dream?" she asked.

Neal sat next to her and leaned his back against the wooden headboard. He took a deep breath and then expelled it. "I dreamed that I was riding through the woods holding Owen, but we both knew the Erlking was after him." Neal ran his hand roughly through his shaggy red hair. "What terrified me was that I knew that no matter how fast I rode, the Erlking would touch Owen and Owen would die. I couldn't see him, but I felt his presence. He began to laugh at us. Then all the trees in the forest grew grotesque faces and joined in the laughter. The trees began to move in together, so the path became narrower and darker, until a huge gnarled elm tree blocked our way entirely. I reined in the horse, Owen screamed, and I woke up."

"Then you bolted out of bed and woke *me* up," Vicky concluded.

"Right."

"It was only a dream, Neal." Vicky said in an exasperated tone, pulling a wayward strand of her blonde hair back behind one ear. "Why do you have to be so damn sensitive?"

Neal answered with an edge in his voice, "Because that's who I am, Vicky. It's part of me. Maybe the question you ought to ask yourself is why you have to be so short tempered and irritable."

"Well, did it ever occur to you that it's been a major strain moving in here and getting adjusted?"

Neal's tone softened, "Yes, I know it has. I'm still adjusting to the house. It's old, with a lot of history, and its atmosphere is filled with impressions and memories from the past, believe it or not. In time, the situation will settle down. So if you'll give me a little leeway at present, I'll do the same for you. Truce?"

She sniffed, "Oh, all right." She stretched and reminded him, "Since our subject is the house, you promised to paint the tower room today, remember?"

"Yeah, I'll paint this morning, early. This afternoon at one, I have to play at Coveland House."

"Great, I'm going back to sleep, but wake me by eight o'clock. Today's Saturday, and I've got a hair appointment. Gotta look good for my job interviews next week." Vicky promptly lay down and turned her back to Neal.

He looked at the back of her head in surprise, "Job interviews? Are you thinking of quitting Ferraday's?"

"I already did." Vicky swiveled abruptly toward him and raised her voice, "Evelyn Ferraday's been on my back for weeks, criticizing everything I do and claiming that I come in late and leave early—saying that everybody—cashiers, stockers, and customers—complained to her that I was unfriendly and difficult. That prune-faced old sow has never liked me—she just manufactured reasons to fire me, so I beat her to the punch—I quit."

"Well why didn't you mention it before?"

"Why should I tell you everything? You're hardly interested. You're so busy working on the house, grading your papers, and catering to Owen, that I'm just an afterthought anymore. The point is that I have interviews—one at Hollander's in the hardware department and there's a lawyer in Coveland that needs a secretary-receptionist."

Neal was taken aback. "Look, Vicky, you are not an afterthought to me; I want to know what's going on in your life." He lifted his hand to touch her shoulder, but then thought the better of it. "Will you be back from your hair appointment by noon to stay with Owen while I'm at the concert?"

Vicky's grunt was unintelligible. She rolled over on her side, turning her back to him. Deciding not to press the issue, Neal got up and went downstairs to brew some coffee. He knew he wouldn't be able to sleep anymore that morning.

Neal had intended to paint the study the weekend before spring break, but the beginning of the year had been hectic for him at the high school. He had less free time on the weekends, and much of that time he spent with Owen. It was also an important time for his son, because it was the first year of "real school" as Owen called it. "Daddy," he said, "I'm growing up. I'm not in kindergarten anymore." The tower room was the last room left to paint, and if the truth be told, he thought, he had avoided the job. The atmosphere distressed him.

After breakfast, he and Owen climbed the stairs to the third floor. Earlier in the week, Neal had washed the walls and covered the floor with newspapers. The cans of paint waited in the middle of the floor. He was going to paint the dark maroon walls ivory in the hope that changing their color would lighten the heavy, unhappy atmosphere of the room.

Neal stopped in the doorway of the tower room and surveyed the ugly maroon walls, the cabinets with empty bookcases above them, the brick fireplace and the large, bare window. The smell of mold was so strong in the room that it coated Neal's tongue, leaving a foul taste in his mouth, and he detected another odor, a faint smell of ashes. The dark walls seemed to repel the light, holding the bright morning at bay, as if desolation ruled there and the light could not enter. The color unsettled him; he didn't like looking at the angry reddish flush of the walls. The empty fireplace was like a gaping mouth, frozen in a scream. Neal clenched his fists— his stomach felt queasy. There was a lingering despair in the study, misery made palpable. He felt it even more strongly as he stood there than the first time he had entered the room when he and Vicky toured the house.

He couldn't stand it another minute. He strode to the window and threw it open. He sat on the wide ledge and took a deep breath of the fresh sea air. Owen followed him, and climbed into Neal's lap. Neal slowly relaxed, drawing comfort from the view, which lay before him in colors as bright as a child's drawing. The oblong backyard, a patch of grass, dried and yellow from the winter, was sandwiched between the dark green walls of the enclosing forest. Beyond the yard was the blue-green, white-capped strait, with seagulls gliding m-shaped above it. The sky was a morning-glory-blue trumpet whose single burning note was the golden, incandescent sun.

Owen seemed as entranced with the view as if he had been a medieval prince in a castle-keep, surveying the kingdom he would inherit. And indeed, at that moment, there was nothing before them to indicate that it was the twentieth century. There were no boats, no airplanes, no power lines, not even the sound of a car intruded. The time could have been two hundred or two thousand years ago.

Neal's eyes were on the view, but his thoughts were about Owen. Owen was still at the age when the earth had not yet fastened its grip on him; he was so light that gravity barely held him. Neal imagined that if he released his arms, Owen would rise upward and glide like a seabird, making his way back toward heaven.

Perhaps amplified by the atmosphere of the room, the thought of losing Owen created a pain so intense and sudden that he felt it physically like a punch in the gut. He had already lost his father and grandfather. If Vicky left him, Neal had no doubt he would survive, but to lose his son would devastate him. Owen and his grandmother Barbara were the only real family Neal had left. His mother had died of cancer when he was nineteen. Ian died of a heart attack. Peter, his father, had never battled alcoholism, but willfully succumbed to it, killed by a drunken driver—himself—in a one-car accident on an icy road north of Seattle.

Owen's head rested under Neal's chin. Neal bent his head forward and touched his cheek to the boy's fine, silky red-gold hair. Owen was normally talkative and sparrow-quick, but the view held him temporarily spellbound.

Neal's thoughts drifted to his grandfather. Ian had been his anchor during his unhappy youth. Blind and mute though he had been, Ian had never been self-pitying or morose. He had, on the contrary, been a cheerful man, full of humor, strongly principled, brimming with an infectious energy and appetite for life. When Neal pondered what it was to be a mature and good man, his example was always Ian. Neal's summers in Scotland with Ian and his grandmother Barbara remained the happiest times of his life.

During the days, he and Ian had taken walks around Edinburgh, down the Royal Mile where Neal had questioned his grandfather about the Palace of Holyroodhouse, home of Mary, Queen of Scots, and its Abbey, and Ian had spun tales about Arthur's Seat, the cliff that overlooked the palace. Neal had learned about the Tolbooth at Canongate and the house where John Knox had lived, and the beautiful cathedral where he had preached, St. Giles, with its open-crown steeple. He had seen the stone heart, the Heart of Midlothian, on the site where the English had placed the old gallows, and he had fallen in love with Edinburgh Castle atop its craggy volcanic rock, the fortress that was symbol and protector of Scotland's power. It had been with Ian, on the streets of Edinburgh that his love of history had awakened.

At night, Neal had lain on the hearthrug, listening to his grandfather play, or watching Ian's hands that took on a life of their own, flickering like flames, or like reels of film, telling stories of Ian's youth, of war, or of Peter, Neal's father, in the happy days before the troubles had begun.

"Daddy, can we go down to the beach later?"

Owen's high-pitched voice brought Neal back to the present. "We can go late this afternoon, Owen. I've got to paint this room now, and then after lunch, your mother will be here with you, and I'm going to play the pipes for the people at Coveland House. I should be back between two-thirty and three o'clock, and then we can go."

Neal pivoted toward the interior of the study and Owen hopped down on the floor. "Why don't you go get your trucks and cars, and play on the landing outside while I paint?"

While Owen retrieved his toys from his second-floor bedroom, Neal stirred the paint and poured it into the pan.

"Sparker decided to keep us company," Owen announced when he returned with his arms full of dump trucks, mini-Mustangs, pickups, and fire engines. Sparker the calico cat sat solemnly just outside the door to the study, surveying the room with her gooseberry eyes and wrinkling her nose at the strong smell of paint.

Neal had wanted to get a dog for Owen, but the apartment in Stone Harbor was very small, and Vicky had warned him, "If we get a dog, you're walking it—I'm not!" Neal had bought Sparker from his colleague Ellie Lawndale, a math teacher at Coveland High. "She's part Maine Coon, I think, but don't ask me what percentage," Ellie laughed. "She's not one of the larger ones, but she's very affectionate."

And so she was. Sparker followed Owen all day when he was home; she slept at the foot of his bed every night, and she was tolerant of his rough affection. Sometimes Owen draped her over his head so that her face with its long, white whiskers was above his, her pure white paws hung straight down his cheeks, her body lay over the top of his head like a coonskin cap, and her bushy gray, orange, and white tail flicked lazily behind his head. "Look at my helmet, Dad!" Owen would laugh as he paraded up and down the house. Sparker's green eyes, one framed in orange, the other in gray, had a patient, mournful bassett-hound look, but she never protested and never bit or scratched Owen.

Neal dipped the roller, and began to paint.

"Brrrrrrrrrrrrrr," said Owen, rolling his tongue to make the sound of the dump truck, as he lay on the old wood of the landing, lost in imagination.

"Brrrrrrrrrrrrrrr," purred Sparker, as her green eyes followed every movement Owen made, occasionally batting at a passing vehicle.

Neal finished painting in less than three hours. The walls gleamed, reflecting the late morning light. "Better—much better," Neal observed, relieved that the ivory paint had lightened the atmosphere of the room. He smacked his paint-spattered hands together, "Let's clean up and eat lunch!"

When he and Owen finished their sandwiches, Neal said, "Where's Vicky? It's twelve-thirty, and I'm supposed to play at one o'clock at Coveland House."

"She went to Oscar's Hair Salon," Owen informed him.

Neal called Oscar's, but Vicky had left there around ten. "Where the heck is she?" He laid the receiver down and said, "Well, Owen, you'll just have to come with me."

"Hooray!" shouted Owen with a gap-toothed grin, "Let's go!"

CHAPTER 5

The Piper Plays

C oveland House was a small retirement community situated in the heart of the village at the north end of Waterfront Street. It was a two-storey brick building on two acres of prime real estate at the edge of Kelly's Cove. The upper floor was the residential area. The ground floor housed the reception area, infirmary, dining room and kitchen, and the large social room, a twenty by thirty-foot space with a polished wood floor, and a grand piano.

Each resident had a private room and bath, but they dined communally, and every day there were group outings or activities. There was a registered nurse available twenty-four hours a day. The residents were a mixture of retired naval personnel, business people, teachers, Boeing engineers, widows, and widowers who could afford the substantial monthly fee thanks to pensions, savings, or the generosity of relatives.

At one o'clock every Saturday, after lunch, there was a one-hour concert or lecture. Valerie Julian was the entertainment director at Coveland House, and when Neal called and said, "I'm a bagpiper with twenty years' experience. Would you be interested in a free bagpipe concert at Coveland House?" Valerie snapped at his offer faster than the King of Bullfrogs could zap a fly out of the air. Before the echoes of "free bagpipe concert" had time to fade, she had him booked. She said, "I'm more than interested. You're on for the third Saturday in April."

Valerie Julian met Neal at the reception area. She was a thin, dark-eyed woman of about forty, Neal guessed. Her youthful face belied her cloud of thick white hair. After she and Neal introduced themselves, Valerie asked, with her eyes on the small, red-haired boy, "And who is this?"

"This is Owen, my son and assistant."

"Pleased to meet you, Owen MacGregor," Valerie said, with a smile of pure sunshine. "Well, men, without further ado, your audience awaits you."

She led them to the social room where they stopped just inside the door. Neal thought he might retire here himself if it meant having daily access to this room. Comfortable sofas lined three walls, but the far wall was a picture window and the picture it revealed was a spectacular view of the cove. Sailboats plied the cobalt waters on either side of the Harbor Pier with its landmark red building, and the hilly shoulders of the far shore glimmered green under a cloudless sky. The Cascade Mountains loomed distant, yet majestic, like purple-robed gods presiding over the scene.

The interior of the room was almost as picturesque. A grand piano near the window mirrored the boats on the bay; its raised black lid was like a glossy sail angling into the wind. The dark wood paneling, the parquet floor, the wooden chairs in the center of the room, and the close proximity of the water created another ship-like effect. As people walked in and the thirty-five or so audience members sat in their chairs, the floor and the joints of the chairs creaked like the murmurings of a ship. At any moment, Neal thought, the whole room might break away from the building and launch out into the bay.

Standing behind the audience, at the entrance to the room, Neal took out the bagpipes and asked Owen to place the case against the wall, by the nearest sofa. When Owen set the case down, a small, plump man sitting alone on the sofa leaned over and extended a short, thick-fingered hand, "Hello," he said, "I'm Murray Appleman. What's your name?"

Neal noticed that Owen held his ground and responded immediately. Although Owen was not really shy, he was reserved with strangers, and normally would have fled at a direct approach. But there was something reassuring in the man's clear, blue-eyed gaze and kind expression that drew Owen. The close-cropped fringe of hair that rimmed Murray's shining pate was as white as Sparker's paws. He had thick, fluffy eyelashes and deep smile wrinkles. Owen shook Murray's hand and said, "I'm Owen MacGregor."

"Would you sit with me during the concert?" Murray asked. "I'm all alone here." He gestured at the empty sofa. "That is, if it's okay with your father."

Owen looked up at Neal, who smiled and nodded. "Okay," Owen said, and climbed up next to Murray. "You're Mr. Appleman?" Owen asked.

"That's right," Murray smiled, pleased that the boy had addressed him with respect.

"Where do you keep them?"

"Where do I keep them?" Murray lifted two snow-white eyebrows.

Owen nodded earnestly. "You know," he said, "the apples."

After a split-second hesitation, Murray slapped himself in the forehead. "Of course!" he said. "Stay here, Owen. I've left them in my room. I'll be right back." He slipped out quietly.

In the meantime, Valerie Julian walked to the front of the room to introduce Neal. Facing the audience, she announced, "I am very pleased today to present bagpiper Neal MacGregor, a history teacher at Coveland High School, a graduate of the University of Washington, and the grandson of Ian MacGregor, one of Scotland's best pipers. Please join me in welcoming Neal."

There was a smattering of polite applause. In the expectant silence that followed, the blast of the drones was comparable to that of an air horn. Two white-haired ladies in the last row cried out and jumped six inches off their chairs. People clapped hands over their ears, and a few others surreptitiously turned off their hearing aids. Valerie Julian's expression, an equal mixture of surprise and fright, telegraphed her fear that she had made a colossal mistake. But as soon as Neal began the tune, he saw her relieved smile.

Neal was a powerful presence as he strode up the center aisle playing "Bonnie Dundee." He walked slowly and carried himself erect. His fair skin and wavy red hair and mustache were in stark contrast to the black blazer and white shirt he wore with the red, black, and white MacGregor kilt. The bag cover under his left arm was black with white trim. The three black drone pipes with silver slides were held together at the top with a thick white rope that ended in a dangling tassel. Kilt and tassel swung to a rhythm of their own, while his fingers danced on the chanter as he played the tune with all its flourishes and ornaments.

When he reached the grand piano at the front of the room, Neal turned and faced the audience. After "Bonnie Dundee," he played "Highland Laddie," "Brown Haired Maiden," and "High Road to Gairloch." Every eye was on him, and after the initial shock of the powerful sound, every man and woman in the room seemed stirred by the music. The men sat up straighter, women smiled, and the eyes of some filled with tears. Feet tapped and heads nodded in time to the martial beat.

Neal had volunteered to play for them because most of the men and some of the women of Coveland House were veterans of World War II. They were of the same generation as Ian, his grandfather. For you, Grandpa, Neal thought, as he played for them.

Neal was playing the third tune, "Brown Haired Maiden," by the time Murray slipped back in to the social room with two apples, one for Owen and one for himself. Owen whispered his thanks and then bit into the red apple with a resounding crunch as Murray looked on smiling. Once Owen was settled, Murray's attention was riveted on the piper. The figure of the bagpiper, and the reedy music quickened his pulse and stirred his blood. Murray had fought in Normandy. He had seen and heard the Scottish pipers, and he knew what battle was like. The music brought it all back; in an instant he relived the past, the thick of fighting, the artillery noise and the taste of fear. He jerked reflexively when the music suddenly stopped and applause crackled like gunfire.

"Thank you," said Neal, bowing and smiling. As the applause subsided, Neal said, "Sorry if I startled you there at the beginning. The pipes are loud and there's no help for it. It's just the way they are, and that's part of their story. The bagpipes are also known as the Great War Pipes of the North. The pipes were used in battle because they could be heard, as you've undoubtedly concluded, over the sounds of battle, whether it was the clash of swords and lances, the screams of men and horses, or the din of artillery.

But more importantly than that, the music of the pipes inspired men to acts of courage, and it put fear into the hearts of the enemy.

"The instrument has a five thousand-year history." He stopped for a heartbeat, "But don't panic, I'm not going to tell you all of it." There were few chuckles. "I'll leave out a year or two," Neal added. The second laugh was bigger than the first. "Well, you know I'm a history teacher. What can you expect?

"Even though we think of the pipes as Scottish, they probably originated in the Middle East. Roman soldiers marched to the bagpipes, and they were used all over Europe in the Middle Ages. Chaucer mentions them in the *Canterbury Tales,* and Shakespeare refers to them in several of his plays. They're associated with Scotland because the Scots just kept playing them long after everyone else.

"The pipes were used in war by the Scottish regiments for hundreds of years. They were used in this country when the Black Watch fought the French at Fort Ticonderoga in 1758. There was even a piper named John MacGregor at the Alamo. Pipers led the Scottish regiments into battle in World War I at the Battle of the Somme, and many other battles at great cost. Over a thousand pipers died in the Great War. My grandfather Ian MacGregor was a piper with the Black Watch at Dunkirk in World War II, in the spring of 1940. Scottish pipers also served at El Alamein, in Burma, Normandy, and more recently in the Persian Gulf."

Neal paused and cleared his throat. "I spent many happy summers in Scotland with my grandparents when I was a boy, and one soldier, a Yorkshireman, who had been with my grandfather in France, once told me, 'Before Dunkirk, I never really cared for the pipes, but when your Grandfather played, I saw the men transformed by the music's miraculous power; it roused their courage, strengthened their exhausted bodies, and they burst out singing, united and defiant in the face of death.'"

And power it has, thought Murray, as he listened to Neal play the rest of the concert; it has, indeed.

CHAPTER 6

The Travel Shop

The business district, for the shopping convenience of the seven hundred and six souls who inhabited the village of Coveland, consisted of two thoroughfares, Ferry Road and Waterfront Street. They formed a T, with Waterfront Street as the crossbar. Hollander's was 'ocated on Ferry Road, along with the post office, a pharmacy, one bank, a clothing store, and a bed and breakfast. The business area of Waterfront Street was two blocks long, from Stacy's Seafood House at the south end to the Harbor Pier and Coveland House at the north. Between them were the Town Tavern, a law office, an art gallery, a candy store, a bakery, Sarah's travel shop, two antique stores, a liquor store, an ice cream parlor, and a Japanese restaurant.

Friedkin's Travel Shop and its neighbors on each side, Stoddard's Antiques and Barrett's Bakery, were as long and narrow and close together as the keys of a grand piano. They could have been C, D, and E, except that none of them were painted white. Stoddard's was teal blue and the bakery was a pale gray-green, so Friedkin's salmon exterior with white trim made a bright buffer between them. The buildings faced Waterfront Street with the bay at their backs. The rear of each building had to be supported by piles the size of telephone poles, since they all projected over the beach, fifteen feet below the street level. Old-fashioned park benches dotted the street, along with whiskey barrel wooden planters overflowing with pink and white petunias, purple pansies, and bright red geraniums, dancing and bobbing in the breeze, as nimble and vivid as harlequins.

The interior of Sarah's shop was white with a polished wood floor and a high ceiling. Thanks to the two plate glass windows on either side of the door, the space held sunlight the way a champagne flute holds the sparkling gold wine. The front of the shop was a display area for the large items Sarah sold: luggage of various sizes, shapes, and brands, attaché cases, carry-on bags, travel clocks, money belts, and other accessories. Travel posters decorated the walls, and in honor of her hometown, there was a framed New York City subway map behind the cash register.

About fifteen feet back there were two glass-fronted cases that extended toward the center of the room, serving as room dividers. The cases were filled with maps that ranged from every American state to the outback of Australia. Sarah also sold historical maps from different periods and places, as well as framed reproductions of medieval maps, some of which she displayed on the walls.

The back area contained racks of travel books, guides, language aids, and lining the left wall was a display case of world music CDs, including Celtic, European, Scandinavian, Middle Eastern, African, Indian, and Far East categories. The door at the back led to a small kitchen-storage area with a restroom.

Sarah stood at the front of her shop and looked out at the sunny, pristine morning. It was Saturday, April fifteenth, one week after spring break, a slow time for the travel business. The Covelanders who had already thrown their yearly sacrifice into the volcano to appease the insatiable IRS god were too broke after taxes and spring break vacations to invest in travel accessories. They frolicked for free outside in the brilliant sunshine and brisk wind under cloudless skies. The gorgeous weather, as all residents of the Pacific Northwest knew, could at any moment revert to the bleak, gray chill of lingering winter, gold transformed into lead in a process of reverse alchemy. Everyone who could walk was out on the beaches, sailing or fishing in the Cove, enjoying the glorious weather.

But if everything worked according to plan, she would lure them in this afternoon.

"Well, he's having a bang-up day." The line at Matthew's Old-Fashioned Ice Cream Parlor extended out into the street. "And we don't even have one looky-look," she lamented. "Well, Bitsy, I hope we get *some* people this afternoon for 'Mysterious England.'"

"Fear not," Bitsy replied, "we will. I demanded that everyone in my family attend. That's two parents, five married siblings and their spouses—try saying that with a lisp—which makes twelve, and five of their assorted children—only the well-behaved ones—which brings the grand total to eighteen, counting me. See? You're sure to have standing room only."

Bitsy, who appeared to be all legs and elbows, topped with a wild mop of auburn curls, was kneeling on the floor in the back, manhandling a carton of books, when she looked up at Sarah and grinned. Her smile was a brilliant white flash through a freckle explosion, and her eyes were two wide-set beacons of green, sparkling with intelligence and humor.

Sarah smiled at her part-time helper. "Thanks, Bitsy, you're a one-girl advertising agency. I'm just nervous about this because it's the first presentation I've tried, and I have no idea what the response will be. Mr. Deel is going to arrive somewhere between two-thirty and two forty-five, and I want his talk to be a resounding success for his sake and mine.

"Well," she added, "since we're free of customers for the moment, let's set up a table with multiple copies of his book, and some English and Celtic music CDs."

"Hey, boss, how about maps of England, too?"

"Good idea."

Thirty minutes later, they had set up a table display for Hamilton Deel's lecture-presentation about the sacred sites and standing stones of England.

"Now that's finished," Bitsy informed Sarah, "you should sit down and have a cup of tea while the inimitable Bitsy Baird uncrates new books, mans the telephone, and just generally disseminates well-being, good cheer, and *joie de vivre!*"

"Good idea." Sarah replied. "I leave it all in your hands."

Bitsy was the youngest in a family of seven children, and because her parents thought she was going to be the runt, Elizabeth became Bitsy. By the time Bitsy had reached her full height of six feet two, it was too late to change the nickname. She was a terror on the tennis courts and the salvation of Coveland High's basketball team. She was a senior at the high school and she worked for Sarah after school and on weekends, except on basketball nights.

Besides being a reliable, hard worker, she was also, like Sarah, passionate about books, music, and travel. She hoped to go to an Ivy League school and major in English. She enjoyed working in the travel shop, partly because she was fascinated with Sarah, the native New Yorker. Bitsy had lived all her life on Darrow Island, "Narrow Darrow," she called it, and she knew everyone in town. Since Sarah was new to the island, Bitsy took it on herself to be Sarah's source of information on the events and people of Coveland, "your guide to the inside," as she put it.

Sarah walked to the back of the shop and poured herself a cup of tea. She sat at a small table in the kitchen next to the windows that overlooked the bay. She tuned the radio to the classical music channel and let her thoughts drift. She was thirty years old, a lover of books and music, neither of which had brought her fortune or fame. She had grown up in Brooklyn Heights and graduated from Brooklyn College with degrees in English and music. For three years, she had played viola in a chamber music group called Musicians of Brooklyn—The MOB. The MOB had changed her life.

She sipped her tea, watching the seagulls flocking in the air near the outdoor café at the end of the Harbor Pier, feeling her spirits sink inexplicably in complete opposition to the buoyant, beautiful day. She found herself humming a tune, with her teacup suspended in mid air. Of course—the music! The radio station was broadcasting a performance of the Beethoven Violin Concerto. That would do it, Sarah thought. That was the last piece she had heard Danny play in New York before he left for Vienna.

Danny Levinson, the first violinist in the Musicians of Brooklyn, was twenty-nine when Sarah joined the group in 1989, five years her senior. Handsome, brilliant, talented, uncommitted Danny. Tall, lean, with sculpted cheekbones, curling black hair, dark, clouded eyes, and a crackling, electric-aura intensity, he was fire and he created a fire in her. They had kept their own apartments, but they had been practically inseparable for three years. In May of 1992, he'd won a position in the first violin section of the Vienna Philharmonic. "Come with me, Sarah. We can live together on my salary, until you find work." She had wanted to go, but as his wife, not as his live-in lover. But Danny had never told her he loved her, and he had never mentioned marriage. Just, "Come with me."

So Danny had left and she had stayed. He went away on a summer's day in August of 1992. He kissed her goodbye that day and ran down the stairs of her fourth-floor walkup, into the steamy Brooklyn morning and out of her life, although she hadn't known it then.

As soon as he could, he had written to her, and she had replied. The long, barren stretches between his letters had been almost unbearable. She had buried herself in work, and by January she had saved enough money for a roundtrip fare to Vienna, so she wrote to tell him that she was going to visit him. His reply had been as swift and sharp as an executioner's ax. Don't come, he had written. He had been weak; he was to blame, but he couldn't commit to anyone. His career was his life, and the woman he lived with was pregnant . . .

In the following six months, Sarah lost ten pounds and developed plum-colored bruises under her eyes from lack of sleep. She was so distracted in rehearsals that Beth O'Leary, the cellist in MOB, grew alarmed. At the conclusion of a rehearsal in which Sarah played wrong notes and got lost three times in a Haydn quartet she had performed twice in the last year, Beth erupted, "That's it, Friedkin! You're coming with me." She towed Sarah to Niko's Coffee Shop, sat her down and said, "Look, Sarah, you've got to pull out of this funk. I know you loved Danny, and he's a handsome, talented guy, but he's got as much character as a cue ball has hair. He's not worth a death spiral. But you—you're made out of integrity; you're worth a thousand Danny's. You've got to take care of yourself. Forget him and move on!"

Sarah's eyes swam in tears. "How do I do that, Beth? For me, there are reminders of Danny everywhere—he's at my apartment, he's in our rehearsals, he's in the concert halls." As her tears spilled over and poured down her face, she pointed to a corner booth. "That's where we sat after rehearsals in this very coffee shop."

"Hell," said Beth, "I'm an idiot. I would have to pick this place." She sipped her coffee, "Look, Sarah, I'm going home to Seattle for six weeks this summer. I want you to come with me, or come and visit me, and get out of New York for a while."

So Sarah had traveled west instead of east. In the month she had spent in Seattle, she had been charmed by the city and the small islands of Puget Sound. With Beth's help, she moved to Seattle in the fall of 1993, landing a job as an editor in a small publishing house. After a year, she had decided to go into business for herself, and had opened Friedkin's Travel Shop on "Narrow Darrow." She knew no one on the island, but soon after, her great uncle Murray had moved up from California to be near her.

So here she was, thirty years old, aching of heart, still single, but surprisingly solvent. Her brother had helped her with the capital to begin the business, but she had repaid him, and her travel shop continued to turn a profit. The shop was unique in the area, and it thrived due to its diversity. Sarah smiled. Know it and weep, all you mega-monster chain stores; there was still hope for American small business.

She finished the last of her tea in a gulp because the little bell on the front door jangled. Two customers entered. A handsome couple, thought Sarah, walking to the front to take her place near the cash register. Would she ever be part of a couple again? Or maybe the real question was, would she ever be able to trust a man enough to risk a relationship again?

Sarah watched the couple idly in a detached way, recognizing the heady signs of infatuation. She and Danny had had that self-involvement that excludes the world. These people were both tall blondes, and they laughed as they browsed. The scent of hairspray wafted over as the woman shook her head and ran her fingers through her artfully cut hair. She was about Sarah's age, sharp-featured, but pretty, and heavily made up, which seemed un-West Coast, as far as Sarah paid attention to style. The woman wore a thin, tight-fitting black blouse, khaki slacks, and leather sandals. Her lipstick matched the blood-red polish on her long fingernails.

Her husband was older, perhaps forty. Although he wore civilian clothes, jeans, a white polo shirt, and a pale blue windbreaker, he had the ramrod carriage and short haircut of a military man. Navy, Sarah guessed. He was a fit, rather attractive man, but there was something dissolute in his hooded eyes with their puffy pouches, his wide mouth and weathered, ruddy complexion. He could hardly take his eyes off his wife.

After fifteen minutes or so, they bought two books, *Paris in Photographs*, and a hunting-and-fishing guide to Alaska. Sarah rang up the cash purchase and said, "Good morning, did you find everything you were looking for?"

The man didn't respond. He didn't even make eye contact; he just tossed thirty dollars onto the counter and whispered something in his wife's ear. She snorted with laughter as she leaned against the counter, keeping her back to Sarah.

Sarah was offended by them both. She made change, but, "Here's your receipt," died on her lips, because by the time she looked up, they were halfway out of the shop, walking so quickly that she thought they were going to break into a sprint by the time they got to the door.

"Did you see that?" Sarah asked. "He didn't even wait for his change!"

Bitsy, who was stocking the new books, replied, "You mean the dashing Captain Jim and his latest conquest?"

"You know them?"

"Well, my sister Janie says he's the Don Juan of Narrow Darrow. But I don't know his girlfriend."

"I thought she was his wife," Sarah said. "They both wore wedding rings."

"They're both married, I'll bet, but not to each other. Janie went to school with him. He's an airline pilot, and his wife is old—over forty. She lives in their house in Seattle. He keeps a small place here that my sister says is his love nest. They probably dashed out," Bitsy continued, in a voice direct from the London Shakespeare Theatre, "for they could not another moment contain their smoldering passion. Heedless of the world and aaaall the consequences," spoken with a sweeping gesture, "they burned for one another, in a love so overwhelming that words cannot—"

"Thank you, Dame Elizabeth," Sarah interrupted her, "for your dramatic rendering. And now, for your encore, could you please help set up chairs for our afternoon entertainment?"

Bearing a striking resemblance to a crane in a mating dance, Bitsy bowed her head, extended her arms, and bent one long leg behind the other in a deep curtsey. "It would be my deep and abiding pleasure, Madam," she replied.

CHAPTER 7

The Real Deel?

After the concert, Owen introduced his new friend to Neal. "Daddy, this the Merry Apple Man. He gave me one of his apples."

"That's me, the Merry Apple Man." Murray laughed and shook hands with Neal. "It's Murray Appleman, actually," he added quietly, "and you have a fine boy here." He touched Owen's shoulder.

"Yes, he is," agreed Neal, "and thank you for taking care of him during the concert."

"My pleasure. You know," Murray added, "I enjoyed the music very much. It brought back old war memories. I served in the Army in Normandy." Murray drew in a deep breath. "I lost a lot of buddies in France. A lot."

"The war was won at a terrible cost, that's for sure." Neal said. "My grandfather came back blind and mute—wounded by shrapnel—but at least he came back. So many men didn't. He was seventy-six when he died this past September. I was very close to him, and now that he's gone, there's a kind of hole in my life. After his death, my grandmother Barbara sent me a journal that he wanted me to have."

Neal didn't know why he was telling all this to Murray, but something about the older man made Neal trust him and feel at ease, as if they'd known one another for years. "I think the journal tells about his experience at Dunkirk, and the aftermath, but I haven't had the heart to read it yet."

Murray simply said, "Well, when the time is right, you will."

"Daddy, can we go get some ice cream now?" Owen interjected.

"Yes, we can when I finish my conversation. Don't interrupt—it's rude."

"You should try Matthew's Old-Fashioned Ice Cream Parlor on Waterfront Street," Murray said. "Take it from the Merry Apple Man, who also has a sweet tooth—they have the best ice cream on the planet."

"I know," said Owen. "We got ice cream there before."

"And another suggestion if you've got time," Murray said, speaking to Neal, "There's a travel shop across the street from Matthew's Ice Cream, owned by my grandniece, my *favorite* niece. At three today, she's hosting a talk called 'Mysterious England,' by an American author who wrote a book about England's standing stones and sacred sites. Sound interesting?"

"Yes it does," Neal replied "When I was about twelve years old, my grandparents took me to see some of the standing stones in Scotland, an experience I never forgot. From my youth, history has been one of my greatest interests. I really would like to attend the talk." Neal held out his hand. "A pleasure to have met you, Mr. Appleman," he said

"Oh, call me Murray, please. Nice to have met you both. Goodbye, Owen. Hope to see you at the travel shop later. Enjoy the ice cream!"

At the front desk, Neal stopped and telephoned home. He left a message on the answering machine telling Vicky that he and Owen were going to eat ice cream and possibly attend a talk at the travel shop on Waterfront Street, and that they would be home by four-thirty or five. Two-fifteen, he thought, where is she?

"Okay, Owen, let's go get some ice cream!"

At two-twenty, forty minutes before Hamilton Deel's scheduled talk on "Mysterious England," Sarah sat at the cash register, mumbling to herself as she checked off items on her to-do list. "Okay, chairs are out, books on display table, clipboard with mailing list on the counter, screen is up, projector—"

"Hey, boss, what does Hamilton Deel look like?" Bitsy asked. She was setting out paper cups for coffee and tea on a card table behind the rows of chairs.

Sarah shrugged. "I don't know. The publisher didn't send a photograph, and there's no author's picture in his book."

"Maybe we'll recognize him instantly by his clothes," Bitsy suggested.

Sarah lowered her pen and looked at her assistant. "Really? Do you think he'll come dressed as a standing stone?"

Bitsy laughed. "I was thinking he might be disguised as a Druid—you know, with beard, flowing robe and rope belt, muttering incantations in Old Celtic."

"Oh that would be swell," replied Sarah. "We'd either be laughed out of town or besieged by all the like-minded nut cases in western Washington."

"Well," said Bitsy airily, "business is business, however it comes. But isn't he supposed to be here now?"

"Yes, he was supposed to be here at two-fifteen."

"By the way, boss, do we have any napkins?"

"Oh, drat," blurted Sarah, banging her fist on the counter, "I knew I forgot something. Look, Bitsy, I'll finish setting up the table. In the meantime, take my bike and five dollars, and go over to Hollander's and buy some napkins, okay?"

"Sure, boss."

Sarah took the money from the cash register and handed it off to Bitsy, who grabbed it as she sprinted past, like a halfback running a sweep. "Hurry!" Sarah called after her, unnecessarily, as Bitsy darted out of the shop, the bell jangling in her wake.

"All right then, into the breach," Sarah muttered to herself, and took up where Bitsy had left off. She set two large urns on the table, one for coffee and one for hot water, with a box of tea bags beside it. On a small tray, she put a bowl of sugar, a small pitcher of milk, and a cup holding small plastic spoons. She placed two platters of assorted cookies, pastries, and doughnuts from the bakery, still wrapped in clear plastic, on the table. She stored a third platter in the kitchen.

For the moment, her work was done, so she sat on her stool at the cash register, biting her lower lip, drumming her fingers on the counter, and wondering first if Hamilton Deel was going to show up, and secondly, if there would be an audience to hear him. It was already two thirty-five, and the shop was as empty as a liquor store on Sunday morning.

Sarah sighed and promised herself a relaxing evening with a cool glass of wine when all this was over. Her nerves pranced like so many high-strung racehorses at the starting gate. Nothing was worse than waiting. She fidgeted and bit her lip, certain that this was the jittery state that drove people to smoke. If she'd been offered a cigarette, Sarah the nonsmoker would have lit it up and puffed harder than the Little Engine that Could. Since alcohol and nicotine were both out of the question, and she couldn't sit still, she walked to the back of the shop to the restroom.

She washed her hands and stood for a moment before the mirror, brushing her springy black hair and applying a fresh dab of lipstick, the only makeup necessary to complement her fair skin and the natural flush of her cheeks. She straightened the collar of her white blouse and stared, blue eyes into blue eyes, pleased with the result. Trusting in the power of positive thinking, she gave her reflection the thumbs-up sign and said, with all the conviction she could muster, "I'm telling you, it's going to be good."

With that thought held in the forefront of her mind like a Crusader's banner, she marched out of the restroom and resumed her lookout position at the counter. Her positive thinking was swiftly rewarded when she saw Hamilton Deel approach the shop. "I'll be darned," she said, with a bemused smile, "Bitsy was right—he did dress the part."

Sarah hopped off her stool and hurried around the counter in order to greet the author. The moment he opened the door, as the bell jangled, she spoke, "Mr. Deel, welcome! I'm Sarah Friedkin."

Hamilton Deel certainly should have sent a photograph, Sarah thought. He was a heartbreaker—attractive in a rugged way and younger than she had expected. He had the slim but muscular build of a tennis player, and his leonine mane of hair tumbled in red-gold waves to his collar. His high forehead bespoke intelligence, and his short, straight nose was underscored by a bristling ginger mustache. His scent was clean and his grip was firm when he shook her proffered hand. But what struck Sarah most was the warmth in his eyes. The irises were a beautiful golden-brown, with a dark outer ring, and they shone with a kind and humorous light.

He smiled and returned her greeting, "Hello, Sarah Friedkin," but his expression was slightly startled. "How did you know it was me?"

"The kilt," she said. "Who else could it be? You're a little late, but you're here at last."

"Late? Doesn't it begin at three?" he asked, looking around the shop. "No one's here yet."

"Well, yes, it begins at three, and we're looking forward to it. I just thought that you would arrive, uh…" Sarah stopped, afraid she might antagonize him if she pointed out that he was twenty minutes late. She waved one hand in the air, "Well, never mind what I thought. And don't worry—I'm sure we'll have an audience shortly. So come in and—oh! Who's this?"

Sarah's attention had been so riveted on Mr. Deel, that she had not even noticed the child behind him. A small, red-haired boy edged his way into the shop, tugged on Hamilton Deel's hand and whispered, "Daddy, I have to go to the bathroom."

"Oh, your son! Let me take him to the restroom," said Sarah, "while you get ready. You can put your briefcase behind the counter if you like."

Sarah took hold of the boy's hand, expecting Hamilton Deel to get down to business, putting slides in the carousel and taking out his notes. But no—good heavens, the man just stood there without making a move! And why had he brought his son with him on a book tour? "You can go ahead and load the projector," she encouraged him, as she took the little boy's hand and led him to the back of the shop.

"Well, actually," he called after her, in a light tone, "I'd rather just look around the shop a bit."

Sarah's blood pressure felt rocket-propelled. First he was late, with no explanation or apology, and now he wanted to lollygag around the shop. She checked her wristwatch and clicked her tongue. Good God—almost a quarter to three, and he wanted to browse! When she realized she was half-dragging the little boy, who was running to keep up, she slowed her pace. "Here you are," she said, opening the door to the restroom for him. What a darling boy he was, but his place was home with his mother, not here on his father's business trip.

She heard the bell jangle and peeked out the kitchen door to see who had entered. Oh, good. Bitsy was back with the napkins and she was conversing with a thin, balding man of middle age who was half a head taller than she. Her uncle, no doubt, or one of her myriad relatives.

The clamor of the bell announced the entry of more customers, and Sarah was gratified to see five people enter the shop. She recognized one of the village council members, Brucie Barncamper. It was impossible to overlook Brucie, a woman so large, wearing a yellow dress so bright, she could have been a landmark in a satellite photograph. Well, thank heavens, thought Sarah, an audience was beginning to materialize. And where was Hamilton Deel? Oh, for godsakes, there he was standing by the wall studying her framed reproduction of the Hereford map.

Deciding that the father was more important at that point than the son, Sarah left her post near the restroom door and approached Mr. Deel in the hopes of spurring him into action, although her actual impulse ran more along the lines of drop-kicking him into place. As she walked through the book and music section, Bitsy waved at her from the front of the shop, crooking her finger and beckoning, but Sarah mouthed the word *wait,* and proceeded in a direct line for Mr. Deel.

As Sarah neared him, before she could open her mouth to speak, Mr. Deel pointed a finger at the reproduction without even a glance at her, and said, "You know, Sarah Friedkin, you have excellent taste in maps. The Hereford *mappamundi* is a very unusual thirteenth-century map. Well, really it's more than that; it's a huge illustration of the medieval world view. Its orientation is different from modern maps. North is at the left and East is at the top, because they believed that on Judgment Day, Christ would rise from the east, like the sun."

"Mr. Deel! Don't you think you should—"

"And see the two angels on either side of the figure of Christ at the top? Their words sound through trumpets. It's a very interesting illustration that the same sound can have different meanings for different people. The angel on the right-hand side sounds the trumpet, announcing to the blessed dead, 'Arise and come to everlasting bliss.' See, here they come, a bishop, a crowned king, a monk, three nuns, and two people arising out of opened graves. In the meantime, the trumpet of the angel on the left-hand side pronounces doom to the lost, 'Arise and go into hell-fire prepared for you.' There are six lost souls, roped together and dragged to the winged, horned devil, to be passed on to an evil spirit and delivered to the mouth of hell, depicted as the open jaws of a monster with menacing teeth and glaring eyes."

Sarah's eyes glared and her mouth gaped in a show of teeth, that, menacing or not, displayed her disbelief that he could lecture like a history professor, unconcerned about the stream of people filling the front of the shop, who were coming to hear his talk on England's standing stones, which was supposed to begin *in five freaking minutes!* "Well, that's all very fascinating," Sarah began in an exasperated tone, "but time is short, and I really think you should—"

"Boss." Sarah felt Bitsy's hand on her shoulder.

Hamilton Deel tore his glance away from the map and said, "Hi, Bitsy."

Sarah was taken aback—how the devil did he know Bitsy?

"Hey," replied Bitsy, with a grin, "I knew you would be here."

"Well, of course he's here," Sarah snapped. "Bitsy, what do you want?"

The girl hesitated at Sarah's tone, but then said, "Uh, well, I thought you might want to meet Mr. Deel. He's been waiting to speak to you ever since he got here."

"What are you talking about? I met him the moment he came in the door. Who is this?" Sarah asked.

The tall, gaunt man who had entered the shop with Bitsy loomed above Sarah like a pine tree overshadowing a toadstool.

"Boss, this," Bitsy said, with a gesture to indicate the tall man, "is Hamilton Deel."

Sarah gasped, "You're Mr. Deel?" She turned to the man in the kilt. "Then, who—?"

"This is Mr. MacGregor, boss. He was my history teacher at Coveland High."

At that moment, the little boy, returning from the restroom, ran up and took his father's hand. "Sarah, this is my son Owen." Mr. MacGregor's brown eyes were amused as he reached for her hand and held it in both of his. "My first name is Neal," he smiled, "not Deel. And you don't have to call me Mister."

Sarah's cheeks burned hotter than hell-fire. She lifted her eyes to the tall man's face, held out her hand, and sighed. For the second time that day, albeit a little more weakly than the first, she said, "Mr. Deel, welcome. I'm Sarah Friedkin."

CHAPTER 8

A Vision

"Did you enjoy the talk, Owen?"

"It was okay, but the two best things were when the Merry Apple Man came and we ate doughnuts at the end." The breeze from the open windows ruffled Owen's coppery hair as they drove home from Friedkin's Travel Shop after the lecture. "Daddy, why are you laughing?"

Neal leaned back in the driver's seat, guiding the car easily with one hand on the steering wheel. "When we first arrived at her shop, Sarah mistook me for Hamilton Deel, the speaker today. When I opened the door, the bell jangled, and I didn't hear her clearly. I thought she called me Mr. Neal, but she actually said Mr. Deel. Even though I saw the flyer in the shop advertising the lecture, and I read Hamilton Deel's name, it didn't occur to me until she came back from taking you to the restroom that she thought I was the other guy.

"So when I figured it out, I played a little joke on her and didn't tell her. I just kept talking about the map even though she wanted me to hurry up and get ready for the lecture."

"She turned red in the face when Mr. Deel came," said Owen.

Neal laughed again. "She sure did. But I made it up to her when I offered to play a few tunes on the pipes while Mr. Deel got ready for the talk."

"She liked that," said Owen. "She watched you and she smiled the whole time you played."

"Did she?"

"Yep, and before we left, she gave me three giant chocolate chip cookies to take home, and this." Owen held up a compact disc. "Songs of the British Isles."

"I didn't know she gave you that."

"She said not to tell you until now."

Neal looked at his son. "She pulled a fast one on me, huh?"

Owen grinned, "Yep, she sure did."

At four forty-five, when Neal and Owen got home, Vicky's Mazda was parked at the end of the driveway. He and Owen hurried into the house.

"Vicky!" Neal said, as they walked through the back door into the kitchen, "We had a good day. How about you? And where have you been?"

She was sitting at the kitchen table sipping a bottled beer and leafing through a travel book with pages of city scenes in glossy photographs. There was an unopened bag of potato chips before her on the table. She raised her eyebrows and looked at Neal.

"And a merry hello to you, too." She set the beer bottle onto the table with a dull thump. "As you well know, I had my hair done at Oscar's, and then I decided to have a manicure. See?" She held out her hands so Neal and Owen could see her fingernails.

Owen set his cookies and CD on the kitchen counter. "Mamma, they're really red!"

"The label on the bottle said Red Hot Mamma." Vicky laughed and wiggled her fingers.

Inexplicably, Neal saw a sudden image of claws dripping with blood. He was so shocked, he blurted out in a loud, angry tone, "But that doesn't explain all the hours you were gone, Vicky. I called here at two-fifteen and you weren't home then. Where else have you been?"

Owen glanced anxiously from his father to his mother, and asked, "Mamma, may I have some potato chips?"

"Take the damned bag and go outside, Owen!" Vicky yelled.

Barely dodging the swat his mother aimed at him, he grabbed the chips and ran for the door.

Vicky scowled at Neal. "I had a pedicure, too, and then I picked up this from the pharmacy." Her shoulder bag hung on the back of the chair, and she took a thick packet out of it and plopped it on the table. "The before-and-after pictures of the house." She thumped the rectangular packet with her middle finger for emphasis, "Following that, I walked out to Ike's on the Pier. I browsed in the shop and bought this book, which I was peacefully reading before your interrogation began." She slammed it shut. "And then—sin of sins—I ate lunch on the dock." She flicked her hair back with one hand. "I had a little fun on my own. What's wrong with that? It was a gorgeous day, so I watched the sailboats on the Cove and ate a leisurely lunch." Vicky shrugged. "I guess I lost track of time. After that, I stopped in at Hollander's and picked up some steaks for dinner."

"Oh," said Neal, unsure of what it was he had expected to hear. "Well," he said, trying to recover himself, "did you take a look at my handiwork upstairs?"

"Not yet," she answered, pulling a blonde hair out of the corner of her mouth.

"Well, come and see. It looked great when I finished."

"You go ahead. I'll be up in a minute after I smoke a cigarette."

"Okay," Neal said. First, he put his bagpipes in the music room, and then he went out the parlor door and bounded up the stairs, glad to release some of his tension in the effort. On the second floor, he hurriedly changed out of his kilt, donning jeans and a sweatshirt. He was eager to see how the tower room looked after the paint had dried.

When Neal got to the head of the stairs on the third floor, the door to the tower room was closed. That's odd, he thought. He'd left the window and door ajar so that air could flow through the room. He opened the door, took one step inside, and stopped. His jaw dropped like a trapdoor.

The white wall on the left side of the fireplace was streaked with blood. Fresh, bright red blood—in places it still glistened. Neal stood staring in disbelief; he couldn't breathe. Unless he'd lost his mind, the ivory white walls had been spotless after he'd painted them just a few hours ago. He forced himself to step closer. There were two distinct hand prints fairly high on the wall that dissolved into twin wavering streaks, smeared down to the edge of the wainscot. And that was not all. Directly below the smears of blood, near the base of the wainscot, there were dents and black scuff marks, as though someone had kicked the wall in fury.

Neal's mind whirled in confusion. What happened here? Who did this? An intruder? The window was closed, also, but he was certain he'd left it open. The smell of paint was very strong in the room. Neal walked over to the window and tried to open it. It was locked from the inside.

He looked back at the wall, hesitating, thinking what to do, and then decided. He rushed out of the room and galloped down the stairs, startling Vicky, who was on her way up.

"Going to a fire?" she asked.

"Going to get the camera." Neal flung the words over his shoulder as he bounded down. He slowed down at the first floor landing and called after her, "Don't touch anything in the study."

When he returned to the third floor with the camera, he found Vicky outside the room, leaning against the closed door with a sour expression on her face. "Is this some kind of joke, Neal?"

He stared at her. "Do you really think *I* did that?" His voice rose in anger. "What would be the point? I don't know who did it or why, but I'm going to take pictures of it so that when I clean it up and paint over it, I'll have evidence to help me get to the bottom of it all."

"What are you talking about?"

"Don't be an idiot, Vicky." Neal pointed at the closed door. "I'm talking about the blood on the wall in there."

"Blood on the wall?" Her expression was incredulous. She grabbed the doorknob and flung the door open.

The opposite wall was as white and unspotted as milk.

"God, Neal, you're hysterical. Go ahead and take a picture. It'll serve as proof that you're losing your mind."

Neal said nothing. His lips were bloodless, pressed together in a straight line. After a moment, he nodded. "I saw. . ." He stopped and shook his head. "No, never mind what I saw." He looked down at the camera in his hand, then said, "Mock me if it pleases you, Vicky, but there's one thing you can't dispute. The window is locked now, but I left it open to air out the room when I finished painting. And the door was shut when I came up here earlier. I left it open as well. How do you explain that?"

"Well, let's see," she said, "it could be leprechauns, unless of course Batman was in the area."

"Very funny. You see, you can't explain it."

"Of course I can. This is an old house, and a draft could have caused the door to slam shut and the vibration could have made the window close." Vicky flung one hand into the air. "What else could it be?"

"I don't know, Vicky, but even if the window fell shut, it didn't lock itself."

"Well maybe someone came in the house and played a little prank. We were gone for several hours."

"Was the door locked when you came home?" Neal asked.

"Yes."

"Well, then," said Neal, "maybe you're right about Batman. Only he could have come through a third-storey window. There's no tree to climb, and we don't have a fireman's ladder. It's a mystery, isn't it?" He massaged his brow with his thumb and fingers. "If an intruder did manage to come in through this window, he didn't go out the same way because it was locked from the inside. The kitchen door was also locked. So maybe someone entered and exited through one of the first floor windows. The front door is always locked, unless you unlocked it for some reason."

"I didn't. It's locked."

"Okay, then. Let's go through the house and check the windows for signs of entry or exit. I'll check the ground outside for footprints or any kind of disturbance."

Vicky's sigh was theatrical. "This is completely ridiculous. You dreamed this up and probably locked the window yourself. If you want to check the house, you do it. I'm not wasting another moment with this charade. I'm going to broil the steaks." She stomped out of the room without a backward glance.

As the sound of her footsteps on the stairs receded, Neal stood unmoving in the tower room. She was right in part—he had dreamed it up; he had experienced another vision, so vivid he'd thought it was real. But unless he *was* losing his mind, he had not locked the window. So who had? It was possible that someone had come into the house. What if that person was still hanging about outside? Neal felt ice at the pit of his stomach. *Owen.* The boy had gone outside.

Neal's heart raced as he tore out of the room and down the stairs to the ground floor. He rounded the banister and continued down the hall into the kitchen. Vicky slammed a cabinet shut, banged a pot down on the counter, and still found time to cast a sour glance at him as he dashed through the room. Outside, as soon as the door closed behind him, he heard Owen's voice nearby. He ran around the alcove and found his son swinging in the swing on the pear tree.

"Owen!"

"Hi, Daddy." Owen pumped his legs and kept swinging.

"Who were you talking to? Who was here just now?"

"Just my friend Tod, but he said he had to go."

"Tod? Who is he?"

"My friend, Daddy."

"Your friend from school?"

"No, he doesn't go to my school. He just plays with me here sometimes."

"Well, where does he live?"

Owen shrugged, "I don't know."

Neal took a deep breath, put his hands on his hips and thought for a moment. When he came around the house, the only voice he had heard was Owen's. He saw no one, and a small boy or even a grown man would not have had time to disappear in the few seconds it took him to run around the alcove. Owen must have been talking to an imaginary playmate. It wasn't the first time. He was an only child, imaginative and sometimes lonely, and he had often entertained himself by carrying on long conversations with his special friends.

Neal tried a new tack. "Well, Owen, did you see anyone else out here while you were talking to Tod?"

"Nope."

"All right then, why don't you hop off the swing and let's take a walk around the yard and maybe go down to the beach for a minute?"

"Wheeeee!" Owen timed his leap for the apex of the swing's arc and landed upright with a grin.

Neal took his son's hand firmly in his own and made a thorough search of the grounds without explaining his purpose to Owen. He looked at the windows and the ground beneath them for any signs of tampering or disturbance, but he found nothing out of order, no evidence that anyone had trespassed on his property.

His search of the house was equally fruitless. The windows were all locked from the inside. Both back and front doors had deadbolt locks, and there were no signs of entry or exit that Neal could find anywhere.

He was stumped. He was also uneasy. He decided to keep Owen supervised at all times. Better not to let him play outside alone for the time being. Maybe someone had played a childish prank, but until Neal knew for certain, he wasn't going to take any chances.

After dinner, while Vicky and Owen watched TV in the den, Neal cleaned up the kitchen. Vicky had begged off; she was too tired from all the uproar. What a day, Neal thought. He put the leftover steak and the salad in separate plastic containers and stored them in the refrigerator. As he loaded the dishwasher, his mind worked faster than his hands, posing questions he could not answer.

If no one had come into the house, who had locked the window? And why had he seen the bloody hand prints on the wall? Was his vision caused by the oppressive atmosphere of the study, somehow linked to its unhappy past? Or, God forbid, had he seen into a frightening future?

Metal clanked harshly on metal as Neal slung a handful of silverware into the dishwasher's bin. What was it about this place? Somehow the house had triggered an escalation of his psychic sensitivity, inducing dreams and visions all disturbing and fearful. And that brought up the final question: Why did people glamorize second sight and call it a gift when what it brought was uneasiness and troubling uncertainty? He slammed the door of the dishwasher shut and remarked to himself, "It's a burden, that's what it is."

Later that evening, when Owen and Vicky had gone to bed, Neal checked all the windows and doors again. Satisfied that all was secure, he poured himself a scotch on the rocks, and then shut the back parlor doors, sealing himself into his music room. Taking advantage of the fact that he was alone, he put on a CD of American songs by various composers, then sat in his recliner and put his feet up.

He wore a gray sweatshirt, faded jeans, and thick white socks. He was tired and worried, but as he surveyed the room, he was pleased nonetheless with a sense of ownership. There were his bagpipes next to the upright piano, his record and CD collection, the phonograph and CD player, all arranged just as he wanted. The warm tones of the hardwood floor and the blues and greens of the rag rug were beautiful and restful. He leaned his head back and gazed at the high ceiling. There was comfort and calm in the generous space and the quality of the structure, made in an age when workmanship was meant to endure, when quality was more important than quantity. In spite of all his worries and all the trouble, he was suddenly very glad they had bought the old house.

Then he remembered the house pictures Vicky had brought home. Neal wanted to see them, but he was too comfortable and too tired to get up. He'd do it tomorrow. He sipped his scotch, closed his eyes, and let the music pour over him. He relived the day, his painting the tower room, the concert at Coveland House, Owen in the ice cream parlor, "Mysterious England" at the travel shop, and then the shocking vision of blood on the wall. Quite a day, but now that it was over and done, he made a conscious effort to let it all go and relax. Breathing deeply and slowly, he made his mind a blank slate and let the music work its soothing magic.

When the last notes drifted into silence, the song that stayed in Neal's mind was Jordan Kittering's *Music of the Waterfall.* It was a simple song, and Neal knew the refrain by heart.

O my love she is fair and she is small,
Her singing, like the music of the waterfall,
So pure, so sweet my heart does call.
O Annie, my fairest, rarest of them all.

The final line and the music kept repeating in his mind: *O Annie, my fairest, rarest of them all.*

"*My fairest, rarest of them all,*" Neal closed his eyes and laid his head back against the chair. "*My fairest, rarest of them all. . .*"

Black hair, gentian eyes, transparent skin. She was fair and she was small. Fairest, rarest. All Neal could hear was the song. And all he could see was the face of Sarah Friedkin.

CHAPTER 9

A River of Gold

At six o'clock on Monday morning, Sarah woke to a world draped in white. Fog was a winding sheet that wrapped both sea and land in its cold, damp embrace. She put on her floor-length terrycloth bathrobe and let Mazie out for her morning run. Then she put the kettle on for tea and toasted an English muffin.

The pot of tea was brewed by the time Mazie barked her let-me-in signal, a single sharp, "Woof!" Sarah opened the back door and the dog bounded in, her curly red-blonde fur beaded with droplets of moisture. Naturally, Mazie waited until she was inside to shake off the water, spraying Sarah and the kitchen in equal measure.

"Mazie! You rotten dog!" Sarah laughed, raising an arm to protect her face.

Mazie smiled back, a big doggie grin, and sat expectantly in the middle of the tiled kitchen floor. "Okay," said Sarah, "I love you anyway, sloppy though you be." She handed Mazie a milkbone and pointed, "On the paper."

Mazie took the bone with a gentle mouth and carried it to a corner of the kitchen near her dog cushion, plopped down onto the newspaper, and crunched away. Sarah poured herself a mug of steaming tea, and then slathered both halves of her toasted muffin with butter, followed by two generous smears of raspberry jam. She took a bite, closed her eyes and said, "Simply heaven."

She sat at the table while she ate, and looked out the window. "Can't even see the trees in the back, Mazie." The dog wagged her tail at the sound of her name. Sarah could feel the chill emanating from the window. She drew the collar of her robe close about her neck, ate a bite of muffin, and took a sip of the hot tea.

"Mmmmmh," Sarah remarked, continuing her one-sided conversation with the dog, "the only thing warmer than a steaming cup of tea on this cold, damp day, Mazie, is the burning memory of Saturday—the day I made a complete fool of myself." It had been a near-fatal case of embarrassment. In spite of Bitsy's promptings, she had ignored Hamilton Deel and almost lost her temper at Neal MacGregor. When Bitsy introduced Hamilton Deel, and Sarah realized her error, her cheeks flamed like coal fires. She blushed all over again just remembering.

What saved her at that moment was Neal MacGregor's gentleness and humor when he took her hand. The memory of his brown eyes, so warm and kind, took away the sting. When he offered to play the pipes, Sarah suddenly realized that he was the bagpiper she had seen on the bluff near the Fritzinger house. His generous offer was one of those moments of grace when something awful leads to something more wonderful than one could imagine. She had loved his impromptu concert, and so had the audience. It set the atmosphere perfectly for Hamilton Deel's lecture, and it disguised the fact that the whole thing began fifteen minutes late.

Well, at any rate, when the real Hamilton Deel emerged, a good-natured survivor of flight delay and mistaken identity, his talk had been a success. Sales had been brisk and the mailing list overflowed. Bitsy had been so excited over their success that Sarah thought she might cartwheel across the floor. The shop buzzed with conversation after the lecture and the crowd had stuck around long enough to eat every last cookie. Well, not every one. Sarah smiled; she had scooped up three big chocolate chip cookies for Owen, Neal's charming son. She couldn't resist giving him a CD to take home. The boy was precocious; he carried on a conversation like an adult, and he had held his own in cheerful banter with her and Uncle Murr.

Sarah laughed. Poor Uncle Murr. It was obvious that Brucie Barncamper, sixtyish widow, had taken a shine to Murray Appleman, seventyish widower. When Owen and Neal left, Brucie had zeroed in on Murray and talked him into a corner for half an hour. Sarah feared Uncle Murr would be the fox to Brucie Barncamper's hounds; she was an outspoken, aggressive woman, known to pursue her interests relentlessly on the village council. It would not be a match made in heaven—Brucie was half a head taller than Murray and outweighed him by seventy-five pounds.

When Murray had taken Sarah to dinner that evening in Stone Harbor, she had broached the subject. "I think you have an admirer, Uncle Murr."

"Oh, you mean the vision in yellow. I'm afraid so," he said. "She's a lotta woman."

"Good luck, Uncle Murr," Sarah said. "My advice is run for your life."

"Don't worry," he had replied, "She's got a size advantage, but she can't touch my speed."

Sarah finished her English muffin and poured herself a second cup of tea. She was delighted with the success of "Mysterious England," and she was filled with a great enthusiasm, the likes of which she hadn't felt since the heady days in New York before her breakup with Danny Levinson.

Danny Levinson. She set down her cup with a bang. "No!" Banish the thought.

Mazie barked—either in agreement with Sarah's sentiments, or in alarm at her tone.

"One way or the other, you get the point, don't you, Mazie?" Sarah laughed and sipped her tea, her thoughts returning to Neal MacGregor. At the reception on Saturday, she had spoken with him and his adorable son only briefly, because they were in a hurry to leave. At closing time, though, Bitsy had told Sarah all she knew about Mr. MacGregor. "He teaches history at Coveland High, and the kids love him. He's funny, and he makes the class interesting. He makes the events of history come alive, but oh God—his tests! They're always essay tests. No multiple choice, true-false, or fill-in-the-blank questions."

"In other words," said Sarah, "you have to know your stuff to pass his class."

"I'll say," Bitsy agreed. "You have to make a real effort, because you can't just memorize facts. He makes you study cause and effect." She paused. "What I like about him is that he expects a lot from everyone, and he doesn't play favorites. Plus sometimes he plays the bagpipes for us at school."

Well, Bitsy, I like him, too. Sarah drained her cup of tea and then changed clothes in her bedroom. She dressed warmly in coffee-brown trousers, a pale-blue button-down blouse, and a cream knit pullover. After fastening the leather band of her watch, she put on gold hoop earrings, and applied a dash of lipstick. She stood before the mirror, brushing her thick, black curls, still exhilarated.

This morning she felt as though she stood atop a mountain, high up where she could see. Somehow she knew without a doubt that she would succeed. Her hard work and attention to detail had created a thriving travel shop. She had made a new home for herself and Mazie here in this charming cottage on this beautiful island. Uncle Murray was here, and her father was in good health back in Brooklyn. So many blessings.

And now Neal MacGregor had entered the picture. He was practically her neighbor. To see him, all she had to do was walk down the beach and around the point. Sarah shook her head and lowered the brush. No, the truth was, to see him, all she had to do was close her eyes. Even though he was not a big man, his physical presence was powerful; he had a quiet confidence about him, an easy, humorous manner with people, and she had felt an instant rapport with him. The warmth of his eyes and his slightly crooked smile had disarmed her from the first. He was musical, intelligent, and kind—it was kindness that prompted him to play the pipes after her embarrassing *faux pas*.

Drat! Sarah rapped the brush on the dresser. Kindness and gentleness were the worst. She squeezed her eyes shut and brushed her hair violently, until it shone glossy, blue-black and her scalp ached from the scoring of the bristles. She finally stopped, dropping her arm and letting her shoulders go limp. Before her hopes arose, she had to kill them.

As far as Neal was concerned, maybe the name of the mountain where she stood should be Nebo, the mount that Moses ascended. And like Moses, she could see into the Promised Land, but she could not go there. There was a river she could not cross, a river of gold that the piper wore on the third finger of his left hand.

Sarah sighed. At least Moses got to die. She had to go on living.

The thought of Neal accompanied her as she drove in to work, slowly and carefully, through the thick fog. In fact, he was on her mind all day.

When Bitsy came in to the travel shop around three-thirty, she observed, "You look pensive, Boss. I thought you'd be sittin' on top of the world after Saturday."

"Well, I am," Sarah said. "I think it's this miserable fog—it's seeped its way into my brain. I really am delighted about 'Mysterious England.'"

"Well, my battalion of relatives sure enjoyed it. Mary Ellen can't wait for the next talk. She said the last time her teenagers were that calm, well-behaved, and focused was back in the days when she breast-fed them."

"There you have it," Sarah remarked, "the power of mystery, the pull of the unknown."

"Speaking of unknowns," Bitsy said, "when are we going to have the next lecture?"

"Well, let's see." Sarah consulted the wall calendar by the front counter, putting her finger on the dates with penciled notations. "We have one about the Alaskan wilderness on Saturday, April twenty-ninth. The following Saturday, May sixth, I have a concert."

"Are we having a concert here at the shop?" Bitsy asked.

"No, it's nothing to do with the business," Sarah replied. "It's one I'm attending personally." She pointed to the calendar and continued, "The next talk after that is on May thirteenth, about kayaking the Colorado River. I think that's plenty before summer. I don't want to overdo it, and lose my audience."

"Sounds good to me. Do you want me to take down the 'Mysterious England' display in the window and put up the publicity for the Alaskan wilderness?"

"No, let's keep 'Mysterious England' a while longer. Just make the display smaller and move it over to the side, so we can put the flyers and books about Alaska in that window as well. Take down the old flyers, but leave the books and the standing stone photographs."

"All right, boss. By the way," Bitsy said, "I'm going to a concert on Saturday, May sixth."

"Are you? What concert?"

"The one at the high school. There's a group from New York coming."

"Well actually," Sarah said, "that's my concert. I'm playing in it."

Bitsy's green eyes popped, "You are?"

Sarah nodded. "The group is called Musicians of Brooklyn; I used to perform with them when I lived in New York. I'm only going to play on one piece, for fun and old times' sake."

"Violin?"

"Viola."

"Are they coming because of you?"

Sarah smiled, "No, they're touring the West Coast, and the cellist, Beth O'Leary, is from Seattle. She's the one who introduced me to the Puget Sound area."

"How cool!" Bitsy began to plan. "The high school auditorium seats three hundred. I'm gonna bring the basketball team, the tennis team, and the mega-monster Baird clan." Her freckled face was alight as she promised Sarah, "You're gonna have a great audience. I'm mobilizing the troops!"

The bell on the shop door jangled, and a small, portly older man walked in. Sarah called out, "Uncle Murr, come have a cup of tea!"

"Tea?" he boomed, "Is that all you've got to offer an old man who braved the fog and walked all the way down here to see you? Bitsy, where does she keep the hard stuff?"

"Darned if I know, Mr. Appleman," Bitsy replied. "I haven't found her hiding place yet."

"Come here, you!" Murray extended both arms toward Sarah, "Give this old man a hug."

Sarah smiled into his dark blue eyes that were so like her own and hugged him, "I will, even if you are rude and sassy."

"How else do you think I lived this long? Nothing lasts like piss and vinegar."

Bitsy laughed.

Under his patina of theatricality and worldliness, her great-uncle, Sarah knew, was a kind, tender man brimming with great enthusiasm and love of life. It was the secret of his perennial youthfulness. Children and animals recognized it instantly and were drawn to him like dancers to music.

"So what's up, Uncle Murr? Can I sell you some luggage?"

"Well, actually, you can sell me a journal. But you'll have to order it. It's called *Intersections: Where Physics and Metaphysics Meet.*"

"Do you know who publishes it?"

"It's a small press in L.A.," he said, and told her the name.

She jotted down the title and publisher. "Okay, we'll get that for you, Uncle Murr. I didn't know you were interested in such subjects."

"Well, since I've got plenty of time (knock on wood)," Murray rapped the knuckles of one hand on his bald head, "I've begun to think about a lot of things I didn't have time for when I was immersed in a career."

"Speaking of careers, Uncle Murr, Bitsy was just telling me about how many people she's going to bring to my concert on May sixth. And she was responsible for fifty per cent of the turnout for 'Mysterious England.'"

"Sounds like a girl after me own heart," remarked Murray.

"That's what I thought, too," Sarah said.

"What do you mean?" asked Bitsy.

"Well, if a career in English doesn't work out for you, Bitsy, you can always go into arts management and become a big-time agent. That's what Uncle Murr did in Los Angeles before he retired."

"Did you?"

Murray nodded, "For forty years."

"That," said Bitsy, "is a distinct possibility. You may be my first client, boss."

"I already am."

CHAPTER 10

Skirmish

Dinner at the MacGregor's began as quietly as an ambush, but quickly escalated into war. It was the one-month anniversary of their move into the house. They sat at the kitchen table in the alcove, Owen hardly touching his meal, while Vicky, distracted and nervous, picked at the grilled salmon and pushed peas around her plate, drinking three sips of wine for every bite she ate. The house payment was soon due, and Neal broached the subject that had been on his mind all day. He asked Vicky, "How's the job search going?"

The opening salvo, once fired, could not be taken back.

Her knife and fork clattered so loudly on the plate that Owen jumped in his chair. Vicky's tone was strident, "Who can find work in this damned village? Other than paper routes and waitressing jobs, there's nothing." She drank half her glass of white wine in one long swallow.

"Well, Vicky, don't you think you've been too hasty? You turned down the receptionist job at the law office because it didn't pay enough, and Hollander's offered you a decent wage, but you said no to them, too."

"Decent wage? What are you talking about? A ten percent pay cut from what Ferraday's paid me, with longer hours? No way."

"Mamma," Owen blurted, "I'm through eating. May I be excused?"

"No, you are not through eating. Your plate is full. You eat a total of three bites at every meal lately. What's wrong with you?"

"My stomach hurts and I can't eat any more."

"Your stomach hurts again? Great—some family we have. You've got stomachaches and your dad's got hallucinations. Well, too bad, Owen. You can get up when your plate is clean."

Owen's face flushed and his lower lip trembled, "Mamma, I can't eat any more. I don't feel good."

"Look, Owen," Neal intervened, "just eat two more bites of the fish and one big bite of peas, and then you can go, okay?"

Owen looked down at the food and nodded his head. A single tear splashed on the plate next to the salmon, but the boy dutifully picked up his fork and ate.

"Still, the job at Hollander's would have helped tremendously," Neal said, returning to the subject of Vicky's employment. "Coveland is not Seattle."

"Oh, really? I hadn't noticed."

"You said it yourself—there isn't much choice here, and there aren't that many management jobs available." Neal scratched his head. "I can't see that you've made any real effort on the job front or here at home."

"What the hell does that mean?"

"Is that good, Daddy?" Owen's brow was wrinkled and his brown eyes were anxious as he pointed to his plate.

"Yes, that's fine. Why don't you go and practice piano now?"

Owen took flight faster than a stone fired out of a slingshot, vanishing down the hall and into the music room in record time.

Neal waited until he heard the sound of the piano, and then said, "What it means is that I've seen no signs that you're looking for work. You don't scan the employment ads, and you've not taken any more interviews. And with all this time on your hands, Vicky, you don't turn a finger toward housework. Look around you—this beautiful house has become a pigsty. The floors need sweeping; there's dust on every possible surface; magazines, books, dirty socks, and shoes litter the floors, and the hampers are overflowing with clothes that need washing."

Vicky poured herself more wine. "Wow, the list of my sins—job, house. Anything else?"

"Yes there is. There's the way you treat Owen lately."

"What's that supposed to mean?"

"Vicky, either you're irritable with him, flying off into sudden rages, or you're remote, preoccupied, and you ignore him. Why do you think he has stomachaches all the time? He's upset."

Vicky opened her mouth to reply, but Neal stopped her. "Wait!" His eyes lit up and he smiled. "Hear that?" It was music, a rippling of notes, like a waterfall, bright and clear. "Do you know what that is?"

Vicky's voice was sullen, "Yeah, it's the piano."

"Sweetheart, it's a sonata by Mozart, and your six-year-old son is playing it with authority. He's talented and sensitive, and he deserves better treatment from you. I don't want him upset anymore."

"Oh, it's always about Owen, isn't it! What about *me*?" Vicky's face was distorted with anger as she stabbed at her chest with her index finger. "I'm twenty-nine years old and I don't have a life. I'm isolated in this house all day while you go to work and meet people." Vicky crossed her arms over her chest. "And when I do meet people, I get criticized. Today, I was talking to a man I know in Hollander's when that human roadblock Brucie Barncamper waddled up to me. She had Owen in tow, and he was blubbering his eyes out. She informed me that I didn't know how to take care of my son. That busybody do-gooder with her greasy brown hair and army tent blouses. So what if he was alone in the parking lot for a moment? No mother can watch her kid twenty-four hours a day. But that's supposed to be the highlight of my life—watching a six-year-old.

"Then I came home, cooked dinner, and next I'll have the privilege of cleaning the damn kitchen, after which I get to sit around the house all evening. When is it my turn? When do I get to do something interesting and fun?" Vicky turned her head away. Her nostrils were dilated, and her mouth was a down-turned slash in a face blotched with red patches. "Life's been a bitch ever since Owen was born."

Her statement dropped like a bomb, exploding between them, stunning them both into silence. Vicky gulped her wine, face averted, and Neal struggled to regroup and focus his thoughts. His emotions swirled like smoke and ashes—sorrow for Owen's sake, mixed with anger and disbelief that Vicky could dismiss the past six years in bitterness so harsh.

Owen was no more a burden to him than wings were to a bird. Neal looked at his wife with uncomprehending eyes. He really didn't know who she was anymore. Her admission about Owen altered everything—it chilled his heart and shook the very ground of their relationship. Suddenly their marriage seemed as flimsy as a house of cards, dangerously close to collapsing.

Vicky poured herself more wine with stiff and jerky movements, and Neal watched her drink. On the surface, she was attractive, but now all he could see was the sharpness of her features, the thin-lipped, unhappy mouth, down-turned at the corners, the short-lashed, light-blue eyes, cold and furious. Any allure she had ever held for him suddenly vanished. Under a thin veneer of prettiness, there was an enamel hardness about Vicky, a brittleness as palpable as an insect's carapace.

He sighed and dropped his gaze. He drained the last of the wine from his own glass, considering his options. Vicky was his wife and the mother of his son, and if she was going through an unstable period, she needed his support. Although he wanted to take her by the shoulders and shake her until she realized how fortunate she was to have a son like Owen, a good husband, and a beautiful home, he knew that would accomplish nothing. He couldn't force her to appreciate her blessings; she had to come to that realization herself. And if he wanted to keep his marriage intact, he had to tread very carefully on the perilous path where they now walked—over treacherous ground that threatened to open up and swallow them alive.

In spite of his anger and sadness, he searched within himself for understanding. He knew that there were times when she had chafed at the restrictions a small child necessarily brought, but he hadn't realized that her own needs were so paramount that she saw Owen as some sort of onus, a millstone dragging her down. He shook his head—how could she think that way? He hoped it was just her momentary anger talking. That had to be the answer.

He finally broke the tense silence between them. "Vicky, I don't believe you really mean that. You're used to going to work all the time and meeting people, and right now you feel isolated. We can go out more together if you like. We can get a sitter for Owen. How about coming with me to the concert up at school on Saturday night? There's a really fine chamber music group from New York—"

Vicky rolled her eyes, "B-O-R-I-N-G, boring! Just like you, Neal." She jerked her chair back and stormed past him.

He tried again, calling after her, "Well, tell me what you want to do. We'll do that instead. You name it."

The only reply he got was the pounding cadence of her footsteps, threatening and angry as war drums, as she stomped up the stairs.

Neal crossed his arms over his chest and slumped back in his chair. He sighed, and gazed upon the untidy remains of dinner, his heart torn, his bones lined with lead, imprisoned by gravity. As he sat, weighed down and unmoving, he gradually became aware of the music, Mozart's music, played by the son he loved. The notes rose and fell in bright waves, clear and transparent, flowing all around him, balm to his wounds. Neal closed his eyes, focusing his mind on the music and the one who played it, and his spirits began to lift. After a few minutes, he rose slowly from the table and went into the parlor.

The inner doors that separated the parlor from the music room were open, and Owen stopped playing when he noticed his father at the far end of the room. But Neal urged him, "Keep practicing, Owen. It sounds terrific. I'm going to sit down here on the sofa and do some grading for tomorrow." He had to read and mark the test papers on the French Revolution, Napoleon's subsequent rise, and his fall at Waterloo for his students on Friday. He picked up his red pen and the stack of papers from the coffee table where he had left them and began to read.

Ten minutes later, after he had read Jack Baird's opening paragraph six times without comprehending anything, he heard Vicky's steps on the staircase. As he set down pen and papers, he caught a glimpse of her red blouse and flowered skirt as she rounded the banister. He walked to the parlor door, and as she whisked past, he caught the scent of her perfume. "I'm going out," she called. "There's a movie in Stone Harbor I want to see, and I'll be back when I'm back. Don't wait up!"

Neal made no move to stop her. He stood with his hands in his back pockets, watching her slender back and the swing of the artfully cut blonde hair as she walked away from him. The slam of the back door was like a slap in the face. He heard the sound of the Mazda picking up speed down the driveway. The squeal of the tires when she turned onto the asphalt made him wince.

He retraced his steps to the sofa, picked up his red pen and the stack of test papers, and stared at them without seeing them. She'd had outbursts in the past, but she'd never walked out before. It was uncharacteristic; she didn't like being home alone or going places alone. He guessed it was a sign of the times—another indicator that their relationship was falling apart.

He heard Owen's voice, "Daddy, I finished practicing."

Neal lifted his eyes from the papers. Owen stood in front of him, his brown eyes searching for approval. Neal smiled and tousled his son's coppery hair. Then he set the test papers down, and hugged Owen. "You rascal—your playing just gets better and better. I'm looking forward to that end of the year recital at Yoshiko's house. Do you know that Mamma and I are very proud of you?"

Owen's eyes were grave. "I know, Daddy."

Neal hugged him again to quell the sharp pain in his chest. How could Vicky mistreat this child? After a long moment, he sat back and held his son at arm's length. "Time for you to take a bath now and get ready for bed. There's school tomorrow. And when you're all cleaned up, if you feel like it, for dessert you can have your choice between strawberry ice cream or liver and onions. Deal?"

Neal held out his hand, and Owen, smiling at last, shook it. "Deal."

Neal had graded four papers by the time his son returned. Owen stood beside the coffee table, dressed in his blue pajamas, his damp red hair sticking up in clumps, with a hopeful expression on his face. "Can I have some ice cream now?" He carefully eased himself into Neal's lap.

"Sure you don't want liver and onions?" asked Neal, thankful for the interruption.

Owen grimaced, sticking out his tongue.

Neal laughed and laid down the stack of papers on the coffee table. Then he wrapped his arms around Owen, and smoothed the boy's hair.

Kids and animals, Neal thought: Hold them and your blood pressure drops.

"Hey, Owen, how was school today?"

"Okay, except right after lunch when Leftheri Gregoris threw up all over his desk in Spelling."

Neal laughed, "Pretty bad, huh?"

"Yeah, it had green chunks in it. He's the only kid in our class who likes broccoli." Owen rubbed his eyes and yawned.

"And how was your stomach today?"

"Not too good."

"Did you eat lunch?"

"I tried but the hamburger got stuck here," Owen pointed to his throat, "and wouldn't go down." He rubbed his eyes and asked, "Why is Mamma mad all the time?"

Owen was just as jangled by the dissonant music of the house as he was, Neal knew, but without the same defenses. Neal wished he could make Vicky see the damage she caused, but she seemed hell-bent on a downward spiral, whipping out of control and concerned with no one except herself.

Neal searched in his mind for an answer that would comfort and reassure Owen. At last he said, "Remember the last time we came back from Seattle on the ferry? When we boarded the boat and went on deck it was a warm, sunny day, but then it started to rain and the wind was blowing so hard, we had to go inside. Then after about ten minutes, the ferry passed out of the rain and it was bright sunshine again all the way home. Well, your mother is going through a bad patch right now, like that patch of rain. She's upset with me, not you. She loves you, Owen. You know that, don't you?"

Owen nodded, and Neal added, "And I have a very important message for you."

Owen's eyes lit up, "What?"

With a certainty born of faith and hope, from having weathered childhood storms himself, Neal said, "Everything is going to be all right."

"It is?"

"Guaranteed. I'm going to make it all right."

Owen smiled and looked relieved, "Promise?"

"Promise. Now tell me something good that happened today."

"Well, Yoshiko gave me two big pieces of sea foam candy."

"And did you eat them?"

"Yep."

"See, the stomach is already better," Neal said. "That was nice. Why'd she do that?"

"I played all my piano pieces except one from memory."

"That's great, Owen."

"I know," he said. He yawned again and asked, "Where's Mamma?"

"Oh, she went out for a while. She'll be back later." Neal decided to end the conversation. "Let's go get some ice cream, but then you'll have to brush your teeth and go to bed."

After one heaping bowl of strawberry ice cream, his favorite, Owen was in bed and asleep by eight-thirty.

CHAPTER 11

Attack

When he was certain that Owen was asleep, Neal went back down to the kitchen and made half a pot of coffee. He really wanted a beer, but he was having enough trouble concentrating, and alcohol would only make it more difficult. He took a mug of the hot, black brew back into the living room and picked up the test papers. If he kept focused he'd finish by ten. He took a sip of coffee, picked up his pen, and plunged into the world of nineteenth-century France.

At ten-fifteen, Neal scrawled a red 86 on Erica Mundy's paper, and blew out a sigh of relief. "Finished at last." He grabbed a beer from the kitchen, and then went upstairs to the tower room to record the grades on his computer. On the second floor, he checked on Owen, and all was well; the boy slept soundly.

The third-floor tower room, which Neal had painstakingly made his study, looked pleasant enough. He had filled the built-in bookshelves in the north wall with his books on history, literature, and music, his set of *Encyclopedia Britannica*, and the *Oxford English Dictionary*, as well as German, French, and Italian dictionaries. The roll-top desk and computer worktable stood immediately to the right of the door, below the bookshelves. Between the fireplace in the opposite wall and the large window, he had placed a leather armchair with a side table and a Chinese lamp.

Neal had had no more visions since the Saturday three weeks previous, when he had seen the bloody streaks on the wall. The white walls of the newly painted room were bright, giving the study an airy, clean quality. And to Neal's relief, there had been no other disturbances in or outside the house. Still, he felt somewhat uneasy in the study, and that chagrined him. It was his house, and he was determined to be at home in every room.

As he waited for the computer to boot up, he glanced around and thought of the before-and-after pictures—especially the ones Vicky had taken of this room. He ought to look at them, just to compare how much the room had improved. Maybe he'd do that tonight.

His mind was brought back to the task at hand by the subsidence of the computer's customary beeps and whirrs, so he brought up the screen with his class roll and recorded the grades. After he shut down the computer, he opened his long-awaited bottle of beer, and sat in the leather chair. It was ten-forty, and Vicky still hadn't come home.

The first sip of cold beer tasted wonderful. He leaned his head back and looked out the window. Vicky had put up drapes, but Neal kept them drawn to the side in order to maximize the light and the view. Far out in the strait, he could see the lights of a ferry making a night crossing. The ship was headed away from him, slowly growing more distant.

Growing more distant, like his wife. It seemed to him that Vicky was going away from him little by little, every day. He had an image of her receding, growing smaller and smaller, and he felt powerless to stop the process. He couldn't turn her around and bring her back. She had to do that herself. Today was May fourth, the one-month anniversary of their move into the house she had wanted, and it had certainly brought her no happiness. In fact the opposite was true; she had grown increasingly moody and depressed. She hardly communicated with him or Owen and her only interests seemed to be television programs and romance novels.

Neal took a sip of beer. Maybe she was going through a temporary letdown after the initial excitement of moving into the house. At first, they had both been elated by the beauty of the old house, the view, all the space, and the proud feeling of ownership. But, more space meant more house to clean, and although the view was wonderful, the house was isolated. At the apartment complex in Stone Harbor, all Vicky's acquaintances had lived in close proximity, making it easy for her to chat with the neighbors. But there were no neighbors in this secluded spot.

He rubbed the cold droplets of condensed moisture from the label of his beer and took a long drink. Or maybe she was depressed over the loss of her job, which meant a loss of position, status, and income. Vicky had always worked—she had never been a housewife, and during the years she was Assistant Manager at Ferraday's she had always been gregarious and social, except apparently at the end of her tenure, enjoying the interaction with customers and co-workers. "She needs a job," Neal muttered, "and not for her sake alone." She'd be out of the house, meet people, and the extra income would help. She had the best chance of finding a management position in Stone Harbor. Beginning tomorrow, he'd help her look. That was the solution; he was sure of it.

Well, that was the solution if she would listen to him and take his advice. Tonight, though, Neal reflected, she hadn't even given him a chance. He had offered to do whatever she wanted, and she had just walked out. If she'd waited, they could have found a sitter for Owen and gone to the movie together. But she had left in anger, with no reply to his offer. The more he thought about it, the stranger it seemed. And earlier at dinner, she had been so preoccupied and jumpy. Very odd.

He drank more beer, and then tapped his fingers on the bottle. Well, there was one positive thing. At least she had begun to wear make-up again, and take care of her hair and nails. Dressed as she was tonight, she looked like the Vicky he had first met, years ago. And the perfume he'd noticed—she hadn't worn that for ages.

Neal looked at his watch. Eleven o'clock. She ought to be home soon. He sat back in the chair and sipped his beer. The best thing about his evening had been Owen's description of his day and the piano lesson. Owen was a talent. Neal recognized it, and so did Yoshiko Katagiri, his teacher. Two times through a piece, and the boy had it from memory.

A scratching sound behind him startled Neal. He pivoted in the chair and looked in the direction of the door. The far corners of the room were filled with shadows, and at first, he saw nothing amiss. But something was wrong—something about the room had changed. The door was shut. He knew for certain that he had left it open.

There was a pause, and then the scratching became more insistent Neal put the half-finished beer on the side table and stood up. He looked and listened carefully. There was nothing in the room. The scratching was coming from outside the door.

His muscles were in fight-or-flight readiness as he crept to the door, careful to make no sound. He took hold of the handle, and opened it with a jerk.

Sparker the cat gazed at him with round green eyes.

Neal laughed, feeling ridiculous. "Oh, you wanted in, did you?" Sparker brushed against his leg and then strolled past him into the room.

Neal fetched two volumes of the *Encyclopedia Britannica* and propped them against the door, to hold it open. "Ah, the uses of knowledge," he said.

But how had the door closed, and closed soundlessly? Maybe the house had shifted slightly and the floor was no longer level. That could cause the door to swing shut of its own accord. He'd check it tomorrow. It was probably nothing. Everyone knew that old houses were full of quirks.

When he went back to his armchair, Sparker was curled up in the seat "Oh, no, you don't, Miss Calico Cat," Neal told her as he picked her up. "This is my chair." He put her on the floor, but the moment he sat down, she leapt up into his lap. Purring loudly, she began to clean herself in the completely self-absorbed, languorous way of cats.

Neal drank his beer, idly petting the cat's long, fine, silky coat. As soon as she finished her bath, she curled up in his lap and went to sleep. After a time, he closed his eyes and listened to the wind rattling the windowpane. The window was open about two inches, and he felt the cold air wrap itself around his lower legs. The wind moaned and the old house sighed and creaked

Neal was sleepy, but he wanted to wait up until Vicky came home. She had her faults, but she was his wife, and he didn't want her to come to any harm. He closed his eyes, "O Lord," he murmured, "let her come home safe."

At that moment, the window slammed shut with a crack. Neal jumped, and the cat, startled out of sleep, spat, hissed, and clawed Neal's leg as she shot out of his lap and leaped halfway across the room toward the open door. There was a growl, deep, long, and menacing, directly behind Neal. He'd never heard anything like it in his life. It was unidentifiable, unearthly. He felt the hair on his head rise, and he froze. He was afraid to turn around.

The second evil-sounding snarl was louder and closer. Neal summoned his courage and rose from the chair. He turned toward the center of the room, and beheld a creature from hell. A huge, black dog, with a deep chest, powerful legs and short, bristling fur stood facing him. It was the size of a small pony. Its hackles were raised and the ears were laid back on the massive, mastiff-like head. Its lips were drawn, exposing double rows of yellow, dully gleaming triangular teeth, wholly unnatural. They were unlike any dog's teeth he had ever seen: they were the lethal teeth of a shark. The largest were two inches long, and they looked razor-sharp. Foam ringed its powerful lower jaw, and Neal smelled its feral, penetrating scent.

He prayed he was dreaming.

The dog growled again. White flecks of froth fell from its lower jaw onto the floor. It lunged forward and stopped, threatening Neal.

He jumped back reflexively and felt the cold glass of the window against his left side and the smooth wall on his right. The molding of the window bumped his spine. He could not retreat further.

As his mind raced, he heard soft laughter. It shocked him as much as the presence of the hellhound. He looked wildly around the room for its source. At last he saw movement in the farthest corner of the room, opposite the bookcase. The shadows seemed to writhe and weave themselves together, coalescing slowly into a wavering, elongated figure, a tall form, cloaked and hooded. Neal recognized the figure he had seen before, in the fog.

The soft laughter came again, followed by a low, seductive, well-modulated voice, "Do you like my pet?" There was more self-satisfied laughter.

Neal, chilled to the core, was riveted by the being's eyes, black holes of malice that threatened to suck him in.

"I think he'd make a nice pet for Owen. Don't you?"

The sound of Owen's name, issuing from the mouth of the vile, malicious being, filled Neal with dread so deep and black and cold that it froze his heart. His nightmare had come to life. Horrified, he thought of his boy, sleeping alone and unprotected one floor below. "You son of a bitch!" Neal's voice was so deep and ragged that he hardly recognized it as his own. He shook with rage and fear for his son, "You'd better not harm Owen, not one hair on his head."

He leaped to his left and pushed the heavy chair at the dog, knocking the lamp and table over in the process. The chair fell harmlessly on its side. The dog merely dodged it and repositioned itself, growling again. Neal was breathing fast and his heart was hammering. He took a deep breath to steady himself; then he raised his right hand and pointed at the dark figure, commanding him in a ringing voice, "Get out! Take your hellhound and get out of my house *now!*"

For one moment, Neal thought he saw the black figure waver and fade, but then he heard the mocking laugh, and two things happened at once. The door slammed shut, propelling the two encyclopedias across the study floor with such force that they banged into the opposite wall, and the black dog lunged at Neal's throat. Neal lifted up both arms to defend himself. The weight and mass of the dog knocked him back with so much force that his head hit the wall with a resounding crack. His whole body sagged, and then he knew no more.

CHAPTER 12

Spirits

Swaying and blinking like a dashboard hula doll, Vicky fumbled with the key until she finally unlocked the kitchen door and let herself into the dark and silent house. "Two a.m.," she explained to no one in particular, "quite late." She shot the bolt behind her and dropped her purse on the floor. "Home—or is it?"

The kitchen whirled around her, kaleidoscopic. She tapped her temple with a long, red fingernail. "Spirits and ghosts, tick-tack! My husband's completely cracked. He lets his good-looking wife lead such a boring damn life." She shook her head, blinked, and wiped a tear from her eye. "Nope, not gonna cry." She stretched out both arms and began to rotate slowly, shuffling her feet. "Not gonna cry, time to fly. See, Neal, I am quite a poet." Still turning, she said "Actually, I am poetry, the poetry of flight." Dipping her extended arms gracefully as a bird (or so she thought), she zigzagged unsteadily down the hall and started up the staircase.

"Been caged but now I'm free, thanks to darlin' Ji—whoops, better zip the lip on that one."

Halfway up, the staircase creaked loudly. Vicky flopped down onto a stair and removed both her shoes. "Actually, Neal, in case you haven't noticed, I am running away. Barefoot on sweet feet." She continued up the stairs, holding her flats in her right hand while she gripped the railing with the left.

She turned onto the landing. "I am getting loosh—loose, you see. You can't catch me. I was twenty when I married you. Twenty. I was found, but now I'm lost." Tears welled up in Vicky's eyes. "Neal has no idea." She finally reached the second floor. "I'm gonna tell him." The door to her bedroom was open. Vicky held her breath, tiptoed in and stopped. The unmade bed was empty. "Where is he?"

She crossed the hall to her son's bedroom.

Vicky rubbed her eyes, trying to adjust to the darkness in Owen's room, and peered at the two single beds. "Owen's asleep, I see." she muttered, peering at her son. "And Neal loves him more than me." She stepped closer to the extra bed and poked at the pile of clothes and stuffed animals. "Where is Neal?"

She dropped her shoes and they clattered loudly on the wood floor. Owen stirred and changed position.

"Shhhh!" Vicky whispered, shaking her head, "Don't wanna wake Owen."

She went out onto the landing. Waggling her index finger in the air, she declared, "Goin' up!" She swayed slightly, facing the staircase to the third floor. "You know, Neal, if we had some s-shush-smashin' passion here, I would never have had to find it somewhere else. But, you see, I did. And that is entirely your fault. Don't blame me."

Gripping the railing, she pulled herself up the staircase and walked into the guest bedroom, looking for Neal. "Oops, forgot! No bed yet."

She retraced her steps and stopped in front of the closed study door. She rapped on the door with her knuckles, "Knock, knock. Who's there?"

Vicky waited. There was no answer. "Well, here I come, ready or not!" She barged into the room, expecting to surprise her husband. The room was empty and dark, but a little light came in from the hall behind her. She wrinkled her nose, "What's that stink?" Hands on her hips, she surveyed the room. "My dear husband had a party and didn't invite me." The leather chair, the lamp, and side table were overturned; books lay on the floor, and there was a pile of clothes by the window. Must've been a wild party if he'd thrown his clothes off!

Vicky blinked several times, puzzled by the disarray in the dim room, then clapped her hand over her mouth. That was no pile of clothes—there was a body on the floor. "Neal?" she whispered. "Neal?" He lay so still that she feared he was dead. She crept closer until she stood over him. When she bent down, she saw the shallow rise and fall of his chest. He lay on his right side, his back against the wall, with his right arm extended in front of him, and his left arm partially covering his face. His head lay toward the fireplace and his feet were near the window, legs slightly bent. An empty beer bottle lay on its side near Neal's outstretched arm.

When she knelt beside him, the smell of spilled beer filled her nostrils. Suddenly it all clicked. "Ha! He's drunk," she snorted. She shook his shoulder roughly. "Neal, wake up!"

When he did not respond, she sat back on her heels in surprise—he was passed out cold! Surprise turned to sudden anger, and her anger made her sober. What right did Neal have to get drunk? *She* was the wronged one, the misunderstood one. She was going to wake him up and let him know a thing or two.

She stood up, righted the small side table, put the lamp back in place and turned it on. "That's better." Then she picked up the beer bottle, and stomped into the guest bathroom, where she filled it with cold water.

She returned, and from a standing height, poured the water directly onto Neal's face. She watched with pleasure as the water ricocheted a foot into the air.

It worked. He spluttered and groaned, reflexively rolling away from the stream of cold water. He lay face up, rubbing his face and eyes with the sleeve of his sweatshirt.

"Serves you right," Vicky snapped. "Lying there dead drunk on the floor like a dirty wino."

Neal sat up with a groan and gingerly felt the back of his head.

"And what did you do to the room? It's a complete mess!"

Neal suddenly froze and gave Vicky a look, wide-eyed and panic-stricken. "Owen! I've got to protect Owen!" He rose unsteadily to his feet and jostled Vicky slightly as he hurried toward the door.

"Owen! What about me? Come back here, Neal." As she started after him, she stepped into a puddle of water. Both feet shot out from under her, and suddenly she found herself airborne. She fell heavily, striking her head against the floor, and landing flat on her back, the wind knocked out of her. Stunned, she stared at the ceiling in disbelief, until tears flooded her eyes. "Damn it!" she howled in pain and frustration, chest heaving with the effort.

As soon as she caught her breath, she rose to her feet and went after Neal. Back and head aching, she descended the stairs to the second floor and entered Owen's bedroom.

Neal stood at Owen's bedside. "Thank God," she heard him whisper. "Owen is safe."

"Why wouldn't he be?" hissed Vicky. "Because of your wild, drunken party, maybe?"

"Party?" Neal shook his head. "I'll explain what happened later, Vicky. In the meantime, don't jump to any ridiculous conclusions, and don't raise your voice. Let him sleep."

The room was shadowy, but Vicky could see that Owen lay on his left side, with one arm on top of the quilt, breathing slowly and evenly. Sparker rose from her place near the foot of the bed, yawned and stretched, and sat observing the proceedings impassively.

Neal leaned forward and stroked his sleeping son's hair. Owen made a small sound and then, with a rustle of bedcovers, turned onto his back.

"What's that?" asked Vicky. There was something cloth-like and dark stuck to the boy's left cheek.

Neal reached over and plucked it carefully from Owen's skin with his forefinger and thumb. He brought it close to his eyes to examine it in the dark room, and then he sniffed it. His sharp intake of breath was audible. "Oh, my God!" He jerked his hand away from his face as if it held a viper.

"What's the big dramatic deal?" Vicky said. "It's not going to bite you. It's a tuft of Sparker's fur."

"No—Sparker's fur is not short, coarse and black like this."

"Let me see it."

"You don't have to see it. All you have to do is smell it."

He thrust it in her face. Vicky jerked her head back, grabbed the tuft of fur, and twisted it out of his grip.

"Vicky, give it back to me."

She dashed out of the room with Neal hard at her heels. Vicky turned and scowled at him on the landing.

"Look, Vicky, there was a dog in the house tonight—"

"Who brought the dog to your drunken party?"

"What are you talking about? There was no party here."

"Of course there was. You were mad at me because I went out on my own and you took advantage of the fact. You invited your friends over and you got drunk! When I came home, I found the study in a shambles and you were lying dead drunk on the floor. You are your father's son, all right!"

"I wasn't drunk. I'd only had one beer. I was alone in the study when I heard a growl in the room. I turned around and suddenly, out of nowhere, there was a huge black dog threatening me. Then I heard a voice and I saw a shadowy figure in the far corner of the room." Neal ran his hand through his hair. "This figure spoke and implied that the dog might harm Owen. Then the dog lunged at me, and I hit my head so hard against the wall that I blacked out."

"Do you really expect me to believe that?" Vicky yelled. Her face was flushed and veins stood out in her neck.

"Yes, I do—the proof is in your hand. You're holding a piece of that dog's fur."

"Liar! You were drunk, and now you're making up some idiotic ghost story to explain why you were out cold! Either that or you're hallucinating again."

"Look at the fur—smell it. The dog stank; it had a foul, penetrating odor."

Vicky held the tuft of fur over the stairwell, rubbing it between her thumb and fingers; then she blew on it, so that it dispersed, winnowing like so much chaff in the wind.

"What are you doing?" Neal's voice rose in anger, and he jerked her around by the arm. "Vicky, you have just destroyed the only physical evidence of the creature."

"Yeah," Vicky's voice was contemptuous, "Sparker is some kind of scary ghost cat, all right."

"It wasn't Sparker's fur!" Neal shouted. "Can't you even consider that I might be telling the truth? In all the years of our marriage, I have never been a liar. Why would I lie now? What do I have to hide?"

He rubbed his face with both hands. "Ah, God. My head is splitting, and I am worried sick about the threat to Owen. And you know something else?" Neal lifted his head, his eyes dark with anger. "I don't give a damn if you believe me or not. Persuading you is a complete waste of time and energy. So, all right, Vicky, if it makes you happy, I was drunk."

"Ha!" she shouted, "I knew it!" She turned and walked toward their bedroom. At the door, she said, "And don't bother to come to bed with me. You can sleep on the floor since you like it so much." Then she flounced into the room and closed the door with a bang. Neal was coming unraveled. Let the poor, deluded fool chase after his ghosts. In the meantime she could do as she wished, and she would keep her secrets. She leaned against the door and smiled; she had never been so satisfied in all her life.

CHAPTER 13

The Violist Plays

Murray Appleman adjusted his tie and took stock of himself in the mirror. He rarely dressed formally anymore, and the sight of himself wearing his navy blue wool suit, the crisp white shirt, and the blue tie with gold flecks was startling. "Not bad for an *alter cocker*," he remarked, running a hand over the top of his bare head where a few lonely silver hairs still gleamed. "The bald eagle is not extinct, and neither am I." He pulled on his beaked nose and laughed. "The old blue eyes still shine."

Eighty years old last June. He could hardly believe it. How could such a thing be? Just yesterday he was a child, growing up in the three-bedroom apartment on Prospect Avenue in Brooklyn with his mother, father, and sister Rachel. It was strange, Murray thought, how the clarity of memory grew sharper in inverse proportion to the passage of time. Scenes from his youth were startlingly clear, while what he had done last Friday seemed beyond recall.

In his mind's eye, he could see the neighborhood of his youth, the three and four-storey limestone buildings lining the avenue across from the green oasis of the park. He could see the candy store where the giant glass jars held their treasures of red-and-white-striped peppermint sticks, black licorice, yellow lemon drops, gum drops, rock candy, jelly beans in all colors, and chocolate bars and pieces, each more delectable than the last. He closed his eyes, remembering the smell of freshly baked bread from the Italian bakery around the corner, shaded by its red, white, and green awning, its shelves piled with long brown loaves and fat round ones with crunchy crusts and soft white insides.

He could see the interior of his father's delicatessen on Atlantic Avenue, the scuffed wood floor, the tables and chairs, and in the glass-fronted cases, the rows of kosher meats and cheeses, the steaming pots of soup, lentil, mushroom and barley, and chicken, and the jars of pickles floating in brine. He thought of his favorite lunch, cream cheese and lox on an onion bagel, and his mouth watered—his nostrils filled with the scent, as his eye delighted in the color of the light brown bagel, the white layer of cream cheese and the lox, orange with pink tints.

"Ha!" said Murray, back in present time, "the bona fide New York bagel. There's an endangered species." It seemed like ages since he'd eaten the real thing, not those fake pieces of crap they sold around here.

He picked up his wristwatch from the dresser and slipped it over his left hand. Seven o'clock. Only thirty minutes until Sarah's concert began.

Murray closed his eyes. Time, where do you go? The seconds ticked past like heartbeats, like breaths that could never be retrieved. Let me do some good, with the time I have left. Let me help Sarah, see her settled, and secure—and then? Then he'd be ready to trade this life for a place beside his beloved Molly.

Murray looked at the picture on his dresser of himself at twenty-two, and his nineteen-year old bride. "You were a gorgeous girl, Molly." The black and white photograph taken after the wedding had captured their youth and her shy innocence. In bright sunshine, they stood on the stoop of Molly's building. Wearing a dark suit with wide lapels, and a full head of hair, he smiled directly at the camera. Molly's dark, heavy hair was gathered in a loose braid and she wore a light-colored, street-length dress, pale yellow, Murray remembered. She carried a small bouquet of roses. Slender and small, she had turned her head slightly to her left, and she looked up at him with a shy smile. He could see the hollow in her cheek, and garlanded by tendrils of her hair, the graceful, delicate line of her long neck.

They had stayed in love for fifty-five years, sharing the joys and enduring the grief that life brought. Their three attempts to have children had ended in miscarriages, each followed by a time of sorrow. And she would have been such a good mother, Murray thought. But that was not to be. So, lacking children, they had focused all their attention on each other. "Ah, Molly," he sighed, "the six years you've been gone have been long ones."

A year after her death from a heart attack, Murray had sold their house, because he could not bear the emptiness where Molly used to be. He had rented a small apartment after that. When Sarah moved from New York to Coveland after the break-up with the Levinson schmuck, Murray got the idea that he might move there, too. She was his sister Rachel's granddaughter, and the only family he had on the West Coast. His remaining relatives still lived in the New York area.

He had visited Sarah and discussed his idea of moving to the island. She had been delighted, so he had made all the arrangements. He'd been at Coveland House for two years. It wasn't so bad. Of course it was quieter than Los Angeles. Coveland compared to L.A. like a stroll in the park to the Indianapolis 500. But who needed all that exhaust? There had been a mild invasion of Angelenos in the Seattle area the last few years, and it amused Murray to see how the Seattle natives hated the big-city ways of the Californians.

So here he was. He lived simply and independently, never intruding in Sarah's life, but present if she needed him. And he tried to help out whenever and however he could. After all, he didn't have money worries anymore. He had a car, his ancient Lincoln, he had a few friends, and—he glanced at his watch. Oh, boy—if he didn't stop ruminating like an old fart, he'd be late to the concert!

He pocketed his keys, and headed downstairs. He had elected to drive himself instead of riding in the van with Valerie Julian, and it was a good thing, too, he thought, when he got to the parking lot, since the group from Coveland House had already left.

At seven-twenty, when Murray entered the high school auditorium, it was less than half-full. Two aisles ran at a gentle slope from the back of the hall to the base of the raised wooden stage. There was a wide seating area in the middle, flanked by two narrow ones. He easily located Valerie

Julian and the contingent from Coveland House. The flock of silver heads, dotted with a smattering of a few bald, shiny ones (like his own), sat about ten rows back from the stage in the middle.

The curtain was drawn, and the stage was empty except for four chairs and four music stands in a semicircle in the center. The house lights burned brightly, and there was a lively buzz of conversation. Murray took a seat alone near the aisle in the left rear of the middle section. He didn't feel like small talk, and he was nervous for Sarah's sake. Who likes to play to a half-empty house? He silently prayed that the hall would fill quickly.

His prayer was swiftly answered. At seven twenty-five, a boisterous group of students surged down the aisle on the right. Murray recognized tall, freckle-faced Bitsy Baird with what seemed like the whole raggle-taggle high school in tow. She talked, laughing and gesturing like the extrovert she was. The students piled into the seats about three rows behind the older people. At the same time, down both aisles, there came a steady flow of couples and families. Murray began to relax and read his program; it would be a good turnout.

At seven thirty-five, the house lights dimmed, and four musicians walked out onto the stage. As the audience applauded, a man and a small boy slipped into the aisle seats on Murray's row. Murray groaned inwardly. Oh no, a kid—fidget, yack-yack, and trouble—he'd have to change seats. But when he and the boy locked eyes, their recognition was mutual.

"The Merry Apple Man!"

"Owen!"

Smiling broadly, Murray moved over to sit next to Owen and Neal as the four string players tuned onstage. He shook hands with the MacGregors, and whispered, "Good to see you both again."

Murray opened his mouth to continue, but before he could say anything else, an amplified female voice announced in ringing tones, "Good evening, everyone. My name is Brucie Barncamper."

Tonight, she was an apparition in red. Tall and broad, she commanded center stage and spoke into a handheld microphone. Murray's eyes widened, and he gripped the armrests of his seat, checking his immediate instinct to flee. Flight being unmanly and out of the question, since nothing would prevent him from attending Sarah's concert, his strategy for self-preservation followed another direction. He lowered his face into one hand and sank into his seat, willing himself into invisibility.

"I am the president of the Coveland Cultural Council," Brucie boomed, "and we on the council are very pleased to present The Musicians of Brooklyn tonight. There will be a reception in the foyer of the auditorium immediately after the concert, and I would like to invite you all to meet the artists there and join us for refreshments. And now please welcome The Musicians of Brooklyn." There was another warm round of applause. Brucie lumbered off the stage, and the concert began.

At intermission, after Owen's restroom break, Murray asked the small boy, "So, did you take my advice the other day and go to Matthew's Old-Fashioned Ice Cream Parlor?"

"Yes, we did and I had strawberry ice cream in a waffle cone with sprinkles."

"Oh, you're making me hungry," Murray complained in mock distress. "And did you enjoy the talk at the travel shop?"

Owen nodded vigorously, "Yep, and we're going to the next one, too. Right, Daddy?"

Neal smiled half-heartedly. "Well, we'll see," he said.

Murray was surprised by the younger man's demeanor. There were dark circles under Neal's eyes, and his face seemed older, scored with deeper lines. Worse than his physical appearance was the aura of gloom and depression that enveloped the red-haired history teacher.

Searching for a conversational topic, Murray held up his program and pointed to the first piece listed after intermission, "See that—the Mozart oboe quartet? My grandniece Sarah—the one who owns the travel shop—is going to play viola on that one."

That statement elicited the biggest response of the evening from Neal. "Really?" he said, sitting up straight and looking closely at the program. "I didn't read the names of the players—only the pieces. I had no idea she was a musician."

"Yes, she is, and a very fine one, too. She played viola professionally with this group in New York before she moved here and made a career change."

"What's a viola?" asked Owen.

"It looks like a violin, but it's larger and has a deeper voice," Murray explained. "It blends in so well in ensembles—groups—that it is sometimes difficult to distinguish its sound from all the others."

"In other words," Owen remarked, "it's nothing like the bagpipes."

Murray laughed, "It certainly isn't. Look," he pointed, "here they come now."

The four musicians entered from the left side of the stage, cellist Beth O'Leary, Sarah, violinist Edward Schultz, and Julie Jacobs, the oboist. After bowing, they sat and tuned. The violinist wore a tuxedo and the three women were dressed in long black gowns. Sarah sat between Beth O'Leary, a large, slightly pudgy woman with shoulder-length caramel-colored hair, and Edward Schultz whose chiseled features, ruddy cheeks, and fall of heavy, straight blonde hair made him look like a poster boy for the *Hitler Jugend*. Julie Jacobs was a small woman with a cascade of curling hair that reached almost to her waist.

As they began to play, Murray could tell that Sarah was enjoying herself. She played with animation, radiating energy and pleasure. She could still be playing professionally in New York if it hadn't been for that characterless schmuck Danny Levinson. No, *schmuck* was too kind a word. Hell, in his case, even the term *asshole* would be a compliment. At least the scum had done Sarah the favor of removing himself from her life, but at the cost of practically destroying her trust in men. She should have a career and she should have a husband and children. She's got it all, Murray thought—brains, talent, initiative, integrity, kindness—all wrapped in a beautiful package. It'll work out for her—it's got to, he reassured himself.

And then he closed his eyes and let the pleasure of Mozart's music, superbly played, supersede all thought.

CHAPTER 14

The Hazards of Romance

After the concert, the audience made its way up the aisles and out the two double doors to the broad but shallow foyer. There were two long cloth-covered tables at one end laden with food and drink. Brucie Barncamper and her minions had outdone themselves for the reception. After a quick survey of the scene, Murray announced to Neal, "I am to food and drink as predator is to prey. Watch this." He patted his round belly, and moved in for the kill, towing Owen and Neal in his wake.

"Look at all the pies!" exclaimed Owen, pointing with one small finger, "Cherry, apple, lemon meringue, blackberry, and chocolate cream."

"And the cakes," added Murray, picking up where Owen left off, "Chocolate, carrot cake, spice cake. And cheeses—Brie, Havarti, Gouda, Swiss, cheddar with fruit and crackers. Mmmmmh! The only problem is where to start."

Murray didn't ponder the problem very long. He and Owen quickly filled their plates, munching as they went. Neal followed them, glad to see his son eating well, but selecting only cheese, crackers, a small cluster of grapes, and a glass of red wine for himself. He and Owen followed Murray, who walked over to the far side of the foyer and stood in the shadow of a tall potted ficus tree.

"This tree is my camouflage," Murray explained, "in case I have to hide from one of my avid admirers."

"I hope I'll have that problem when I'm your age," Neal replied.

"You'll retract that statement when you see who I mean."

Murray glanced at Neal's untouched plate. "Not hungry?" he asked. "Here I am, setting you and Owen an excellent example of how to be a hearty eater, and you've hardly even touched your food."

Neal smiled wanly. "Ah, well, I've no appetite tonight," he said. But the truth was, his hunger was of another order.

Neal scanned the crowded foyer, looking for Sarah. Watching her during the concert had reminded him of the time he and a high school buddy had played hooky to go salmon fishing. It had been a beautiful day on the river, but his exhilaration and deep pleasure had been marred by nagging guilt and a secret jealousy when his buddy caught the bigger fish. While Sarah played the Mozart, Neal had relished the chance to watch her, and his attraction grew with every small observation. He noticed how her hair, the color of night, set off the luminous quality of her skin so that it seemed to glow like day. He had watched her sparkling eyes, the small smile turning up the corners of her generous mouth, and the concentration and play of expressions on her face as she bowed the viola and made eye contact with the other members of the group. Guilt had descended when the thought of Vicky flickered across the horizon of his mind like heat lightning, but he ignored it; he needed a respite from that storm. What had surprised him was his sudden envy of Sarah's colleagues. He found himself longing to be with her onstage like the other musicians. He wanted to share the experience with her as they did.

Neal was drawn, too, by Sarah's warmth and the guileless quality she possessed. The day he'd met her in the travel shop, her intensity and sincerity had come shining through, just as clearly as it had onstage tonight. Sarah—the name meant princess. Fitting, Neal thought. She was like a jeweled crown—not anything large, overdone, or gaudy, no—like a circlet of gold, simple and elegant. A symbol not of worldly power, but of that which is perfect and true.

Perfect and true Sarah, who was for him completely unobtainable. Well, he thought, no one could stop him from looking. Cold comfort though it was, he would memorize her, every feature, every gesture, every glance. Neal shook his head and blew out a noisy breath. One more frustration to endure: the flare of desire—a feeling he hadn't experienced for a long, long time—checked by the knowledge that he could never pursue her; he was a married man. Neal's shoulders slumped. From fire to ashes—his surprise and elation at seeing Sarah at the concert turned to acute sadness.

"You seem preoccupied or worried," said Murray. "I can't tell which."

"Oh, just a little weary," Neal said, and meant it. He held a half-eaten cracker with a smear of Brie on it, still searching the crowd. Although he'd recovered from the physical shock and blow to the head he received during his harrowing experience in the study two days earlier, he was very tired—still mentally and emotionally shaken. The goose egg on the back of his head had subsided, but he'd had a splitting headache all day Friday, which had made teaching a literal hell.

Murray sipped his red wine, and then, speaking loudly in order to be heard over the noise of laughter and many conversations, he said to Neal, "The last time we talked, you spoke about your grandfather's journal. Did you ever read it?"

"No, not yet," Neal said slowly. "Now that you mention it, I think I will read his journal—very soon," he said. He smiled at Murray, "Thank you for reminding me. The past two weeks have been rough. It'll be good to read what he had to say."

"You know," Murray said, "if I can ever be of help to you, or if you just need a sounding board, call on me. Solomon I'm not, but eighty years of life have given me a little bit of wisdom." Murray suddenly bent from the waist and showed Owen the top of his head, "See this bald spot? The brain was always cookin'! It just got too hot for the hair."

Owen laughed.

"Ah," said Murray, straightening, "here come the musicians. And heaven help me, Brucie Barncamper, is with them." He looked resignedly at Neal. "I'm afraid I'll have to leave my tree and take my chances in the open ground. Wish me luck."

Neal laughed and said, "Best of luck, Murray, because if she's the one, you'll need it. Remember, fortune favors the brave."

Murray took Owen's hand and said, "Let's go and talk to Sarah." He led the MacGregors through the press of the crowd. Speaking to Sarah, as they realized when they approached the group of musicians, was not going to be easy. She was surrounded by Bitsy and the combined high school athletic teams. They ringed her like the Himalayas around Shangri-La. Murray sought passage by reaching up and tapping Bitsy on the shoulder.

"Mr. Appleman!" she exclaimed, turning around. "Wasn't Sarah great?"

"She certainly was."

"Want to squeeze in here and talk to her?"

Murray nodded.

"Okay, watch this," Bitsy whispered, and then in a virtuoso demonstration of crowd control, she turned and shouted, "C'mon guys, let's go get some more food!"

When the thundering horde raced to the tables on cue, Bitsy gave Murray the thumbs-up sign and remarked as she sauntered off, "More effective than screaming *Fire!*" She left the field clear for Murray, Neal, and Owen, and Brucie Barncamper, who was closing in at a high rate of speed.

Sarah, now that they could finally see her, was radiant.

Murray's smile was just as luminous. He said to Neal, "Isn't she a beauty?"

"Uncle Murr!" Sarah threw out her arms and embraced him. "Did you enjoy the concert?" she whispered in his ear.

"Absolutely, doll. You were wonderful." He kissed her cheek lightly, still holding her in an embrace and then said, "See who's here?"

"Yes, the MacGregors, and all in red, your would-be flame."

"Wasn't your niece marvelous, Mr. Appleman?" The blast of Brucie's voice could have led a big parade all by itself. Compared to it, seventy-six trombones would have withered in shame.

Murray released Sarah and turned to face the music.

"Ah, good evening," he said "Yes, indeed, Sarah is marvelous, as a musician and in every way, Mrs. Barncamper."

"Oh, heavens, call me Brucie," she bellowed, taking Murray by the arm and dragging him back to the refreshment table. "Have you tried my apple pie?"

Sarah shook her head as she watched them go, and then she offered her hand to Owen. "Hello, Owen, my friend."

"Hi," said Owen, "You are very pretty."

"Well, thank you!" she laughed. Then Sarah looked up at Neal.

"So, Sarah Friedkin, do you recognize me when I'm not dressed in a kilt?" he asked, taking her small hand in both of his. He noticed the slow flush that crept up her throat to her face.

She tilted her head slightly and answered, "Yes, kilt or no kilt, I remember you, Neal. Believe me, our time together in the travel shop was something I'll never forget. When I realized you weren't Hamilton Deel, my face felt so hot that it must have been the color of Brucie Barncamper's dress."

"Well, let's say you had a quite a glow about you," Neal replied.

Sarah's laugh bubbled up hearty and deep. Her eyes shone up at Neal. "Thank you again for playing the pipes at my shop. It was a perfect introduction to Hamilton Deel's talk. But, you know, it wasn't the first time I'd heard you play."

"No?"

"No, I was walking on the beach one day this spring, when I heard bagpipes, and I saw someone—now I know it was you—playing up on the bluff behind the old Fritzinger house. It sounded so good that I sat on a log and listened for a while."

"Well, thank you. That's my new home, and I didn't know I had an audience that day, but I'm glad you enjoyed it. If my playing was good, yours tonight was wonderful," Neal declared. "I thought you were a businesswoman; I had no idea that you were a professional musician."

Before Sarah could reply, Owen piped up, "Daddy has a recording of the piece you played."

"Does he?"

"Yes, 'cause I remember this part." Owen sang a lilting melody.

Sarah's eyes widened in delight. "That's the oboe theme from the third movement. Good for you!" She laid her hand on Owen's shoulder and looked at Neal, "Speaking of professional musicians, I think you've got one in the making right here."

"I just might. He's studying piano and doing very well."

"Come and meet—"

"Would you like—"

Sarah and Neal laughed; they had spoken at the same time. Neal suddenly felt lighter, as though gravity had relinquished some of its pull.

"Ladies first," said Neal with a half-bow.

"I was going to ask you to come and meet my friends, the other musicians."

"And I was going to ask you if you would like something to drink. I'll get it for you."

"Oh yes, thank you, I'd like some wine."

"Coming up," Neal said. Then he looked at Owen "Do you want to come with me?"

"I'll stay with Sarah, Daddy."

"Okay, I'll be right back."

"Oh, and Neal," Sarah suggested, "maybe you can rescue Uncle Murray. He's over there by the table. Ever since Brucie met him at my shop and found out he was a widower, her mating instinct has gone into overdrive. She has him collared, and from the looks of it she may try to drag him off to her lair at any moment."

"That seems to be a possibility," Neal replied. Speaking from experience, he added, "There's nothing more fierce than the female of the species."

All he could see of Murray was the gleam of his bald head poking up just over the top of Brucie's red shoulder. She had him backed up against the wall and she carried on a continuous monologue at the top of her voice, the sound of which was audible from a distance, rising and falling like the baying of hounds.

"She's so determined," Sarah said, "that he'd have to be outright rude to get her to back off, and I know he won't do or say anything offensive. He's too kind."

"All right," Neal laughed, "I'll see if I can pry them apart without resorting to plastic explosives."

"Thank you. In the meantime, I'll introduce Owen to my friends," Sarah said, taking the boy's hand in hers.

Neal met several people he knew as he walked toward the refreshment table to get Sarah's wine. Valerie Julian, the program director of Coveland House, waved at him from across the room. In the middle of the foyer he shook hands with Owen's piano teacher, petite, black-haired Yoshiko Katagiri and her tall Swedish husband Ingemar Lindahl.

"Quite a program, wasn't it?" Neal said to Yoshiko.

"Oh, we enjoyed it so much. I wish we could have a concert like this once a month," Yoshiko replied.

"Owen liked it, too. He's over there with the musicians."

"Yes, I see that little red head; we'll go talk to him before we leave. I'm so glad you brought him; it's great for him to hear players of that caliber. By the way, Neal, he's been telling me how much he likes the new house," Yoshiko said. "He loves his new room and the swing you made for him, the big yard, and the beach. That house has such a beautiful setting. Before Miss Fritzinger died, I used to visit her there and play piano for her sometimes."

"That's right!" Neal said. "Peggy Williams, our real estate agent, told us that. I had forgotten it. You know, Yoshiko, I made a lot of repairs and the house looks great now."

"Do you have pictures?" Ingemar asked.

"Yes, as a matter of fact, we do. Vicky had some developed, but I haven't had a chance to look at them yet." Neal's impulse was to invite Yoshiko and Ingemar over to see the house, but he refrained; the situation at home was too turbulent.

"Bring them with you next week to Owen's lesson," Yoshiko suggested. "We'd love to see them." Then she pulled on Ingemar's arm and said, "Let's go talk to my favorite student."

Responding to a tap on his shoulder, Neal turned to see Peggy Williams with a tall, handsome younger man.

"Did I just hear you mention my name?" she asked.

Neal smiled, "Yes, I was talking about my favorite real estate agent."

It was Peggy's turn to smile. "Neal, meet my son Bill," Peggy said. "Cherish your boy Owen while you can—my son's been away for four months. He's the chief engineer on a commercial fishing boat."

"I know about that rugged life," Neal told Bill, as they shook hands. "My father worked on the boats out of Seattle, too."

"How is everything at your new home?" Peggy asked.

"Well, I completed most of the renovations." Neal replied. He told her about some of the improvements he had made and let that suffice. He didn't have the heart to tell her any more news of his house.

He walked slowly, still pondering what he could do to help Murray, when he heard someone call his name. It was his friend and colleague Ellie Lawndale, the teacher who had given him Sparker the cat. As he spoke to her briefly about the concert, a plan came to him. "Ellie, are you leaving soon?"

"No, I'm on the clean-up committee." A gap-toothed grin split her broad, kind face, "I'll be here 'til the bitter end."

"Well, could you do me a favor in the next few minutes?"

"Sure."

He quickly explained the problem with Brucie and Murray, and then told her his solution.

"Good idea," she smiled. "Just tell me when."

Neal hurried out to the parking lot and moved his car. As soon as he re-entered the building and got Ellie's attention, he nodded.

Ellie approached Brucie and whispered a message in her ear.

Brucie's jaw dropped, and then her demeanor changed with the force and speed of an atomic reaction. Her brows collided; the corners of her mouth dived; her color darkened, and she swelled in girth and height like a mushroom cloud. "What?" she exploded, causing more than a few heads to turn. After one last remark to Murray, she marched to the center of the foyer, leaving him standing alone in the corner.

Neal took the opportunity to deliver his own message to Murray. "I created a diversion, Murray, so run for your life."

"Blessings on your head, my boy. Where's the nearest exit?"

As Murray slipped out the front door of the auditorium, Brucie clapped her hands above her head several times, subduing the crowd into silence. In her most authoritarian voice, *fortissimo*, with an edge of righteous indignation, she announced, "Someone has blocked the *only* exit of the parking lot. Would the driver of a red Mustang—and you know who you are—please move his car immediately!"

Following Brucie's orders, Neal dashed out and re-parked his car, allowing Murray to escape in his ancient Lincoln. Mission accomplished, he returned to get Sarah the drink he had promised her.

Eternity was shorter than the food and wine line. As Neal waited impatiently behind two small white-haired ladies, he glanced at his watch. It was almost ten, an hour and a half past Owen's bedtime. Neal really wanted to stay and talk to Sarah, but he knew that as soon as he met her friends, he'd have to take Owen home.

Home—that uncertain, unpredictable place. He didn't know who or what he'd find when he got there. Vicky might be there or not, as it pleased her. She had refused to come to the concert, going instead to another movie in Stone Harbor. She was barely speaking to him after their row in the middle of the night on Thursday. And then who knew what nonhuman presences he might encounter in the old house.

Vicky hadn't believed anything he had told her about the huge black dog and the shadowy figure in the study, even though the episode on Thursday had seemed entirely real to him. But was it? Well, he hadn't lunged back against the wall in a fit of self-destruction. The dog had attacked him. The blow to his head had been severe enough to knock him unconscious for three hours. And the other bit of evidence, to his mind, was the stinking clump of fur he had found on Owen's cheek. Even though Vicky had rubbed the tuft of fur into oblivion, the dog's fetid odor had remained on Neal's fingers until he washed it away later with soap and hot water.

Was it all real or was he coming unhinged, as Vicky seemed to think? He had the proof of his own senses, but he knew very well that the senses could lie. He could never prove his case in a court of law—judge and jury would laugh at him the same way Vicky did. Maybe he *was* losing his mind. And yet, even if he couldn't prove anything, there was the fact that Thursday night was the second time he'd seen the dog and the hooded figure. His experience in the study was related to the first vision he'd had in the fog, the day he had played the bagpipes. On that day in March, he had believed for a moment that he saw an animal moving in the mist below the bay window, only he had thought it too large to be a dog. And that day, too, the hooded being had materialized out of the darkness and spoken, calling his name.

His two visions were at least connected and coherent, making him more and more certain that there was a presence in the house, something supernatural. Or maybe that was the wrong word. *Super* implied a superior force or power. This power, he was sure, was not from above, but from below. There was some sort of inferior influence, something discordant and foul, reeking of dissolution, in his house. He had felt the disharmony from the very beginning, and it seemed to be growing in influence and power, invading not only his house, but his very life. Grandpa, he thought, I need your strength—and your advice now. He would read that journal tonight when he got home.

He hoped his grandfather's words would be a solace in his cheerless home. Neal sighed heavily, thinking of Vicky's hostility. She had excluded him from her bed Thursday night, which was a hardship in name only— they had not made love for months. The truth was that he had never intended to sleep in his own room after the shadowy being threatened Owen. He feared for his son, and that night, before Vicky had said anything, he had already decided to spend the night in Owen's room.

In fact, he thought, as he finally got to the head of the line and poured a glass of red wine for Sarah, from now on, he was going to spend *every* night in Owen's room.

CHAPTER 15

The Journal

O wen fell asleep in the car before Neal drove out of the school parking lot. Even though it was early May, and the season was spring, it felt like winter. The night was chill and the gusty wind pushed ragged clouds across a sable sky. Through the clearings between the clouds, Neal could see here and there the white fire of an occasional star. The glimpses of light brought him a measure of comfort as he drove down the narrow back island roads lined by trees that seemed to be the ominous forward flanks of an advancing army.

His very life seemed headed into a future shadowed on two fronts—the threat to Owen on one hand and the snowballing disintegration of his marriage on the other. In the face of the gathering gloom, the thought of Sarah heartened him. Nothing could take away the brightness of the evening—rediscovering her, the warmth of her presence, hearing her play, seeing her in the context of her friends, and present, whether he willed it or not, pulsing over and under and through it all, the stir and pull of sweet attraction. There was no denying it—and he knew she felt it, too.

Her friends were as warm, intelligent, and likable as she. At the reception, Julie Jacobs, the oboist, and Sarah, both dog lovers, had traded stories about their pets. Julie had brought her dog Tipper along with her on the tour, and she and Sarah regaled Owen, who dearly wanted a dog of his own, with funny anecdotes about their pets. To surprise Sarah,

Edward Schultz had presented her with a package of fresh bagels he had ordered, shipped out express from New York. Amid the laughter and bagel-tasting, Neal had enjoyed talking to them all, but he had conversed the most with Beth O'Leary, the cellist. Forthright and expansive, Beth had made plain how very fond of Sarah she was. In fact, all the musicians had bantered with Sarah and teased her in a display of such warm camaraderie that Neal wondered why she ever chose to leave the group.

Downshifting as he turned into his driveway, he found himself comparing his wife's barren social life with Sarah's rich one. He could not imagine anyone outside of family holding Vicky so dear, or treating her with such transparent love and affection. He wished fervently that Vicky were a woman whose friends held her in high regard, but she was so critical and oftentimes so rude, that she had only short-lived, superficial friendships with other women, and none at all with men, whom she regarded solely in sexual contexts.

The porch light was on, but the house was dark when Neal drove up. Seeing that Vicky's Mazda was gone, he felt a surge of relief, followed immediately by a backwash of guilt. But the truth was that after talking with Murray, he'd decided to read his grandfather's journal that night, and with Vicky gone, he'd have some peace in which to do it.

There was no peace in Vicky's presence. Wrapped in her aura of anger, she was cold and silent, ignoring him, and snapping at Owen. Since Thursday, she had gone out each evening, returning in the wee hours. She was asleep when Neal and Owen ate breakfast and left for school. In fact, she had stopped eating with them altogether, and what's more, he thought, she had almost stopped functioning, shrugging off her responsibilities as a wife and mother. Over the course of the past month, Neal had gradually taken over the cooking and the laundry, which left no time for cleaning. He was saddened and dispirited by the atmosphere of neglect that accumulated as tangibly in the untidy house as the dust bunnies, the strewn clothes, and the mildew on the bathroom walls.

As his path and Vicky's crossed more and more infrequently, their communications descended into accusations and defensive replies, barbed and laced with poison, like the darts and arrows of two enemy camps.

Any negotiations seemed out of the question. If Neal tried to discuss her behavior, she simply hurled epithets at him or refused to talk at all.

Their relationship was so strained that he saw her in a completely different light. Vicky had always been a fine-featured, pretty blonde, but now it seemed to Neal that her prettiness was as scabbard is to blade, a thin sheath for the merciless hardness and raw edge of steel.

Neal got out of the car and went around to the passenger side. As he lifted Owen to carry him in, the boy woke momentarily. "Are we home?" he asked, wrapping his arms around Neal's neck and his legs around his father's waist. He lapsed into sleep again as soon as he laid his head on Neal's shoulder.

Neal carried him through the kitchen and up the stairs to bed. He pulled back the bedcovers with one hand and then laid the boy down gently. After easing off his son's shoes and trousers, he covered Owen with the sheet and blanket and kissed him on the forehead.

"Night, Daddy," Owen murmured and turned on his side.

"Goodnight." Neal left the room, closing the door behind him, and then climbed the stairs to the study to retrieve his grandfather's journal. His muscles were tense and every nerve was on edge as he opened the door and turned on the overhead light. He surveyed the tower room. It was the first time he'd returned to the study since Thursday.

The chair, lamp, and table were back in place. The only sound was the rattle of the windowpane, shaken by the gusting wind. Neal waited, watching and listening for several minutes, but the only activity he detected was a draft of cold air near the floor. Tonight the room seemed blank, empty—there were no presences. No, there was nothing. He relaxed a little.

He opened the roll-top and pulled a slim, leather-bound journal from one of the horizontal slots in the desk. The size and weight of the book felt good in his hand. He closed the roll-top, turned off the light and went down to the front parlor.

He laid the journal on the coffee table, and then he took off his jacket and tie. To ward off the chill in the room, he made a fire. When the logs were burning brightly in the fireplace, Neal sat down on the sofa and took the slim book in his hand. As he opened the journal, a letter from his grandmother Barbara, one he had read in the past, but forgotten, fell into his lap. The stiff paper crackled as he unfolded it and read it again.

Edinburgh, Scotland
October 1, 1994

Dearest Neal,

Before he died, your grandfather Ian asked me to send you this journal. I should have given it to you when you were here for the funeral last month, but in the midst of all the arrangements and my grief, I overlooked it. The words of the journal are his, exactly as he dictated it to me. He knew that when he was gone, you might need it; he hoped it would afford you protection and guidance in troubled times.

The other matter I am writing about is that upon my death, our property, our house here in Edinburgh, and all its contents will be yours. You'll always have a place in Scotland, as you have always had a place in our hearts.

I hope this finds you, Vicky, and Owen in the best of health. I am well, but I am missing my Ian sorely, as I know you do. Let me hear from you.

All my love,
Grandma Barbara

Neal leaned back and crossed his arms, staring into the fire. *He hoped it would afford you protection and guidance in troubled times.* Well, troubled times: he certainly had that—he was under siege. Vicky was more adversary than wife, and either there was a threatening, infernal presence in his home that he had no idea how to combat, or else he was insane. Oh, how he wished he could talk to his grandfather! Ian had always been a source of security and strength for him. Neal prayed that Ian might help him now, even after death.

In a way, he already had, Neal thought. The very touch of the smooth, worn leather had a calming influence, an assurance that somehow, things would be all right.

Neal folded his grandmother's letter and placed it carefully inside the cover of the journal. Then he turned to the first page and began to read.

This is a true account of my extraordinary experience in May of 1940, which I have revealed in full to no one but my wife Barbara. I, Ian MacGregor, was a piper with the Black Watch when we were attacked and overwhelmed by the Germans.

Outside, the wind gusted, and the clouds flew past as the damp chill of the Pacific Northwest enclosed the house in its clammy embrace. In the living room, the logs burned and shifted; the fire flared and crackled as Neal read, transfixed by Ian's description of the early days of the war and the series of disturbing visions he had had as the British Expeditionary Force advanced over the battlefields of Flanders. With mounting intensity, Neal read Ian's account of how the *Totenkopf* SS massacred the British soldiers and how the towering supernatural figure had stood behind the commanding officer, delighting in murder. Pulse pounding, Neal gripped the journal with stiff, white-knuckled hands as he read Ian's description of what happened next.

Suddenly aware of my presence, the black-shrouded being turned and fixed me in his gaze, a look filled with such hatred and naked malice that it froze my heart. With a cruel smile, the creature raised an arm and pointed one finger at me. In that instant, a shockwave of hot, searing pain shot through my entire head. The pain was unimaginable; a flash of red scorched my eyes and then burned my throat and lungs, as though I breathed in and swallowed fire. My knees buckled, and I collapsed, unconscious before I fell to earth. Hours later, I awoke in the cornfield, blind, mute, and alone.

Dumbfounded, Neal lifted his head and stared unseeing at the fire. Christ, so that was what had injured his grandfather, not shrapnel as he'd been told. He didn't know what was more shocking—Ian's description of the demon, or the fact that his grandfather had withheld the truth. Incredibly, the man he trusted most in the world had lied to him. He squeezed his eyes shut—that was a stinging blow.

As his emotions swirled, he tried to think through it all. He rubbed his face with both hands. Had his grandfather told him the truth, Neal might have laughed at him; he certainly wouldn't have believed him—no, not until now, when Neal had had his own eerie experiences. Was the cloaked figure he had seen in the study the same being that had blinded his grandfather? And if so, why was it here? God, he wished he could talk to Ian!

Then it struck him—he'd do the next best thing—he'd call his grandmother, ask her help, maybe even invite her over for an extended stay. Knowing Ian's story, she would believe him. She would need no explanation to understand how much he feared for Owen's safety in the house, and she could be present with Owen when Neal could not. At seventy-five, she was still an active, vigorous woman who seemed decades younger. She would help with the housework and cooking—no one was tidier than his grandmother. She would be a motherly, cheerful presence for Owen, and a morale booster for him. And being here would ease Barbara's loneliness and give her purpose.

"That's it," he decided. He checked his watch. Eleven-twenty. He'd call her after midnight, when it would be early Sunday morning in Edinburgh. Neal hoped she would want to come; his grandmother was a rock. The downside of that was that if she refused, God Himself wouldn't be able to persuade her. What would he do if she didn't come? He tapped his fingers on the open page of the journal. No, he brushed the ridiculous doubt aside; he refused to let his fears dictate his thoughts. He knew his grandmother better than that; her love and loyalty would send her across the ocean posthaste.

He felt suddenly light and hopeful. He wasn't alone in this any longer and his help would come from someone very dear to his heart. Neal smiled, thinking of his grandmother, her aureole of thick white hair, and her bright brown eyes, intelligent and good-humored, the windows of her unsinkable spirit.

Then he immersed himself in his grandfather's journal once more. He read about Ian's encounter with the piper, whom he saw only with his inner vision, and how Ian followed the sound of the wild fantastic music northward, through the blasted fields and villages of Flanders toward Dunkirk. Ian recounted the meeting between himself and Jack and Ed, the two Yorkshiremen.

"Of course!" Neal exclaimed—he had met Ed. He was the one who had described the power of the bagpipe's music, how it miraculously transformed the exhausted men, giving them new strength and rousing their courage so that they burst out singing, united and defiant in the face of death.

Neal read Ian's description of the last day on the beach at Dunkirk, when Jack was killed by a strafing Stuka. Ian had stood up in defiance and played his pipes amidst the death and destruction on that terrible beach, rallying the spirits of the British soldiers, and leading them to the rescue ships.

There the journal of Ian's war experiences ended. The last entry consisted of a few lines of music, notated by hand. It was an unusual bagpipe tune, one quite unfamiliar to Neal, with no title or composer listed. What followed surprised Neal even more. He turned the page and found a letter his grandfather had written him.

CHAPTER 16

The Letter

The letter was not enclosed in an envelope; it was written on the pages of the journal. Neal read it, oblivious of time, place, or anything but the words on the page.

Neal, my lad,

When you read this letter, I'll be dead and buried. When you were a child, I thought it better to tell you that I was wounded by shrapnel, than to trouble you with the story of a supernatural being. Now that you have read the account of my experiences at Dunkirk, I hope you will understand and forgive me. As fantastic as it may seem, it happened just as I described it. It is all true.

Unfortunately, I knew that last day on the beach, when I played the pipes and was assailed yet again by the spirit, that it was not over. What I didn't know was how or when the creature would come after me the next time.

Your grandmother Barbara and I were newlyweds when I left Scotland to go to war, and although I didn't know it then, she was already expecting a baby. As you know, our only child, your father Peter, was born in January of 1941. For the rest of the war years and for three years after, there were no more incidents. I had no visions and no sense that the evil being was near us.

But when Peter was seven years old, he began having nightmares. The dream was always the same. It was night and Peter found himself walking alone in a forest, lost and far from home. Because he was frightened, he began to walk faster, trying to find his way out of the forest. As his panic grew, he suddenly heard someone calling his name softly, seductively. The voice was always behind him. When he forced himself to turn and look, he saw in the distance a figure hooded and cloaked in black, with one arm outstretched toward him. It filled him with terror. He would wake screaming and flailing, pupils dilated, heart hammering, his pillow soaked with sweat.

The nightmares happened only occasionally when he was seven. As the years went by, the dreams persisted, but they occurred more frequently, and with one difference. Each time, the cloaked figure came closer. Peter was terrified that it would finally touch him.

In the final dream, when Peter was fourteen, the figure loomed over him and enveloped him in the cloak. Peter didn't wake screaming; he was unconscious and impossible to wake for several hours. When he did, the darkness was no longer on the outside, it had invaded Peter himself. That was the beginning of our waking nightmare. Peter began to drink secretly. He stole whiskey from our liquor cabinet at first. He kept a flask in his room, and he'd drink himself senseless each night. Later, he used money he earned from his part-time job at the fish market to bribe an older employee there, Alan Reed, to buy the whiskey for him.

By age fifteen, Peter was an alcoholic. At eighteen, he married your mother Sally, and you were born in December, 1961. Peter was always dissatisfied and restless. For him, Scotland was a tomb—cold, dreary, damp, and depressing. He and Sally moved first to Vancouver, Canada, and later to Everett, Washington, where you grew up. Your father eventually got work on the commercial fishing boats that shipped out of Seattle, and you know the rest.

Neal leaned back on the sofa and gazed at the ceiling. Yes, he knew the rest all too well. During the weeks when his father shipped out, his mother Sally, a waitress who worked nights at a truck stop on Highway 5, left Neal home alone, which petrified him. In the early evenings when she left for work, he locked all the doors and windows and turned on every light in the house. He ate dinner alone, did his homework, took his bath, and put himself to bed.

When his father came home from the fishing expeditions, temporarily flush, his parents indulged every desire, spending the money on clothes, new appliances, new furniture, and always cigarettes and liquor. His mother took off from work so she and Peter could go out and drink together. Sometimes they invited their friends home to drink with them. Neal remembered the loud parties that went on until three or four in the morning. The pounding rock music, harsh male laughter, and the squeals of women frightened him badly. He barricaded himself in his bedroom and slept with the pillow over his head.

The mornings after the parties, the whole house stank of cigarette smoke, spilled beer, and whiskey. More than once he'd had to step over and around the sprawled bodies of his father's snoring buddies who slept in drunken stupor on the living room floor.

The wild parties ended for his mother when she was only thirty-nine, during Neal's freshman year at the University of Washington. Her persistent, hacking smoker's cough was diagnosed as lung cancer in March. They buried her in June. His father never remarried, but lived instead with a succession of younger and younger women who drank and partied with him.

The car accident that killed his father had occurred almost two years ago, four days before Christmas on a curving, icy stretch of highway north of Seattle. Peter's car veered off the road at an extremely high rate of speed and slammed into a tree. He died of massive head injuries before they could extricate him from the car. Tests showed that his blood alcohol content was more than twice the legal limit.

Neal did not shed a tear before, during, or after the simple funeral. He took care of all the arrangements, and sat numbly between Vicky and his grandparents during the brief graveside service. His father had been absent from his life physically and emotionally for so long that he hardly missed him. But now after reading Ian's account of Peter's childhood, Neal understood that drinking had been Peter's escape, but an escape that led from tormented life to sudden death.

Given his father's history, Neal thought, it was no wonder that Vicky had accused him of drinking, then making up some fantastic ghost story to explain why he was unconscious in the study the other night. "Well, I wasn't drunk," Neal said aloud to himself, "and grandfather's journal and letter prove that I'm not crazy either." No, he thought, Grandfather's tormentor, who became my father's tormentor, and now mine, is real. Frighteningly real.

There was a popping sound from the fire and a display of sparks as the burning logs shifted. Neal rose, banked the fire with a poker and checked his watch. It was eleven forty-five. Soon after he finished reading the letter, it would be time to call his grandmother.

He sat down again on the sofa and resumed reading.

It was our idea to keep you here with us in Scotland every summer because we knew that Peter and Sally were incapable of providing you with a stable home. We'd have kept you year-round if we could. But despite all the adversity, Neal, or perhaps because of it, you have become a trustworthy, courageous man of whom I am very proud.

My purpose in writing this letter is to warn you. I fear that this evil being will focus next on you and Owen. Beware as your boy approaches seven, Peter's age when the creature began to haunt his dreams. What grieves me is that I can offer no real strategy for defense.

I pray God and hope with all my heart that my fears for you and Owen never materialize. But should the worst happen, there is this— the tune that Barbara notated for me as the last entry of the journal is all that I could recall of the shining piper's music. It is but a shoddy imitation, for no mortal man could write or recreate that sublime music; it is no better than a penny candle attempting to represent the sun. But, small though it be, even a penny candle may light the way in darkness. In any case, the tune is something, and maybe it will help you in the future; I do not know. But this I do know—you are a man of keen intelligence, and so perhaps this account of all my experiences will lead you in a direction in which, for the good of all, you can somehow overcome this foul menace.

Though I cannot be with you in person, know that I am with you always in spirit. Be brave, my lad, and may help come to you at greatest need.

All my love,
Grandfather

Struggling to comprehend his suddenly topsy-turvy world, Neal closed the journal and laid it in his lap. Fact had become illusion and illusion fact. A demon, not shrapnel, had caused his grandfather's war injuries, then somehow possessed Neal's father. This shadow-creature was real and now it had come for him and Owen. In short, his grandfather's revelations had rewritten Neal's history.

But history, he thought, has its uses. At least Grandfather had forewarned him and armed him with knowledge. He would simply have to make a quick adjustment to a new set of facts. Somehow, although truly alarmed now that he knew the threat was real and not imagined, Neal felt a kind of calm take hold. His visions had been real and true; he was not deluded. Because he no longer doubted his own perceptions, he could focus all his energy on banishing this creature from his house and his life. As a father, he was bound to protect his son and somehow he would. And now it was time to take the first step. Girded with a steady resolve, Neal walked into the kitchen to call his grandmother. He dialed her number and waited for her to answer.

"Hello, Grandma," he said, "are you the Scottish cavalry?"

"Well," Barbara replied, not missing a beat, "I'm not mounted on horseback, but I'm an army of one and I'll do anything I can to help you."

Neal said, "I've read Grandfather's journal and his letter."

"Have you now? Well, if you're needing the cavalry, you're obviously under siege, so tell me how I can help you, laddie mine."

"It's here in the house, Grandma, in the tower room."

Neal heard her sharp intake of breath. He continued, "I've seen it on two occasions, and the second time it threatened my son. It's Owen I'm worried about. Vicky and I are going through a bad patch—the worst of our marriage, in fact—and she's never around. So what I'd like is for you to come and stay with us until I can figure out a way to resolve the situation. I need someone who understands the threat to be here with Owen when I can't. I don't want him alone in the house—ever."

"When shall I come?"

Neal laughed in relief. "Can you get here in an hour?"

"No, but I'll call John Campbell at the travel agency and get it all arranged in two blinks of the eye. I'll ring back tomorrow and let you know when I'll arrive in Seattle."

"God bless you, Grandma, and thank you so much. I feel better already."

"Ah, I know Ian would tell me to go, Neal. Peter's gone and it's just you and my great-grandson left. For whatever it's worth, the cavalry is on its way!"

"Thank heavens," Neal said when he replaced the receiver. Just the sound of her voice was a tonic against depression and fear. Her presence would bring calm and lend a normalcy to the household, something sorely missing almost from the day they moved in. She was stubborn and strong of spirit, his grandmother, and she would be a staunch ally.

He felt heartened, practically buoyant, taking the stairs two at a time to Owen's room. The room seemed chilly, so Neal pulled the blanket up over his son's chest. "Only sweet dreams, Owen," he whispered. "No other kind."

He lingered a moment, watching his son. Owen breathed slowly through his mouth, his chest rising and falling rhythmically, one small hand palm up on the pillow, his delicate eyelids feathered with long lashes. A child drenched in sleep, so vulnerable. How could any person or any being in the universe desire to injure such innocence?

Standing there, Neal wished he were versed in the Mysteries like a high priest of ancient times, one who could chant words of power in ritual rhythms to create a seal of protection about this child, a defense against all evil. But though that was beyond his ability, he knew that the one great power he had was his love for his son. He could only offer the protection of his own mind, hands, and heart. He touched the top of Owen's head lightly. He would do whatever he had to do. If it took his life, Neal would give it, that Owen be left unharmed.

CHAPTER 17

Blows Are Struck

It was a measure of his fatigue that Neal, an early riser, slept solidly, undisturbed by dreams, until eight-thirty the next morning. After his midnight conversation with his grandmother, he had fallen asleep, sinking like a stone into the waters of forgetfulness, and lain in the same position all night. When his consciousness surfaced, it took him a moment to get his bearings, but then he sat up immediately and looked across the room to see that his son was all right. Owen lay on his right side in the other bed, snoring gently. The fuzzy ball of tri-colored fur lodged in the crook of Owen's knees was Sparker, loyal sidekick, faithful feline.

Satisfied that all was well, Neal yawned and stretched, then lay back down again, arms clasped behind his head, while a kaleidoscope of thoughts shifted through his mind in quick succession as he recalled the events and experiences of the night—attending Sarah's concert, reading his grandfather's journal, and his decision to ask his grandmother to visit. His world had changed. Beginning today, he had to plan a course of action, try to devise a strategy to combat this thing that had taken up residence in his house, threatening him and his son.

He also had to tell Vicky that he'd invited Barbara to come for an extended stay. He didn't look forward to that conversation—he'd probably need to invest in a suit of armor first. He guessed Vicky was home, but he didn't know for sure. She hadn't returned by the time he'd gone to bed last night.

Forsaking the soft comfort of his bed, Neal got up, padded barefoot across the hall, and opened the door to Vicky's room. He was greeted by a scent all too familiar from childhood, the sour smell of cigarette smoke and liquor mixed with stale perfume. Vicky lay sprawled diagonally across the unmade bed, still dressed in the white linen slacks and green silk blouse she'd worn last night. She slept face down with her bare feet sticking out over the edge of the bed. Her shoes lay upside down on the floor where they had fallen.

Fallen was the word, he thought. Pity struggled with anger as Neal stood silently over his prostrate wife. He was sorry to see her descending into chaos and yet she did it by choice. She was a grown woman with responsibilities she chose to ignore. He wanted to wake her, literally and figuratively, but the confrontation could wait. He decided to let the dragon sleep.

Neal dressed quickly and silently, drawing on some old jeans and a light blue sweatshirt, taking care not to wake Vicky. He put on clean socks, tied the laces of his sneakers, and slipped quietly out of the bedroom.

In the kitchen, he brewed coffee and made toast for himself. After he ate his breakfast, he lingered at the table with a second cup of coffee, enjoying the view. The day was bright and the gusty wind of the night before had won the blue field of the sky, routing the clouds in complete victory. The wind persisted, nudging the fir trees into motion. They swayed and nodded like tall, dignified dancers against the background of azure. Vibrated by the wind, the house hummed its own music in small creaks, rustlings, and murmurs while the old kitchen basked in sunlight.

Neal thought about what he had to do. On Friday, after the harrowing incident of the night before, he had made Owen promise to stay out of the study by concocting a story about the dangerous unscreened tower window. But he wanted more assurance than a six-year-old's promise. Tomorrow was Monday; he'd buy a padlock and install it on the door. He had to make certain that Owen never entered that room, and that the boy was never alone in the house. Of course when Barbara came, that would be much easier.

The telephone rang and Neal grabbed the receiver before it could ring twice. It was his grandmother.

"Neal, I've made my travel arrangements, and I'll arrive a week from tomorrow, on Monday, May fifteenth at six-twenty in the evening. I know you wanted me as soon as possible, but in order to close the house and prepare for a long absence, I need a little time to put everything in order."

"Grandma, that is fine. We'll have time to get one of our bedrooms ready for you." He'd also have time, Neal thought, to break the news to Vicky. He'd have to pick his moment well. "What airline?"

"British Air. All right then, lad, I'll ring off so I can get cracking with my preparations. I will see you soon, and lend whatever aid I can."

After thanking Barbara, Neal replaced the receiver and sat down at the table again. Sunlight poured through the clear panes of the windows, turning the old kitchen an antique gold. The polished oak floor gleamed, and the eggshell-white walls held the light.

He closed his eyes and let the sunlight warm him. He felt the presence of the house all around him. He heard the sound of the wind pushing against the walls and windows, making the old wood creak and murmur, rustling the curtains. The house contained its own music, he thought. Like a violin, it was a wooden structure that enclosed a space—a space with its own resonance. And in an old house like this one, the thoughts and emotions of all its inhabitants, the sound and tenor of all its years pressed on its walls, floors, and ceilings, its very fibers, and remained. One could hear it, feel it; all one had to do was listen.

He knew that the house, like any instrument, needed tuning. From the beginning, his ear had caught discordant overtones, echoes of the past. He wished his grandfather were here now, so that he could tell him about his dreams, his visions, and what he sensed about the house. But that couldn't be.

Barbara would help him with the housework and with Owen, but the problem remained: what could he do about the evil presence itself? He wished there was a friend he could trust here and now, someone with whom he could discuss a strategy. Neal sipped his coffee. How does a man fight a supernatural being? And more importantly, how does a man fight such a being and win? He couldn't afford to lose; Owen's life hung in the balance. What could he do?

Unable to sit still longer, he rose from the table and stood at one of the windows, gazing at the fine day. Dew shimmered on the grass and on the trees in the orchard. At the tip of one of the branches of the pear tree, Neal noticed a single drop suspended, ready to fall. When he moved slightly, changing his angle of vision, the rising sun was suddenly mirrored in the dewdrop, causing it to shine blindingly bright, a brilliant daystar.

For some reason, Murray came into his mind. What had Murray said last night? *Solomon I'm not, but eighty years of life have given me a bit of wisdom.*

Neal smiled. He liked the old man; he had warmed to him from the first. Maybe Murray, with his fund of life experience would first believe him, Neal thought, and then be able to help him. "It's worth a try," Neal said with a nod, as he turned from the window. "I'll call him later today." He rinsed out his coffee mug and put it in the sink.

At the same moment, he heard two wall-shaking bangs in quick succession from upstairs. Adrenaline shot through his body like a high-voltage current. Neal sprinted down the hall toward the staircase. At the base of the stairs, he heard Vicky's ear-shattering scream. His leg muscles were steel springs; he vaulted up the stairs to the second floor, and then stopped in his tracks.

Owen cowered on the floor against the far wall. Vicky towered over him, her right arm raised to strike.

"Don't hit him, Vicky!" Neal shouted.

She turned her head and glared at him. Her hair was tangled and unkempt; mascara streaked her face in black rivulets under her red-rimmed, bloodshot eyes.

There is another creature from hell in this house, he thought.

"This little idiot slammed his damned trucks into the wall and woke me up. He deserves to be punished, and I'm gonna do it. After I've slapped the shit out of him, maybe he'll think twice before waking me up again."

Neal sprang forward and grabbed her upraised arm before she could strike Owen. Furious, she pivoted and smacked Neal in the eye with her left fist.

In an instantaneous and unthinking reaction, he shoved her against the wall. The blow knocked the wind out of her, and she slumped to the floor.

Neal's eye watered and the whole right side of his face stung, but it was biting anger and the stab of regret that pained him most. In a low, harsh voice, he said, "I'm sorry, Vicky. I didn't intend to do that—it was a reflex reaction." He pressed his palm over his right eye and then removed his hand, blinking rapidly. "But don't ever strike me again, unless you want to fight like a man. If you do, I guarantee you'll lose."

Vicky squeezed her eyes shut and bent forward, gasping for air.

Neal looked at Owen and softened his tone somewhat, "Stand up, son. First of all, you should never have slammed your trucks into the wall. Apologize to your mother."

Owen's bottom lip quivered and his brown eyes shimmered with tears, "I'm sorry, Mamma. I won't do it again."

Vicky turned her head away. She was still gasping for breath.

"All right," said Neal. "Your mamma's just extra upset because she didn't get much sleep last night. Go down to the kitchen and I'll be there in a minute. But first put the trucks back in your room."

Neal wished he could erase the entire episode in the hall for everyone's sake, but especially for Owen's. It saddened him that Owen had witnessed the violent scene between his parents. When the boy left, Neal waited a moment, watching his wife and struggling to calm himself. Eyes closed, she sat on the floor with her head leaning back against the wall, breathing heavily. She had lost weight; Neal could see the outline of her Adam's apple. Her arms were bony, and the veins stood out in her hands.

"Vicky, I'm going to help you up."

Her eyes opened and she growled, "Keep your hands off me."

Neal sighed. "What time did you come home last night, Vicky? Owen shouldn't have slammed his trucks into the wall, but he's not responsible for your lack of sleep or your foul humor."

"I got home around four, not that it's any business of yours."

"It certainly is my business, since, although you may have forgotten it, you are my wife, and the mother of our son. You told me you were going to a movie, and that was fine with me. I want you to enjoy yourself. But where else did you go? What did you do after the movie?"

"I went to Dill's Dance House."

"And?"

"And that's all. I had a few drinks and danced."

"Your eyes are awfully bloodshot for just a few drinks."

"Go to hell, if you don't believe me. You're the one who makes up the fantastic stories."

"All right, Vicky. You had a few drinks and danced. You had a good time, which was your objective, so why are you in such a foul mood?"

"Because my life is dull, boring, and unimportant, just like the man I'm married to." She heaved herself off the floor, rising unsteadily to her feet. "And if you'll excuse me, I'm going back to bed now so I can forget my life and you for as long as possible." She teetered into the bedroom and slammed the door behind her.

Neal stood unmoving for a moment, his eyes on the bedroom door, his mouth a thin white line. He took a deep breath, released it, and then went downstairs to make breakfast for his son.

When he walked into the kitchen, he found Owen standing beside the refrigerator, drinking a glass of orange juice. The cat sat at the back door, waiting patiently to go out.

"Is Mamma okay?"

"Mamma's fine; she just doesn't know it," replied Neal. "Let Sparker out, Owen, while I make you some oatmeal." Neal poured water in a pan and turned on the gas burner. "After breakfast, I think we'll take a walk on the beach. Sound good?"

Owen let the cat out the kitchen door. "Yep," he said.

Neal thought of the week ahead and hoped he would survive until Barbara's arrival. Vicky's total abdication of her roles as wife and mother made Neal in effect a single parent. He had to carefully orchestrate his schedule for the week to include all the errands he had relied on her to do. As he stirred the oatmeal, eye still stinging from the blow his wife had given him, his mind was on the week ahead. He asked Owen, "When is your next piano lesson?"

"Um, it's on Thursday."

"At what time?"

"Um, six-thirty."

"Okay, good," Neal said, "I can take you."

And that was the extent of their conversation. Owen ate his breakfast, and Neal drank another cup of coffee in silence, both subdued by the episode with Vicky.

Later, after Owen was dressed, they walked down to the beach. Sparker accompanied them to the bluff's edge, and then followed as they descended the wooden stairs to the white sand below. The temperature was below fifty degrees, Neal guessed, and the cool air felt wonderful on his face after the heat of the house. He was thankful to be out in the bright sunshine, breathing the clean, strong smell of the sea, borne on the spanking breeze. He hoped it was in the fresh wind's power to transport the image of that scene in the hall to somewhere distant, a place past all remembrance.

CHAPTER 18

Meeting on the Beach

Neal's desire to race down the beach was strong enough to make his muscles itch. He wanted to release his anger and frustration in a burst of violent physical motion. But that was out of the question, since Owen would never be able to keep up. So instead, he jogged to the water's edge and picked up several flat, rounded stones of various sizes.

"What are you doing, Daddy?"

"Watch." Neal held a gray and white speckled stone between the thumb and index finger of his left hand. He drew back in a wind-up like a major league pitcher, and flicked the stone side-armed, low to the water. It glanced off the blue surface, just past the crest of a wave and skipped three times before it lost momentum and sank.

Owen clapped his hands and laughed. "Do it again, Daddy!"

Neal kept skipping stones until his arm ached to match his throbbing eye and pounding head. His world had changed, all right. Physical violence had never been a factor in his marriage before this episode, although for many days now, he had been tempted to shake Vicky until her teeth rattled to snap her out of her self-centered, self-pitying funk. She had the house she wanted, a faithful husband, and a fine son, Neal thought, flicking stone after stone into the sea. Surrounded by such riches, how could she be so unhappy?

After throwing a few stones into the sea himself, Owen had wandered about fifty yards down the beach toward the point. Neal saw him playing at the water's edge, poking about in the rocks with a long thin stick, slapping the water, and playing tag with the waves.

Neal kept hurling stone after stone into the water. Maybe when he'd thrown the last one, and the beach was denuded, he'd be over his anger and frustration. As he wound up to throw again, Owen screamed, "Daddy!" Neal jerked his head toward the point and saw a big blonde dog running straight at his son.

Stone in hand, he sprinted towards Owen from the opposite direction. The dog got to the boy first, leaping up at him, knocking him down onto the rocky beach, and straddling him. Neal, running full tilt toward his son, drew his arm back to throw, but restrained himself, fearing that he might hit Owen instead of the dog.

The next thing he saw made him glad he'd held his fire. The dog licked Owen's face and nudged him in a playful manner with its nose. Owen turned his head from side to side to avoid the wet doggie kisses.

Neal slowed to a fast walk. "It's okay, Daddy," Owen said, as Neal approached. "He's a friendly dog."

"I can certainly see that," Neal said, giving Owen a hand up, and then stroking the dog's thick, curly fur.

"He just surprised me, that's all." Owen petted the grinning, happy dog.

Neal took a closer look at the dog and said, "I think he's a she, Owen." The dog wore a collar with current tags. "Where is your owner and what kind of dog are you?" Neal asked. He lifted the dog's head and looked into her golden-brown eyes. "What's your name, pooch?"

"Mazie." The reply surprised both MacGregors. The sound of the wind and the sea had covered Sarah Friedkin's approach.

"Sarah!" Neal exclaimed. "Is this your dog?"

"Yes, she's mine," she said. Under a faded denim jacket, she wore a thick white turtleneck sweater that set off her glossy black hair and blue eyes. She tucked her hands into the pockets of her jeans, and added, "She's half German Shepherd and half Nova Scotia Duck Tolling Retriever."

"I didn't know you had a dog, much less a halfbreed Nova Scotia Duck Tolling Retriever," said Neal.

"You mean you've heard of that breed?" Sarah asked, surprised.

"Sure," Neal smiled, "Five seconds ago. Actually, I think you made it up. I know you're creative, but this time you've outdone yourself."

Sarah looked at Owen and asked, "Do you think I make up stories, Owen MacGregor?"

"Well," Owen answered, "you're so smart, I think you could."

Neal guffawed, and Sarah smiled. "Well, thank you for your confidence in me, Owen, but you'll have to come to my house sometime and see the dog book I have. It has pictures of Nova Scotia Duck Tolling Retrievers, and they look a lot like Mazie. By the way, Owen, I'm sorry Mazie knocked you down. She's got more enthusiasm than manners."

"Oh, she didn't hurt me."

"Hello there!"

At the shouted greeting, everyone looked toward the point. Murray waved and approached with short, quick steps.

"He moves well for a man his age," remarked Neal, "It's a good thing too, because the last I saw of him, he was in full flight from Brucie Barncamper."

Sarah laughed, "I heard about that. She is just impossible."

Murray wasn't sporting the latest fashion in beach wear; he wore a black overcoat and a fedora that Neal thought would have looked perfectly appropriate on the streets of New York forty years ago.

The older man, reading Neal's thoughts, asked, "Like my *chapeau*?" He smiled at Owen, and tapped the crown of his hat, "Gotta keep the old dome warm." Turning his attention to Neal, he said, "What a nice surprise to see you here. Whereabouts do you live?"

"Up there," Neal replied, pointing to the blue and white Victorian house on the bluff.

"Ah, very nice," said Murray.

"Actually there's something about the house that I'd like to discuss with you, Murray."

"Shoot."

"Well, it's rather complicated, and I'd prefer to speak to you, uh, in other circumstances." Neal nodded toward Owen in a meaningful way.

"Ah," said Murray, placing the index finger of his right hand alongside his nose. "In that case, why don't we meet for a drink at the Town Tavern on Tuesday night?"

"I'd like to, but this is a sensitive matter, and I'd rather not discuss it in a public place."

"How about your house?" Murray asked.

"Definitely not there."

"Well, if I can butt in," said Sarah, "I make a mean lasagna. You two can have dinner at my house, and afterwards while you have your discussion, I can show Owen my dog book."

"It wouldn't be too much trouble?" Neal asked.

"None at all. It'll be both my pleasure and my opportunity to vindicate my good name. What about Thursday?"

"Well, I've got to take Owen to his piano lesson on Thursday. What about next Tuesday instead?"

"Let's see," said Sarah, doing mental calculations, "that's May ninth. That should be fine. How about seven-thirty—no, seven? It's a school night."

"Perfect," said Neal.

Then they spoke simultaneously.

"Your wife—"

"My wife—"

They laughed, and Sarah blushed.

"—is also invited," she finished lamely.

"Thank you," said Neal, "but she's not interested in the topic of discussion, and I know she won't want to come."

There was an awkward pause.

Seeking to defuse the tension of the moment, Murray reached into the inner pocket of his overcoat, whipped out a thin, folded magazine, and brandished it in the air. "My new journal, *Intersections: Where Physics and Metaphysics Meet*, ordered for me by my favorite niece. See that comfortable log over there? The one without too many bumps? I intend to sit there and read this while you youngsters cavort on the beach." Without another word, Murray walked to the log, parked himself, and began to read. He glanced up and saw that they were watching him and hadn't moved. "Don't worry about Owen and Mazie. I'll keep an eye on 'em. Shoo!" he shouted.

Laughter released them. "Well, I don't know about cavorting, but shall we walk?" Neal asked Sarah.

"Yes, we shall—the beach is ours. It's just us and the seabirds this morning," she replied.

"Let's go this way," Neal suggested, gesturing away from the point. He was intensely aware of her physical presence and he noticed how her head came just above his shoulder. They walked in a relaxed, steady rhythm, their strides matching easily, as if they had strolled the beach together for years.

"What did you think about last night's concert?" he asked.

In her animated way, smiling and gesturing, Sarah talked at length about the music itself and her pleasure in performing again, while Neal drank in her presence like a tonic. There was an aura of health and vitality about her, like the beach itself and the young day not yet at its noon, that was a potent antidote for his troubled spirit. With every step, his dark mood dissipated. He forgot himself completely, and simply enjoyed her company.

He quietly observed the dark blue of her eyes, the heightened color of her cheeks in the wind, and the lustrous sheen of her black hair. As Sarah told him more about her New York friends Julie, Edward, and Beth, it seemed to Neal that the rise and fall of her low, lightly-accented voice against the surf's steady bass made perfect music. He watched the sun strike blue fire in her hair while he breathed in the scent of the ocean and the fragrance of Sarah herself. As he searched in his mind for a metaphor to describe the molten sea-colors of her eyes, he realized he was in trouble.

Confound it all, he thought, glancing out at the white-capped strait, why does life have to be so damned complicated? This woman's pull on him was tidal. He dearly wished he had met her earlier in his life when he had been free to follow his desires. Under those circumstances he would have taken her hand in his; he might even have stopped her then and there with a kiss. Now, of course, that was entirely out of the question. He jammed his hands into the pockets of his windbreaker and kicked a piece of driftwood out of his path with more force than necessary.

Irritated at fate and suddenly impatient, Neal stopped. He took hold of Sarah's arm so that she turned to face him, and interrupted her monologue. "Look, Sarah, I enjoyed meeting all your friends last night, and now I know a lot about them. But what about you? What's your story?"

A faint, startled look crossed her face, and after a moment's hesitation she replied, "Well, I'll tell you my tale—but only if you reciprocate."

"Done," said Neal, holding out his hand. They clinched the deal with a handshake. It was a long handshake. Sarah released her grip first.

"We walked awfully far down the beach," she said. "Uncle Murr looks like a large black bump on his log. Let's turn around and on the way back, I'll tell you the story of Sarah." She laughed, "Sounds like the title of a B movie, doesn't it?"

"Sounds exciting to me," Neal replied. "You know—like *The Perils of Pauline*." He was gratified by her hearty laugh. He glanced at her, "So tell, Sarah, is there a dastardly villain and a railroad track in your history?"

"Oh, of course. New York teems with dastardly types who live to tie sweet young things like me to railroad tracks." She shrugged and held both hands palm up, "What else are subways for?"

Smiling up at Neal, she said, "Well, first things first: I was born in Brooklyn in 1965, and according to my brother, I was not a pretty baby. He said I looked like a red-faced hairy monkey," she laughed. "Mark is seven years older than I. He's a graduate of Harvard Law School, and now he's a trial lawyer in Manhattan. He lives on the Upper East Side with his wife and three kids. Thanks to a loan from him, I was able to open the travel shop. While I was in school, he helped me with homework, especially math. I did well in all the other subjects, mostly because I read the way a beluga whale feeds—everything in sight and fifty pounds a day. I was an active kid, too—I skateboarded, roller-skated, and biked all over Brooklyn Heights."

Sarah chewed on her bottom lip. "Well, what else? My dad lives in the brownstone where I grew up on Clinton Street. My mother died five years ago in July and I miss her still." She paused and looked at Neal, "Keep going?" she asked.

It seemed to him that her eyes married the sapphire sea with the dusky blue of evening. They were the horizon, the meeting-place of sea and sky, where he dearly longed to go. "Yes, tell me more," he said.

"I brought home stray dogs, played the violin and later the viola, went to art museums, movies, concerts, and after enduring the usual awkward adolescence, I graduated from Brooklyn College with a double major—music and English."

"And then you performed professionally with Musicians of Brooklyn?" Sarah nodded.

"But why did you move to the West Coast to open your travel shop?"

"Now that," said Sarah, gliding around the issue as precariously as a windsurfer around a reef, "will have to be the next installment in the continuing story of my life. Look, here we are. Uncle Murr, we're back!"

Murray looked up from his journal and then rose, a little stiffly, from his perch on the log. To Neal, the combination of Murray's hat and black overcoat, so incongruous on the beach, with his slightly stiff and jerky movements seemed comical, Chaplinesque. Murray lifted his hat in wordless greeting, reinforcing the effect.

Neal laughed and said, "Murray, the way you moved just now—well, it looked like you stepped out of a silent movie."

"Or maybe we stepped into one," Sarah suggested.

"Either way, I'm of the correct era," Murray answered, "but the two of you, red-haired Neal and blue-eyed Sarah with the light in her eyes, are definitely Technicolor."

He folded his journal and slipped it back into his inner pocket, "In fact, he added, "to my experienced and impartial eye, I'd say you could be a Hollywood happy ending. And here come the boy and dog to complete the picture."

Mazie ran up and circled Sarah, while Owen followed, running toward them as fast as his small legs could churn. When he reached them and caught his breath, he looked expectantly at the group of three adults and asked, "So where are we going now?"

Glancing at Sarah and Neal, Murray laid a finger aside his nose and answered, "That, my boy, is the pertinent question."

CHAPTER 19

Quite a Story

N eal brought himself, Owen, and a very good Italian red wine to dinner at Sarah's on Tuesday. Owen brought a large rawhide bone.

"For you, Mazie," Owen said, presenting the bone to a well-behaved, but madly tail-wagging dog. Mazie barked her thanks, and then took the bone gently from Owen.

"On the paper," commanded Sarah. Mazie obediently took the bone to her corner in the kitchen, lay down beside her dog cushion on the front page of *The Island Gazette*, and gnawed like a tundra wolf.

Thanks to a late Pacific cold front that had moved in overnight, it was raining and cold outside, but in Sarah's kitchen, all was warm and bright. The table by the window was set for four. The lasagna sat steaming in its pan and beside it there was a basket of hot garlic bread and a large bowl of Caesar salad.

Murray inhaled deeply and said, "If the lasagna tastes as good as it smells, I may either cry with happiness or burst into song."

"Let's hope you cry with happiness," Sarah remarked. "I've heard you sing."

After his first bite, he looked at them and said, "What'd I tell you?" His eyes watered, and he addressed Sarah, "An Italian must have sneaked into our line somewhere back in time, doll. Thanks to him, you can cook, and I can appreciate it. Ah, I am a happy man."

Neal smiled and said, "It's delicious, Sarah. What do you think, Owen?"

"It's better than pizza."

"There you have it:" Neal laughed, "a five-star rating, if I ever heard one."

Sarah beamed, "Thank you all very much, but save some room for dessert."

For a few minutes, all conversation stopped as they ate their meal. The only sound other than chewing was the regular drip of the faucet in Sarah's sink.

"By the way," asked Murray, swallowing the last of his lasagna, "what's for dessert?"

Sarah laughed, "Uncle Murr, if you love life the way love food, you'll live to be a hundred and fifty."

"Oh, I intend to," he said. "Someone's got to look after you. But you still didn't answer my pressing question, Sarah. Dessert?"

"I've got homemade apple pie and ice cream."

"Oh, I love apple pie!" exclaimed Owen. "Daddy, when Grandma comes, will she make apple pie?"

"She might. She's a wonderful cook."

"Is it your mother who's coming, Neal?" Sarah asked.

"No, actually she's my grandmother, Owen's great-grandmother Barbara. She lives in Scotland—Edinburgh. She's coming next week for a long stay."

"Oh," said Murray, "she's the one who recently lost her husband."

"Yes, my grandfather Ian died in September," Neal explained to Sarah. "It was he who taught me to play the pipes."

"Does your grandmother come to visit regularly?" Sarah asked.

"No, she doesn't. She's coming because I asked her, due to the same situation I'm here to discuss."

"I see," said Murray, although he didn't. "What airline is she flying?"

"British Air."

"Good. Did you see that Northwest suspended one of its pilots without pay for drinking while on duty?"

"Really?" said Neal.

"Yes, I read that in Saturday's *Island Gazette*. The pilot's a local man but he's based in Seattle. Can't remember his name—it's something Scandinavian."

"Well, I'm glad Grandma is flying British Air."

"Ready for dessert?" Sarah asked. "And yes, I know *you* are, Uncle Murr."

Owen and Murray ate pie and ice cream, but Sarah and Neal decided to wait until later. In the meantime, Sarah made a pot of coffee. Neal joined her at the kitchen counter and pointed to the dripping faucet "Needs a new washer."

"It does."

"It's easy to fix. I can do that for you on the weekend. I've got my own tools and I'm free." He smoothed his mustache, and lifted his brows at the unintentional irony. *Free?* If only I was, he thought.

"Really? You wouldn't mind fixing it?"

"Be happy to. How about five o'clock on Saturday?"

"That will work. Thank you, Neal."

"Finished," said Murray. "The pie was delicious." He came over and gave Sarah a kiss on the cheek. "Thank you, lovely child." Taking Neal by the arm, he said, "Come on then, Neal. Let's talk."

Sarah quickly cleared a space at the table for her book *Dogs of North America*, and then turned on the radio. Opening the book, she said to Owen, who was petting Mazie, "Come, let's take a look while your dad and Uncle Murray talk." When he sat next to her, Sarah said, "Okay, brace yourself, my boy. You are about to see a picture of the famous Nova Scotia Duck Tolling Retriever."

Murray led Neal into Sarah's small living room. Cold rain pelted the windows, but the room was warm; a bright fire burned in the small fireplace. There was a sofa, a loveseat, and an armchair upholstered in a deep green fabric, all grouped around the hearth. A cream-colored cotton rug lay on the dark hardwood floor before the fire. Two tall bookcases filled to capacity stood at one end of the room while on the other end, a black music stand with its companion music cabinet stood sentinel beside the shiny, black upright piano. Plants of various sizes lined the window or sat in large orange clay pots on the floor. Two lamps lent a golden glow to the room. It was a comfortable, inviting space, full of warmth and altogether charming—just like Sarah, thought Neal.

When they were settled, with Murray on the loveseat, and Neal to his left on the sofa, they were silent for a moment, listening to the crackle of the fire in counterpoint to the rain's steady patter. Neal stared into the fire and silently prayed that he was doing the right thing in telling his story to Murray.

Taking a deep breath, Neal began, "The day you and I met at Coveland House, Murray, we talked about the war, and I mentioned that my grandfather was wounded by shrapnel. That was what I had always believed. Well, when I read his journal, I discovered that in May of 1940, at Dunkirk, he was blinded and rendered mute by a supernatural being. And this creature has plagued our family ever since." Neal kept his eyes on the fire, afraid to look at Murray for fear that the older man's reaction would be ridicule or complete disbelief.

Neal cleared his throat self-consciously and then hurried on. "As I told you, my grandfather was a piper with the Black Watch. He served with the British Expeditionary Force in Flanders, when they were overwhelmed and forced to retreat by the German advance. In addition to his talent for music, he had the gift of second sight, and in the journal he described a series of visions he had at that time.

"In one vision, German SS soldiers herded about eighty unarmed British infantrymen into an open-ended cowshed, and then lobbed in stick grenades. Then the SS fired at will, slaughtering them. In the second vision, Grandfather saw a group of about one hundred British soldiers and officers trapped by the *Totenkopf* SS in a burning barn. When the British soldiers fled the fire, the enemy surrounded them and then marched them into the barnyard. Once the soldiers were lined up, the SS machine-gunned them at point-blank range.

"During the second massacre, Grandfather saw a very tall, black-clad figure standing beside the German commander, unbeknownst to the officer. Grandfather sensed that this being derived great pleasure from the murders and the victims' terror. When the creature became aware of Grandfather's scrutiny, it turned all its malice on him. It raised an arm, pointed at him, and in that instant scorching, searing pain struck Grandfather's eyes and burned his throat. He fell unconscious in a coma-like state, and hours later when he awoke, he was blind and mute. In the meantime, the Black Watch, in flight from the enemy, had left him for dead.

"He found himself alone in a cornfield behind the German lines. It was the middle of the night, and he didn't know what to do. But then he heard the sound of bagpipes. Assuming the piper was one of his own, he struck out after the sound and followed the music for days, stumbling along as best he could. He never caught up with the piper, and the piper never spoke to him. Grandfather finally realized that the piper was also a supernatural being, but one whom he could trust implicitly. In his mind's eye, the piper shone with light. The piper led him in the right direction until eventually Grandfather met two Yorkshiremen who helped him get to Dunkirk where the massive rescue by sea was in progress.

"On the beach at Dunkirk, Jack, one of the Yorkshiremen, a very kindly man, was killed by a strafing Stuka. Grandfather was so angered by Jack's death that he stood up and played his pipes in an act of defiance against war and death, and the soldiers followed him down the beach. That was the moment the evil being assailed him again; the cold malice of it almost stopped him in his tracks. But he suddenly heard a phrase of the shining piper's music, and the evil presence fled."

Neal raised his eyebrows and chanced a look at Murray. The older man sat staring at the floor with his arms folded across his barrel chest and his chin pulled down. "Go on," Murray said.

"Well, Grandfather had a feeling that it wasn't over, and he was right. For a very long time, there were no more incidents. Not until his son, my father Peter, was seven years old."

Murray sat motionless, eyes fixed on the floor as Neal told him how the creature had destroyed his father's life.

"My father was an alcoholic by age fifteen. I remember him drunk almost every night of my life. He died just before Christmas of 1993, when he lost control of his car and ran off the road into a tree. His blood alcohol content was more than twice the legal limit."

Neal paused and took a deep breath. "All that I've told you so far, Murray, is what I read in Grandfather's journal. None of it, except my father's drunkenness, was my direct experience. Before I go on, though, I should tell you that I inherited more than my red hair and piping abilities from my grandfather. Like him, I had the sight as a boy, but as I grew older, my visions tapered off—that is until a few months after we bought the old Fritzinger house.

"Even before we moved in, it seemed that the house triggered an awakening of my psychic abilities. I had a series of experiences there that unnerved me and made me very afraid for Owen. One afternoon in March, when I was working on the exterior of the house, I decided to take a break from painting and play the pipes on the bluff near the ocean. I stopped playing when a sudden fog came in off the sea. Walking back toward the house, I thought I saw a huge black dog moving in the mist below the parlor bay window, and then I saw a shadowy figure materialize out of the mist and darkness at the level of the tower room. I even heard it call my name—MacGregor.

"The very first week I spent in the house, I dreamed of a young blonde boy weeping in the tower room. He was enclosed in shadow. The shadow dissolved into him somehow, and when he looked at me with demonic eyes, full of hatred and malice, he became Owen. Then there was an upsetting incident the same day I played at Coveland House, the day I met you, Murray. I had a vision in the tower room in which I saw bloody handprints on the wall.

"The last incident was the worst. I saw both the dog and the shadowy figure for the second time inside the tower room. This happened just last week on the Thursday before Sarah's concert."

Neal described the hellhound and the apparition in the study. "The creature spoke to me, and I can't tell you if I actually heard its voice, or if the voice sounded in my mind. He asked if Owen might like his pet. When I heard him say *Owen*, I was horrified, and then I felt such rage that I commanded him to leave. 'Get out of my house!' I shouted. For just a moment, the apparition seemed to waver, but then the dog lunged and knocked me into the wall with such force that I lost consciousness.

"When my wife woke me later, the dog and its master had gone. I remembered the threat to Owen and raced down to his room. Thankfully, he was sleeping peacefully, unharmed, but not untouched, because on his cheek there was a tuft of black fur."

Neal looked at Murray. "I know this story sounds crazy, but that's what I'm facing. I am afraid that since my father's death, this thing is looking for a new target and it has come for Owen. In June—next month, Owen will be seven. That was my father's age when this creature came for him. It would destroy me if anything happened to Owen, but I don't know what to do. Will you help me find a solution, Murray?"

Neal watched Murray, waiting for him to speak. Murray's chin almost touched his chest, and his eyes were still focused on the floor. Neal sat agonized while a full minute passed. At last the older man stirred. "That's quite a tale," he said in a soft voice.

"You don't believe me."

"Now, wait a minute, Neal. I didn't say that. There are several possibilities. You could be lying."

Neal stood up abruptly. "Damn it, Murray, I knew this was hopeless."

"Sit down, Neal, and hear me out. I have to think through *all* the possibilities—not just the ones that please you. Calm yourself and don't interrupt. I listened; now it's your turn."

Neal sat down and crossed his arms over his chest.

"As I said, you could be lying," Murray continued. "Or you could be mentally ill. Schizophrenics hallucinate and hear voices. Or maybe you hallucinated under the influence of alcohol or drugs."

Neal stared into the fire. "My wife would agree with the last bit. She thought I got falling-down drunk last Thursday and then created a ghost story to cover the fact."

"But why would you carry the charade this far—asking me for help when all you really wanted was to deceive your wife?" Murray asked. "It would make more sense if she was present tonight as a witness. The question is: what do you have to gain from this story? There's nothing to gain from me, and if the story is a lie, you'd lose my respect and my friendship.

"I don't really know about your alcohol or drug habits," he continued, "but I imagine if you had a problem to the degree of hallucinations, it would have affected your job by now. And in a village like Coveland, addiction, or mental illness for that matter would also be common knowledge.

"That leaves the third possibility, which is the strangest one." Murray ran a hand over his scalp. "You could be telling the truth."

Neal sat as tense and immobile as a man on trial for his life, listening as the judge read the verdict.

"In fact," Murray continued, "I think you *are* telling the truth."

Neal exhaled noisily through his mouth. "Well thank God for that."

"I don't think you'd create a story so detailed, involving four generations of your family, to cover one drunken night."

Murray leaned forward. "It is a strange story, but there is more to this world than meets the eye," he said, "and believe it or not, I have thought a lot about things seen and unseen. Have you ever noticed how the visible proceeds from the invisible?" he asked.

"What do you mean?"

"Idea precedes manifestation. The mental design of a house comes before the actual building of the structure. Everything created has its origin in the invisible world, and that includes human beings.

"Although we humans appear to reign supreme upon this earth, we are actually in the midst of a hierarchy, a chain of living beings, with some below us like the animals and plants, and some above us, from angels and archangels to the Cherubim and Seraphim, and the Creator himself."

"Well, I agree with you, but where are you going with this, Murray?"

"Patience, my boy, I'm getting to the point."

Leaning back, Murray laced his fingers together over his round belly. "They had it all sorted out in the medieval period. In the journal Sarah ordered for me recently—the one I read on the beach the other day— there was a picture of a twelfth-century manuscript, showing the ascent of the soul through a series of concentric spheres. The soul was pictured as a human being rising from earth, the visible world, through the psychic worlds, represented by the starry heavens, to the spiritual realm above the stars, the Empyrean, which represents the prime mover or the Divine Intellect. Each sphere contained within it the one below, linking all creation together in a grand order.

"As my understanding is above that of an animal, so there are beings above me. Can an ant comprehend mankind? Can I understand the Cherubim?" Murray paused for a moment and scratched his scalp. "I guess what I am trying to say is that we live in the midst of a great mystery, and there are realities independent of time and space, which human reason or rational sense alone cannot comprehend."

Murray shrugged and held his hands palm up, "I've never seen a supernatural being, but then I've never seen a virus, either." He laughed, "Hell, I can't even see the salt in saltwater, but it is there."

"The world is full of strangeness and mystery, that's for sure, and fantastically diversified forms of life," said Neal.

"Exactly," replied Murray, "and for some reason, Neal, I think you and your grandfather encountered a being from the psychic domain, the world of subtle manifestation—and not every such entity is benevolent. But, as I said earlier, in the overall world view, the psychic realm is *below* the spiritual and subject to it."

"Well, what good is that?" Neal asked.

"Do you remember the story about Moses and Aaron confronting Pharaoh? When Pharaoh asked for a miracle, Moses did as God had commanded him—he told Aaron to throw down his rod. Aaron did, and it became a serpent.

"Then Pharaoh called for his magicians and sorcerers, and every man of them cast down his rod and they all became serpents, too. But Aaron's serpent swallowed them up, and the reason it did is that the serpents of the sorcerers were made of magic, while Aaron's serpent had spiritual power. That's my point. The Spirit always prevails over the psychic. So even though the being that attacked your grandfather has formidable powers, there are greater forces than it. The good news is that there must be a way to defeat it."

Neal raised his eyes skyward, "Oh, Murray, you give me hope."

"Well, we still have to figure out a plan of action." Murray sat up straight and looked at Neal, "And I think we should include Sarah. I trust her and she's as intelligent as they come. We are going to research this problem before we're done, and we may need her resources. What do you think?"

Before Neal could answer, there was a polite knock and then Sarah poked her head into the room. "May I come in?"

"What do you say, Neal?" asked Murray.

Understanding the broader meaning of Murray's question, Neal gave his assent. "Yes, come in, Sarah," he said.

She entered the room and said, "Owen and I looked at my dog book, but he kept rubbing his eyes with his knuckles and yawning, so I asked him if he wanted to lie down on my bed and rest. He said he wanted to play with Mazie. By the time I had loaded the dishes in the dishwasher, he had fallen asleep on Mazie's cushion."

Neal smiled and glanced at his watch. "It's eight-thirty, his bedtime, and he got so excited about coming over here that I guess it did him in."

"I covered him with a blanket," Sarah said. "Do you want to leave him there or move him to my bed?"

"Let me take a look," Neal said.

In the kitchen, they found Owen lying asleep on his right side on a red, black, and white plaid dog cushion. He was covered by a white thermal blanket, and his face was turned toward Mazie, who lay beside him with her head on her paws. The dog's eyes were alert, and she followed Neal and Sarah's every movement.

"I think he's fine where he is," Neal said. "I'll just let him sleep until it's time to go. By the way, Sarah, you have good taste in dog cushions."

"I do?"

"Yes, indeed. That's the MacGregor tartan."

"Well, of course," laughed Sarah, "in honor of Mazie's roots. Her breed, or half of it anyway, although you didn't believe me, is from Nova Scotia—New Scotland. Do you want to see my dog book?"

"Yes, but first I have to tell you something important." Neal's expression was serious, and he gazed into Sarah's eyes, the blue horizon which fate denied him. He said, "Although I have not known you and Murray very long, Sarah, I felt comfortable with both of you from the first, and I felt that I could trust you, which is why I confided in Murray tonight. I asked his help with a very serious problem, and I want your help as well."

The atmosphere was charged with a sudden solemnity, and Sarah's smile faded. She stepped forward impulsively and took his hand in hers. "Of course I will do whatever I can to help. And I trust you, too, Neal. You are . . ."

She stopped, suddenly flustered, and released his hand. "Um, I mean you are—well . . ." She smiled, "Well, one can always trust a man who wears a kilt—he's out there in the open somehow."

Although he suspected she meant to say something entirely different, Neal laughed, breaking the tension. "Yes, you've got that right."

"And of course," Sarah added, "you are exactly right about me. Proof of my utter honesty and reliability awaits you." She pointed to the table where the open dog book lay. "But only after you take a look, and have some pie and coffee, may you tell me your story."

"Yes, ma'am," said Neal. "I am your obedient servant."

Murray gave a low whistle and remarked to Neal, "No wonder Bitsy calls her *Boss*."

CHAPTER 20

The Erlking

S arah allowed Neal a full minute to study the photographs and written description of Nova Scotia Duck Tolling Retrievers before she demanded that he atone for his sins. "Now, sir, you may state your humble, heartfelt, and truly abject apology for doubting me."

"Sarah," Neal declared, "I done you wrong. There is such an animal, and you got one over there in the corner. I do apologize."

"Apology accepted."

"Now that the air is cleared," Murray reminded them, rubbing his hands together, "it's time for pie and coffee."

Sarah laughed, "Seconds, Uncle Murr?"

"Always, doll."

Sarah served pie, then poured coffee for them all.

After finishing his pie, Neal asked, "Do you mind if we talk in the living room?" He looked over at his sleeping son. "I don't want Owen to hear any of this, even in his sleep. He's been complaining of stomachaches at school, and twice lately I had to pick him up early because he threw up. There's a lot of tension in our house, and I don't want to upset him any more than he already is."

"The poor boy," said Sarah. "Of course we can talk in the living room. Take your cups with you. I'll pour the rest of the coffee into a thermos and we can finish it in there."

Sarah brought the thermos and a box of thin chocolate-covered mints into the living room. Murray unwrapped a mint, bit into it, and groaned with pleasure.

"Okay, Uncle Murr," said Sarah, "suppress your rapture, and let the man continue."

After rolling up the sleeves of her blouse, she kicked off her shoes and sat cross-legged on the opposite end of the sofa from Murray.

Neal stood by the fire and retold his story. After Murray explained his thoughts on the matter, Sarah, like her great-uncle, sat with downcast eyes, thinking. Then she lifted her head and said, "I do have a question, Neal. How do the bloody hand prints in the tower room and the nightmares you had relate to the evil being?"

"I truly do not know how or even *if* the bloody hand prints relate to the creature. I can only tell you what occurred." Neal explained how he had painted the study white, only to find it streaked a few hours later by hand prints that descended into wavering smears of blood down to the wainscot. "There were scuffed dents at the base of the wall, as though someone had kicked the wall in violent anger. I had no idea it was a vision until I went out to get a camera, came back, and found the wall smooth and untouched. However, one mystery remained. The window I had left wide open to air out the room was shut and locked, and not by me. I searched for signs of an intruder—broken or unlocked windows, open doors, footprints outside, but found nothing. Maybe this creature was playing with me, but I still don't know for certain.

"As to my dreams, the nightmare about the weeping boy may not relate to the evil creature; I don't really see how it does. But the second nightmare was triggered by Schubert's song *Erlkönig*, and the story is related to my predicament. I found some old LP-records in the attic of the house and I listened to the song that night just before I went to bed. Do you know it, Sarah?"

"Of course, the *Erlking*." She quoted the first stanza:

> *Wer reitet so spät, durch Nacht und Wind?*
> *Es ist der Vater mit seinem Kind;*

Er hat den Knaben wohl in dem Arm,
Er fasst ihn sicher, er hält ihn warm.

Sarah looked at Murray, *"Verstehst du?"*

He laughed, "I understand. Most of it, anyway, thanks to Mamma, Papa, and Molly Picon."

"What do you mean?" asked Neal.

"Yiddish," said Murray, "the language of my youth. It's close enough to German that I could survive, God forbid it should be necessary, in downtown Berlin. But other than a father holding his son safe and warm as they ride late on a windy night, what is the song about?"

Before Neal could explain, Sarah said, "Wait. I've got the whole text in German and English on the liner notes of a Schubert CD." She rifled through a stack of CDs on a bookcase shelf.

"What'd I tell you?" Murray asked, palms lifted skyward. "She's already a resource."

Sarah came back and laid the liner notes on the table in front of Murray. "There," she said, "you can read it for yourself."

Murray looked at Neal, "Would you mind if I listen to the recording? I don't know the song."

"I don't mind."

Sarah inserted the CD and Murray scanned the English translation of the lyrics, while Neal crouched in front of the small fire and worried it with a poker. Sarah sat on the sofa beside her uncle and explained, "Schubert wrote the music, but Goethe wrote the words. The Erlking is a fearful supernatural creature. After the narrator sets the scene in the first verse, there is a dialogue between the father and son, and later the Erlking speaks to the child alone."

She touched the remote control, and the foreboding minor key piano introduction darkened the atmosphere, as though a cold wind swept last year's leaves, reminders of death, into the room. Then the singer, a baritone, told the story of the father riding through night and wind with his small son. The child hides his face in fear and tells his father that he sees the Erlking. It is only the mist, says his father. The music changes to a major key as the Erlking coaxes the child to come with him, to a beautiful place where they will play games. Dark music returns when the boy tells his father how the Erlking whispers to him, but the father says it is only the dry leaves rustling in the wind. The Erlking promises that his daughters will sing to the child and rock him to sleep. The boy's voice rises higher, asking his father if he sees the Erlking's daughters hiding in the shadows? Again, the father reassures the boy, and then the Erlking tells the child that if the boy won't come willingly, he'll take him by force. Frantic, the boy cries out that the Erlking is seizing him, hurting him. Finally, realizing that the danger is real, the father, in great fear, spurs the horse as the boy begins to moan. When they arrive at the courtyard, the child is dead.

"Quite a macabre story," said Murray, when he lifted his eyes, "Each time the boy cries out, there is more fear in his voice until he's frantic."

"Yes," said Sarah, "the tension rises throughout. The insistent, repeated piano notes are like the pounding of hoofs against the turf. When the hoofbeats stop, the child is dead." She shivered, "The song gives me goosebumps."

"It gave me a nightmare," said Neal.

He replaced the poker and moved from the fireplace to the loveseat. "I dreamed I was the father, and Owen the son. We rode at night through a forest in which the trees seemed to close in on us.

"In the song," Neal continued, "the father is unaware, or else refuses to believe the Erlking is present. What was so frightening in my dream, was the fact that both Owen and I knew the Erlking was real. I was convinced he would take Owen in the end; Owen was going to die." Neal's voice shook on the last word.

He paused and poured himself more coffee from the thermos. After he took a sip of the strong, hot drink, he said, "To make matters worse, the Erlking felt our terror. It delighted him; he burst into a loud, mocking laugh. Then the trees grew grotesque faces, and they, too, laughed at us as they closed ranks. We were forced into a narrower and narrower opening until the way was blocked by an ugly, gnarled old elm. When Owen screamed, I woke up."

No one spoke. Only the crackling fire and the pattering rain conversed.

Finally Sarah stirred. She set her coffee cup down on the floor beside the sofa and said to Neal, "So, you think this creature or being. . ." She stopped, clicked her tongue, and then blurted, "What shall we call it? The nameless evil?"

"How about the Erlking?" Murray offered in a soft voice, his eyes on Neal.

Neal nodded agreement.

"What is it that you think the Erlking will do?" Sarah asked.

"I'm not sure, but all the prospects are frightening. I think Owen is his target. I know from Grandfather's experience that the Erlking has the power to cause severe injury in an instant. And my father's addiction proves that the Erlking can create lifelong misery. I'm certain he has the power to kill."

Neal hunched forward on the loveseat and rubbed his eyes with his thumb and forefinger. "I think he's targeted Owen because he knows that to hurt my son would injure two generations at one blow. If harm comes to that child, I will come undone." Neal stared into the fire and then added, "The Erlking thrives on fear and destruction. The more terror his victims feel, the more pleasure for him."

Another heavy silence descended on the room. At last Sarah asked, "Do you think it would help if you moved out of the house, or sent Owen away?"

"I've thought of that," answered Neal, "but I'm certain that the house is not the issue. Grandfather was miles away from the SS troop that slaughtered the British soldiers, and he was struck down like a lamb. That happened in France. My father grew up in Edinburgh and later moved to America. So Coveland or Katmandu makes no difference. The common denominator has not been *where*—it's been *who*—MacGregor males."

"Good God!" exclaimed Sarah. "If I were Catholic, I'd call an exorcist."

"That occurred to me as well," said Neal. "But I'm not Catholic either, and I think in cases like this, getting the Church to move is like pushing a two-ton boulder up the slopes of Mt. Rainier. I need a solution quickly. I'm afraid for Owen every day. He's six, but he'll be seven a month from today, on June ninth. That was my father's age when the Erlking invaded his life."

Sarah said, "You're awfully quiet over there, Uncle Murr. What are you thinking?"

Murray cleared his throat. "I'm wondering if there may be a connection with a place, at least within the house. Doesn't all the supernatural activity seem to happen in and around the tower room?"

"Yes, and I've made that room off-limits for Owen. I've even padlocked the door. But Owen was asleep on the second floor when I found a tuft of that black hellhound's fur on his cheek."

"Did you keep the fur?"

"I intended to, but when I showed it to Vicky, she took it out of my hand and, well, you have to understand that she doesn't believe any of my story. Anyway, she was angry at me, thinking I was lying, so she destroyed the evidence. She rubbed it between her fingers and then blew on it so that it dispersed and drifted away down the stairwell."

Murray frowned.

"What is it, Uncle Murr?"

"I wish we had some kind of concrete evidence."

Neal opened his mouth to speak, but Murray cut him off, saying, "I do believe you, Neal, but I'd feel better if we had some physical proof."

"Neal," Sarah asked, "exactly when was it that you saw the Erlking the first time?"

"It was back in March, almost at dusk, when a dense sea fog surprised me as I was playing the bagpipes on the bluff."

Sarah snapped her fingers, "Of course!" she exclaimed. "Uncle Murray, there is this bit of proof. I can corroborate some of Neal's story, because Mazie and I were on the beach below his house that day."

Sarah addressed Neal, "That was the day I told you about—I saw you playing as I walked on the beach. I heard the pipes first, and then I spotted you up on the bluff. I was intrigued by the music, so I sat down on a log and listened for a few minutes. I sat with my back to the sea, and the fog surprised me; it enveloped me in an instant. I remember the cold, clammy feeling very well. Something about it upset Mazie, and she began barking wildly, with raised hackles."

Recognition lit Neal's face, "Yes! I remember hearing a dog barking in the distance."

"It was the way she barked that frightened me," said Sarah. "She wheeled around, barking furiously in different directions, growling and snarling. And then the fog itself alarmed me; it was impenetrable, completely blinding. I was so disoriented that without Mazie, I couldn't have found my way back toward the point. It was just eerie; I was completely unnerved."

"Maybe that fog marked the arrival of the Erlking. Maybe he even created it," said Neal, "and Mazie sensed his presence."

"It's possible, I guess, because I've never seen her behave that way before or since," said Sarah. "She was spooked."

"I'm still curious about the house," said Murray. "It's a beautiful old Victorian. Do you know its history, Neal?"

"I know a little about it from Peggy Williams, the real estate agent who sold it to us. It was built by a German logging tycoon named Fritzinger around the turn of the century. His daughter lived there until her death in 1993."

"I think we ought to find out as much as possible about the history of the house and the people who lived there."

"I'll do that," said Neal.

"Good. And for my part, there may be someone at Coveland House who grew up here and who knew the Fritzinger family. I'll ask around and see what information I can glean. Another thing we can do is try to verify your grandfather's visions. If the SS regiments did actually massacre British troops in two separate incidents, there might be some record of those events, and that would give more credence to his vision of the Erlking. Sarah, could you do that research?"

"Yes. I'll start with books about Dunkirk, and there must be volumes written about Nazi war crimes. I should be able to come up with something."

"Thanks, doll. One last thing, Neal," Murray said.

"Yes?"

"If you have no objection, I would like to visit the tower room."

"Don't think you're going without me, Uncle Murr!"

Neal's grin was lopsided. "Of course, you're both welcome to see it."

"Great!" said Murray, rubbing his hands together, "When?"

"Well, my grandmother Barbara is arriving on Monday from Edinburgh and it will probably take us most of next week to resurrect the house from its current catastrophic state, so what about a week from Friday, on May nineteenth?"

"That's fine with me," said Murray. "And by then we can compare notes—we will have had time to do our research." He looked at Sarah, "Is that date good for you, doll?"

"Yes," she smiled, "my social calendar is blank as usual."

"Well, now that it's settled," said Neal, "I had better take my son home." After thanking Sarah and Murray for their help, Neal scooped up the sleeping Owen. As he carried him out to the car, Sarah sheltered the boy with her umbrella, and Murray opened the car door.

They stood side by side in the rain as Neal drove away. Sarah said, "What do you think, Uncle Murr?"

He shook his head and puffed his cheeks as he blew out a noisy breath, "There goes a good man with a formidable foe. We've got to use all the information we can gather to figure out a practical solution. And then that solution had better be the right one," he said, running a hand over his bald spot, "because in a confrontation with a creature like that, we will only get one chance." He shook his head, "Somehow, I feel like a man about to brave a typhoon with only a parasol for protection." He put his arm around his niece, and said, "Speaking of typhoons, come on, doll, let's go in out of the rain. Maybe things will look better in the morning."

CHAPTER 21

Pranks

Vicky wore the new black satin negligee with spaghetti straps and a low-cut, tight-fitting bodice, Jim's gift. Sitting before her bedroom mirror, she gathered up her shoulder-length blonde hair in a twist and observed the effect with satisfaction.

Jim Nordquist. How nice to have a real man in love with her—a man she could respect, a pilot who worked in Seattle for a major airline, who could buy her expensive presents like the negligee. A man who enjoyed the same things she did.

Vicky pulled on her dressing gown and leaned forward to inspect herself more closely. She clicked her tongue at the crow's feet fanning out at the corners of her eyes and the fine lines underneath. Her thirtieth birthday loomed only six months away—November twentieth. She sat up straight and squared her shoulders; life would not pass her by. No—she wouldn't let it. She was getting frown lines, too. She smoothed the deep vertical trenches between her eyebrows with her fingers, pushing them away. She sat back suddenly and laughed, remembering the day she met Jim Nordquist.

Her life had mirrored the endless gray and sodden January weather until Jim walked into Ferraday's that chilly Friday afternoon. Old Prune-Face Evelyn Ferraday said, "May I help you?" as he entered. The tall, attractive man gestured at Vicky, and said, "No, thank you, my cousin there in the aisle will help me." What is he up to, Vicky wondered, watching the fortyish, self-confident man approach with a military bearing and stride. No uniform, but had to be career Navy, she thought.

"Hi, Cousin," he grinned and lowered his voice, "hope you don't mind. With a choice between Age and Beauty, I chose Beauty."

Vicky flushed with pleasure.

He offered her his hand. "Jim Nordquist, Northwest Airlines," he said, and then reading her name tag, added, "Glad to meet you, Vicky MacGregor, Assistant Manager." He held her hand just a tad too long, while she took in his height and smelled the musk of his cologne.

She helped him find the drill and hinges he needed for the fishing cabin he kept on the island. He talked to her like she was the only woman in the world and kept her laughing. The store seemed darker when left.

Jim came in several times the next week, charming her, telling her funny stories, and making her laugh. She began to look for him every day, disappointed if he didn't appear. Eventually he asked her to eat lunch with him.

In late February, he asked her to lunch with him at his fishing cabin, only ten minutes away. Once there, Jim offered her a drink, and then he kissed her. She fell into his arms, ripe and juicy as an apple. Lunch was forgotten, and she arrived back at Ferraday's twenty minutes late, duly noted by Prune-Face. Thereafter, Vicky's long lunches and early departures from the store became habitual.

Vicky brushed her hair, thinking about the last eight years. How naïve she had been when she had envisioned that marriage to Neal would include adventure, fine clothes, and jewelry. Her laugh was bitter, "Hardly." Their first apartment near the University of Washington was apparently designed for pygmies. The living room was the size of a walk-in closet. They slept in a room so small that there was only a maximum clearance of sixteen inches around the double bed, and they had to put their chest of drawers outside in the hall.

When Neal got the teaching job on Darrow Island, they did go kayaking on the cove once, and there were a few long, romantic walks on the beaches. But they lived in a cramped apartment near the naval air base in Stone Harbor, where the cold, howling wind competed with the continual roar of jets taking off and landing at all hours of the day and night.

Her pregnancy, a few months after their first anniversary, had been a tiresome, puking ordeal. At first, after the baby was born, everyone had said he was as cute as his mother. Relatives and friends brought presents; her sisters came to help out. But after all the attention died down, the drudgery and lack of sleep had exhausted her. She spent lonely days with the baby waiting for Neal to come home. She tried to read, but the baby interrupted her so often that she gave up. Her nights were hellish: changing stinking diapers, heating bottles, and sitting dead-tired and frustrated in front of the TV while Neal cooked pasta or graded papers and she rocked the colicky, screaming child.

Everything seemed to decline after the baby. She really did love Owen, but he was a burden, the death of her freedom. And apparently the death of Neal's pathetic bank account as well. From then on, there had never been enough money for vacations or anything else. Before the baby, she and Neal had at least gone to an occasional restaurant or movie. Afterwards, well, thank God for TV—for a few hours she escaped into the world of the wealthy, the sleek, and the sophisticated, the world of fashion magazine publishers, attorneys, and doctors with glitzy offices, elegant apartments. She identified with the beautiful women whose tall, handsome lovers brought passion and adventure into their lives.

When Neal did come home, she begged him to go out, but he didn't want to pay for a sitter—all he wanted to do was hold the baby and play with him. He talked to Owen as though the child were an adult and could understand him. He'd stand at the window holding the baby in the crook of his arm, saying, "Look, Owen, there's the world laid before you like a gift. See the ocean? Someday you'll go down there and sail a boat, or swim, or fish, or dig for clams. See up there," Neal would say when another damned plane droned so loudly she'd had to turn up the TV, "that's an airplane. Who knows? You may travel in one of those to Scotland, Russia, India, China, or Japan. You might even fly one someday."

Well, Owen might not be the only one to fly. Maybe it was her turn now. Motherhood was not for everyone. She had fed Owen, bathed him, dressed him, taught him to ride a bike. But shouldn't there be more to life than taking care of a child with a husband duller than lint? Didn't she deserve adventure and passion? The spark had long since gone from her marriage—she couldn't remember the last time Neal had touched her. Of course, that didn't matter anymore—now she had Jim.

God, the house was silent. Vicky brushed her hair, feeling suddenly small, aware of the empty space all around her. She didn't like it. The old house was a big place to be in alone—it was almost spooky. She began to notice little creaking noises, the moaning of the wind, tapping rain, a branch scraping against the window. How had that ancient Fritzinger woman lived here by herself all those years? Ugh—that was the last thing Vicky wanted to think about—a sad, withered old crone, tottering and decrepit.

Where were Neal and Owen? It was almost nine-thirty on a school night. Not that she cared, really. The only reason she was home was because Jim had gone to Seattle for a business meeting tomorrow. Something about that ridiculous suspension. So he'd had a couple shots of whiskey in a New York bar two hours before a flight. He was an experienced pilot. Hell, she'd felt safe with him in his pick-up truck on narrow, unlit back roads at three a.m., after they'd spent the entire evening drinking. Jim could hold his liquor. "Management is overreacting, like a gaggle of hysterical geese," he'd said. He'd ride it out; it would all blow over and he'd soon be back in the cockpit.

I'll drink to that, thought Vicky. She padded down to the kitchen and poured herself a tumbler of orange juice. Then she carried the glass upstairs to the third floor. This was Neal's fault, too. He'd criticized her drinking, so now she had to hide it from him. When she reached the third floor landing, her eyes widened in shock. The door was padlocked. A chill ran through her body. Had Neal discovered her bottle?

Then she remembered—he put the lock there because of the ghost. What a crock—Neal was so pathetic, caught up in his fantasies. Well, let him delude himself; at least it kept him occupied. In the meantime, she was free to pursue her pleasures; she could meet Jim and drink to her heart's content. That is if she could get to her damned bottle. She rattled the door and then in a burst of frustration, she jerked on the padlock. To her great surprise, it popped open.

"Weirder and weirder," she muttered. Why did he padlock the door and then leave it unlocked? He was on a trip for sure, light-years farther into la-la land than even she had guessed.

She shrugged, and then unhooked the lock, put it in the pocket of her dressing gown, and entered the tower room. She pulled a fat book about the Lincoln-Douglas debates (God, who'd ever read that?) from the second shelf of the bookcase, and there was her lovely bottle of vodka.

She poured a hefty slug into her orange juice, replaced the bottle, and then sat down in the armchair that faced the big window. "Mmmm," she murmured, taking sip after sip in quick succession. Nice. Such a warm, soothing effect. She could feel her muscles relax. She laid her head back in the chair and hummed tunelessly.

She hadn't been in the study since the day after she'd found Neal drunk on the floor, the day she had straightened up the room and hidden the bottle. It was a pleasant room, she thought, looking at the ivory walls and the bookcases, but so chilly. Outside, the cold rain persisted, and a strong draft entered through the one-inch crack of the open window. Vicky got up to close it.

"You're getting drunk."

She froze. How had Neal snuck up on her like that? She decided not to look at him or answer his accusation. "Go to hell!" she said.

"I live there."

Her mouth dropped open and frown lines furrowed between her brows. Well, what's got into him? He couldn't talk to her like that. She was ready to turn around and slap his face, when she heard a car pull into the driveway. She knew the sound of that motor. It was the Mustang.

Vicky blinked. If Neal was in the room, who was driving his car?

She whirled around. No one was there.

"What the hell?" she whispered. She gulped the last of her drink and then ran down the stairs, dashed into the kitchen, and stopped. She heard the rattle of a key in the lock, and then the door flew open. In walked Neal, bearing a sleeping Owen in his arms.

"What are you doing here?" Vicky demanded.

"I live here."

"How'd you do it?"

"I bought the house and then I moved in. Simple."

Vicky stamped her foot. "How did you sneak up on me like that?"

"It was easy: I opened the door and walked in."

"Then who drove the car?"

Neal kicked the door shut behind him. "Well, since Owen doesn't have his license yet, I confess I did."

"Very funny, Neal. You put one over on me, but you're not as smart as you think." She took the padlock out of her pocket and held it at arms-length between her thumb and forefinger. "You forgot to lock it." She released her grip, and the padlock fell to the floor with a loud *whump*.

She left the room smiling, but undecided as to what pleased her more—the fact that the heavy lock dented the floor, or that Neal's face blanched whiter than the ivory walls of the study.

Fifteen minutes later, Vicky heard Neal enter the darkened bedroom. Feigning sleep, she lay unmoving on her stomach under the bedclothes, trying to control her breathing.

"Vicky, we need to talk."

She waited for him to go away.

"I know you're awake."

He turned on the overhead light. "I've invited my grandmother Barbara to come for an extended stay next week. I'm picking her up on Monday evening."

"So thoughtful of you to inform me," she said, turning over and squinting against the light. "Wonderful of you to make these masterful decisions on your own and then tell the little wife as an afterthought."

"I would have told you sooner, but I have hardly seen you for days. You screamed at Owen on Sunday morning, and you've been gone ever since."

"Oh, I've been here."

"Yes, you're here between three or four in the morning until sometime after Owen and I leave for school. Speaking of communication between a husband and wife, where do you go, Vicky?"

"I told you. I go to see—"

"Movies." Neal finished her sentence. "Well, you see more movies than all the New York film critics combined, and each one is as epic as Wagner's Ring Cycle."

Vicky wrinkled her brow, "What are you talking about?"

"They're long, Vicky—real long. Like seeing the *Star Wars* trilogy topped off with *Braveheart*."

"That's right, Mr. Superior—put it in terms your stupid wife can understand." Vicky's tone was caustic. She sat up in bed and raised her voice, "You think you're so much smarter than me, Neal, but you're not. You're a deluded fool, lost in a shadow-world of your own making. Well, while you're wandering in circles, chasing mirages, I'm going to have a life. What I do is none of your business."

"Isn't it?" Neal sighed, and then an odd expression crossed his face. He said nothing, but something about the look in his eyes made Vicky uneasy. She suddenly remembered she was wearing the new negligee, so she pulled the sheet up around her throat.

"Why is Barbara coming?" she asked, not that she wanted to know, but in order to change the subject.

"I asked her to come because while you are out at the movies, I need help with Owen. Although you don't believe me, I told you the truth about my experience in the study."

"Your ghost story."

"That ghost threatened Owen. I want someone here all the time Owen is in the house, and Barbara is willing to help me."

"Fine. Let her. That gives me more freedom. How long is she staying?"

"I really don't know. She'll be here until I can resolve the situation."

"With the ghost."

"Exactly." Neal held up the padlock. "I did lock this, Vicky."

"Oh, really? Then why was it unlocked? And why the hell did you padlock the study anyway?"

"I want to keep Owen out of that room, as I already told you."

Good, thought Vicky, he doesn't know about the bottle.

"And I don't know why it was unlocked," Neal continued.

"Maybe the ghost did it," Vicky laughed.

"I believe he did," Neal replied, unsmiling, and then walked out of the room.

Vicky was miffed. "At least he could have turned off the light," she said. She threw off the covers, and was three steps from the light switch when she heard a brief, sharp sizzle as the bulb burned out. "Damn it to hell!" she spat and then her hand flew to her mouth. She could have sworn that in the distance she heard faint laughter.

CHAPTER 22

Realization

S tanding in the hall outside Vicky's room, Neal regarded the open padlock in his hand. Knowing that it was probably a vain act, he walked up the stairs and put the lock in place on the study door again. He snapped it shut and tugged on it roughly to test it. "Solid as my marriage," he said, "with an equal chance of holding."

He walked downstairs as slowly and stiffly as an old man riddled with arthritis. His stomach felt knotted and volatile at the same time; he thought he might vomit. He went into the kitchen and made himself a whiskey on the rocks.

He took the drink into the parlor and sat down on the sofa in what felt like slow motion, as though he struggled to move on the bottom of the ocean, in a cold, dark, alien world under tons of pressure. Now it all made sense. Vicky's erratic behavior, her clothes, her perfume, the new hairdo, the manicures. He knew now why she'd dressed with care, worn a red silk blouse with a flowered skirt, overdressed for a spur-of-the-moment movie; he knew the reason for all the late nights and flimsy excuses.

Vicky was having an affair.

As he spoke to her in the bedroom, it had ambushed him suddenly, silently, like an aneurysm. Hand curled around the glass, he sat stricken, betrayed. Droplets of condensation rolled down the side of the whiskey glass onto his forefinger, overflowed down and across his knuckles to wet the arm of the sofa, while he sat unmoving, a man of stone.

Though his body was still, his thoughts churned, chaotic as the sea surface in storm. She'd been unhappy ever since Owen was born. He'd hoped the new house would please her, and it had, briefly, but once the novelty wore off, Vicky's old unhappiness returned. All the signs of an affair had been present, but he'd been too preoccupied or too blind to read them. No—he hadn't wanted to read them. Vicky with another man. Neal gagged and felt stomach acid burn his throat and the back of his nose. His eyes watered. He sniffed and sipped the whiskey.

He remembered Vicky at twenty, a bubbly, pretty sophomore when they met at a Halloween party, of all places. Neal had normally shunned parties. They reminded him of all the frightened, unhappy nights he had spent barricaded in his bedroom while his parents and their drunken friends caroused. But he'd let himself be persuaded by a fellow grad student. Vicky had charmed him. Vivacious, fun-loving, she drew him out. They had married the following June. Their powerful physical attraction had been as spectacular as a fireworks display, and just as brief—a brilliant, electrifying array, followed by darkness. He stared into the ashes of the cold fireplace. His marriage was ashes; it had been years since the fire burned out.

He knew that Vicky's affair was only a symptom of their troubled marriage, not the cause. Her unhappiness, like his own, resulted from their basic incompatibility. Harnessed together like two stubborn oxen, they had pulled in opposite directions, managing only to chafe each other raw.

Somehow, over the years, her desire for "fun" had eclipsed her loyalty to husband and child, and Neal's attributes, what she had named as his calm strength and maturity, had lost all their appeal. Now he was dull and boring, while Owen was a burden—perceptions fueled in part by her deep fear of aging. Vicky wanted to live in that uninhibited, exhilarating freedom of the very young, without the weight of duty and responsibilities. Neal shared neither her interests nor her desire to return to adolescence.

He shook his head, seeing everything in the painful clarity of hindsight. In the beginning their incandescent sex life had masked the fact that their values and priorities in life were completely different. And now those differences emerged like islands rising from the sea, solid, unavoidable, inescapably altering the map of their world.

Sadness that it had all turned out this way overwhelmed him. He felt a great weight pressing down on him; he didn't think he could rise from the chair. But what surprised him was how little anger he felt on his own behalf. It was Owen who bore the brunt. In Vicky's hot pursuit of her own pleasure, she had neglected and mistreated Owen. The boy was sick all the time now with stomachaches and nausea. In the event of a divorce, Owen was the one who would be the most vulnerable and the most hurt. That was the part Neal hated the most.

In the days to come, Neal knew he would have to confront Vicky about the affair and then decide what he wanted to do about the marriage. His biggest task would be to shield Owen from the fallout.

At that moment, Sarah Friedkin popped into his mind, and he felt a twinge of guilt. Yes, he had been attracted to her; he had wanted to pursue her, but he had not acted on his desires. He had not committed adultery. But Vicky had.

God, the nausea surged back with a vengeance. He took three sips of whiskey in quick succession, then put the glass down. He slowly shook his head. Well, regardless of what Vicky had done, adultery was still out of the question for him. That was a line he would not cross no matter what the state of his marriage.

But Sarah—he couldn't help thinking of her. She was like music to him—a melody, pure and ascending, that drew his heart and made his spirit rise. She was a kindred soul, and her presence was a delight. Just being with her had shown him how numb he had been, for years, really.

But this was not about Sarah. Neal tapped his glass. Much as he would love to, he couldn't think about her now; he had to put her out of his mind. This crisis concerned himself and Vicky and Owen. He hoped he would have the wisdom to do the right thing for all of them, especially Owen.

Everything came down to Owen, Neal thought, the lightning rod for all the tension in the house. He tightened his grip on the glass. He would protect his son as far as humanly possible. At least he had taken certain measures on Owen's behalf. Thank God Barbara was coming. She would be cheerful, a calm and gentle maternal presence, all that Vicky was not. And now, thankfully, he had Murray and Sarah to help him with the other problem he faced.

Neal sipped his drink, and then laid his head back. His eyes sought the ceiling. Yes, the matter of the Erlking. Up above him, at the top of the house, what future waited? Somehow he had to exorcise the threat from his house, his life, and the MacGregor line. There had to be a confrontation with whatever it was that occupied the study. But what if he failed? What would happen to Owen then?

No, he couldn't think like that. There was only one acceptable conclusion. He sat erect, downed his drink, and spoke, "Failure, as they say, is not an option."

He heaved himself up from the chair and put his empty glass in the kitchen sink. Next, he checked on Owen, and satisfied that all was well with him, Neal took a shower. The hot water felt wonderful. He washed his hair and scrubbed himself clean. He dried off with a thick blue towel, and changed into a clean T-shirt and pajama bottoms. His stomach was no longer roiling, and he felt a little better. He lay down in the twin bed across from Owen's, and prayed he'd feel better in the morning.

When his eyes flew open at six a.m., Neal rolled over on his side toward the window, pulled back the curtain, and peered out. It was gray and still raining. He placed his palm against the cold glass. He had slept fitfully, and now that he was awake, the thought of Vicky's betrayal returned like the pain of neuralgia, a deep, dull ache. He sighed, pulled his hand away from the chilly windowpane, and sat up.

Rubbing the sleep out of his eyes, he thought about his day. Wednesday. School. About five weeks till summer vacation. The annual teacher-student countdown was on. What kind of summer would the MacGregor clan have? He dropped his head into his hands. Better not get too far ahead, Neal thought. *Sufficient unto the day is the evil thereof.*

As always, when he was in trouble, Neal thought of his grandfather. He rose from the bed, thinking about Ian and the pipers of the past world wars, how they marched into gunfire, playing their pipes. Well, war was not always pitched battles with guns and artillery blazing. Sometimes it was just getting up and facing one's fears and bearing the heartaches. That was his lot, this day at least.

He padded into the bathroom to relieve himself and shave before he woke Owen. After shaving, he washed his face and dried himself with a towel. His comb-defying red hair was uneven and tangled as usual. After a struggle to subdue his wayward locks, Neal gave up, as he did every morning, and smoothed his bushy mustache.

Back in Owen's room, he dressed quickly in olive green slacks, a yellow button-down shirt, and why not? A green, red, and yellow tropical tie. He was absurdly pleased by the warm, bright colors of the banana trees, parrots, and mangoes.

He touched Owen's shoulder and said, "Time to get up." Owen's eyes fluttered open and he sat up. "Good morning," smiled Neal.

"Morning. Is it Wednesday?"

"Yes."

"Good. Today's our field trip. Mrs. Burton is taking our class to the Island County Museum. They've got a real blockhouse, Indian canoes, and totem poles. I can't wait!" Owen leaped out of bed, startling the sleepy cat, and ran for the bathroom.

"Meet you downstairs," Neal called after him. He glanced at Vicky's closed door as he went out into the hall. Still sleeping, he thought.

Owen appeared in the kitchen five minutes later, fully clothed and bouncing with anticipation.

"How about cereal for breakfast?" Neal asked.

"What if I want eggs, bacon, and toast?" Owen asked.

"Well, in that case, you'd get cereal," Neal replied as he took out two bowls and Sparker brushed against his pants leg.

"Okay," Owen laughed, "I'll get the spoons."

"And feed your cat."

After breakfast, the two MacGregor men donned their anoraks, and then with briefcase and backpack, faced the elements. With headlights lit and windshield wipers keeping time, Neal drove the Mustang through the rain and chill of early morning. He dropped off Owen at the elementary school, and then drove another half-mile to Coveland High.

The small school had been built over seventy years ago. Neal entered through the heavy double wooden doors and was greeted by the unmistakable school smell, the mingled odors of old wood, wax, chalk dust, soap, sweat, furnace oil, and fevered adolescence. He greeted students and other teachers in the wide, high-ceilinged, busy hall on the way to his classroom.

Entering his room, he closed the door to preserve the early morning quiet before the first surge of students. His large wooden desk, front and center, faced the twenty student desks, an optimistic number, he thought, since his largest class had only fifteen enrolled. There was a blackboard behind him and another on the left wall as he faced the room. Four windows on the right, banked with a profusion of green houseplants, let in a good deal of natural light. A single supply closet, set in the center of the back wall, was flanked on both sides by tall bookcases overflowing with history texts, biographies, and stacks of videos. Almost all the available wall space was covered with maps of Europe, America, and Asia in various time periods.

As Neal opened his briefcase and took out his textbooks and notes for the day, he realized he felt a little better. Morning helped, he thought. So did his job, and the atmosphere of the school. He was going to assign a long-term project for his American History classes. He had no idea what the students' reactions would be. He thought the project was a good idea, and who knew what might come of it?

He sat down at his desk, smoothed his gaudy tie, and awaited the onslaught of young humanity, the cocky ones, shy ones, pretty ones, the insecure, the sarcastic, the defiant, the intelligent ones, daydreamers, gigglers, the lively and the dull. He thought of his students with glad anticipation. He wanted to do his job and do it well, his own difficulties be damned.

He laid his palms flat on the desk, and for the second time that morning, the image of his grandfather sprang into his mind. Now there was a man: cheerful and brave, never bitter in the face of towering obstacles. Suddenly overwhelmed with a fierce defiance toward all negative forces, Neal hit the desk a resounding blow with both hands, deciding in that moment that neither danger, depression, nor fear would bring him down—he wouldn't allow it. No, he had Ian's example before him and the example of all brave soldiers in all the wars across time.

Feeling a rush of energy, he smiled. He would be a positive force; today he would try to spark an interest in his students. He hoped to ignite a love of learning in them that would burn, an illuminating flame, through all their years.

Neal rose and walked to the windows. He looked out at the gray curtain of rain. It still falls on us, he thought, as it fell on Caesar's Rome, on Joan of Arc's campaign, as it fell on Napoleon's troops, on London during the Blitz, on the Salish Indians native to Darrow Island before the Europeans came, a mere two hundred years ago. History, the story of humanity, its glories, its shame, its excesses, its heart. He and his students were all a part of that story, Neal thought, and today he would help them discover their connections to history, how the long arms of the past reached out and touched the present.

The bell rang, doors opened, students surged through the halls, dust flew, voices merged in jangling cacophony: the school day had begun. Ten minutes later, when the fifteen students who were his first class were settled in their seats, Neal said, "Good morning. Today, I am going to assign you a project that I call 'Links.' What does that suggest to you?"

Hands shot up.

"Golf."

"Chains."

"In German, *links* means left."

"A big cat."

"Sausage."

Neal smiled, but made no comment. Then he asked, "What about the word *connections*?" Several students nodded.

"Well, the project is related to our study of World War II. I want each of you to interview a relative, family friend—someone from Coveland or elsewhere that fought or was involved in the Second World War in some way, and then I want you to show in what ways their war experiences are directly connected to your lives. For example, my grandfather's injuries during the war made him blind and mute. He had to learn sign language, and so did I in order to communicate with him."

Jack Baird raised his hand, "What if we want to write about someone who didn't come back from the war? Could we do research on men who were killed?"

Neal shook his head. "No, this is an interview, Jack, with a living soul, not a ghost. Anyway, among all you Bairds, there must be one veteran in the family who came back alive." Neal smiled, "If you don't know anyone personally, we've got a naval air base on the island, and at Coveland House, I'll bet there are several veterans. The written interviews are due on Friday, May twenty-sixth. We'll use the rest of the term to June tenth, to put together a book that shows how Adolf Hitler's decision to subjugate Europe is linked in some way to each one of you. Links."

Neal gave them the requirements regarding the length of the written interviews, and then he explained that he was going to put the book together on his home computer, and print out copies for the class. The students were quiet, taking it all in. Neal watched them and sensed an interest, the spark he'd hoped for. He smiled at them, the spotty, bespectacled, tentative faces of the future, who were soon to find out how inextricably they were all linked to the past.

CHAPTER 23

Pasta, Piano, Pictures

"Daddy, you said we had to buy groceries today after school, and you just passed Hollanders."

"That's right. Hang on." Neal waited for a lull in the Ferry Road traffic, and then whipped the Mustang into a tight U-turn. "Sorry about that, Owen. I've got too many things on my mind—I can't seem to remember anything lately. Let's hope I don't forget anything else," he remarked as he drove into Hollander's parking lot. "In fact, you can help me out," Neal said. "Tonight—Thursday night—is three-P night. Remember these words: pasta, piano, pictures."

"Pasta, piano, pictures," Owen repeated.

Inside the store, Owen stepped onto the back axle of the grocery cart, gripped the bar and rode standing between his father's arms as Neal zipped down the aisles. "Pasta, piano, pictures," Neal muttered under his breath. "Guess which one's for dinner."

"The piano."

"Well," Neal replied, "that was my first choice, too, but pianos are tough to fit in the oven, and then you have leftovers for days. You have to eat fried piano, piano sandwiches, piano soup, and ugh, pickled piano. So I decided against it. Guess again."

"You said *piano* because my lesson is tonight."

"You got it, but what are we having for dinner?"

"Pasta."

"Right you are. Pasta is so good-a," Neal told Owen, "you eat more than you should-a." They stopped in front of the pasta shelves. "Straight or curly?" Neal asked.

"Curly."

Neal tossed a package of spiral pasta into the cart.

"Why did you say *pictures,* Daddy?"

"I have to remember to bring the pictures of the house to show Yoshiko and Ingemar at your lesson tonight. Yoshiko was curious about the repairs and improvements I made, because she used to visit the house and play piano for Emily Fritzinger, the former owner."

"Oh. Can we get some candy, Daddy?"

"Green beans, did you say?" Neal grabbed a can off the shelf.

"Daddy, I said candy."

"Well, if you say *candy* in Czechoslovakian it means green beans."

"It does not."

Neal stopped the cart abruptly and fixed his gaze on Owen. "Okay, you're right. It doesn't mean green beans. It means meat sauce."

"Candy, Daddy."

"Candy is dandy, as the poet wrote, but meat sauce is boss." Farther down the same aisle, Neal selected a jar of ready-made sauce, and added it to the contents of the cart.

At the checkout counter, Owen tried again. "Can we get some candy?"

"Will you eat your dinner?"

Owen smiled and said, "Pasta is so good-a, I'll eat more than I should-a."

"Then candy," said Neal "will be dandy."

From the muffled blare of the television, Neal knew Vicky's whereabouts when he and Owen arrived home. He had Owen feed the cat while he boiled the pasta and heated the meat sauce and green beans. After draining the pasta, he took three plates and glasses and placed them on the counter where Owen could reach them.

"Owen, set the table while I talk to your mother for a minute. Here are the plates and glasses, and the silverware is in the drawer. Forks on the left, knives on the right. We'll eat shortly, and remember—no candy until after dinner."

Leaving the bright, fragrant kitchen, Neal pushed open the swinging door to the den and found himself in another world. The room was like a dim, smoky bar, reeking of alcohol and cigarettes. It took a moment for his eyes to adjust, since all the drapes were closed and the only light came from the blaring television. Blinking rapidly in the darkness, he peered through the acrid haze of smoke and saw Vicky lying sound asleep on the couch, and beside her, littering the floor, four empty beer bottles and an ashtray overflowing with crumpled cigarette butts.

Bursts of canned laughter, tinny and shrill, erupted intermittently from the television, but Vicky slept, oblivious to the noise. Breathing heavily through her mouth, she lay on her right side in the fetal position, facing the screen. Her hair was disheveled, and a few loose strands veiled her face. The two deep, vertical lines entrenched between her brows gave her an angry appearance even in sleep. In the flickering light from the television her flesh took on a ghastly, gray hue.

Neal's shoulders slumped. He rubbed his eyes and then let his hands fall heavily to his sides. Where Vicky was concerned, his heart remained a battleground between anger and pity, and for the moment, seeing her so unlovely and vulnerable, pity had the upper hand. He hadn't seen her since his revelation about her affair. At some point he knew he had to confront her about the infidelity. That he dreaded—but he had to face it—they had to face it together.

At the same time, he intended to tell her that he had not given up on the marriage. Reconciliation might still be possible. For his part, Neal knew that if he didn't make an effort to set things to rights, he wouldn't be able to live with himself. Of course reconciliation was only possible if Vicky desired it, too. But before anything else, he had to ease some of the hostility she felt toward him.

He turned off the television, and then touched her shoulder gently, "Vicky."

"Why the hell did you turn off the TV?" her low voice had a rattle in it. Keeping her eyes closed, she coughed to clear her throat.

"Well, you weren't watching it," Neal replied. "Why don't you come and eat dinner with us? I made pasta with meat sauce."

"Not hungry."

"Vicky, you haven't eaten with us for days. In fact, we've hardly seen you. How long is this behavior going to persist? You've got a son and husband who love you and need you."

"Oh, sure." She rolled onto her back and stared at the ceiling. "Translation: please be our maid and babysitter. No way—I want my freedom."

"You'd better consider what you're saying, Vicky."

She laughed, "All afraid you'll lose your unpaid servant, are you?"

"Damn it, Vicky!" Neal barked. "You know I don't think of you in those terms."

"Frankly, Neal, I don't care how or what you think of me."

He softened his tone, "Look, I don't want you to cut yourself off from us like this. Let's be a family again. Please come and eat with Owen and me."

She shook her head. "Go away, Neal."

"Well, before I do, there's one important thing I want to say. As I told you, my grandmother Barbara will be here next week, and in spite of the anger you feel toward me, I want you to treat her with respect."

Vicky chuckled.

"She's arriving on Monday, the fifteenth, and she'll be staying in the guest bedroom next to Owen's room."

"Good luck, Neal. I hope your imported maid is more satisfactory than your domestic one. As far as treating her with respect, there'll be no problem, since I'll see her as infrequently as I see you." Vicky rose from the couch in one smooth motion and said, "I'll be going out in a little while."

Neal watched her walk toward the door nearest the stairs. "Going out is easy," he called after her. "Why don't you stay home and grow up instead?"

Her answer was succinct, "Go to hell."

It was an indication of the state of affairs in the MacGregor home that Owen never questioned why his mother no longer ate with them. Neal didn't mention Vicky either, though her vacant chair and empty plate were eloquent enough. Nor could he find it in himself to return to the jocular mood he'd maintained earlier in the evening, so dinner was a quiet meal, quickly eaten.

Afterwards, while Owen practiced in preparation for his lesson, Neal searched unsuccessfully downstairs for the photographs of the house that he wanted to show Yoshiko and Ingemar. Vicky had had them last, and he didn't know where she had put them. He would have to ask her; he couldn't avoid it.

He went up to Vicky's room and knocked, but there was no response. He peeked in the room, and wished he hadn't; her room was more disheveled than the rest of the house. The unmade bed was the sloppy centerpiece, surrounded by a floor littered with clothes, shoes, books, crumpled cigarette packs and overflowing ashtrays. Well, he thought, one more outward and visible sign of her inner turmoil. Maybe she was in Owen's room.

He walked across the hall and opened Owen's door. The sole occupant was Sparker, who sat on the windowsill, enjoying the sea view. Seeing Owen's yellow windbreaker on the bed, Neal decided to take it with him, thinking Owen might need it by the time they returned from the piano lesson. He picked up the light jacket and stopped for a moment, hearing a noise above him.

Someone was walking in the tower room. Owen was downstairs practicing and Vicky didn't have a key to the padlock. Neal held his breath— could it be the mysterious intruder? Or was it the Erlking himself? Either way, he had to investigate.

Sparker followed him out of the room to the base of the stairs, where she sensibly stopped. Stomach knotted with tension, Neal continued up, taking care to make no sound. The padlock hung open, and the door was very slightly ajar. There was no sound coming from the room. He took a deep breath to steady himself, then he charged into the room and almost tackled his wife, who shrieked in surprise.

He pulled up short and blurted, "Vicky! What are you doing in here?"

She answered his question with an angry one of her own, "Why did you burst in here like that?" Grimacing, she asked in a sarcastic tone, "Looking for your ghost?"

"As a matter of fact, yes."

She opened a drawer of the rolltop desk and took out a yellow legal pad. "I am in here because I wanted a piece of paper."

"How did you get in without a key?"

Her smile was unpleasant, "Well, wouldn't you like to know?"

"All right, Vicky, I don't have time to play games. It's getting late and I have to take Owen to his lesson. Yoshiko and Ingemar would like to see the photographs you took of the house. Where are they?"

"Under your nose," she said, pointing to the packet that lay in plain view in the open drawer, and without another word she walked out of the room.

Neal picked up the packet and closed the drawer. When he heard the slam of her bedroom door, he shook his head. Taunting, flamboyant, foul-mouthed and rude—her behavior seemed designed to provoke him. Placating Vicky's hostility would be as easy as deflecting bullets with his bare hands. Well, he'd just have to add that impossible task to his other one. He looked around the room that was the Erlking's haunt, wondering when he'd have to face that danger next.

Neal ran a hand through his hair and smoothed his mustache, hoping he would be strong enough, smart enough, and where Vicky was concerned, patient enough, to undertake the job. "Oh, Lord, help me," he murmured. On his way out, he locked the padlock, testing it to see if it was truly engaged. Satisfied, he checked his watch. It was six-fifteen, time for him to take Owen to the piano lesson.

Yoshiko and Ingemar lived on the east side of Coveland, about seven miles from the MacGregors. Their small wood frame house, painted a quiet, pale green, lay within walking distance of Waterfront Street. The grassy front yard was enclosed by a red cedar fence. Ferns lined the inside of the fence, and the two cherry trees, now past full bloom, stood on either side of a blue-gray slate path bordered by stones from the sea. Beds of purple iris bloomed at the base of the veranda.

Neal and Owen entered through the gate and walked up the gently curving path to the small veranda. Music greeted them—the delicate, ethereal sound of a wind chime suspended outside, and from inside, the clinker-studded, elephantine pounding of Amanda Watson, eight-year-old reluctant pianist nonpareil. The front door was kept unlocked, so the MacGregors entered the house and sat on a bench in the hall just outside the living room, while Amanda ripped her way through a Beethoven minuet.

Though she had the musical sensitivity of a carrot, Amanda was a good-natured child, friendly, outgoing, and intelligent, the star of her soccer team. Since her parents, refusing to recognize the obvious, insisted on private piano lessons, Yoshiko, with the patience of water dripping on stone, dutifully tried to mold the adamantine Amanda.

Amanda concluded the minuet with a stunning flourish of sour chords, for which Herr Beethoven, Neal was sure, would have flayed her alive. But since she had Yoshiko for teacher instead of the temperamental German, Amanda emerged, skin intact, with an enormous grin that revealed simultaneously her good humor, her relief that the lesson was over, and the glitter of an impressive amount of metal covering her teeth. After greeting Owen, she made her escape, bouncing down the path, sneakers slapping the slate, blonde ponytail flapping in her wake, to the getaway car, her mother's 1992 Chevy.

Yoshiko appeared in the hall looking fresh and surprisingly unperturbed. She greeted them with a serene smile, "Hello, Owen. Good to see you again, Neal. Come in," she said.

Neal marveled at her composure. He was in sore need of a similar equanimity in the face of difficult circumstances, and to a music teacher, Amanda would qualify as a vicissitude of the first degree. Wondering what the secret to Yoshiko's serenity might be, he followed her into the simply furnished, uncluttered living room where she kept her Steinway grand.

"It's a seven-foot B model—the kind I like best," Owen had once informed Neal.

While Owen sat down and adjusted the height of the piano bench by turning the circular knobs with expert efficiency, Neal said, "Yoshiko, I brought the pictures of the house." He held up the packet in one hand.

"Oh, good. Let's look at them after the lesson. Owen is my last student this evening, and Ingemar will be home then. I'll make you some excellent green tea—Japanese style. And I have some juice and cookies for you, Mr. Owen."

Seating himself in a comfortable armchair near a window, Neal had a pleasant view of the yard. If he wished to read, there was a low table with Ingemar's natural science journals and other magazines an arm's length away. But reading required calm and concentration, both impossible for him at the moment. As if the anxiety about the Erlking was not enough, every encounter with Vicky seemed one notch shy of mortal combat— guaranteed to leave him shaken and drained.

It was a relief to be in someone else's home. Closing his eyes, Neal leaned back in the chair. He laced his fingers together and stretched out his legs, crossing them at the ankles. For one hour he would simply listen to Owen play. Maybe if he kept his mind on the music, his muscles would relax and his blood pressure would return to a level somewhere below red alert.

Yoshiko sat in another armchair close by the piano where she could see the keyboard, and the lesson commenced. By seven-thirty, Owen had played his pieces, receiving praise and careful criticism, too. Yoshiko gave him his assignments for the following week, and then the lesson ended. "Time for tea," Yoshiko said.

In the kitchen, Yoshiko poured a glass of juice for Owen and set a platter with cookies on the table. She filled a teakettle with water. "Someday when we have more time, Neal, I'll invite you for the full Japanese green tea ceremony. As you probably know, the ceremony includes a meal, and takes from three to five hours to complete. I use a brazier to heat the water, but tonight I'll use the stove since I will make the tea without the ritual."

"Will the tea make me as calm as you, Yoshiko?"

She smiled and answered, "Actually, the tea ceremony has its roots in Zen Buddhism, and its true significance is symbolic and spiritual. One of its goals is harmony. It creates a calm state of mind, which can then serve as a preparation for meditation." She took out a tea canister, a bowl, and a bamboo whisk while she heated the water.

"Everything involved in the ceremony, from the setting to the utensils is carefully chosen," Yoshiko continued. "Even the host's hand and arm movements are ritualized and choreographed. The simplest things have a symbolic meaning. For example, the brazier represents yang and the water jar yin, with the shelf beneath symbolizing the harmonizing of the two energies. To enter into the ceremony is like stepping out of the world, into a place of tranquility, and it makes one mindful of the present moment."

"And mindfulness of the present prevents worries about the future," Neal remarked.

"Yes."

Watching her in the spare, simple kitchen, it seemed to Neal that the peace surrounding her, or, more precisely, emanating from her, was almost palpable. A measure of that quiet serenity seeped into him and he noticed it physically; his breathing slowed and his taut muscles relaxed.

Ingemar came home about five minutes later. "Well, hello," he said, stopping in surprise when he saw Neal and Owen seated at the kitchen table. "What a pleasure to find you two here!" The tall, slender Swede, a writer for an environmental journal, first shook hands with Neal and then tousled Owen's hair. "How's the piano playing going, Owen? Is Yoshiko treating you all right?"

Owen smiled and glanced at his teacher, "Well, you know she can be a little picky sometimes."

"What!" exclaimed Yoshiko, feigning distress.

Ingemar laughed.

"But she helps me a lot," Owen added.

"She helps me, too," said Ingemar, greeting his wife with a kiss.

"Ingemar, Neal brought the photographs of the Fritzinger house."

Sitting down across the table from Neal, Ingemar said, "Great. Let's have a look."

"I haven't even seen them myself," Neal admitted as he opened the packet and took out the pictures. "Let's see, Vicky took some of these before the renovations and some after." He glanced at each photograph and then passed them to Yoshiko, who sat beside Ingemar.

"Oh, the parlor floors look magnificent, Neal," Yoshiko commented, "and I like the paint you used in place of the wallpaper. It makes the rooms look brighter and larger. Look at this, Ingemar—these must be the second and third storey rooms." In a smooth habitual motion, Yoshiko tucked a strand of her black, shoulder-length hair behind one small ear. "You know, by the time I met Miss Emily, she had closed off the upper floors, so I never got to see that part of the house."

Owen scooted his chair over closer to his piano teacher. He pointed to the picture she held in her hand, "That's my bedroom," he said with a proud smile.

"What a nice space," Yoshiko replied. "I like your room."

"Me, too."

"Good heavens," exclaimed Ingemar, pointing at the next photograph Neal handed Yoshiko, "what an ugly room!"

"That's the 'before' picture of the tower room, which is now my study."

"Mr. Fritzinger used it as his study, too, according to Miss Emily," Yoshiko told Neal. "She said that after her father died, she closed off the third floor because the memories were too painful. She later closed the second floor because it was too expensive to heat. It was difficult for her, being all alone in that house."

"She must have missed her father," said Neal. "But I'm curious—did she say anything more about the house?"

"She loved to sit on the porch and look at the sea, and she especially loved her music room and the kitchen. That's all I remember. I didn't ask too many questions; I thought it was impolite."

"Her father Gunter had eccentric tastes, I think—at least his choice of maroon paint was strange." Neal handed Yoshiko another picture. "Here's what the room looks like now."

Ingemar gave a low whistle in approval. "From the inferno to *paradisio* with one paint job. Immensely better."

"Oh," said Neal, "here are the photos Vicky took of the house's façade. Most of these were taken in progress, before I finished the exterior." He glanced at them cursorily and then handed the entire group of photographs to Yoshiko.

With a piercing whistle for attention, the teakettle announced that the water was boiling. Yoshiko handed the photos to Ingemar and got up to make the tea.

"May I watch?'" Neal asked her.

"Of course."

"Me, too," said Owen.

Yoshiko put nine spoons of powdered tea into a small ceramic bowl. Then she ladled a little hot water onto the tea. She took a bamboo whisk and beat the mixture into a thick paste. Next she added more water and whipped it to a frothy consistency. "Let's sit at the table and we can drink it."

Yoshiko held the bowl in both hands and set it on the table before Neal's place. "Honored guest first."

Ingemar, still studying the photographs of the exterior, said, "Neal, I'm so impressed with the work you did on this house. It's really amazing. If I ever want renovations done here, I'm going to call you."

"Thanks, Ingemar, it was a huge job." Neal felt the heat on his fingers and palms as he lifted the bowl to taste the green tea. Before he drank, he inhaled the delicate aroma.

Yoshiko sat down beside her husband and took a look at the photograph he held. "The new paint makes the house look young again. But what's this?" She took the photo from Ingemar and examined it more closely, drawing her brows together.

Neal put the bowl to his lips and tasted the tea.

"Oh, Neal, you must have been in the tower room when the picture was taken. I can see your shadow."

Neal coughed and put the bowl down abruptly.

"The tea is bitter," said Yoshiko.

"Yes, it is," Neal agreed, although it was not the tea that made him cough.

"May I see that photograph?"

Yoshiko handed him the picture, and Neal studied it carefully.

"Do you see your shadow?" Yoshiko asked.

"Yes," Neal nodded. "Yes, I do."

After sharing the bowl of tea, Neal thanked his hosts and wished them a good night. He and Owen walked past the wind chime and down the slate path to the car. Neal carried the packet of photographs as reverently as a Tea master, a man keenly aware of the profound significance of simple things.

CHAPTER 24

A Misstep

S tanding impatiently at the tail-end of the line, Sarah glanced at her watch. Four-thirty already. The hassles of big-city life were supposed to be unknown in tiny Coveland, but here she stood, stuck in Hollander's Saturday-afternoon rush hour. There was only one open register, and the three people ahead of her seemed to be stockpiling rations in preparation for the end times. She fidgeted and chewed her lower lip. The unbelievably lethargic cashier, a middle-aged woman, checked the groceries with the ponderous motions of an armor-suited diver at the bottom of the sea. Sarah had to look away before she screamed in frustration.

Leaving the travel shop in Bitsy's charge, she had slipped out well before closing time. Neal was coming at five to fix her leaky faucet, but at this rate she wouldn't even be there to meet him. She glanced at the measly contents of her shopping cart. She had bought beer, which she hoped he liked, pistachios, which she adored, and cheese and crackers, if all else failed.

Motion caught her eye. Looking up, she saw another cashier open a second register. Sarah reacted like a NASCAR driver; she pushed her cart fast enough to leave skid marks. Success! She got there first—no one else could match her speed.

After she finally paid for her groceries, she loaded them into the Jeep. She slowly negotiated her way through the congested parking lot, back onto the road and sped away. Halfway up the hill to Beach Road, she noticed the flashing lights of a police cruiser directly behind her. "Drat!" she blurted, and pulled the Jeep over onto the narrow shoulder.

The short, chubby policeman walked to her window and asked, "In a hurry, Miss? You were driving fifty-seven miles per hour in a thirty-five-mile zone."

Sarah's jaw dropped, "I was?" She grimaced.

"Afraid so. May I see your license and insurance, please?" After checking the validity of every possible document save the tags on her clothing, he took forever to write the ticket. He finally handed it to Sarah and said, "Have a good evening."

"Uh, thank you." She drove away, careful to keep the speedometer on a steady thirty-five. She turned right onto Beach Road, oblivious to the scenery. She was an idiot, foolishly excited and rushing home to see a married man. Sarah tapped her thumbs on the steering wheel. Well, she rationalized, that married man was going to fix her dripping faucet. And being married, he posed no risk. She could enjoy his company with no complications. No involvement—no risk. Simple.

Sarah checked the speedometer. She was driving fifty miles an hour.

At five o'clock sharp, Neal knocked at the door. Sarah had beat him home by all of six minutes. Mazie barked and ran ahead of her to greet the visitor. "Come in, Neal," she said as she opened the door.

"Hi, Sarah. I probably won't need all this," he held up an oblong gray metal tool box, "but I came prepared." His grin crinkled the corners of his long-lashed brown eyes.

"Where's Owen?"

"His friend Leftheri Gregoris invited him to a birthday beach party on the Cove this afternoon. I don't have to pick him up until seven."

Sarah hardly heard what he said. She was so pleased to see him that her body felt light, as though it had lost all weight and density. Hang all the research, she thought, *delight* is the key to anti-gravity. He was truly a pleasure to behold. The green polo shirt showed his broad shoulders and chest to good advantage, and the tight-fitting jeans emphasized his narrow waist and hips. The red-haired Scot wasn't a tall man, nor was he as pretty-boy handsome as Danny Levinson, but his carriage was princely. And what a crown, she thought. His red hair was a comb's nightmare, but a woman's delight, tumbling in unruly waves to his collar.

Sarah restrained an impulse to put her hands on his chest and kiss him. Mazie, however, exercised no such restraint. She jumped up, propped her front paws on his chest and licked Neal's face.

"Welcome, from the Friedkin family," Sarah said. "Down, Mazie, you rotten dog."

Neal laughed and wiped his face. "Don't let her kid you, you're a good dog, Mazie."

"Well," said Sarah, "bursting with affection anyway."

"Believe me," Neal remarked, "there are worse traits."

Sarah smiled, "I guess so. Come into the kitchen."

Neal set his tool box on the floor by the sink and examined the leaky faucet. "This should be simple." he said.

"Would you like something to drink?"

"Sure."

"I've got coffee, tea, soda, and beer."

"A cold beer would be great soon's I'm finished." He took out the old washer and searched in the tool box for the same size replacement.

After setting out a big bowl of pistachios on the kitchen table, Sarah sat down and observed Neal. "How did you get to be so handy?"

"Well, my father worked on the commercial fishing boats out of Seattle. He was gone for months at a time, leaving my mother and me on our own. If something broke at home, I was the one who had to fix it. I learned little by little, and I enjoyed working with my hands—I have a knack for it. It's a good thing, too, because I did the repairs on the Fritzinger house myself." He fitted the new washer in place, screwed the metal piece back on and turned on the tap. He turned it off and waited. "Ta-daa!" he sang after a moment, "No drip."

"Thank you, Neal. Sit down and have some pistachios. I hope you like nuts."

Neal smiled, "Oh, I do—all kinds, pistachios, pecans, walnuts, Friedkins..."

Sarah laughed, "You really hit the mark with the last one."

She took two beers out of the refrigerator, handed him one and joined him at the table. "By the way, Neal, remember that day we walked on the beach? You promised that if I told you my life story, you'd reciprocate."

Neal ate a pistachio, "I did, didn't I?"

Sarah nodded, "So tell."

He took a sip of beer. "Better wet my whistle." Then he told her about his alcoholic father Peter, his mother Sally, who left him alone while she worked nights as a truckstop waitress, and their wild, drunken parties. "That was the unhappy part of my childhood, the poison. But it was mitigated by the antidote—my summers in Scotland with my grandparents Ian and Barbara. They gave me the warmth, security and love my parents could not.

"Those summers were magic. I loved Scotland, and I learned so much. Grandfather was an outstanding piper and a marvelous storyteller. Not only did he teach me to play bagpipes, he knew all about Scottish history and he taught me that, too. They lived in Edinburgh—my grandmother still does. It's a wonderful city, the Royal Mile, the castles, the whole atmosphere. My times there were the happiest part of my childhood." Neal took another sip of beer. "And that's why I mourn Grandfather's passing more than my father's or mother's. I lost my mother to cancer in 1980. Grandfather died last September, and my father was killed in a car accident on December twenty-first, 1993."

"Good heavens," said Sarah. She fiddled for a moment with a pile of pistachio shells until she mustered the courage to ask Neal, "How did you meet your wife?"

At the question, Neal's expression seemed to dim, and he sighed, "I met Vicky at a party when I was a grad student at the University of Washington. She was a sophomore there, but she dropped out as soon as we got married. Although she was never interested in school, she's very intelligent. She worked for several years as an assistant manager at a hardware store in Stone Harbor," Neal said. "Vicky likes pop culture—TV, movies, rock music, parties. I'm not a party man myself." His eyes looked troubled and he took long drink of his beer. "Vicky and I don't have too much in common."

"Well, you have Owen," Sarah said. "A beautiful, bright boy with quite an ear for music."

Neal's smile was immediate. "He is a great kid, and he does have a fine ear, doesn't he? You ought to hear him play piano."

"I'd love to. If he decides to study music when he's grown, he could probably be a professional musician."

"Definitely," agreed Neal. "And speaking of professional musicians, Sarah, you never did explain why you left your playing career in New York to come out to the West Coast and open a travel shop. Were you dissatisfied with your career or your chamber music group?"

"No, I love playing music and I liked the other performers in my group very much. You met them—they are all good friends of mine."

"Well, what happened?"

Mazie barked. The dog stood expectantly at the back door, wagging her tail.

Sarah, reluctant to answer Neal's question, was grateful for the interruption. Stalling, she drank the last sip of her beer. "It's time to take Mazie for a run," she explained. "We usually go down to the beach. Would you like to come along?"

"Well, all right," Neal said, "but before we go out, I have something to show you." He took something out of his tool box. "Remember when we talked the other night after dinner, and Murray remarked that it would be good to have concrete proof of the Erlking?"

Sarah raised her eyebrows, "Do you have evidence?"

Neal said, "Well, what I do have, is a very interesting photograph of the house that Vicky took the day after I saw the creature for the first time."

"Can you see him in the picture?" Sarah asked.

"In a manner, yes. The day you heard me play the pipes up on the bluff, when the fog bank suddenly moved in from the sea was the first time I saw the shadowy figure of the Erlking, in front of the tower window. The next afternoon, when Vicky and Owen came out to see the exterior, which I had been painting, she photographed the house from all sides. I didn't look at the pictures until Thursday when I brought them to show Yoshiko, Owen's piano teacher, and her husband Ingemar. Take a look."

Neal handed her the photograph.

Sarah studied the picture for a moment. "There's a tall shadow on the glass of the tower window."

"Yes. Yoshiko thought it was my shadow, but I was outside when Vicky took the picture. There was no one in the house at all."

"It's a huge, looming shadow, isn't it? I can see the outline of the hood. Could there have been a ladder in the room, or something tall, like a floor lamp, with a drop cloth on it?"

"No, at that time, the room was completely empty. I didn't start renovating it until after we moved into the house in April."

"What amazing luck to capture this image. But it's very disturbing, isn't it?" She shivered. "Ugh, I remember how frightened I felt in the fog that day. I can't imagine how you must feel with the Erlking in your house."

As Sarah handed the picture to Neal, Mazie barked insistently.

"We'd better go out now," Sarah said, "but by all means hold onto this photo. It's the best proof we have, and I know Uncle Murr will want to see it."

Sarah put Mazie on a leash, and then she and Neal followed the excited dog down Harlech Road and across Beach Road. At the top of the bluff, Sarah glanced at Neal and asked, "Ready for blast-off?" She released the dog, and Mazie rocketed down the path to the beach.

"I see what you mean," laughed Neal.

They followed Mazie down the steep, diagonal sandy ledge carved out of the face of the bluff, picking their steps slowly and carefully so as not to slip. The strong, invigorating breeze off the dark blue, white-capped water tousled Sarah's black hair and lifted the collar of Neal's shirt.

When they reached the rocky part of the beach, Sarah was silent, so Neal prompted her, "And you were saying?"

"What?"

"You know—about why you came to Darrow Island."

"Do you really want to hear that?"

"Yes, I do. Spit it out, Sarah."

She set out walking at a brisk pace. "Funny you should say that. The whole thing left an awful taste in my mouth, and I wish I could spit it out and be done with it forever." She kicked a piece of driftwood into the cold water. "Well, my reasons weren't professional; they were personal." She told Neal how she had fallen in love with Danny Levinson, the brilliant, handsome first violinist of Musicians of Brooklyn, and how he had betrayed her with another woman when he got the job in Vienna. "He kept up a correspondence with me while he was living with her. I didn't have a clue, until I saved up enough money to visit him, and he was forced to tell me about her then. She was pregnant." She winced, "After three years, it still hurts to talk about it."

Sarah shrugged, "Maybe I should have moved there with him in the first place. He asked me, but I didn't want to go as his live-in lover, and when I told him that, he didn't ask me to marry him."

"So then you came here?" Neal stopped and picked up a small green stone.

"After a near nervous breakdown. I had the classic symptoms of depression. I couldn't eat, sleep, or concentrate. My playing went to hell. That's when Beth O'Leary, the cellist you met, stepped in and offered to take me along when she visited her parents in Seattle. I went with her mostly to get away from New York because so many places there reminded me of Danny. Out here, there were no memories of him. I loved the area, so I took an editing job in Seattle in the fall of 1993, and then I opened the travel shop here on the island last year. I guess you could say I'm a risk-taker. I wanted to be my own boss."

"Have you dated anyone here?" Neal asked, and tossed the stone into the water.

Sarah shook her head. "No, I haven't even had any offers." She chafed her arms, wanting to end the conversation. "I'm getting cold, Neal. Let's go back to the house." Mazie was down the beach sniffing at the base of a white driftwood log. Sarah whistled, and the dog immediately came running.

They retraced their route along the beach. Mazie scrabbled up the twenty-foot embankment and waited for them at the top. Sarah climbed up ahead of Neal. They were over halfway to the top when a chunk of sandy earth gave way under her left foot and she slid down, out of control, into Neal, dislodging his footing. As they slid, Neal managed to keep her and himself upright, holding Sarah in one arm, while using the other as a buffer between their bodies and the cliff face. They landed on their feet with a jolt, both facing the bluff.

"Are you okay, Sarah?"

She turned to face him, a little breathless, "Yes, are you?"

Neal nodded, but didn't move away from her. He kept his arm around her and his eyes on hers.

Sarah was aware of his touch along the entire length of her body. Flustered by his close proximity, and the intensity of his gaze, she said, "I'm sorry. I slipped—I didn't mean to fall. . ." She left the sentence unfinished, because Neal stopped her lips with his mouth. The kiss was soft, but electric, and he followed it with many more. His arms encircled her and he pressed his whole body against hers. Time stopped while Sarah's hands held his face; her mouth drank his kisses, and she knew nothing but his touch and his warmth.

Then Mazie barked.

It was like the stroke of midnight at Cinderella's ball. Gold turned to dross, riches to rags, all magic ended. "Oh," said Sarah, pushing Neal away and catching her breath, "she's up near the road, alone. I have to go get her." With adrenaline surging through her veins, and distress like a fire at her heels, Sarah turned and ran up the cliff face with little effort.

Neal scrambled after her. He caught up to her as she and Mazie crossed Beach Road. "Sarah, I'm sorry," he said.

Biting her lower lip, Sarah simply nodded. The great, aching lump in her throat blocked all speech.

They strode quickly back to Sarah's house in an awkward and painful silence. After Neal collected his tool box from Sarah's kitchen, she walked him out to his car. They stood together beside the red Mustang.

"Sarah," Neal said, "I am truly sorry. I shouldn't have kissed you. I am a married man and it was wrong." He hesitated, "But please don't be afraid to be with me in the future. It won't happen again. You know I like you;

how could I not? How could anyone not?" He lifted his hand as though he wanted to touch her cheek, and then he let it drop. "I respect you, and I want your friendship, and I will never do anything to jeopardize that."

His honest brown eyes smiled into hers, and that was the moment she understood how little she had lost with Danny Levinson, and how much she stood to lose here.

"Will you forgive me?" he asked.

Tears welled up in her eyes, "No," she said, "I won't, because there is nothing to forgive. I was a willing participant." She laughed, and two fat, salty drops rolled down her cheeks. "But you're right. We can't let that happen again." Sarah wiped her face with the back of her hand. "We'll forget that it ever happened and we'll be friends."

"Good," Neal said. "Sarah, you can count on me. I will always be your friend." He held out his hand, "Shake?"

Blinking back tears, she shook his hand, and then he got into the car.

She lifted her hand in farewell to the married man who could not possibly hurt her. To stand there and watch him drive away was an exercise in agony. He was everything she wanted, but she had to let him go. The bittersweet memory of his kisses would haunt her days and nights, a tantalizing taste of the love fate denied her. She had loved Danny and he had betrayed her, and now she had betrayed herself. She wanted to be the lover of a married man. And that would never do. As much as she loved Neal, she would not commit adultery to have him.

She shook her head slowly and wiped away the salt tears. No, she had lied to Neal; they could never be friends. To be near him would be to endure the same pain over and over again. She simply couldn't bear it. Sarah took a deep breath, lifted her head, and straightened her shoulders. She knew what she had to do. Steeling herself like a battle-weary soldier, she trudged back to the house, knowing that her only course of action was to shun him entirely.

CHAPTER 25

The Cavalry Arrives

The note lay in the center of the kitchen table on Monday evening when Neal and Owen returned from the airport with Barbara. Neal saw it as soon as he set Barbara's luggage down inside the kitchen door. It was a lined piece of notebook paper half-covered in Vicky's childish, looping scrawl. She had used a red felt-tip pen and ignored the lines. *Since you've got another woman in the house, I'm out of here for good. I'm with Jim now.* No signature and no telephone number.

"What's that say, Daddy?" Owen came in behind Barbara.

"Oh, it's an old grocery list your mom wrote." Neal grabbed the paper and crumpled it in his right hand before Owen could read it.

Barbara already had. She stood near the table with her coat over her arm, her eyes on Neal. Their eyes locked for a moment, and then Neal instructed Owen, "Take Grandma's coat up to her room and put it on her bed."

"Thank you, love," Barbara said, handing Owen her coat.

Owen smiled up at her, "Grandma, your room is right next to mine."

"Is it, then? Well, I know we'll have a jolly good time together from now on."

As soon as Owen was out of earshot, Neal said, "Sorry about this, Grandma. It's not a very festive welcome for you." He turned up one corner of his mouth in a weak half-smile.

"Ach, don't trouble your head about me, lad. I've got all the welcome I need just from you and your bonnie boy. I'm thankful and very happy to be here with the ones I came to see."

"Despite her note," Neal said, "Vicky's leaving has nothing to do with you. This has been brewing for quite some time, and she's using your arrival as an excuse to walk out. I've known for a while that she was having an affair."

Barbara took his hands in hers. "And very sorry I am to hear it. But I believe that eventually this will work itself out. It's going to be all right, Neal. This is a painful moment, but it may be that Vicky's done you a great favor. She's gone, but she's taken half the tension in the house with her."

"True," Neal said. He threw the balled up note into the trashcan under the sink with more force than was necessary. "Would you like some tea, Grandma?"

"Tea?" Barbara tilted her head, brown eyes gleaming. "Having just crossed an ocean and a continent, and seeing how we've both got darker waters to navigate before we're done, I think we need a snort more ripping than tea, don't you?"

Neal laughed, "Yes I do. I surely do."

"Root beer for me, Daddy." Owen came in and sat at the table.

"Comin' up."

At six forty-five the next morning, after a shave and a shower, Neal went down to the kitchen. The smell of frying bacon made his mouth water.

Barbara was standing at the stove tending two frying pans. "Grandma, you should have slept in."

"At my age, I don't lie in. Besides, you and the wee lad look like you could use a few hot, home-cooked meals."

"Well, you're right about that."

"Good morning, Grandma. What's for breakfast?" Owen rubbed the sleep out of his eyes.

"Morning! Well, you're a fine sight, all dressed for school." Barbara held out her arms, "Come, give your grandma a kiss." Owen smiled and planted a wet one on Barbara's cheek. She gave him a fierce hug and tousled his silky red-gold hair. "For breakfast we've got eggs, bacon, scones, and all the black currant jam you can eat, Owen, my lad."

"Boy, I hope you stay forever, Grandma."

By Thursday, Neal had brought Barbara up to date about his visions and the entire series of events before and after his family had moved into the house. As they sat at the kitchen table drinking coffee after their early dinner, he explained how Owen had suffered in the past weeks as Vicky grew angrier and more distant. "And as you know," he said, "she has not bothered to contact us since she left the note on Monday. She is so taken up with her lover that she shows no concern at all for her son."

"That is a great pity, but it happens," said Barbara, shaking her head. "Sometimes a woman gets overwhelmed by the circumstances of her life and thinks a lover will change everything. She's usually mistaken. It will be no surprise to me if Vicky soon realizes she traded all she owned of value for base counterfeit. After all, what kind of man would break up another man's marriage?"

"The whole thing is painful to discuss," Neal confessed, taking a sip of his coffee, "so let's talk about something else—you, for example. Grandma, you saved the day for us—your presence is a blessing. Owen hasn't complained of stomachaches all week, and I'll bet the house must look better now than it did even in its glory days at the turn of the century."

Barbara's energy since her arrival had been simply remarkable. She had cleaned the house within an inch of its life—the floors and cabinets gleamed, the dust bunnies had been sent packing, and mountains of dirty laundry had been washed.

"Well, the benefit is mutual. I feel needed and important and useful the way I did when Ian was alive."

Barbara sipped her milky coffee. It was only five o'clock, and the late afternoon was so sunny and mild that they had opened the back door and the windows to the breeze. They relaxed in comfortable silence while Owen played outside near the pear tree. They could hear him talking.

"That boy of yours has quite an imagination," Barbara said. "He keeps a running conversation, even though he's alone."

Neal smiled, "Imaginary playmates. I think I did that, too. He's an only child, so he creates his own company."

"He chirrups like a bird. The first time I heard him, I was cooking dinner in the kitchen and he was playing with some of his lorries on the rug in the parlor. You were upstairs working on the computer. I heard voices and rushed in there, thinking someone was with him." She shrugged, "But it was just Owen. I asked him who he was talking with and he told me it was his friend Tod."

"Well, I'm glad that it was only his imaginary playmate. I've been on edge and worried about his safety ever since the last episode in the study when the shadow-creature threatened Owen."

Barbara pressed her lips together and nodded. "But since then have you had any other incidents?"

"Not really. The only thing is that the padlock on the study door seems to spring open mysteriously. Vicky found it open, and I hadn't unlocked it, but other than that, nothing." Neal smoothed his mustache. "What I fear is that this could be the calm before the storm."

"And Friday we're going to discuss the whole situation with your friends?"

"Yes, I've invited them for dinner. Sarah and her great uncle Murray are looking forward to meeting you."

"As I do them."

"I've entrusted them with the whole story, including Grandfather's experience at Dunkirk and everything that's happened here in the house. They want to see the study, the place this demon inhabits. My hope is that by putting our heads together, we can devise a strategy to exorcise it from the house and from our lives."

"Aye," Barbara said, putting her cup down. "Enough is enough. The bloody creature has given us grief for far too long. I would give anything to see you and Owen happy and safe. I only hope there is some way I can help."

"You know about Grandfather's experience during the war, so you may be able to help us there."

Neal stood up and rinsed out his coffee mug. "Well, I shouldn't sit here any longer. I want to play the pipes a while before I take Owen to his piano lesson tonight, and then later I've got tests to grade.

"By the way, Grandma, I've assigned one class a project, which is due next Friday. The students have to interview various people who are veterans of World War II or else have related stories to tell. You might be interested to read some of them."

"Why, yes, I would like that," said Barbara.

"Well, let me go outside and play the pipes," Neal said. "It's the first time in weeks I've felt like it."

"Ach, I'll be delighted to hear it, lad—at a distance, mind. It'll be like a wee bit of home."

The light breeze ruffled Owen's hair as he played with his trucks, cars, and airplane in the landscape he had created under the pear tree. With a garden trowel, he had dug up a heap of dirt and hard-packed it to make a mountain. The hole where he had scooped it was his lake. After he had poured a glass of water in the hole, he'd turned the plastic glass upside down and placed it at a slight distance from the mountain. It was the tower for his airport.

"What are you doing, Owen?"

The voice was soft and light. He recognized it at once. It was Tod. Owen didn't look up. "Car chase on the mountain." He rolled his tongue to make motor sounds as the cars chased each other up, down, and around. The fresh dirt smelled good and it felt soft and cool on his hands. His jeans were dirty, but he didn't think Grandma would mind.

"Who are the people in the cars?"

"I'm in the red one and Daddy's in the blue one."

"Are you going to win the race?"

"It's not a race. We're just having fun going fast up and down the mountain."

"What about the truck over there?" Tod pointed to the pick-up truck in the long grass near the base of the tree.

"That's Africa. The jungle. My mom is hiding there. She went there on a trip, but she's afraid of tigers and snakes. That's why I have the airplane ready to take off. After while, Daddy and me are gonna fly over to Africa and bring Mommy back."

"Is that your grandmother in the car in the lake?"

"No, Tod. Grandma is in the control tower. She's going to guide us in and out of the airport. We'll be in radio contact."

Something white caught Owen's eye. He turned his head and saw Sparker, his calico cat, walking down the driveway near the corner of the house. "Sparker," he called, "come. Come here, girl."

Sparker answered with a cry and ran toward him, tail high in the air. Owen held out his hand to pet her, but when she passed the pear tree and saw Tod, she turned into a Halloween cat with arched back and stiffened tail. Ears laid flat, she hissed and spat, then bolted back around the corner of the house.

"That's funny. Why'd she run away?" Owen asked.

"She probably smelled my dog's scent on me."

Owen's eyes lit up. "You have a dog? Where is he? My dad and me wanted a dog, but mamma said no, it was too much trouble. I love dogs. Where is yours?"

"Well, I don't know. He wanders off on his own sometimes. Want to help me look for him?"

Owen nodded, "Yeah, let's look for him." He stood up and brushed off his hands and the knees of his jeans.

"Let's go this way," Tod said.

Owen followed him around the opposite side of the house from the driveway.

Tod stopped in the shadow of the house and looked toward the water.

"Do you see him anywhere?" Owen asked.

"No. He probably went in there." Tod pointed to where the forest and underbrush bordered the grass of Owen's yard. "Or maybe he went down on the beach. Let's go look over the edge of the bluff."

"No, Tod. Daddy said I can't go alone to the edge of the bluff. I better stay here."

"You're not alone, Owen. You're with me."

Owen knew that Tod was older, but he couldn't tell how old he was. Tod was funny that way. He wasn't real tall, but he seemed sort of grownup, like a small man. He looked young, but there was something about his dark eyes that seemed old. And he knew a lot—that was like a grownup, too.

"Well," Owen said slowly, "if I'm with you, then I guess it's okay."

Tod smiled. "C'mon," he suddenly shouted, "let's run!"

"Wait for me, Tod!" Owen sprang after him, running as fast as he could. He hoped they'd see the dog on the beach. Oh, he couldn't keep up. He was halfway across the yard, but Tod was still ahead of him. Tod disappeared over the edge of the bluff

"Wait, Tod, wait!" He pumped his legs as fast as he could. He was catching up, almost to the edge.

"Owen, stop!" Daddy shouted in his angry voice.

At the last second, when Owen realized he was going to fall, fear shot through him like a laser. He lost his footing and tumbled forward, sliding on the grass toward the edge of the bluff. As his hands slid out into space, he felt a strong grip on his leg that caught and held him.

"What do you think you're doing? What have I told you about going to the edge of the bluff by yourself?"

His daddy, breathing hard, grabbed his arm and pulled him to his feet, away from the edge. "What were you thinking? You almost fell off the bluff! If I hadn't come out here to practice and caught you, you might have really hurt yourself."

"Ouch, Daddy, you're hurting my arm." Owen squirmed. "Don't be mad—I wasn't alone. I was with Tod. We were looking for his dog."

"Tod?"

"My friend Tod. He thought his dog might be on the beach. We were running to see if he was or not."

"Owen, you know Tod is an imaginary friend."

"No, he's not, Daddy. He's real."

"Well where is he?"

"He ran ahead of me. I guess he went down to the beach."

"Where? I don't see anyone on the beach. Look, Owen, no one's there. No person, no dog."

Owen scanned the beach. Except for seagulls, the rocky shore was empty.

"Well, he was here before."

Neal looked down at him, "I know you have a good imagination, son, but this is going too far. You can go to the bluff with Grandma or me. No one else. Is that clear?"

Tod was real and Daddy didn't believe him. Owen blinked back the tears, "Yes, Daddy."

Neal laid the bagpipes down and gave him a big hug. "I'm not really mad, Owen. I got upset because you scared me. I don't want you to get hurt. Understand?"

Owen nodded.

"Good." He picked up his pipes. "Let's get you back to the house, and then I'm going to practice a while this afternoon, while it's nice out."

The next time he played with Tod, Owen thought as he walked back toward the house, he wouldn't tell anyone. From now on, it would be his secret.

CHAPTER 26

Another Vision

Leaving his bagpipes on the porch, Neal escorted Owen into the kitchen and found Barbara loading the dishwasher. Neal told her what had just happened. "So, Grandma, after he almost slid off the cliff, I decided that Owen may only go out to the edge of the bluff accompanied by you or by me. No one else, and that includes his playmate Tod."

"I think that's an excellent plan," Barbara replied. "Owen, since you've been playing in the dirt, why don't you go and wash your hands, and then sit down at the table and have some dessert? You can have apple pie or scones, and we can have a cup of tea together. Would you like that?"

"Yes, Grandma, a scone with jam, please." He went to the bathroom under the stairs to wash the dirt from his hands.

"I'm going to practice now," Neal said, turning to go out again.

Barbara stopped him. "Before you go, lad, I have an idea. Since you're going to play the pipes, well, it occurred to me, and it's just a thought, but have you by any chance tried playing that bit of music in Ian's journal?"

"To tell the truth, I had forgotten all about it. I realized it was bagpipe music, when I first looked at it, although it seemed a strange sort of tune." Neal smiled, "But it never crossed my mind to play it. Good idea, Grandma; I'll try it out on the chanter first. Once I get it under my fingers, I'll play it on the pipes."

While Barbara made a pot of tea and served Owen his dessert, Neal retrieved Ian's journal from the tower room. To his chagrin, the padlock hung open. "Fat lot of good you are," Neal remarked, removing the lock and opening the door. He knew there was nothing wrong with the lock. He felt certain that the Erlking was toying with him.

As Neal took the journal from its slot in the roll top desk, he felt a wave of icy air envelope him. Instantly aware of another presence in the room, he stiffened when he heard moaning and sobbing behind him.

He turned around and saw a young boy, perhaps ten or eleven years old, with hair so white-blonde he could have been Scandinavian. Holding his flayed and bleeding hands before him, the boy knelt on the floor, next to a large desk on the left side of the fireplace, rocking back and forth, grimacing and crying in pain. The palms of his hands were lacerated, oozing blood.

The boy seemed somehow familiar. His straight hair was chin-length, with short bangs in front, and he was dressed in an old-fashioned style, wearing a white long-sleeve shirt with a round collar, brown shorts and knee-socks, and narrow, ankle-high leather shoes, tightly laced. He seemed completely unaware of Neal. He looked, Neal thought, like a sepia-toned photograph come to life.

"What happened?" Neal asked.

At the sound of his voice, the boy vanished.

This time, although Neal was shaken, he was not deceived. He knew that he had had a vision, and from the way the boy was dressed, he knew he had witnessed a scene played out in the past, many years ago in this very room. He had recognized the fireplace, the wainscot, and the maroon walls. The large desk was unfamiliar—but all the former furnishings of the house had been removed long ago.

The icy air had vanished with the vision. Neal sat down for a moment in the armchair near the window. Where had he seen the boy before? He snapped his fingers—it was the weeping boy from his dream, older now. And the bloody handprints he had seen on the wall in an earlier vision now made sense. First he had seen the prints; now he had seen the bloody hands. The boy must have bloodied the wall with his hands and kicked the baseboard in anger. To Neal's knowledge, the only boy that had lived in this house was Gunter's son Heinrich. But why were his hands lacerated? Would Gunter have punished his boy that way? What kind of man would do that to his son?

Neal smoothed his mustache. He had a truckload of questions and no one to answer them. He gazed thoughtfully around the study, Gunter's study. The episodes that had taken place here had left their mark. Neal remembered how the oppressive atmosphere had affected him the day the realtor had shown him into this room—the constricted feeling in his throat and the tensing of his solar plexus, as though he prepared himself for a blow. Maybe that was because many blows, physical and psychological, had been struck in this room.

Old houses had their own resonances, and this house was almost one hundred years old. The Fritzinger family had lived here a very long time; they had left their stamp on this place. Powerful emotions left their traces, and the echoes here were discordant—Neal had sensed that from the first. He was more and more convinced that the life of the Fritzinger family had been sad and full of strife, perhaps even tragic. He would never know the whole story, because every member of the family was dead, but he thought he had a better picture now.

He sprang up from the chair abruptly, with a strong desire to get out of the room and the house, too. He wanted to go outside into the sunshine and leave the sadness that had reverberated here for decades. Gripping the journal, Neal closed the door and snapped the padlock shut.

Owen and Barbara were chatting over tea when Neal got back to the kitchen. Neal carried his chanter in one hand and the journal in the other. "You know, Grandma, I think I'll have a cup of tea out on the porch. Why don't you keep me company for a while?"

"I'm going to practice for my lesson," Owen announced, getting up from the table.

"First rinse your cup and plate," Barbara directed Owen, "and put them in the dishwasher, there's a good lad." Then she answered Neal. "Aye, I'll have another cup of tea with you," Barbara said. "It's a beautiful evening."

While Owen practiced his piano pieces, Barbara and Neal took their tea down the hall and out the front door to the porch where they could see the strait. Neal propped the front door open, so they could hear Owen playing, and then, quickly and quietly, told his grandmother about the vision he had just had involving the boy he believed to be Heinrich Fritzinger. "I'll tell Murray and Sarah about it tomorrow night when they come for dinner. That's why they want to see the tower room—most of the supernatural activity has taken place there."

"I wonder what connection there is between the Fritzinger family and the creature that has plagued our family all these years," Barbara mused.

"Maybe there is none; maybe it is just a coincidence that we bought an old house with its own ghosts."

Barbara pushed a curling wisp of her white hair away from her face. "You could be right, but it may well be worth investigating—to find out all we can about the previous owners and see if that throws any light on our problem." She smiled, "Although I risk sounding like a Scotland Yard detective, I say let's not rule anything out yet, particularly if it is knowledge imparted by one of your visions. Remember that so far the visions you've had about the creature have been connected, and the two visions about Heinrich are connected. Who knows—maybe a little more background information will provide a common denominator."

Neal snapped his fingers. "Owen's piano teacher used to come here to visit Emily Fritzinger, Heinrich's sister. I think I'll take Yoshiko to lunch this week. Maybe you could come, too, Grandma, and we'll ask her to tell us as much as she knows about Emily, and if there's anything at all that Emily might have said regarding Heinrich or Gunter, their father. I'd invite Yoshiko here, but I don't want to talk about any of this in front of Owen. In fact, this is urgent enough that I'll try to meet with her tomorrow."

"That's a fine idea, Neal. The sooner we can answer all our questions, the better. Now what about playing Ian's strange tune on the chanter before it gets too late?"

"I'll give it a whirl," he said.

Later that evening, at Owen's piano lesson, Neal asked Yoshiko to have lunch with him and Barbara the next day. He decided that it was worth it to take one day off from school in order to get as much information as he could about the Fritzinger family, and an interview with Yoshiko, a first-hand source he could trust, was a priority. She agreed to meet him and Barbara Friday at eleven-thirty at Ike's on the Pier, the outdoor café on Coveland's historic wharf.

When he and Owen returned home at seven forty-five, Barbara was in the den reading a book while Sparker snoozed beside her on the sofa. "Neal, you had a telephone call."

"Vicky?" he asked.

"No," she replied, "it was Sarah Friedkin. She asked me to tell you that she cannot come here to dinner tomorrow evening."

"Did she say why?"

"No, she just said she couldn't come."

"What are you reading, Grandma?" asked Owen.

"A book about Winston Churchill, who was Prime Minister of Britain a long time ago." She patted Owen on the shoulder, "Time for you to go upstairs and get ready for bed."

"Already?"

"Already. Bedtime at eight-thirty." She pointed in the direction of the stairs, "March, me bonny boy. That's a direct order."

Owen smiled and saluted, "Yes, ma'am."

Neal was still puzzled about Sarah's message. He scratched his head and asked, "Well, did she want me to call her back?"

"She didn't say so."

"Oh." Neal's tone was flat. "Well, that's a disappointment. I wanted you to meet her, Grandma."

"Don't worry, I'm sure I will sooner or later," Barbara replied.

"I think I'll call her anyway," Neal said.

Feeling ridiculously nervous, he went into the kitchen and got himself a beer, the last one in the refrigerator. After a few sips, he called. He waited through four rings and the recorded greeting on Sarah's answering machine. Struck dumb by the sound of the beep, he hung up.

Neal sat down at the kitchen table to finish his beer. He had tests to grade, but he had to collect his thoughts first. Sarah's cancellation bothered him. He drummed his fingers on the table in a nervous tattoo. Why did she cancel? If she had some kind of schedule conflict, she would have said so. If she was ill, she would have explained. God, he hoped it wasn't because he'd kissed her that day on the beach. The last thing she'd told him on Saturday was that they would still be friends. No, there must be some other reason. He took a long sip of beer. Well, tomorrow he might get the whole story from Murray.

He pushed back his chair so suddenly that the wooden legs squealed against the floor. "Grandma," he said, as he hurried back into the den, "Is Murray still coming tomorrow?"

Barbara took off her reading glasses. "Why, yes. Sarah said her Uncle Murray would be coming without her."

"Well, that's good." Neal held up the beer bottle and said, "You know, this is the last beer we've got, and Murray might like one tomorrow. It's only eight o'clock, so I think I'll drive over to Hollander's and get another six-pack. I'll be back before Owen goes to bed."

"Can't you do that tomorrow?" asked Barbara.

"Yes, but I might want another one myself tonight."

"All right, then," she said. "You could buy a few tins of cat food, as well." She stroked Sparker's long fur. "This one brought me a dead field mouse today. We have to keep her happy."

On the way to Hollander's, Neal resisted a great temptation to drive by Sarah's house. He had to remind himself of who he was—he was a teacher at a high school, not a hormone-driven student. He was a married man, a father. Self-lecture over and out.

Shit! He slapped the steering wheel. He wanted to see Sarah now.

Somehow, without seeing the road, he made it to Hollander's. As he turned into the parking lot, he saw Sarah's Jeep. What luck! "No wonder she didn't answer the phone," he said to himself. He pulled into the empty space next to her vehicle and hurried into the store with spring in every step.

He expected to see her immediately, but he did not. Smiling in anticipation, he glanced down each aisle as he made his way to the back wall where the cold beer was kept in the refrigerated cases. He grabbed a six-pack of longnecks, and then went to the pet food aisle where he picked up four cans of Sparker's favorite food.

Hollander's was only a nine-aisle store, so he walked to the back and continued toward the opposite wall, scanning each aisle. Brucie Barncamper, an eyesore in a blinding orange pantsuit, blocked his view of the paper products aisle. Beer in one hand, cat food in the other, Neal moved on, with no result.

Approaching the checkout counter, he saw Sarah leaving. She carried a paper bag in the crook of her arm as she walked toward the exit.

"Sarah!" he yelled, waving the cat food high in the air to catch her attention.

She glanced back and saw him, he was certain, but she gave no sign of recognition. In fact, she increased her pace.

Neal waited impatiently at the counter for the middle-aged cashier to ring up his purchases. He handed her a twenty-dollar bill and ground his teeth while she made change in slow motion. He pocketed the money and sprinted toward the exit, not bothering with a bag. He made it to the edge of the parking lot just in time to see Sarah drive past him.

He saw her clearly through the windshield. Unsmiling, eyes glittering with unshed tears, she glanced at him with what appeared to be anger.

Mouth agog, Neal watched her drive away. As the taillights of her Jeep disappeared around the corner, his shoulders slumped and he shook his head. *Ouch.* He stood rooted to the sidewalk in front of the store, while it all became clear to him. She wasn't busy tomorrow; she wasn't ill. Those stolen kisses had spoiled their friendship. Well, who could blame her? She had been burned badly by that jerk in New York, and now she had to fend off the advances of a married man, or so she believed. She'd had second thoughts and decided to flee. He laughed—there was something Sarah had in common with Vicky after all. She wasn't coming to dinner because she just didn't want to be near him.

"Must you block the sidewalk, young man?"

Neal started. Brucie Barncamper, bearing two loaded sacks in her massive arms, waited to pass him, and the sidewalk, four feet wide, wasn't big enough for the two of them. "Oh, sorry," he apologized and stepped off the curb into the parking lot to let her pass.

"Hmph," she grunted, barging down the sidewalk like a tank in full possession of a captured road.

Neal walked to the Mustang, put the groceries in the back seat, and sat behind the steering wheel. He smoothed his mustache in a single motion. Well, here was the score: his wife had left him; Sarah was avoiding him, and his son was threatened by some sort of demon, but on the upside, he was well-stocked with cat food and beer. Laughing to keep from crying, like a doomed man on the way to the scaffold, Neal drove out of the parking lot.

CHAPTER 27

Family Portraits

At eleven-thirty on Friday, Yoshiko met Neal and Barbara for lunch outdoors at Ike's on the Pier, Coveland's landmark restaurant. The T-shaped wooden pier extended its sturdy shaft one hundred yards from Waterfront Street, ending in the crossbar which supported a majestic red-painted building with white trim. Originally a warehouse with a twenty-foot ceiling, the structure currently housed a gift shop with an outdoor café on the far side. Dominating the view of the horseshoe-shaped cove, it ruled over the briny green waters like Neptune.

As he sat on the deck with Yoshiko and Barbara, Neal's pleasure in the day was tinged with guilt at skipping school. To divert himself, he kept an eye on the lone sloop with bold tri-colored sails cruising the waters of the cove. He needed a sign that he was on the right path, that fortune might yet smile on him. So he deemed it a favorable omen that the red, white, and black of the boat's sails were at once the respective hair colors of himself, Barbara, and Yoshiko, and the hues of the MacGregor tartan.

The fair weather he took to be another benevolent augur. The ever-capricious clouds of Puget Sound huddled on the northern horizon, ready to make mischief, but for the moment the sun reigned on high, keeping order like a gracious, good-hearted king, showering them with light. The cooling breeze carried the Cove's salt smell, ruffling their hair and teasing the sparkling green waves. Seagulls banked into the wind above them, hoping for handouts, while the low tide revealed mussel beds and constellations of orange and tan starfish around the bases of the barnacle-encrusted pilings supporting the wharf.

The café was moderately busy with a talkative lunch crowd of tourists and regulars from the village. Yoshiko and Barbara ate shrimp salads with crusty chunks of white bread, while Neal opted for a ham sandwich on rye with a side order of vegetable soup. After introductions, the two women chattered about Owen, who was dear to them both. But Neal quickly steered the conversation to his topic of interest.

"Grandma and I are very curious about the history of the Fritzingers and the house itself," Neal explained, "and I thought you could supply a few more details for us, Yoshiko, since you knew Emily."

"Well, I can try," Yoshiko replied.

When she sipped her water, the sun shimmered in her black hair, and Neal was reminded of Sarah, who was at work less than a hundred yards away. He glanced at the rear of her salmon-painted travel shop, which was so close that he could see into the kitchen window. With equal measures of hope and fear, he wondered if she might come to the café for lunch.

Yoshiko interrupted his reverie. "Vivian Fischer, the Home Health nurse who looked after Miss Emily, encouraged her to go out to concerts and take part in other village activities, but Miss Emily refused. That's where I came in; I began to visit Miss Emily and play piano for her at the nurse's request. Miss Emily loved music, and she must have been a fairly good pianist at one time. She had a Steinway grand and she included some of the Bach Preludes and Fugues, and sonatas by Mozart and Beethoven in her repertoire. But when I met her, she was in her nineties, suffering from arthritis, and she couldn't really play that type of literature anymore."

"What was she like as a person?" Barbara asked.

"She was quiet and shy, probably because she had a slight stutter. She was reclusive really—she hardly left the house. But if something amused her, she had a real belly laugh—I loved to hear it." Yoshiko smiled at the memory. "We talked mostly about music and nature. She loved houseplants and gardening. The orchard was her idea, by the way."

Yoshiko paused, thinking. "I had the impression that her spirit was strong, but that her life had been very difficult."

"In what way?" Neal asked. "She certainly had no financial worries."

"No, there was no lack of money—but a great lack of love from her father, I think. Miss Emily and I had a brief conversation concerning her family life once. You see, there were portraits of her mother, her brother, and Miss Emily herself hanging in the parlor. I asked if there was also a portrait of her father, and she said, 'Ja, and I burned it in that fireplace on the night he died. My father made a fortune and he built this beautiful house, but he was an unkind, angry man who made life hell for everyone around him.'"

"She didn't mince words, did she?" Barbara remarked. "Did she tell you how he made their lives difficult?"

"No, not specifically."

"Could you describe her brother's portrait?" Neal asked.

"Well, the portrait was painted when Heinrich was a boy of eight or nine. He was dressed in a sailor suit, and he was handsome, with light blue eyes and flaxen hair. He bore a strong resemblance to his mother, except that her hair was wavy and his was straight, like mine."

"Did Emily resemble her brother?" asked Barbara.

"No, I think she must have resembled her father. Emily was fifteen when the portrait was painted, she told me. She was blue-eyed like her brother, but her hair was brown, and she was rather plain, not pretty like her mother." Yoshiko rubbed the condensation on her glass of ice water. "The most striking thing about all the portraits was the quality of sadness the painter captured in their expressions and their eyes."

Yoshiko ate a bite of salad and added, "As far as I know, Miss Emily spent very little time in the parlor. She even seemed uncomfortable talking about the portraits. I think they saddened her; maybe they reminded her that she was all alone—the only Fritzinger left. The only other memorable comments she made concerned her revulsion for her father's study—the tower room."

Neal grew excited. "What did she say?"

"She said it was a place of terrible memories, a place of pain, and the one time she talked about it, she stuttered so badly that she could barely articulate her thoughts."

"So just talking about that room triggered powerful, unhappy emotions," said Neal.

"Oh, yes. That's why she closed it off. She associated it with her father and his anger, and as far as I know, she never set foot in the room again after his death."

"She must have been a strong woman to live alone in that great house," said Barbara.

"Yes," agreed Yoshiko, "although I think she drew comfort from the house itself, especially her music room, and from the peaceful and majestic view of the sea and the forest. Perhaps all that she had suffered at the hands of her father made her isolation a solace." Yoshiko smiled, "Of course I'm guessing when I say that—I don't know for sure."

"Peggy Williams, our real estate agent, told us that Emily willed her piano to a children's foundation in Seattle," Neal said. "Do you know anything about that, Yoshiko?"

"I remember the name of the foundation because it is the same as Ingemar's middle name, Reinhold, but I don't know anything about its goal."

Yoshiko checked her watch. "I have a student at one o'clock," she said, "so I think I'd better go."

"Let me give you a ride," Neal offered.

"No, stay and have dessert," she said. "It takes me only seven minutes to walk from here, and I enjoy the exercise. Thank you for lunch, Neal, and it was a pleasure to meet you, Barbara."

After Yoshiko left, while Neal and Barbara had coffee and strawberry shortcake, he sketched out his plans. "I'll drive you home, Grandma, and then I'm going to the courthouse to do as much research as possible on the Fritzingers this afternoon. In the meantime, could you please call the

Reinhold Foundation in Seattle, and see what you can find out about them?"

"I shall," Barbara agreed. "I'm rather curious myself as to why Emily would leave her piano, which must have been of great emotional value to her, to a children's foundation. And later this afternoon, I must set the house in order for our guest tonight."

"Thanks, Grandma, but don't worry about dinner. I'll do the cooking."

Barbara smiled, "Jolly good idea, love. In that case, I'll have time for a long, relaxing soak in that fine old clawfoot tub of yours."

That Friday evening, the house looked lovely thanks to Barbara. She had done, as she said, "a smashing job," and Neal had dinner under control. His theory was that a chef should be to cooking as Louis Armstrong was to music—a master of soulful improvisation. Consequently, Neal made up his own recipes and never measured. Of course, he could never duplicate his successes, "but what the hell," he liked to say, "where's the fun if every meal is predictable?" For the evening's repast, he had prepared Mediterranean chicken, with olive oil, lemon juice, and rosemary, baked potatoes, corn on the cob, and salad.

At seven, when Murray arrived, Neal was elbow-deep in salad greens, and Barbara was setting out food for Sparker. Owen answered the door, and the older man came into the kitchen, bringing a gust of the damp, chill night air with him. He carried a white cardboard container, and he doffed his fedora when he came in. "Greetings, all," he said.

Neal introduced Murray to his grandmother. "Nice to meet you, Mrs. MacGregor."

"Ach, call me Barbara."

Murray, looking bemused, took Barbara's small hand in his, "My pleasure, Barbara MacGregor." He cradled her hand in his for a long moment while he drank in her slim, elfin appearance, the halo of thick, white curly hair, and the merry brown eyes. His reverie was interrupted when Owen tugged on his coat sleeve.

"Hello!" said Owen. "What's in the box?"

"Oh, dessert," answered Murray, coming to his senses. "Direct from Matthew's Old-Fashioned Ice Cream Parlor—an ice cream cake."

"Sometimes my stomach hurts, but not today. I love ice cream cakes!"

"Me, too," Murray confided. He leaned toward Owen and whispered, "Let's put it in the freezer until after dinner. Then we'll eat the whole darn thing."

"Good idea," said Owen.

Neal took Murray's coat and hat and hung them in the hall closet beneath the stairs. When he returned, Barbara was setting the table while Murray sat in one of the kitchen chairs with Owen on one knee and the cat on the other.

"Let's eat first," Neal said, "and later I'll give you a tour of the house."

"Your kitchen is certainly charming," said Murray, watching Neal toss the salad. "And what's more, it smells like my hope of heaven," he added with a broad grin, "which of course means baked chicken with rosemary and garlic."

"Listen to that, Grandma," Neal said, "we don't even have to announce the menu."

"No," Murray chuckled, tapping himself on the nose, "not with this analytical schnozz."

Neal's improvised dinner turned out to be a spicy success, and Murray's ice cream cake proved to be a cool, delicious complement, wrapping up the meal like the tag of a jazz tune.

Afterwards, Owen helped Neal build a fire in the parlor. In the meantime, Murray wandered around the ground floor, inspecting the music room and the den, while Barbara made coffee in the kitchen.

"These old wood floors are wonderful," Murray said, returning to the parlor. "Did you refinish them yourself?"

"Yes, I did," said Neal. Satisfied that the fire was well lit, he stood up. "It was a lot of work, but worth the effort."

Barbara came in bearing a tray loaded with a thermos of coffee, three mugs, and containers of cream and sugar. Murray rushed to help her, "Let me carry that for you."

"Why, thank you, Murray. But, you know I was a nurse for years, and I had to lift some heavy patients. I'm pretty strong."

Murray took the tray and smiled at her, "Your strength I'll take on faith, but the pretty is self-evident."

Barbara said, "Go on with you," but her cheeks were two bright roses.

Murray set the tray on the coffee table and poured coffee for everyone, beginning with Barbara. He and Barbara shared the sofa, while Owen knelt in front of the fire.

Neal took his mug of black coffee from Murray and sat in the armchair. "I spent this afternoon at the county courthouse researching information on the Fritzinger family," he told them. "In 1899, Gunter Fritzinger, a logging magnate, built the house for his wife Maria. Their children were born here: Emily in 1901, and Heinrich, six years later. Maria died in 1930, and Gunter never remarried.

"When Gunter died in 1955, Emily inherited the house and lived here, a spinster, until her death in 1993. According to Yoshiko, Owen's piano teacher, who knew her, Emily closed off the third floor when her father died, and later closed off the second floor to save heating costs, living on the parlor floor the last years of her life. She made the den, originally the dining room, her bedroom. The house grew shabby, but it was structurally sound when we bought it. It was well built and well maintained until the last few years. My repairs were really cosmetic."

"Well, it certainly looks terrific now," said Murray.

"Yeah, it's the best house I ever lived in," said Owen, ending his statement with a huge yawn.

"It's the only house you've ever lived in," Neal replied, "and I think it's time for you to hit the sack."

"Not yet, Daddy."

"Yes, it's late. Time for bed."

"Goodnight, Owen," said Murray.

"Goodnight," said Owen, with another enormous yawn. "Thanks for the ice cream cake, Uncle Murray."

"Glad you enjoyed it. Sleep well," said Murray.

The Piper's Story

Owen gave his grandmother a kiss, and then Neal took him up to bed.

As soon as they were out of earshot, Barbara said, "So you're Owen's Uncle Murray now?"

"Yes, I guess so," laughed Murray. "The first time he met me, he misunderstood my name and thought I was the Merry Apple Man. He's a darling, precocious boy; I'd be proud to have him in my family."

Barbara smiled, "He's a treasure."

When Neal returned, Murray told him, "I've talked to some of the people at Coveland House about the Fritzingers, and I discovered a few interesting facts." He set his coffee down on the table. "There's a ninety-year-old woman at Coveland House named Margaret Casey who grew up here and went to school with Heinrich Fritzinger. She said he had few friends and he didn't do well in school. Since the Fritzingers spoke their mother tongue at home, Heinrich had a heavy German accent, and the kids made fun of him. She still remembers how they taunted him, saying 'The worst in the class is Heinie, the ass.' He was very blonde and tall. Margaret said he was shy and rarely smiled.

"According to her, the Fritzingers kept to themselves for the most part. She said that Gunter was a very domineering man. The rumors were that he ran off any boy that tried to court Emily, and he and Heinrich apparently argued over politics. Gunter loved America—he was a very successful capitalist, as this house attests—but Heinrich was critical of this country and very pro-German. In fact, when he was twenty-one, he moved to Germany."

"What year was that?" asked Barbara.

"He was born in 1907," answered Neal, "so he would have been twenty-one in 1928."

"Good heavens," said Barbara, "Nineteen-twenty-eight wasn't too great a time in Germany, was it?"

"Well, up until 1929," Neal answered, "Germany was able to pay her war reparations and she prospered economically, largely due to huge sums of money borrowed abroad. In 1929, foreign bankers saw that Germany might not be able to repay her loans and they stopped extending them. The collapse of the New York stock market that year and the general world

242

depression made things worse. Things got very bad—high unemployment and terrible inflation.

"As you know, in 1933, Hitler and the Nazi party came to power. In the next five years, Hitler cut unemployment from about six million to less than five hundred thousand." Neal grinned, "Guess I sound like a history teacher, don't I?"

Barbara smiled and Murray said, "According to Margaret Casey, Heinrich supposedly fought for the Nazis during World War II."

"Probably so," said Neal, "because in 1935, Hitler reintroduced compulsory military service, in violation of the Versailles Treaty, which limited Germany to a professional army of one hundred thousand. Provided he was physically able, Heinrich would have had to serve in the German military."

Neal slapped his thighs. "Enough of the history lesson. You're here to see the study. But first, let me show you the photograph that Sarah may have mentioned to you, Murray. Grandma has already seen it." Neal took the color photograph out of his shirt pocket and handed it to Murray. Barbara leaned over and the two of them examined the picture, while Neal explained the circumstances.

"Vicky took this photograph and several others the day after the strange fog enveloped me. The photograph shows the front of the house. You can see the bay windows on the parlor floor, the square tower above, and the wraparound porch. It was a clear, sunny day, and the resolution is very sharp."

"Very curious," said Murray. "The shadow in the tower window is clearly visible. Are you certain that there was no person or object in the room that could have cast a shadow on the glass?"

"That day in March, the room was completely empty. I hadn't begun working on the interior at all, and Owen and I stood beside Vicky as she took the pictures."

"Well," Barbara said, "unlike Ian, my late husband, I never had visions, and although Ian described it for me, I never saw the evil creature itself. I only saw the effect this creature had on my husband and my son Peter. This photograph is the first visible proof of it."

"Unfortunately, I *have* seen it with my own eyes," said Neal, "and that shadow-creature is here in this house." He stood up. "So now, without further ado, come and see the study."

Neal led them up the stairs to the tower room and inserted a small key into the padlock. "I have found this mysteriously unlocked a few times. I think the creature toys with me and opens it at will."

He opened the door and snapped on the overhead light. Murray and Barbara followed him into the room. No one spoke. Neal and Barbara stood near the door while Murray looked around the room. He was drawn first to the bookshelves and then to the large window. Murray ran his hand over the top of the leather armchair. "Just an ordinary room, isn't it?"

"Seems so now," answered Neal, "but it's an unhappy room," he declared. "It feels—I mean, I feel—great unhappiness here. A gray, depressed atmosphere. And now I think I know why. Yoshiko told us this morning that Emily described this room as 'a place of pain.' She closed it off because of the bad memories she had. I didn't want to say all this earlier in front of Owen.

"Yoshiko also described individual portraits of Emily, Heinrich, and their mother Maria, that used to hang in the parlor. When Yoshiko asked about Gunter's portrait, Emily said her father made their lives hell, and that she had burned his portrait on the night he died."

Then Neal reminded Murray of his vision involving the bloody handprints and the scuffed dents in the study's wainscot. "Well, just recently I had a second vision in this room. A young boy, about ten years old knelt right there." Neal pointed to a spot just left of the fireplace. "He moaned and wept, holding his flayed, bloody palms."

Barbara winced, and Murray asked, "Who do you think it was?"

"It had to be Heinrich. He had white-blonde hair, and he was dressed in an old-fashioned, European way, much as Yoshiko described the boy Heinrich in the portrait."

Neal encompassed the study with a sweeping gesture, "Places, rooms, houses have their own feel or atmosphere, especially old houses like this.

When people have lived in a place for years and years, their actions and thoughts and emotions leave their mark, an invisible imprint.

"When we first moved in, the atmosphere of this room was so thick you could touch it," said Neal. "The walls were painted maroon. The only person this place could have cheered up was the Marquis de Sade. The sadness and depression struck me with such force that it was like a physical blow—I could hardly breathe in here."

"Who knows what took place in this room, anyway?" said Murray. "If only the walls could talk."

"I don't know," declared Barbara, "I might not want to hear their story."

"What do you think could have happened here?" asked Murray.

"I think Gunter beat his son to the point of torture in this room," said Neal. "He must have used a ruler or some sort of rod to beat Heinrich's hands until they were raw and bleeding. And he very likely browbeat both children, as well, abusing them psychologically. According to Yoshiko, Emily stuttered, and when she talked about this room, her stutter grew so pronounced that it almost stopped her speech."

"Good heavens," exclaimed Barbara, "that makes everything fall into place! I forgot to tell you, Neal, that I rang the Reinhold Foundation today. Among other charities, they have a home for abused children, which is where Emily donated the Steinway. That gives more credence to the theory that she and Heinrich were themselves abused."

"I suppose it's all possible," said Murray, "although Margaret Casey never mentioned anything about Emily or Heinrich being physically abused. But the fact that the Fritzingers kept to themselves and Gunter ran off all of his daughter's suitors, could mean that he abused her psychologically. And if so, that abuse must have happened in this room."

"Are we dealing with two separate hauntings here," Neal asked, "or do you think there is a connection between the Fritzinger family and the Erlking?"

"If there is a connection between the Fritzingers and the Erlking," Murray replied, "I have no idea what it could be." He ran his hand over his scalp, "Unless the lingering unhappy atmosphere created by Gunter makes this room inviting to a malicious spirit."

"It's malicious, all right," said Neal in a low, troubled voice.

"It's common knowledge that if one is worn down and exhausted physically, one becomes more susceptible to disease," said Barbara. "If that occurs on the physical level, why couldn't it happen on the psychic plane? If Heinrich was subjected to constant abuse, he probably grew unbalanced and neurotic, a perfect target for negative psychic influences. If those negative influences concentrated themselves in this room, they may have left, as it were, a residue."

"And perhaps that negative energy drew the Erlking here?" said Neal.

"Maybe," said Barbara. "It's a very tenuous link at best, but it's the only connection I can surmise."

"Well, time will tell," said Murray, "but for the moment I've seen enough."

"How about a little cognac or brandy downstairs?" asked Neal.

"Good idea," said Barbara. "I could jolly well use a drink."

She and Murray waited on the landing while Neal turned off the light, put the padlock in place and snapped it shut. "If only locks could hold off the supernatural," he remarked.

Murray sighed and clapped Neal on the shoulder, "I'm afraid, my boy, it's going to take a lot more than that."

CHAPTER 28

Seeking Solutions

"How can I get rid of this unholy Erlking?" Neal asked, his eyes on Murray. He sat hunched forward in the armchair, with a wrinkled brow. "What can I do?"

Murray drank a sip of his cognac and swirled the amber liquid in his glass, while Barbara, sitting with her feet tucked under her, stared into the red-orange flames of the fire.

"I don't have an answer," Murray said at last.

"Exorcism?" offered Barbara.

Neal shook his head. "Grandma, we talked about that before you came. The procedure of the Catholic Church is too bureaucratic and slow. It might take months before we see action. No, I'm not going to call an exorcist."

"Let's think about the original events in this story—what happened to your grandfather," Murray suggested. "How did he get rid of the Erlking?"

"He didn't," replied Barbara. "The bloody creature left him lying blind, mute, and unconscious in a cornfield. Ian didn't do anything to make it leave him. It injured him and left of its own accord."

"True," agreed Murray, "but later the mysterious piper came and protected Ian, led him to safety. The only threat to him after that was on the beach at Dunkirk."

"When the Stuka strafed the beach," Neal said.

"Well, yes, but after that, the Erlking almost paralyzed Ian again, until the mystical piper played and dispelled the spirit."

Barbara spoke, "Do you mean we ought somehow to summon the piper?"

Murray smiled and shook his head. "I have no idea how to do that, Barbara. No, my point is that maybe there's a protective power in the music itself, provided the player has the right intent."

"Do you really think music could overpower the Erlking, Murray?" asked Barbara.

"It did on the beach at Dunkirk." Murray sat forward on the sofa and set his glass on the coffee table. "Music, as you know, is a powerful force. Joshua flattened the walls of Jericho with the help of the sound of trumpets. David played the harp and sang for Saul, the King of Israel, to soothe him and restore his peace of mind. In fact, music is used all over the world in different traditions for healing. Sufis, Hindus, Native American shamans, Tibetan monks, and Jewish mystics have used music for healing."

Murray sat back and put one finger aside his nose. "Music certainly came to the aid of Ian. Maybe there is some way it could help us, too."

For a moment, there was silence, except for the crackling fire.

Murray spoke again, "Another example comes to my mind. I remember when Miriam, Sarah's mother, was dying of cancer. Sarah visited Miriam at the hospital one evening, after she had played a concert. Miriam lay there in a coma, emaciated, pasty-white, eyes closed, breathing very slowly, with tubes attached everywhere. Sarah said she spoke to her mother, kissed her face and held her hand; she even rubbed her feet, but there was not the slightest response.

"For a long time, Sarah sat in the chair beside her bed and prayed for peace and healing for her mother and guidance for herself. Then she took out her viola and played Bach, very quietly." Murray looked up at the ceiling and then at Neal and Barbara. "It brought Miriam out of the coma. She opened her eyes and said, 'Sarah, I heard you playing.' She remained lucid all the next day and she died the day after."

Murray's voice was quiet. "The power of music."

Barbara agreed, "Too true. I know that music can lift the spirit and give people courage. Why else did the Scottish regiments take the pipes to war?"

Neal stroked his mustache in a quick, nervous motion and said, "I've read that *feng shui* space-clearers use hand-clapping and the continuous sound of a pure, clear bell to dispel bad thoughts and purify a space." He cleared his throat, "We all agree that music has power, but how can I get this supernatural infestation out of my house? I don't think hand-clapping and bells will have much effect on the Erlking."

Murray sighed noisily and said, "Why don't we think about possible solutions or strategies for a few days and compare notes next week? Sarah invited all of us to dinner at her house next Saturday."

"She did?" Neal said, eyebrows raised.

Murray slapped his forehead. "Good heavens, I should have told you first thing. Sarah sends her apologies for not coming tonight, but she said she just needed a little time to think."

"I see," Neal said.

"You'll come to Sarah's for dinner won't you?" Murray asked.

"Yes, we will," Neal answered.

"But Neal," Barbara said, "do you think it's a good idea to take Owen there, too? You don't want him to hear any of that discussion, do you? Maybe I should look after him here."

"Grandma, I want you there. You know the entire story and your experience and knowledge may help us greatly."

"Barbara," said Murray, "Bitsy Baird, Sarah's assistant, can look after Owen and keep him occupied in another room while we talk. She's a senior in high school and a former student of Neal's. Very reliable and used to kids. She comes from a large family."

"All right, then," said Barbara.

"Well, now that we've got that settled, let's call it an evening," said Murray. "I need to do some thinking and rest my weary bones. Thank you for dinner and showing me the study."

Murray and Neal stood up at the same time. "My pleasure," said Neal.

While Barbara walked Murray into the kitchen, Neal collected Murray's jacket and hat from the foyer closet. As he closed the closet door, he heard the high whine of the Mazda's engine coming up the driveway. Stomach knotted, he hurried into the kitchen, just as Vicky threw open the door, lurched into the room, spun three hundred-sixty degrees, and landed with a hard thump in a kitchen chair. A thick lock of her shaggy blonde hair lodged in the corner of her mouth, and she spat it out explosively, "Well, dear Neal," she said, "looks like you're havin' another party without me."

She thumped the bottle of cognac on the table, uncapped it, and took a deep swig.

"Ahhh," she sighed. Her eyes focused on Murray. "Who's the escapee from the Old Folks Home?" She cackled and slapped the table.

"Vicky!"

"And how about you, Barbara? Enjoying my house—taking my place?"

Hurled lances, heavy, sharp, and spinning, could not match the steel glinting in Barbara's eyes. Holding Vicky in her stern gaze, the older woman took her time before answering. When she did, she simply spoke the truth in a quiet voice, but even so, it seemed to scorch the air. "You are Owen's mother, Vicky, and no one can take your place. You have a beautiful house and the only reason I am in it is to take care of your fine son, something you should be doing, instead of getting drunk and making a bloody fool of yourself."

When Vicky's gaze faltered, Barbara addressed the two men. "Goodnight, to you both," she said. "Murray, it was a great pleasure to meet you. Now, please excuse me." Barbara turned and walked out.

Neal said, "Murray, I apologize for my wife. She is rude and drunk—please ignore her. Let me see you out." He opened the kitchen door.

"Yeah, see him out. Do that, Mr. History Teacher. I'll just sit here and get more rude and drunk in the meantime."

White-lipped Neal accompanied Murray out into the chilly night. "I am so very sorry," he said. "Vicky's been very volatile lately, and as you saw, tonight she's not herself."

Murray fitted his fedora to his bald head and said, "No harm done, Neal. Don't worry about it." He offered Neal his hand and said, "Thank you again for dinner and a very interesting evening." He smiled and opened the door to his Lincoln, "We'll see you at Sarah's place next weekend."

"Speaking of Sarah, Murray, I don't know if she's told you or not, but I'm sure the reason she didn't come tonight is because I kissed her the other day on the beach. I didn't plan to; it just happened. I apologized to her that day and told her that I respect her and value her friendship, but I guess she had second thoughts."

"I guessed something was wrong between the two of you," Murray replied, "but I didn't know what exactly had happened. Sarah's probably just overreacting. You know she had a very bad experience with her former boyfriend in New York."

"Yes, she told me about Danny Levinson, which makes me feel even worse that I offended her in that way."

"Look, Neal, I know you wouldn't harm Sarah intentionally. Tomorrow, I will tell her about the study and what we discussed tonight, and I can also reassure her about you. I think it will help her to talk about it and clear the air, but I'm certain Sarah will be fine. As I told you, she just needed a little breathing space. So don't worry about it anymore. You have enough on your hands with the situation here."

"All right then," Neal replied, as the older man climbed into the driver's seat. "Thanks, Murray."

Neal watched the red taillights of Murray's Lincoln recede down the driveway and then disappear behind the trees that lined the road. Seeking comfort, he looked up at the glittering night sky. At that moment, had it been possible, he would have traded a decade on earth for a split second's serenity in the realm of the silver stars, above all earthly cares. Heavy-hearted and angry, knowing that he had to calm himself before he confronted Vicky, he took deep, slow breaths, willing himself to relax. He kept his eyes on the stars, breathing slowly and steadily. After a few minutes, he unclenched his fists, and felt the tension recede from the muscles of his stomach. Having regained a measure of equilibrium, he took a last deep breath and returned to the house.

When he opened the kitchen door, Vicky still sat at the table, chin propped on her hands. Neal's tone was low and calm, "Vicky—"

"Don't yell at me!" She slammed both palms down on the table and turned abruptly to face him. "Who was that man, and why didn't you tell me he was coming?"

"How could I tell you, Vicky? You've been gone, remember? You walked out and moved in with someone else, who and where I don't even know." Neal sighed and continued, "That was Murray Appleman. I met him at Coveland House the day I played the pipes there. Owen sat with him during the concert, and afterwards we all hit it off. Then I met him again at the concert at the high school. Anyway, I talked to him about my experience here with the evil spirit."

"Evil spirit?" Vicky snorted. "What bullshit. You got drunk one night, fell down and hit your head. The only spirits you met were inside a beer bottle. Several beer bottles. You are ridiculous, Neal, and now you've got two more suckers involved." She shook her head, "Maybe they'll make a movie about you—The Three Stooges Morph into Ghostbusters."

"Just drop it, Vicky. We need to discuss the trouble between us, because we can't go on like this, for ourselves or for Owen's sake."

"You're right about that, buddy-boy. But I didn't come here to talk. I came to pick up the rest of my clothes."

"Well, we're going to talk anyway. You owe it to me and your son. We haven't even heard from you in five days, so the least you could do is give me five minutes now that you're here. For all our sakes, we either have to make this marriage work or end it."

Vicky drummed her fingers on the table and regarded him with a small, strained smile, "You know, I can't even remember the last time we slept together. In case you haven't realized it, Neal, our marriage has been over for quite some time."

"Not in my mind."

Vicky turned her head away.

Neal rubbed his eyes with his thumb and forefinger. "Look, before I read your note, I knew you were having an affair."

She stiffened, keeping her eyes averted.

"I don't know and I don't care who the man is. I forgive you for it because I know that I drove you away in bits and pieces by," Neal swallowed, "well, when I didn't realize how constricted you felt and how unhappy you were."

Vicky's hair was disheveled and she sat so slumped and still that a vision flashed into Neal's mind. He saw a bunch of daffodils, browning and wilted, in a garbage pail.

He felt a surge of pity. "I'll make things better, Vicky. Come home; be part of our lives again. We can see a marriage counselor."

Vicky stood up so abruptly that the chair fell over backwards with a harsh clatter.

Her face was flushed and the corners of her mouth worked up and down. "You see a marriage counselor, Neal. I'll be damned if I waste any more of my youth and energy on this mismatch. You're damned right I'm having an affair, and you can shove your forgiveness up your ass. I've met someone who likes what I like and who loves me for who I am. He's a real man—someone I can respect. Unlike you, Mr. Superior History Teacher."

"Well what about Owen, then?"

"I'll file for divorce and get custody," Vicky flung at him. "That's what about Owen." She stormed out of the room and stomped up the stairs to her bedroom.

Neal remained standing in the kitchen, alone with a single thought: Divorce, yes, but custody of Owen, never.

CHAPTER 29

Music and Bagels

A s soon as he returned to Coveland House from his visit with the MacGregors, Murray telephoned Sarah. "Hi, doll. I'm back."
"How was it?"

"Well, it was an interesting evening, but I'm too tired to go into all the details now. Why don't I tell you over breakfast at Ike's outdoor café tomorrow? If we meet at eight that gives us an hour before your shop opens."

"Sounds good," said Sarah.

"Now go to bed," he told her, "it's late for a thirty-year-old working girl." Her soft laugh was precisely the effect he wanted.

After his telephone conversation with Sarah, Murray took his own advice. He stripped down to his undershorts and climbed into bed. Lying on his back with his arms on top of the covers, he closed his eyes. No good. He turned on his left side, then rolled over onto his stomach. After a moment he tried lying on his right side. Hopeless. His mind was more jumpy than a flea circus and sleep was impossible.

How could he help Neal get rid of that infernal infestation? Such a frightful foe in the house, twelve feet above the little boy's bedroom. Murray looked up at the dark ceiling of his own room and shook his head. He feared for Neal and Owen. Of course he knew that fears were magnified at night, but what to do?

His thoughts kept returning to the fact that the piper's music had saved Ian on the beach at Dunkirk. That was the key; therein lay the solution, he was sure of it. The piper's music was the one thing that dispelled the evil spirit. And there was something else he remembered. Somewhere he had seen a related article about music and patterns or designs. Was it in the Seattle newspaper or the news magazine he read?

Hell, now he'd have to get up. He had to find that article. He put on his bathrobe, turned on a lamp in his sitting room, and found his reading glasses. The light of the lamp cast a warm, golden glow on the small, tidy room with its worn but beautiful Persian rug, the dark blue sofa flanked by a low-backed wooden rocking chair and a leather armchair. There was a large, old wooden chest that served as a coffee table.

For ten minutes, he scanned *The Seattle Times* cover to cover. Nothing. He picked up the last two copies of his news magazine and thumbed through them both. Not there either. Murray scratched his head, wondering where he had seen that article. Maybe he had watched some sort of documentary program on TV. He took off his glasses and rubbed his eyes. No, he had seen it in print, he was certain.

His stomach growled. Well, when at an impasse, one should always check the refrigerator. Murray opened the half-size fridge that he had bought for his Coveland House apartment, and took out a package of cream cheese. Next, he rummaged around for some crackers on the small table where he kept his snacks, but except for boxes of cookies, all he could find was a package of those fake, crappy bagels. He was ashamed of himself for buying them. He picked up the package reluctantly, and there underneath it was his journal *Intersections*. Ha! That's where he'd seen the article.

Well, first things first. Murray spread a thick layer of cream cheese on one half of his fake bagel, and then took his snack and the journal back to the sofa. He found the article and got so engrossed that he almost forgot to eat. Almost. He took a hefty bite of the pitiful, spongy thing covered in cream cheese. It was the texture that was all wrong. A true bagel was a worthy chew, the tongue's delight, and a challenge to the teeth and the muscles of the jaw.

Murray chewed with concentration. Well, at least the cream cheese was the real thing. Still munching, he continued to read. The article described the work of Ernst Chladni, an eighteenth-century scientist and amateur musician who, naturally, was interested in the effects of sound. Chladni covered thin black metal plates with a fine layer of white sand and vibrated them by drawing a violin bow across the edge. As the plates vibrated, the sand organized itself into geometrical patterns: crosses, diamonds, star patterns, and other more complicated designs. Sometimes the lines were straight, sometimes wave-shaped and complex. Chladni showed these figures to a gathering of scientists in 1809, and Napoleon had the demonstration repeated for himself.

Studying the picture of the Chladni figures, Murray forgot to chew.

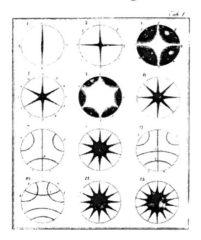

Figure 1. Chladni figures.

The second part of the article was about Hans Jenny, a Swiss scientist of the twentieth century. Before reading it, Murray took a huge bite of his cream cheese covered snack. "Damn," he remarked, looking at the remaining morsel. "This is an expensive proposition." The no-good excuse for a bagel had made him so hungry for the bona fide item, he'd have to book a trip to New York. And he might have to stay there, he thought, if he didn't find a solution for Neal. So on he read.

Hans Jenny expanded on Chladni's research with modern technology and a greater variety of materials and vibrations. He used crystal oscillators, which could regulate pitch and volume precisely, and he experimented with sand, plant spores, iron filings, liquids, and viscous substances. His experiments also produced geometric patterns, and the patterns became more complex as the frequencies were increased. When he vibrated fluids, he found they produced wave motions, spirals, and wavelike patterns in continuous circulation. And when he tilted the plate as it vibrated, the liquid didn't run off; it stayed on the plate and kept constructing new shapes. But when he stopped the vibrations, the liquid ran off, which showed the anti-gravitational effect produced by vibrations.

God, what were the implications of that, Murray wondered, as he tried to digest the awful bagel and the awesome meaning simultaneously. He'd have to tell Sarah about this tomorrow. Maybe when she played her viola, she produced all kinds of beneficent effects. Hell, what were the practical implications of sound? Maybe mankind could counteract earthquakes, and calm storms at sea. Maybe aircraft could fly without fuel, propelled by the vibrations of anti-gravitational devices.

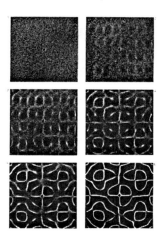

Figure 2. Hans Jenny, 1967: Photographs in sequence showing a sand figure taking shape on a metal plate, activated by a crystal oscillator, frequency 7,560 cycles per second.

Murray studied the illustrations and then continued reading. He discovered that Jenny made an instrument he called a tonoscope. It was a simple device into which one could speak or sing. The vibrations of the voice affected a thin rubber diaphragm at one end, on which sand or powder was placed. It made the human voice visible, without any electronic device intervening. When one sang wordlessly into the tonoscope, figures formed on the diaphragm according to each individual pitch. Lower pitches produced simple figures such as circles, while the higher pitches created more complex patterns, almost flowerlike, such as a hexagram enclosing a circle. As the notes of the melody changed, the figures transformed fluidly, like a living thing. But the same pitches always created the same patterns.

Murray raised his brows and murmured, "Order and beauty created by sound."

The third part of the article began with a quote translated from the Mandukya Upanishad, one of the Hindu sacred scriptures. "OM. This eternal Word is all: what was, what is and what shall be, and what beyond is eternity. All is OM."

Of course Murray had heard of the syllable OM. He knew it was used in meditation, but he had never learned what it symbolized. According to the article, it represented the archetypal primordial sound, the creative, sacred power from which the entire physical universe, all objects, all beings, was generated and sustained.

Translation, thought Murray: *And God said, Let there be light: and there was light.* God spoke, and the sound became form; the world came into being.

The article ended with a quote from Isidore of Seville, the sixth-century saint, the first Christian to write a *summa* of universal knowledge in which many fragments of classical learning were preserved. "Nothing exists without music," Isidore wrote, "for the universe itself is said to have been framed by a kind of harmony of sounds, and the heaven itself revolves under the tone of that harmony."

It reminded him of a psalm. How did it go? *The heavens declare the glory of God. . . Their sound is gone out into all lands; and their words into the ends of the world.* "The music of creation," Murray remarked, "confirmed by the Greeks and Romans, as well as the sacred traditions, Hindus, Jews, and Christians alike, with a reaffirmation by modern scientists." He laid the journal on his lap and thought for a minute. What it all meant was clear: creation is a song—one that was still going on. And if that song should ever stop, the world would in an instant cease to exist.

"Which means, Mr. Erlking, that you will find it very hard to kick against the pricks. You are out of harmony with the universe, and somehow, like Ian's mystical piper, we're going to rout you."

All right, so we don't know exactly how, Murray thought, but we'll get there. He turned off the lamp and returned to his bedroom. He draped his bathrobe across the foot of the bed and lay down, covering himself with the sheet and blanket. Neal had no father or grandfather, and he, Murray, had no son or grandson. He thought of Ian, a man of his own era, how courageously and defiantly he had played the pipes on the beach at Dunkirk, and how fiercely he must have wished to protect his son Peter, his grandson Neal, and little Owen. Murray sighed. He couldn't take Ian's place, but he would do what he could to help the MacGregors.

In the movies, he thought, the good guys always win. The trouble was, this was no movie. He pictured Neal and small, red-haired Owen in his mind. Well, the good guys had damn well better win this time. There was just too much to lose.

Murray put his hands behind his head. There had been a bibliography at the end of the article. Tomorrow after his talk with Sarah, he was going to the library to do a little more research. For the moment he had done all he could. He closed his eyes, turned on his side, and an hour later, breathed in his dreams the fragrance of warm bagels, New York, bona fide.

CHAPTER 30

Morning Revelations

"This is the best time of day at my favorite place in Coveland." Sarah seemed tired, but her eyes, as blue as the heart of the ocean, smiled at Murray. They sat at their corner table on the pier, six feet above the high tide, sipping coffee in the brisk air and bright sunshine. "What a good idea to meet for breakfast, Uncle Murr. Waterfront Street is so empty this early in the morning, especially on Saturday, that we can have the café all to ourselves."

Sarah had driven in to work an hour early, and Murray had walked down from Coveland House to meet her at the Harbor Pier. They were the only two customers on the deck at Ike's outdoor café, and the owner himself had served them coffee, but Ike had not yet brought their food. Sarah had ordered two of Ike's homemade biscuits with bacon, while Murray had chosen the Captain's breakfast, a hearty meal guaranteed to keep him satisfied until eleven at least.

The brilliant light of the rising sun transformed the waters of the cove into glittering blue sapphires and fiery diamonds. Sarah, squinting into the double light of sky and reflecting sea, watched two catamarans east of the pier, one with a white sail, one with a green, racing each other parallel to the coastline. The white-sailed boat led the other craft slightly, their sails angled toward the far shore. The boats skimmed over the water, running before the crisp breeze in the same way that the seagulls plied the air currents overhead, with speed, grace, and agility. Sarah turned up the collar of her light jacket in the wind and warmed her hands on her mug of hot, steaming coffee. As Ike returned with their food, Sarah asked, "What do you think of the view, Uncle Murr?"

"Beautiful," he grinned, pointing to the landscape of his breakfast plate, the twin gold suns of his two fried eggs, the steaming, shimmering sausages, and the golden-brown mound of pancakes that he doused with maple syrup. After the first few bites of egg and sausage, so tasty they bereft him of speech, he regained his focus and told Sarah about his evening with Neal and Barbara, describing the study and their conversation about the history of the Fritzinger house.

"We had quite a surprise at the end of the evening," Murray said. He took a sip of coffee. "Neal's wife Vicky showed up. That is one *meshuginah* woman."

Sarah stopped buttering her biscuit. "Really? Why so?" But before Murray could answer, she continued, "What does she look like? Maybe I've seen her in Hollander's, or maybe she came into the travel shop."

Murray rubbed the side of his nose. "Well, she's a thin blonde, fine-featured, and probably pretty under normal conditions, but last night she was as wild-eyed and disheveled as a raving lunatic, two steps away from foaming at the mouth. She came in drunk and belligerent in a whirl of blonde, shaggy hair just as I was about to leave. In less than fifteen seconds, she managed to insult everyone, including Barbara."

Murray put his fork and knife down, and sat back with a smile. "Barbara. Now there's a real woman for you." Murray laughed, "She didn't take any crap from Vicky. Barbara let that girl have it with both barrels. She told Vicky she ought to take better care of Owen and to quit making a damn fool of herself." Murray clasped his hands together and rested them on his round belly. "Barbara faced her down, she sure did. It was beautiful to behold.

"I left then, and I don't know what happened after that." Murray shook his head and clicked his tongue. "Neal surely has his hands full. He's got one demon in the study and another in the bedroom. It's a good thing Barbara is there now."

"Sounds like it," Sarah remarked. "Did you invite them to my house for dinner next Saturday?"

"Yes, and they are coming, although Barbara was concerned about bringing Owen. But I suggested that Bitsy Baird could keep him occupied in another room while we talk after dinner."

"Oh, yes, that's a good idea, Uncle Murr. I'll ask Bitsy when she comes in to work today." Sarah sipped her coffee and then added, "Maybe you could call Neal today and see if he survived his wife's sound and fury?"

Murray looked into her eyes a long moment before speaking. "He's a good man, and maybe he'll be free someday, doll. I like him, too."

Sarah drew her eyes away and nodded mutely.

"When you told me you couldn't go to the MacGregors, without any good reason," Murray explained, "I suspected that something had happened between you and Neal. Last night, just before I left, he told me that he kissed you on the beach."

"Yes." The color rose in Sarah's cheeks.

"He said that he never intended to make an advance—it just happened and it will not—"

"All right, Uncle Murr!" Sarah raised her voice, stopping him with one hand lifted. "He told me it wouldn't happen again, and I believe him. The problem is me. To put it directly, Neal is everything I want in a man and I know I can't have him." Sarah leaned forward and pounded the table with her fist, rattling their plates. "What a fool I was and what a fool I am. Danny Levinson wasn't worth my affection—he was a scumbag. Now I'm in love with Neal who is a good man, but married. What fine irony is that? The gods must be amused." She slumped back in her chair, deflated, all her energy and anger dissipated.

Sarah brushed back a strand of hair from her eyes. "To love Neal and not be able to love him—it's killing me. I am battling with myself, trying to accept that he and I can be friends—and *only* friends."

Murray reached out and took her hand in his. "Easy, doll. I just wanted you to know that Neal is not on the make. He's not that kind of a man, but you already know that."

He patted the back of her hand. "Are you going to be okay having him over next weekend?"

"Yes, I think so. I just need a little time."

"Well, that's exactly what I told him, and he accepted that."

Murray released her hand and sat back. "But you know, I have to disagree with you about the gods being amused. Never mind about them. I think the one true God is smiling, but not in amusement. Upon honorable people like you and Neal, He smiles only in blessing." Murray laid his two palms flat on the table and gazed intently into her eyes. "Sarah, we cannot see the future or know the ends of all our actions, but it is always best to do the right thing, even if it is painful in the short term. You have done that all your life, doll, and I'm proud of you, and I believe that somehow, this situation will come out all right in the end."

Blinking back the rising salt tide in her dark blue eyes, Sarah smiled wanly at her great uncle. "I don't see how, but I certainly hope so," she said.

Murray decided to change the subject. "But back to Neal's predicament. Have you found any information on the two massacres Ian saw in his visions?"

Sarah took out a tissue from her purse and blew her nose. "Well, I've got a stack of books at home, but honestly, I've been so distracted I haven't looked through them yet. I promise I will after work today."

"Well let me know if you find something. I'm going to the library after breakfast to do a little research of my own."

"Really? Research on what?"

"Have you ever heard of the Swiss scientist Hans Jenny?" Murray asked.

Sarah shook her head.

"Well, he performed experiments showing the effect of pitches on inanimate objects. In his book *Cymatics*, he described how he placed sand, iron filings, wood pulp, and various other substances on a surface and vibrated them with different pitches, with the results that the sand gradually formed itself into geometric figures and other intricate patterns. In my journal *Intersections*, I saw some of Jenny's work, beautiful photographs illustrating how music moved inanimate objects from disorder to order."

"Oh yes, the journal I ordered for you."

"Exactly. Music is a powerful force, I tell you."

"Every musician and sensitive person would agree with you, Uncle Murr, but how is that relevant to Neal's problem?"

"Well, after thinking about Ian's story over and over, I'm convinced that the solution to routing the Erlking lies in the episode on the beach at Dunkirk when the demon came after Ian the last time. Remember that Ian was on the verge of collapse until he heard a phrase of music from the mystical piper. It was music that banished the demon."

"True, but how does that apply here?"

Murray shrugged and laughed, "Hell if I know. But that's why I'm going to do more research, using the bibliography at the end of the article. Then maybe I'll have a sudden inspiration and know what to do next."

"Well, what I have to do next," said Sarah, checking her watch, "is open Friedkin's Travel Shop for Saturday morning business."

"Oh no you don't!" Murray grabbed her hand and squeezed it. "Far be it from me to stand in the way of commerce, doll, but I'll only release you if you tell me you're feeling better."

Sarah's glad smile warmed his heart. "Even a Jewish girl knows that confession is good for the soul, Uncle Murr." She glanced at her wristwatch. "As of eight-fifty-three a.m., I'm a new woman." She stood up and kissed him on the cheek. "Thanks for the talk and for breakfast."

Ten minutes later, when Bitsy arrived at the travel shop, Sarah asked her if she would babysit Owen at Sarah's house the following Saturday evening.

"Sure, boss. Does that mean I get dinner, too?" Bitsy smiled and bent her tall, gangly self over the counter, leaning on her elbows and propping her chin in her hands. Her comb-resistant, auburn hair and her sprinkling of freckles gave her the look of a giant-size Raggedy Ann doll come to life.

Sarah sat on the stool behind the counter and laughed, "I think you're secretly related to Uncle Murr. Yes, of course you can have dinner, and we're going to pay you twice the going rate."

"Great!" Bitsy's green eyes shone and a smile lit up her freckled face. "You're helping me save up for my Ivy League career."

"Career as in basketball, tennis or academics?"

"Tennis, as in a tennis scholarship at Columbia, and academics, of course. You're looking at an Ivy League English major come September."

"Bitsy, what great news!" Sarah exclaimed.

Bitsy's green eyes shone. "I got the letter of confirmation yesterday. Goodbye, Narrow Darrow—New York City, here I come."

"Congratulations. Before you move, I'll give you tips on life in my hometown. But you're such a great help around here that I'll be sorry to see you go."

"My mother, on the other hand, will be ecstatic. I'm the last of the brood to leave the nest. The poor woman is practically giddy with anticipation."

Sarah laughed. "Bitsy, she is not and you know it."

"Okay, have it your way, boss. So what shall I do to earn my keep today?"

"Well, dust everywhere, and then give the place a sweep. I'm going to check inventory and make a list of what books, CDs, and maps we need to order."

At twelve-thirty, Sarah sent Bitsy out to pick up lunch for both of them from Stacy's Seafood House. After eating their crab cakes and fried shrimp at the table in the small kitchen at the back of the shop, Sarah said, "Bitsy, it's been a slow Saturday, so I'm going to dash home and pick up a few books. Can I leave you in charge for a little while?"

"Fear not, boss. I'll man the helm. I can handle everything except earthquakes and bad referees."

"Well, with earthquakes, you just have a giant clean-up job, so the real thing to fear is bad referees. There's no help for that," Sarah replied. "I'll be back in twenty minutes."

Sarah drove home and picked up the three most promising books about World War II that she had checked out from the library, plus one tail-wagging, pleading-eyed dog named Mazie.

Bitsy was delighted when Sarah returned to the shop with the grinning, shaggy dog. "Mazie, how are you, pretty girl?" Bitsy knelt down in the luggage display area and hugged the dog and stroked her head. "You have the most beautiful dark brown eyes I ever saw."

"And the biggest appetite," Sarah added.

"Oh, I'll give her some of your crab cakes, if it's okay with you," Bitsy offered. "You didn't eat them all, and I exercised astonishing self-restraint after you left. Instead of devouring them in two gulps, which was my first intention, I put them in the refrigerator."

"Your virtue astounds me, Bitsy, and yes, you can give Mazie the crab cakes."

"Okay, boss." Bitsy's expression grew grave, "But tone down the virtuous talk. You don't want to ruin my badass reputation."

While Mazie devoured the crab cakes in two seconds flat, Sarah set her books on the table.

"Good grief, boss. Looks like you've got more homework than I do."

"I'm doing research on World War II for a friend."

Bitsy pretended to spit into the palms of her hands, then rubbed them together vigorously. "Want some help?"

"All right. It's so slow this afternoon, I think we can do a little research back here. We'll hear the bell if anyone comes in."

Sarah explained that she was looking for any references to or descriptions of the massacre of British troops by the Nazis in or around May of 1940, in France or Belgium. Bitsy chose one book; Sarah opened another, and Mazie found a comfortable spot underneath the table. After what seemed like only a few minutes, Sarah's concentration was interrupted by the jangling of the front door bell, and she glanced up. A tall, slender woman wearing jeans and a halter top entered the store. She was a young attractive blonde with shoulder-length hair in a layered cut, and Sarah thought she seemed vaguely familiar.

"Want me to help her, boss?"

"Yes, please."

When Bitsy got up to take care of the customer, Sarah refocused her attention on the book she was scanning, a chronological account of the events leading up to Dunkirk. After skimming over the pages describing the early days of the war without finding any pertinent information, Sarah got up to check on what had transpired with the customer. The blonde woman had chosen a small leather overnight bag and she brought it to the counter just as Sarah got to the front of the store.

Sarah rang up the purchase. "That'll be thirty-two thirty-five. Cash or credit?"

Without answering, the woman laid a checkbook on the counter, bent her head over it and wrote the amount in a large, looping script. Sarah wrinkled her nose as the smell of the woman's perfume enveloped her. At that moment, the clamoring bell heralded the entrance of a tall, middle-aged man with droopy eyelids and a military bearing. As soon as she saw him, Sarah realized that he and the blonde woman were the lovebirds who had visited the store on another occasion, the infatuated couple who were so completely self-involved that they had ignored her. He had paid for his purchase in cash and left without waiting for change, she remembered.

As the woman handed Sarah the check, the man came directly to the counter and snaked an arm around his girlfriend's waist, drawing her toward the door. "Let's go, babe," he said, "I'm double parked."

Sarah tore the receipt from the cash register and reached down to get a sack, but before she could hand them to the woman, the man grabbed the overnight bag and the couple rushed out the door, the bell jangling in their wake.

"There they go again," said Sarah, "dashing away like the first time I saw them."

"*Dashing* is the word," remarked Bitsy. "Captain Jim and his latest lovely."

Sarah wadded up the receipt and threw it in the trash. Then she glanced at the check she still held in her hand. "Oh, my God!" she exclaimed.

"What's the matter?" asked Bitsy.

"Oh, I, uh, I, um, noticed the date on the check and realized that all those books I checked out from the library are overdue."

"You're a real outlaw, boss."

"An outlaw. Good choice of words, Bitsy," Sarah commented, although the lawbreaker she had in mind was not herself. Feeling cold in the pit of her stomach, she quickly put away the check before Bitsy could see it. It was drawn on Island Marine Bank in the correct amount, payable to Friedkin's Travel Shop from the joint account of Neal and Vicky MacGregor.

CHAPTER 31

An Imaginary Friend

The morning after Vicky's disastrous, drunken reappearance, Neal sat at the kitchen table with his head in his hands and his breakfast barely touched. His toast and jam tasted like cardboard and glue. He had hardly slept; his eyelids were lined with steel wool, and even though the sun shone brightly, the forest and sea view from the kitchen windows appeared to him to be out of focus and drained of color, like a blurred black-and-white photograph overlaid with a pall of gray. His head and heart ached in equal measure with the memory of the previous night. Not only had Vicky embarrassed him in front of Barbara and Murray, but she had threatened to take Owen from him. After insulting and upsetting everyone, she had collected her clothes and left, slamming the door on the way out. He had to accept that she had no intention of coming back, and their marriage was over.

The one bright moment of the morning was when Murray called to check on him. "Yes, I'm fine," Neal lied. He apologized again for Vicky's behavior and told Murray that he looked forward to seeing him and Sarah again next Saturday. Neal kept the conversation light. He simply couldn't bring himself to tell Murray that Vicky had left him. He replaced the receiver with mixed feelings. The thought that a new friend like Murray had more concern for him than his wife of eight years was painful.

His weekend was a mental ordeal. He kept himself from dropping into depression by sheer will, like a man suspended over an abyss, traversing an endless rope, one determined handhold after another. He graded papers, chopped firewood, washed the car, and he would have mowed on Sunday if it hadn't rained all day. He even took Barbara's place in the kitchen to keep himself busy. He was relieved when he made it to Monday and he could go to work. Teaching grounded him, gave him a frame, a purpose, and a sense of worth. The grayness of his inner vision receded a little.

That evening, after dinner, while Owen played on the porch, he and Barbara sat in the den. Neal told his grandmother about the situation, and Barbara responded, "Vicky has made her choice, lad, and a poor one it is, too. But remember it is more about her than about you. You have been a good husband, scads more tolerant than most. You have provided her with a lovely home, and never given her reason to doubt you. Believe me, a better man she will never find. She herself, not you, is the cause of her unhappiness. This man she has run off with is not the solution to her problems. She is looking for happiness outside herself, and I'll wager she'll have a bumpy ride down a long road before she discovers that happiness does not depend on outer factors or other people. It depends on oneself, on one's sense of self-worth and code of honor.

"So I say, the best thing for you to do is to look forward, not back. Go about your business, Neal, and begin your new life free from the atmosphere of bitterness and hostility."

As Barbara paused, they heard Owen's voice through the open front door. "There it goes!" he shouted, followed by a loud clatter and his high-pitched laugh.

"What's he doing?" asked Neal.

"Oh, he's been having a jolly good time talking to his imaginary playmate, and constructing things with his wooden building blocks. I think he built a tower or something and then gave it a tumble."

"Sounds like it," Neal agreed.

"Let's make it higher this time, Tod," Owen said in an excited tone of voice.

Neal and Barbara could hear every word. "We'll make a hotel with a swimming pool." They heard the sound of blocks being stacked. "What?" Owen asked. "Okay, we'll make a restaurant, too."

"What an imagination the lad has," remarked Barbara. "And speaking of Owen, I can't imagine the court would award Vicky custody when she is the one who left her son, Neal. You are employed and she is not, and you provide a good home for Owen, which at the moment, she certainly cannot."

"I hope you're right, Grandma, but traditionally in cases like this, judges award custody to the mother."

They heard Owen run down the hall toward the kitchen.

"But it does seem obvious that I can provide a more stable environment than Vicky. Hope the court will see it the way you and I do, Grandma." Neal rubbed his face in his hands. "I'm going to try to take your advice about looking forward, not back. The first shock is over with, and I feel much better today than I did over the weekend. But my mind is like a dog chained to a tree, running and running in tiresome circles."

Owen raced back down the hall and out to the porch again.

"He's busy tonight, isn't he?" Neal remarked. "I worry about him and the custody battle, and then about him and that damned Erlking. My mind goes round and round. I wish I could control my thoughts. At least at school, I am able to focus. My classes—"

"Neal," Barbara interrupted him, frowning. "I smell smoke."

He sniffed the air. "Did we leave something cooking on the stove?"

"No. Oh, my God, it's coming from the porch!"

They sprang up at the same time, but Neal got to the door first. "What the hell?" he blurted. Owen crouched against the wall of the house avoiding the smoke while flames consumed one section of the two-foot tall playhouse he had built.

"I'm sorry, Daddy." Owen was wide-eyed with fright.

Barbara rushed to Owen's side, while Neal dealt with the fire. He kicked the burning blocks toward the front steps with his insteps, guiding them deftly like a soccer player, until he had booted all the burning pieces of wood out onto the lawn. Then he ran around the side of the house and returned with a garden hose. After he soaked all the blocks and one charred potato with water, he hosed down the porch for good measure.

In the meantime, Barbara had taken Owen into the den and extracted the whole story. "He's unhurt," she told Neal when he came in and sat down on the sofa next to his son.

A worried-eyed Owen did not wait for Neal to ask what happened. "Daddy, I didn't mean to do it. I'm sorry. I didn't know the fire would get that big. I built a hotel with a restaurant, and I wanted to make a meal, so I put cooking oil on a potato and I got matches from the kitchen to light the fire. And then the fire whooshed up and got big real fast."

"What possessed you to pull a stunt like that, Owen?" Neal's anger welled up like a geyser, surprising him by its suddenness and strength. "That's not like you. If Grandma and I hadn't smelled the smoke and got there in time, that fire could have burned you and destroyed all or part of the house."

Owen's lip quivered. "I know."

"Don't ever light a fire again alone like that."

"But Daddy, I—"

Neal raised his voice, "And don't tell me you were with your friend. We've been through that one before—he's an imaginary friend. Never, ever play with matches by yourself. If I am there with you, you can help light fires in the fireplace or bonfires down on the beach, but never by yourself. Is that perfectly clear?"

Owen nodded. "I'm sorry."

Consumed with worry about his son's safety for weeks, Neal found it infuriating that Owen had so foolishly endangered himself. It was the crowning irony in the series of recent events, the equivalent of building a great dike to protect the city against the sea, only to have the same city torched by its own inhabitants. Neal thought he might explode with anger. He hoped his fuse was long enough to last until the boy left the room. Narrowly controlling himself, he hugged his son, "It's all right, Owen. I know you didn't mean any harm."

Barbara, sensing Neal's agitation, hurried Owen out. "Well, lad," she told the boy, "It's been a busy evening, and I think the safest place for you now is bed. Let's go, quick march."

As they left the room, Neal's fury flared. Was there a safe place for Owen in this infernal house? Maybe he should have let the goddamned place burn to the ground. Mentally and emotionally tired from the disintegration of his marriage and all the worry and fear about Owen, the looming custody battle and the threatening Erlking, his mind whirled round and round, round and round. At school, he was able to focus; his classes had his full attention, but it was another matter at home. Home was supposed to be safe, but no, not here. Here on the third floor was the prime danger. Wasn't it enough to have to fight for his son against the boy's own mother without having to battle a demon, too, the son-of-a-bitch?

Neal couldn't sit still any longer. He went to the kitchen and got a beer, but his real desire was to take a baseball bat and beat the hell out of something. After a moment's thought, he chose the next best thing. From the laundry room, he got his long-handled ax, then he left the house and walked to the edge of the forest. He found a fallen tree, and after a long pull on his beer, he put the bottle on the ground and set to work. He hacked at the log in a fury, hurling blow after blow, grunting with the effort. He exulted in the feel of the ax in his hands and the violent, satisfying impact when the blade bit into the wood. Let the goddamned chips fly where they may, he thought, pounding the log with rage and frustration in every stroke. He stopped fifteen minutes later, sweat-soaked and leaden-armed, with blisters on both hands, spent.

Heaving for breath, he finished off the beer. Then with the ax propped on his shoulder, he walked to the bluff and looked out at the sea. The water, overlaid with mother-of-pearl, glimmered iridescent in silvery blues and pinks in the fading light. He stood for a long time, breathing hard, listening to the rhythm of the surf, and letting his own fatigue and the serenity of the great open space calm him. He tried not to think at all. He wanted to forget himself and blend into the picture before him, to be part of it, to partake of the immense peace, not as a separate entity, but to actually *be* the cool, salt-laden currents of air and the vast, red-gold sunset sky mirrored in the deep waters.

He sat cross-legged on the grass, slowed his breath, and concentrated. By focusing on his breathing, he stopped his thoughts and entered that still inner world where who he was seemed to expand and somehow contain the outer world. There he remained for as long as he could, until his breathing returned to normal.

With his equilibrium restored, he felt steady, centered. His mind was clear, and he felt better prepared to deal with his problems. It dawned on him then that if a man had to fight an enemy, the more knowledge he had about that enemy, the better chance that he might prevail. What was a demon? It might help to define the term.

Neal returned to the house, put away the ax, and climbed the stairs to the study. To his surprise, the padlock was engaged. Was the Erlking bored with his usual game? Or had he found another one? Neal wondered briefly why there had been a lull recently in the demonic activity. Not that he wished for more. But it worried him a little; maybe it was like the eye of a hurricane, an unnatural calm before the storm struck again with greater fury. Well, he didn't know, and he couldn't control circumstances. All he could do was prepare for the battle.

After unlocking the padlock, he took down a dictionary, and looked up the word *demon*. The dictionary gave the first root word as the Latin *daemon*—spirit, evil spirit. The Greek word *daimon* meant deity, tutelary divinity, genius, and later evil spirit. A supernatural being of Greek mythology, Neal read, holding a place between gods and men; an inferior deity; often an attendant or indwelling spirit; an animating influence of irresistible power.

Well, not completely irresistible. The mystical piper had dispelled the creature on the beach at Dunkirk. The Erlking therefore was very powerful, very evil, and very possibly deadly, but an inferior deity, holding a place between gods and men, not omnipotent, not unconquerable. Neal remembered in Murray's description of the three worlds, corporeal, psychic, and spiritual, that the demon belonged to the psychic realm and was therefore not as powerful as spiritual beings. It gave him some hope. But so far the Erlking had won every battle. How could he, Neal, win the war?

Ah, God, he needed inspiration. There's a word, he thought. He picked up the dictionary and found the word *inspire*. From the Latin *inspirare*, in

+ breathe. To breathe or blow into or upon. (obs. or archaic: as to inspire a musical instrument); also, to breathe or blow (air, etc.) into or upon something.

"Hmph," Neal grunted, "a reference to music." Murray was right—the only time the Erlking had been banished, he had been routed by music. The demon, an invisible entity, had been dispelled by music, invisible energy. But where that led, Neal didn't know. Nowhere, really. He still didn't know what to do; he had no answer, no solution.

"What do you think, Grandma?" He and Barbara were alone in the parlor that night after Owen had gone to bed.

She placed her glass of red wine on the coffee table and fingered the small gold Celtic cross she always wore at her throat. "A demon, an inferior deity," she mused. "And the other word," she said slowly, "the word *inspire* is a reference to music, to breathe or blow upon." She paused in thought, brow wrinkled and eyes gazing into space. After a moment, she glanced at Neal, and there was hope in her eyes. "To breathe or blow upon. Breath or wind is the symbol of the Holy Spirit."

Neal was not moved. "But Grandma, how does that help us?"

"First by prayer, and then by faith. God is sovereign over all things, and somehow He will lead us aright."

"I hope so," he said. But his hope seemed like a tiny ship on the churning dark sea of his fear for Owen.

To sooth himself that week, and for diversion, he played the bagpipes. "Outside, mind you," ordered Barbara. "They're too earsplitting in the house."

"Yes, ma'am," said Neal.

He liked to play at dusk, the loneliest hour of the day. He played medleys of marches, reels, slow airs, and strathspeys. He played *pibroch*, ceremonial music for the bagpipes, consisting of a slow theme or ground, followed by a series of increasingly complex variations. He practiced the fragment of music Barbara had notated in Ian's journal, the tune Ian reconstructed from memory after his harrowing experience at Dunkirk. In that music Neal found an added measure of comfort because he felt a connection to his grandfather, who was often on his mind that week. Neal wore a path in the lawn, pacing back and forth, in sight of the sea, and somehow, the music conspired with nature to give him moments of peace and solace. He played daily, taking his comfort where he could.

But it was not only comfort he gained from playing, it was also physical fatigue, which made it easier to sleep at night. Playing the bagpipes was a battle in itself, a real workout. He had to blow continually into the bag to keep it inflated, while maintaining constant pressure on it with his left arm so the wind flowed out steadily against the double reeds. It was the irresistible force (the air) against the immovable object (the bag). It all had to balance perfectly to produce the music.

Balance, the element that was missing in his house and his personal life. Vicky was gone and though the marriage had limped along for years, its sudden death had shocked Neal. But he and Owen were adjusting. During the first week of Vicky's absence, Owen had asked about her often, "When is Mamma coming back?" But as time went on, his questions dwindled and then ceased, primarily because Barbara created such stability in the house. Owen shadowed his grandmother and thrived under her care. Meals were certain and on time; Owen and Neal had clean clothes to wear, and the house shone.

As Barbara had predicted, Vicky's departure released a great deal of tension from the house. Free of Vicky's screaming outbursts and the strain caused by her steady, simmering hostility, the three MacGregors settled into their own peaceful routine. In the evenings after dinner, Owen practiced piano; Barbara read and sometimes watched television with Owen. Neal began to read and grade the interviews his students e-mailed him for the *Links* project, which were due on Friday. Otherwise, he played the pipes, and listened to music. Sad it was, thought Neal that they were better off without Vicky.

Late on Friday afternoon, after dinner, Barbara suggested that they take a walk.

"Let me check my e-mail first, Grandma. All the interviews of World War II veterans are due today," Neal said. He ran up to the study and came down after fifteen minutes or so. "I've got them all except one," he told Barbara as they walked with Owen across the lawn to the staircase at the edge of the bluff. "Jack Baird, Bitsy's cousin, hasn't sent his in yet. There's always one who misses the deadline."

"Well, put work out of your mind for a while, and let's enjoy the evening," his grandmother suggested. Barbara, whose zest for walking equaled a greyhound's delight in running, was as spry as a woman half her age, and Neal was pleased to see that she had no trouble negotiating the wooden stairs. As they strolled along the strand, she remarked, "Be thankful for all your blessings. It's a beautiful place you have here, Neal, the house and the property. You have a spectacular ocean view, and your orchard is going to provide you with heaps of fruit later in the year, plums, cherries, apples, and pears. It makes my mouth water to think of it," Barbara laughed. She took his arm as they walked, "You know, Ian would have been delighted that you used the money from him as a down payment on the house."

"I had hoped so."

Barbara looked ahead down the beach where Owen poked among the rocks. "And the wee, red-haired lad is a corker. He's so bright, talented, and handsome. Of all your blessings, he is the chief one."

"That he is, Grandma. And my chief fear is for him."

"I know, lad. I pray every night that we'll find a way." She clasped the small gold Celtic cross at her throat. "We'll see what the four of us can come up with tomorrow night."

"You'll get to meet Sarah tomorrow, Grandma. She's a corker, too."

"Is she now? She must be if she's related to that blue-eyed charmer Murray Appleman."

Late that night, as was his custom, after Owen and Barbara had gone to bed, Neal listened to music, everything from Renaissance madrigals to Handel operas, classical symphonies, Dixieland jazz, and ragtime. The last song he always played was, "Music of the Waterfall," with its haunting refrain:

O my love she is fair and she is small,
Her singing, like the music of the waterfall,
So pure, so sweet my heart does call.
O Annie, my fairest, rarest of them all.

Not Annie, but black-haired, blue-eyed Sarah called his heart. Kissing Sarah that day on the beach had been inevitable. Night after night, he relived the moment. She stood so close to him in the circle of his arms that he could smell the scent of her hair. She had been out of breath, cheeks flushed from her slide down the bluff face. Her pupils were dilated and her lips were slightly parted. As she had apologized for falling, he hadn't been able to restrain himself a moment longer, and he had kissed her mid-sentence. And, oh, how she had responded. Surrounded by wind, sea, sand, they had been unaware of anything but each other.

He hated the terrible awkwardness that arose between them afterwards. It grieved him to think that he had offended Sarah in any way. She had avoided him since then, he knew, declining to come to his house for dinner. The worst memory from the day he kissed her was the sadness in Sarah's eyes when he left. He wanted so much to make those eyes shine with delight.

And maybe sometime soon he would get his chance to do just that, now that Vicky had moved out and told him she wanted a divorce. Sarah didn't yet know that his wife had left him. On Saturday, the day after the dinner he'd hosted, after Vicky's outrageous behavior, when Murray had called him to find out how he was, Neal hadn't told Murray either. By then Vicky was gone, but the separation was still too new and too raw for him to discuss. But he would tell Murray and Sarah soon. Very soon.

Neal went up to bed. He would see Sarah tomorrow, on Saturday, for dinner at her house with Murray, Barbara, and Owen. They would put their heads together once more to try to find a solution. As he lay in bed, looking forward to seeing Sarah again, his heart beat faster. Then his mind drifted to the purpose of their meeting, finding a solution to the Erlking, the infernal infestation here in the house, and his stomach knotted up. Was there a solution? Or would Owen's life be forfeit on his seventh birthday? And the absent Vicky—why did she have no concern for her son? Her neglect of Owen galled him mightily. "Damn it," he muttered.

His thoughts ran in circles, like a dog chained to a tree. Owen, the Erlking, Vicky. Round and round, round and round, getting nowhere.

Neal turned on his side, punched his pillow, and tried to sleep.

CHAPTER 32

A Scenic Detour

V icky wiggled her freshly painted fingernails in the air to dry. The long, rounded nails shimmered in brilliant, enamel red, like foil party balloons. She loved the color red. It was fun, flamboyant, just the way life should be. The way her life was beginning to be. Five-thirty on Saturday and here she was on Jim's deck with margarita number three right beside her, buzzed and enjoying it. Nothing wrong with that. She had not a care in the world. She picked up her cigarette gingerly from the ashtray beside her and put it between her lips, then took a deep drag and practiced blowing smoke rings.

She had left Jim inside watching the Mariner's game, drinking beer and reclining on the couch in his shorts. Vicky was no fan of baseball. The one-bedroom house, a former fishing cottage, seemed too small for the blaring television clatter, so she had gone out to the deck. The house, perched in isolation on a hillside among the trees, faced the strait, halfway between Coveland and Stone Harbor. Jim had built the small deck and furnished the interior with comfortable furniture.

Vicky enjoyed the warm afternoon even though the bright sun created a glare on the water that made her squint. She sat on the deck planking with her feet on the steps. When the stupid game ended, they were going out to eat at a good seafood restaurant in Stone Harbor. She smiled as she flicked the ashes off her cigarette. In just two weeks together, they had eaten dinner at six different restaurants, gone dancing twice, and seen three movies. Quite an inventory. And *ooh-la-la*—Vicky chuckled and blew on her fingertips, the sex was terrific. Like mangos and papaya after a life of lima beans. Nothing in her marriage could compare to this week with Jim Nordquist.

Only during her childhood, as the baby in the family of three girls, had she been the object of so much attention. Marilyn, the oldest, was the smart one, plain Annie was the funny one, but she, pretty Vicky, was the cute one. Everyone said so. She had Daddy wrapped around her little finger. And he wasn't the only one; males of all ages took notice of Vicky Stevenson. From the sixth grade on, the boys had telephoned. In high school she never lacked for admirers, and it thrilled her still, remembering the night she reigned as Homecoming Queen. Who would have thought her life would be anything but more of the same?

Her sisters' destinies, on the other hand, were predictably humdrum. Marilyn the lawyer had married bald, pudgy Harold the accountant. Annie's husband, pale, moon-faced Derek, was an agent at the insurance company where Annie was a secretary. Vicky crossed her eyes. Oatmeal was more exciting.

In comparison, attractive, red-haired Neal MacGregor had seemed to Vicky like some sort of prize. What a royal mistake. Vicky covered her face with her hands. Her life with him was more of a dead end than either Marilyn's or Annie's dull existences. Neal had disappointed her in every way. He didn't make enough money; he didn't appreciate her—oh no, Owen was more important to him than she was. Hell, *history books* were more important to Neal than his wife. Some marriage—their sex life had long since dwindled to nothing. Not to mention the last bit—his half-cracked hallucinations about effing ghosts.

Ah, God, she didn't want to waste another moment thinking about her marriage. She wanted to stay in the present, where life was good again thanks to tall, sexy Jim Nordquist. What a prince! He had money, he enjoyed the same things she did, and unlike boring Neal, he knew how to treat a woman. She was Jim's sexy lover, not some sort of combination house maid, cook, and mother.

Mother. "Damn it!" Vicky squeezed her eyes shut. Why'd she have to think about the kid and spoil all her fun? She stubbed out her cigarette and gulped the rest of her margarita. *Owen.* She licked her lips and set the glass down. She'd get custody of Owen, but not just yet—she needed time off, time to enjoy life while she was still young. But eventually she'd get custody. It would all be okay. Jim was going to divorce his wife and she'd divorce Neal. Then she and Jim and Owen would make a new life.

A tinny television roar went up inside the house and Jim came out onto the deck. "Game's over," he said and drained the last of his can of beer.

"Who won?"

"Mariners by two." He walked a little unsteadily to the edge of the deck and pitched the beer can into the trees. He sat down heavily beside her, grabbed a handful of her hair at the back near the crown and pulled. When her head snapped back and her chin came up, he ground his mouth into hers. Vicky squirmed away, breathing hard, "Ouch, Jim, you hurt me." She rubbed her scalp with one hand and touched her lips with the other.

"Did I?" He put an arm around her waist and whispered in her ear. "Hey, pretty baby, I thought you liked it rough." He nibbled at her ear, then took her hand and brought her to her feet. "Let's go inside, and I'll make it up to you." With his arm around her, he propelled her toward the door. Inside, he fell onto his back on the sofa and drew her down on top of him, hands roaming over her body.

"Let me close the door and turn off the TV," Vicky said, pushing away from him.

"No, stay here," Jim answered, holding her down with one arm while he unbuttoned her blouse. "Nobody's out there. It's just you and me in the wilderness, baby, and I'm in a hurry."

An hour later, Vicky stepped out of the shower and draped a towel around herself. When she walked into the kitchen, Jim was standing at the counter, drinking another beer and watching the sunset through the open doorway. He beckoned to her with one finger.

When she walked over to him he kissed her lightly, running a finger back and forth across the curving line of her breasts at the top edge of the towel. Then he gave her a sip of his beer and leered at her from under his heavy eyelids, "Ready for another go?"

He stood in a rectangle of light cast by the setting sun. The light gilded the blonde hairs of his arms and chest and Jim squinted against the glare, making his pupils invisible. When he threw back his head and raised the can to his lips, the movement of his angular, elongated shadow caught Vicky's eye, passing like a specter against the wall behind him, a distorted, monstrous caricature.

She jerked involuntarily and shivered with a sudden chill. "Ooh, shut the door, Jim. I'm cold." As she turned to go into the bedroom to change, she gripped the towel with white-knuckled fingers and snapped, "And don't stand there drinking all day. Let's get to the restaurant. I'm hungry."

By the time they left for the restaurant in Jim's pickup truck, the sun had dipped below the treetops. He zigzagged erratically along the narrow track through the woods toward the road at a high speed, veering abruptly from side to side in the gathering darkness, steering perilously close to the trees and laughing whenever Vicky shrieked. When they turned onto the road, he drove toward Coveland instead of Stone Harbor.

Vicky wrinkled her brow and looked at him, "Where are you going?"

Jim glanced at her and smiled, "A little scenic detour."

Sarah skipped a stone off the crest of a small wave, watching it bounce high into the air and then plummet out of sight beneath the water. Up, then down, like the course of her emotions. Tonight was the night she would see Neal—she couldn't delay it any longer. Anticipating dinner with the MacGregors gave her enough butterflies to send her aloft and keep her there for days, like a blimp. Spending time with Neal again was what she longed for and feared most, because she could not predict her inward reaction, and she was afraid she might go into a funk again. Well, she had to face him sometime, and that sometime would be in the next half hour or so.

It had been one week since she'd asked Neal and his family to dinner. Seven days had passed as swiftly as a night's sleep: close the eyes and it was morning. To Sarah, the week had been like a rampart, a defense against the pain of seeing Neal again, and each day's passing chipped away at the wall. Tonight the wall was gone and she stood naked of cover.

During the past week, Sarah had occupied herself with her World War II research, work at the travel shop, walks with the dog, and playing the viola, but thoughts of Neal were as persistent as the island's ever-present wind, a fact of life. Well, Sarah thought thankfully, the business they had to discuss would help divert her mind from personal matters, and there was much to consider. Murray had shown her some fascinating material he had found in his research. For her part, after sifting through ten books, she had discovered accounts of the massacres of the British soldiers in May of 1940, by two different authors, and she intended to present her evidence tonight.

Her preparations for the evening had been painstaking. The house was immaculate, and almost all the cooking was done—the salad in the refrigerator, two blackberry pies cooling, and she'd left the salmon baking in the oven under Murray's supervision. All she had to do when she got home was change clothes, heat up the peas, and pop the dinner rolls in the oven.

"Time to go home, Mazie," Sarah called. It had been a beautiful day, but now it was dusk, and in spite of her warm clothes, she was beginning to feel the cold. The wind whipped off the strait, and the beach was deserted. The dog was far down the shore digging at the base of the bluff, but when she heard Sarah call, she wheeled and bounded back up the sand, her long, reddish-blonde fur and plumed tail streaming in the wind.

Sarah smiled. Mazie ran open-mouthed with her red tongue hanging out to one side, all energy and unrestrained joy in fluid motion.

When Mazie rushed up to her, Sarah leaned down and ran her hands over the dog's head and down her sides, smoothing the soft, thick curly fur. Mazie looked up at Sarah with her beautiful brown eyes. "Good girl. You've had a nice run, so let's go home now. We've got guests coming for dinner."

Mazie ran easily up the steep slope of the bluff ahead of Sarah, dislodging small clods of earth. She waited at the top while Sarah clambered up as quickly as she could. When Sarah, breathing hard, reached the top of the bluff, Mazie had already crossed Beach Road. But instead of heading for Harlech Road and home as she usually did, she wandered over to a semicircular clearing between the trees, about thirty yards away down Beach Road. She was eagerly sniffing around some low bushes at the back of the clearing. Rabbits, Sarah guessed. Mazie thought they were the best game in town.

Sarah stayed on the narrow shoulder on the beach side of the road and cupped her hands around her mouth. "Mazie, come!" But the dog was too interested in the scent to heed Sarah. The light was fading fast, but Mazie's blonde fur was clearly visible in the gloom.

Sarah noticed a white pickup truck approaching as she jogged across the road. At this time of day, he should have his lights on, she thought. As she walked toward the clearing, the pickup truck gathered speed and began swerving from side to side. There were two people in the cab. Oh great, Sarah thought, it's probably some kid out to impress his girlfriend. "Mazie!" she shouted, "Mazie!" Still the dog sniffed and pawed in the bushes in the deepest part of the clearing, about fifteen feet away from the edge of the road.

When the pickup truck reached the far edge of the clearing, everything seemed to happen at once. Sarah saw the driver point at the dog, and then the truck lurched forward with a roar, veering sharply to the right, off the road into the clearing. He's joyriding, showing off; he'll make a squealing U-turn, Sarah thought. But she was wrong: he had no such intention. He barreled directly at the dog.

Sarah, powerless to stop the driver, watched in horrified disbelief. Mazie stood still, like a deer caught in headlights, and then, too late, bolted toward the trees. Sarah heard a sickening thud and Mazie's high-pitched yelp as the right side of the pickup struck the dog. The driver gunned the motor and then made a roaring U-turn in the clearing. With a squeal of tires, he rocketed back onto the asphalt and shot off into the gloom.

CHAPTER 33

Pythaǧorus and Company

Now Rhea, as Ceres, in Hymn XIV, is called "brass-sounding" and "drum-beating." This has reference to the mystical results of certain sounds and rhythm, part and parcel of what the Hindus call Mantravidyâ. I remember reading a curious old French book in the Bibliothèque de la Ville of Clermont-Ferrand, one of the books confiscated from the Minime Monastery of the same town, at the time of the Revolution. This work dealt with the magical properties of music, and described for what especial purposes the various instruments of music were used in the Temple-service of the Jews. Now Iamblichus (De Mysteries,III.ix) goes into the matter of the so-called Corybantic and Bacchic "frenzies" produced by musical instruments in the Mysteries of Ceres and Bacchus; and in his Life of Pythagoras (xxv) he, further, tells us that: "The whole Pythagoras school went through a course of musical training, both in harmony and touch whereby, by means of appropriate chants, they beneficially converted the dispositions of the soul to contrary emotions. For, before they retired to rest, they purified their minds of the [mental, says Quintilian] confusion and noises of the day, by certain songs and peculiar chants, and so prepared for themselves peaceful repose with either few or pleasant dreams. And again, when they rose from sleep, they freed themselves from drowsiness by songs of another character. And sometimes by means of melodies without words they cured certain affections and diseases, and this they say was the real means of "charming." And it is most probable that the word "charm" (epode) came into general use from them. It was thus, then, that Pythagoras established a most salutary system of regenerating the morals by means of "music."

289

M urray laid down G. R. S. Mead's slim volume entitled *Orpheus*. There it was in black and white: exactly what he had been thinking about. Exactly what we need, he thought. We're in the business of curing Neal MacGregor's house of a disease, and we can use the most powerful "charming" available. If only Pythagorus were here to direct us, we'd be in business.

More and more convinced that music was the key, Murray was as mystified as ever about what practical application would produce the desired result. Here and now in the twentieth century, who could know what melodies Pythagorus sang?

Deciding he could use a little liquid mood enhancer at the moment, Murray got up to pour himself a small glass of red wine. Returning to the kitchen table, he sipped his wine while he thought about some of the material he had found in his week of research. One of the most fascinating concepts, found in cultures the world over from antiquity to the present time, was that music had the power to levitate and transport heavy stones. There was the Greek myth of Amphion, the son of Zeus and Antiope, who was given a lyre by Hermes. To fortify the city of Thebes, Amphion played his lyre and the music made the stones fall into place in the city's walls. Similar legends existed about the building of Pre-Incan fortresses in the Peruvian Andes. There was even the eyewitness account recorded in the twentieth century by Swedish engineer Henry Kjellson, who described Tibetan monks levitating a block of stone that measured one and one-half meters long, one meter high and one meter wide, two hundred-fifty meters up the face of a cliff by chanting and playing thirteen drums and six trumpets. And of course, Hans Jenny's research with liquids pointed to the same conclusion, the anti-gravitational effect of music.

Murray had much to tell Neal. Picking up a thick volume of *The Golden Bough* that he had bookmarked on page fifty-four, he said, "And what do you have to say, Sir James George Frazer?"

But what function, we may ask, did string music perform in the Greek and the Semitic ritual? Did it serve to rouse the human mouthpiece of the god to prophetic ecstasy? Or did it merely ban goblins and demons from the holy places and the holy service, drawing as it were around the worshippers a magic circle within which no evil thing might intrude? In short, did it aim at summoning good or banishing evil spirits? Was its object inspiration or exorcism? The examples drawn from the lives or legends of Elisha and David prove that with the Hebrews the music of the lyre might be used for either purpose; for while Elisha employed it to tune himself to the prophetic pitch, David resorted to it for the sake of exorcising the foul fiend from Saul.

The oven timer buzzed and the doorbell chimed at the same moment. Murray was so surprised he dropped the book on the kitchen table. He looked at the oven, stood up, hesitated, took a step toward the front door, and then stopped. "When in doubt," he muttered, index finger pointing skyward, "food always comes first." He turned in the direction of the door and yelled, "Be there shortly!"

He turned off the timer, and after looking in three different drawers, he finally found a pair of oven mittens. He took the sizzling salmon in its shallow baking pan out of the oven and set it carefully on top of the stove. Then he hurried to answer the front door.

"Hi, Mr. Appleman."

"Come in, Bitsy." She was an exuberant presence. Murray, looking up at her, was charmed by her auburn mop of curls, coast-to-coast smile, and sparkling green eyes. "Sorry it took me a minute, Bitsy. The timer buzzed and I had to take the fish out of the oven."

"No problem." Bitsy walked in and sniffed, "Mmm, smells delicious. Boss is a darn good cook. Where is she?"

Murray shut the door. "She took Mazie out for a run on the beach. They should be back any minute now."

"Well, is there anything I can do?"

"Actually, yes. Could you check the salmon to see if it's done? As much as I love food, a chef I'm not."

"Sure," said Bitsy.

In the kitchen, she took the fork Murray handed her, broke off a pinkish-orange piece of the steaming fish and impaled it on the fork. "Looks done," she said, "but only tasting will tell."

"A girl after my own heart," said Murray.

"Mmm," Bitsy sighed, with her mouth full of fish, "perfect—a feast for the gods."

"Good," said Murray, "but how 'bout a taste for the older generation?"

Bitsy laughed and speared him another small morsel. "Here you are, Mr. Appleman, but don't tell on me."

"Absolutely not," Murray assured her. He ate his bite of salmon and rolled his eyes heavenward. "Scrumptious."

"Maybe we should put it back in the oven to keep it warm," Bitsy suggested.

"Good idea."

The doorbell chimed again. "Oh," said Murray, "that must be the MacGregors."

Bitsy said, "If you want to answer the door, Mr. Appleman, I'll take care of the fish."

"Yes, thank you, Bitsy." Murray hurried to the front door. When he opened it, Neal, dressed in a forest green shirt and khakis, proffered a bottle of cold white wine. "Hi, Murray. This is for dinner." Owen wore jeans, a light blue polo shirt, and his yellow windbreaker. He held a tall, white, fluted vase with a single red rose in it. "And this is for Sarah," he said.

"Hello, Murray Appleman," said Barbara.

Murray was aware that Neal said something, but he didn't hear another word after Barbara greeted him. He had looked forward to seeing her again, but when she shook his hand, an electricity that he thought he'd never feel again in this life shot up his arm directly into his heart. She was his type, small, slim, and lithe. Her thick, curly hair was a soft, glowing white halo that framed a face with strong, high cheekbones, beautiful skin, and two warm, dark-brown eyes whose clear, steady, intelligent gaze was locked with his. In fact, that gaze was rather amused, Murray realized, because he was standing in the doorway with his mouth open.

"Heavens, come in, all of you—I didn't mean to keep you standing on the threshold." He moved to the left of the door and extended his arm, ushering them in.

Bitsy came out of the kitchen and there was a round of introductions by Neal, who was glad to see his former student. "Grandma, this is Bitsy Baird, one of my best students at the high school, and first cousin to the renegade Jack Baird who has yet to turn in his history project."

Bitsy smiled, "Unlike myself, who was always punctual with assignments in your class."

"True," agreed Neal. "I remember it well."

Murray stood behind the trio of MacGregors, keeping his eyes and thoughts on Barbara. Seems about sixty, but was married at the beginning of World War II—about fifty-five years ago, he calculated. Must be close to my age. Sweet figure and moves like a girl.

Suddenly everyone turned to face him. Murray's eyes widened. Oh, hell—Neal had asked him a question and he hadn't even heard it. "Uh, what was that, Neal?"

"I asked about Sarah. Where is she?"

"Oh, she took the dog for a run down on the beach." Murray checked his watch, and looked up, puzzled. "Seven-fifteen? I didn't realize it was that late. She should have been back by now."

"Maybe I should go look for her," Neal said. "It's getting dark out there."

"I'll go with you, Mr. MacGregor," Bitsy offered. "I've been with her before and I know the route she takes when she walks the dog."

"Me, too," said Owen.

"Oh no, lad. You're not going gallivanting in the dark," Barbara declared. "You're staying here with me and Murray Appleman."

"Shoot!" said Owen.

"Come on, then, Bitsy," Neal said, opening the door for her. "Let's go find our hostess."

CHAPTER 34

In the Gloaming

S arah's heart pounded with fear as she ran through the fading light in the clearing toward the deeper gloom between the trees. Mazie lay unmoving where she had been thrown, about fifteen feet back into the woods. The dog's stillness was so profound that Sarah halted a few feet from her and approached very slowly and carefully.

"Mazie?" Even though Sarah spoke quietly, her voice cracked.

The wind moaned in the treetops, but the dog made no sound.

Sarah reached her dog and knelt down next to her. It was chill on the ground in the darkness and the smell of the firs and cedars was strong. The dog lay on her right side as though she were sleeping. The left side of Mazie's muzzle was torn and bloodied, but Sarah could see no other marks or wounds on her. She reached out with trembling fingers and gently stroked the dog's head.

"Mazie? Good girl, Mazie." Sarah touched the dog's ears and found them cold.

"Mazie? Mazie?"

There was no response.

Sarah lightly stroked the rough, curly fur of Mazie's shoulder and back, and then held her hand against the dog's side, feeling for breath, praying for movement. But there was none.

She squeezed her eyes shut and felt the burn of tears. She leaned forward, cradled the dog's head against her breast, and dissolved into sobs.

How could this be? She remembered Mazie flying down the beach just a few minutes ago, the light shining in her brown eyes, a picture of joy, and the sharp image, knifelike, ripped her heart. She buried her face in the dog's fur and let sorrow sweep over her like a floodtide.

After a while Sarah sat up and wiped her eyes. In the midst of her sadness and pain, she felt a rising anger. Why did this happen, for what? She gritted her teeth and clenched her fists. What possessed the driver to commit such an act of senseless, cruel malice against an innocent animal?

The wind picked up and Sarah began to feel the cold. She laid Mazie's head gently on the ground, sat upright and wiped her face. She'd have to walk home and get the Jeep, drive back and pick up the body. She had guests coming for dinner. Her face contorted in a spasm and she bowed her head and endured another fit of weeping. At last she stood up, wiped her face again, and whispered, "I'll be right back, Mazie. I'm going to take you home."

Her legs trembled as she walked unsteadily back through the clearing toward the road. It was fully dark and there were no streetlights.

"Sarah?"

As she reached the road, the man's voice surprised her, and for an instant she couldn't place it. When she looked toward Harlech Road, she saw Neal, and Bitsy was with him. They were running toward her, waving to get her attention. Sarah waited at the edge of Beach Road because she was afraid her trembling legs could not support her for even one more step.

"Sarah?" Neal's smile died when he saw her state. "What's wrong? You've been crying."

"Boss," said Bitsy, "where's Mazie?"

The question undid her. Sarah opened her mouth to speak, but instead of words, a low moan issued from it. Her face crumpled and she bowed her head.

"She's dead."

Bitsy gasped, and Neal took a step forward, lifting his hands slightly as though he was going to embrace Sarah, but then he stopped.

"She's dead," Sarah repeated in a flat tone. She turned her face toward Bitsy and said, "A pickup truck hit her." Her voice wobbled, "The man drove off the road to hit her on purpose. She's lying back there in the trees where she was thrown," Sarah pointed, "several feet back from center of the clearing."

Sarah looked up at Neal, "I didn't want to leave her alone, but I have to go get the Jeep. She's too heavy for me to carry and I've got to bring her home."

"Sarah, do you have the keys to the Jeep with you?" Neal asked.

"Yes."

"Then give them to me. I'll run back and get the Jeep. In the meantime, Bitsy can wait here with you and . . . and Mazie."

He took the keys and touched Sarah lightly on the back to guide her. "Come away from the road. It's dark out here, and I want you out of danger." He dropped his hand, and he and Bitsy escorted Sarah back toward the trees.

Deep inside the clearing Neal stopped and said, "Sarah, I know you feel unsteady, so hold onto Bitsy's arm and go with her."

Sarah obediently gripped Bitsy's left arm. "I'd like to stay near Mazie."

"All right, Boss. Let's walk."

"I'll be back as soon as possible," Neal said. He turned and ran for the road, clutching Sarah's keys in his hand.

Sarah directed Bitsy to the place where Mazie lay. The blonde fur of the dog gleamed, a bright spot in the darkness. "I think I have to sit down," Sarah said. She sat at the base of a fir tree, about five feet from Mazie's head. She closed her eyes and leaned back against the tree trunk. "I'm exhausted," she breathed.

"Well, rest there a little, Boss. Mr. MacGregor won't be long."

Bitsy crouched beside Sarah and looked at the body of the dog while the wind sighed in the treetops. "Do you remember anything about the truck?"

"It was white—an older model. A Ford, I think, but I'm not good at recognizing trucks."

"Did you notice the license number?"

Sarah shook her head. "I was so horrified—" her voice caught and she had to stop before finishing her sentence. After a moment she said, "I didn't even think about it."

Bitsy looked at the dog. "Who would want to hurt such a beautiful animal?"

"I think it was a guy trying to show off for his girlfriend. The bastard. It was dusk and I couldn't see clearly."

"And now it's dark and I can't see clearly," said Bitsy, her eyes on the dog, "but just now, I thought Mazie—"

Sarah looked up when Bitsy stopped speaking abruptly. "You thought Mazie—what?"

"Moved." Bitsy's voice wobbled. She cleared her throat and pointed, "Boss, Mazie moved."

"What?" Sarah shot to her feet and bounded over to the dog, falling on her knees beside her.

"Mazie!" Sarah was wide-eyed. "Bitsy, she's breathing—she's alive. Oh, thank God." She touched the dog's side gently and Mazie opened her eyes and lifted her head.

"She must have been knocked unconscious," Bitsy said.

Mazie scrabbled to her feet, but when she tried to walk, her rear end faltered on the left side.

"Oh, she's injured," Sarah said. "Looks like her left leg or hip is broken." Sarah commanded, "Down, Mazie."

The dog barked and lay down, breathing rapidly. Sarah knelt on one knee beside Mazie and gripped her collar with one hand and put the other arm around the dog's back and side. "Bitsy, when Neal gets here, I want him to drive the Jeep as close as possible to us. We've got to keep her from moving too much and aggravating the injury. Would you run out to the road and direct him?"

"Sure thing, Boss." She sprinted away on her long legs.

Sarah laid her cheek against the side of Mazie's face and spoke in a quiet tone, "It's okay, girl. You're alive and we're gonna take you to the vet. Just hold on." And please God, she thought, closing her eyes and wishing with all her power, please don't let us injure her any more on the way.

It was only moments later when Sarah heard the familiar sound of the Jeep's engine and then saw the approaching headlights. Neal parked as close as possible and left the lights shining into the woods. He and Bitsy vaulted out of the Jeep. They smiled as they approached on the run.

"How great that she's alive, Sarah," Neal said. "Do you think she can walk to the Jeep?"

"No, I don't. I'm afraid she'll injure herself more. There's something wrong with one of her back legs."

"I could carry her," Neal suggested.

"Oh, could you, please? Lift her from the right side. It's the left side that's injured."

"Bitsy," Neal said, "go open the back of the Jeep."

"And, Bitsy," Sarah added, "there's a blanket in the back. Could you make a pad to lay her on?"

"Sure."

Neal knelt on the right side of Mazie. "Hey, pretty girl, we've got to get you in the Jeep." He stroked the side of her muzzle with the back of his hand. "I'm not going to hurt you." He moved down and placed one hand under her chest and the other under her hindquarters. The dog growled, low in the throat, but she didn't snap at him.

"It's all right, Mazie," said Sarah. "She's hurting," Sarah told Neal, "but I don't think she'll bite you." She reassured Mazie in a quiet voice as Neal carried the dog to the Jeep.

Neal laid the dog on the pad Bitsy had prepared.

"If you drive, Neal, I can stay back here with her," Sarah said.

"Okay."

"Let's go back to my house and I'll call the vet," Sarah said. "His office is closed, but the answering machine gives an emergency number."

"All right," said Neal. "Hop in the front, Bitsy. Let's go get this dog mended."

CHAPTER 35

Fractures

It was a thirty-minute drive from Sarah's house to the Stone Harbor Animal Clinic, but Neal intended to get there in less than twenty. The clinic always had a veterinarian on emergency call after-hours, and one of the vets was on his way to meet him and Sarah there. He kept his foot heavy on the accelerator and his eye on the road ahead, intermittently checking the rearview mirror for cops, as he drove eighty in a sixty-mile-an-hour zone. Sarah rode in the back of the Jeep with Mazie, as they sped down the curving, narrow two-lane road that bisected the hilly, sparsely inhabited area between Coveland and Stone Harbor. The headlights illuminated stretches of forest interrupted at intervals by the cleared land of dairy farms and berry fields.

Neal's anxiety about the dog was like an icy wind at his back, worrying him and hastening him along. Although Sarah's spirits soared when she discovered that Mazie was alive, Neal was well aware that the dog might have internal injuries that could yet kill her. It angered him and grieved him greatly to see Mazie injured, and Sarah's distress and sorrow had touched him just as deeply. When he and Bitsy found her in tears near the road, he had wanted to enfold her in his arms, but he had restrained himself for fear of offending her again. This time, thankfully, he was not the cause of her suffering, but he intended to discover who was. He'd get the son-of-a-bitch fined or jailed and make him pay the cost of Mazie's medical treatment.

"How's Mazie doing?" Neal called to Sarah.

"She's holding her own. No worse, I think. Just breathing too fast."

They had left Bitsy with Murray, Barbara, and Owen at Sarah's house. Sarah, relieved that her dog was alive, had urged them all to eat dinner, putting Murray in charge. She had promised to call them after the vet examined Mazie.

As the road curved to the right, Neal passed a cluster of houses on the hill to the left and entered Stone Harbor. He drove down Harbor Street toward the naval base. At Highland Street he turned left and found the Animal Clinic in the second block on the right. Sarah waited in the Jeep while he rang the lighted doorbell. He got no response. When he peered into the crack between the window and the mini-blinds, all he could see was part of a dimly lit waiting room. But the room suddenly flooded with light, and Neal could hear the sound of steps as someone hurriedly approached the door from the inside. He heard the snap when the deadbolt was retracted, and then a massive man with a full black beard and a shaved head opened the door. Under the green gown he was tying together, he was dressed in jeans and a sweatshirt.

"I'm Dr. Ruderian. Where's the dog?"

"In the Jeep."

"Let's bring her in."

On a metal table in the back, Dr. Ruderian examined Mazie gently and carefully while Sarah explained what had happened to the dog. "When I found her lying so still, I thought she was dead," Sarah finished.

"Well, she was unconscious and her breathing was probably extremely shallow. You are very lucky she's alive. She may have a fractured pelvis, but to be sure I'll have to take some x-rays." He smoothed his beard with his left hand. "I've got to treat Mazie for shock, and give her fluids, and that will take time. There's nothing more you can do here." The vet paused and said to Sarah, "Why don't you eat some dinner and try to relax?"

Sarah's hair was windblown and there were blotches of dried blood on her blouse. "Do you think she'll be okay?"

"I hope so. Of course the x-rays will tell me what I need to know. There's always the chance of internal injuries, and she may need surgery.

We'll know in a few hours. But a young dog in good health like this is a healing machine. She'll recover in leaps and bounds. I'll call you when I know exactly what needs to be done. In the meantime, I suggest you go home and get some rest."

Sarah gave him her home telephone number and told him to call no matter what time of night. There were tears in her eyes as she told Mazie goodbye.

Out on the street, Sarah wiped her eyes and told Neal, "I'm so weary, I feel like *I've* been hit by a truck."

"Well, let me drive you back to Coveland. And why don't we stop somewhere on the way and get you some coffee or tea?"

"That would be great."

They climbed back into the Jeep, and Neal started the engine. As he pulled away from the curb, it seemed to him that the vehicle had become a soundproof chamber: the silence in the cab pressed on his ears and jangled his nerves. In effect, it was like the changing of the guard, Neal thought; they had swapped one kind of tension for another. He was relieved that the dog was taken care of, but without Mazie, he and Sarah were left alone with each other, tense and tongue-tied. Neal's palms sweated and his mouth felt drier than Death Valley. As he made a quick U-turn and drove the Jeep up Highland Street, retracing their route, he wondered if Sarah was as nervous as he.

Since they were alone and could talk privately, Neal wanted to tell her about the collapse of his marriage, but he hesitated. Twice he opened his mouth to speak, but no words came out; he was unsure what Sarah's reaction might be. He finally decided on a wait-and-see strategy. Besides, as much as he was attracted to Sarah, he was a little reluctant to enter into another relationship so soon after his wife left him. A man had to protect himself. Wait and see—definitely the best plan.

Sarah cleared her throat. "Well, I didn't anticipate that seeing you again would be quite like this," she ventured. She clasped her hands tightly together and chewed on her lower lip.

"No, of course not. I'm sorry for the circumstances, but I am very glad you agreed to see me again and have all of us over for dinner."

"I um, well, I guess I overreacted that day on the beach. You know what I mean, and I just couldn't—"

Shaking her head and wringing her hands, she looked so distressed that Neal interrupted her. "Sarah, you don't have to explain yourself to me. Anyway, the fault was mine, not yours." Neal glanced at her and met her eyes. "Why don't we just let it go? That was then and this is now. Our current mission is to get you some coffee, agreed?"

"Agreed," she said.

Her smile pleased him inordinately, and the sudden lifting of tension in the Jeep was like the relief of a warship's crew when the All Clear sounded after a torpedo watch. It was damn near palpable, thought Neal.

Turning right onto Harbor Street, he told Sarah, "This is where we'll find a coffee shop." He drove slowly, scanning for a place to stop. "Hey, I know," he exclaimed, "there's Braverman's Seafood House. How about a cup of their clam chowder? It's the best on the planet. That'd be better than coffee on an empty stomach and it'll hold you until you get home. By the way, I've been looking forward to tasting your salmon and the blackberry pie."

Sarah smiled, "I hope you get the chance. It's possible Uncle Murr may have devoured it all."

Neal laughed, "Yet another reason to have some clam chowder: just in case."

"Okay, I can call Uncle Murr from the restaurant to let him know about Mazie and I'll find out if he left us a morsel or two."

Neal parked at a meter on the next side street. As they walked toward the restaurant, he tried to reassure Sarah, even as he resisted his impulse to take her hand in his. "I think Mazie will be all right. I had a good feeling about Dr. Ruderian, and I liked the way he examined her so thoroughly."

"I liked him, too. I love that dog and I hope she'll be all right." Sarah shook her head, "What kind of person would go out of his way like that to hit her?"

"A good question," he answered. "Coveland's a small town, a village, really. I bet we'll find out who did it eventually. What kind of pickup truck was it?"

Sarah shrugged, "I'm not sure. It was an older truck—white or a very light color." She scanned the vehicles parked along the street. "See that white pickup parked at the corner by the furniture store? It was similar to that."

"That's an old Ford and the guy who parked that truck needs driving lessons. It's about three feet from the curb and crooked to boot. Maybe he was in a hurry for Braverman's clam chowder," Neal said, opening the door to the restaurant for Sarah.

The warm, fragrant interior of the restaurant was paneled in dark wood. They entered a narrow foyer where a young hostess with cropped brown hair waited at her station to greet them. Beyond her was the bar, and the restaurant, small and intimate, opened out to the right, all its square, white-draped tables occupied. "Saturday night," said Neal, "and a full house. At least no one is waiting to be seated."

In the foyer, he explained to the hostess that he wanted two cups of chowder to take out, and Sarah added hot tea to the order. While Sarah called Murray from the hostess' station to report on Mazie, Neal observed her. There was an untamed quality in her disheveled, windblown hair, the curling tendrils darkly framing her fair face. Neal smiled to himself—add a garland of flowers and she could be Titania, Shakespeare's Fairy Queen. There was even a faint fragrance about her of the outdoors, like a wild creature. He noticed the cuplike hollow at the base of her throat and the curving line of her generous mouth. She was the perfect size for him; her head would fit in the crook of his neck.

In the midst of her telephone conversation, she glanced at him and smiled. There was something so direct and open and free in her eyes that Neal felt himself tumble, out of control. How can it be, he wondered, that a whole world can unveil itself in a single glance? And in that moment he was lost; the fortress of his heart was overcome without a struggle.

"We'll be home in about forty minutes," she told Murray. "See you soon." Replacing the receiver, she said, "Neal, I'm going to the restroom to clean up a little. I want to wash my face and hands and comb my hair. I'm a mess."

Disarmed as he was, Neal changed his strategy. Wait-and-see became seize-the-moment.

"Come here first," he said, beckoning her to follow him out of earshot from the hostess. "I have something important to tell you."

"What is it?" asked Sarah.

He faced her, gazing into her blue eyes, trying to find the right words. Having nightly relived the moment he had kissed her, he knew from Sarah's eager response on the beach that her desire matched his own. Convinced that her distress arose solely from the fact that he was a married man, he wanted to tell her without further delay that his wife stood between them no longer.

"Sarah, I—"

"Well, if it isn't Mr. History Teacher and Miss Shop Clerk."

Neal stiffened. What damned misfortune—it was Vicky, and she was with a tall, blonde, middle-aged man with hooded eyes and a red, flushed face. They had eaten and were leaving the restaurant. By her acid tone and loose demeanor, he knew she was drunk.

Neal forced himself to respond in a civil tone, "This is Sarah Friedkin, who *owns* the travel shop, Vicky. She is my friend."

"So nice to see you out with my husband." Vicky's smile was a mere showing of teeth.

Sarah's color bloomed, but she held Vicky's eye.

"Stop it right there, Vicky." Neal's voice rose, and he lifted his chin. "Unlike you, Sarah is completely blameless in this, and I won't hear one word against her. You've made your choice, for good or ill, and you'd better save your energy for dealing with the consequences."

"Yeah, and what about your consequences, little man?" Vicky's escort stepped too close to Neal and looked down at him from his six-inch height advantage. Neal could smell the alcohol on the man's breath.

"And who the hell are you?" Neal shot back.

"Jim Nordquist," Vicky retorted. "He's an airline pilot and twice the man you are." She pushed past Neal abruptly, and a wave of her perfume washed over him. Jim followed her, casting a malignant glance back at Neal, and then they were gone.

Neal stood staring straight ahead, clenching and unclenching his jaw. "I'm sorry you had to witness that scene, Sarah. I wanted to tell you about the situation myself, but now you know. That was my wife Vicky with her new boyfriend."

Sarah didn't respond, so Neal glanced at her. The expression on her face was apologetic.

"Neal, I've seen them together before."

He was startled, "You have?"

"Yes, they've been in my shop a couple of times, but I didn't know she was your wife until she paid with a personal check last week."

Neal crossed his arms over his chest and sighed, "I've been a fool. Their affair is probably old news in Coveland. The signs have been there for weeks, but I didn't want to read them."

"Well, no matter how or when one discovers infidelity, the impact is always staggering. I've been blindsided, too, and I know you're hurting." Sarah touched his arm. "But I'll tell you this: I think her taste in men has really plummeted. And her math is wrong. He's not even half the man you are. Not only does he look debauched, he looks really mean to me."

Neal gave Sarah a thoughtful glance. "He did look really mean, didn't he?" He snapped his fingers. "That's it!" He quickly took a twenty dollar bill out of his wallet and handed it to Sarah. "Take this in case the food comes. I'll be right back. Wait for me inside the restaurant, Sarah." He flashed a grin at her. "We've got lots more to discuss."

He dashed out the front door of Braverman's and saw Jim and Vicky walking unsteadily and out of step in the direction of the furniture store. He kept his distance, following them. He smiled when they got into the old white pickup truck. When Jim turned on the ignition, Neal backed into the recess of a storefront doorway to conceal himself from the truck's headlights. As the truck pulled away from the curb, Neal scanned it with the intensity of a sniper.

Seeing a pay telephone on the next block, he ran to it, fed it change, and got the number he wanted from information. He put in more coins, dialed the number, and spoke clearly and briefly. He was smiling broadly as he walked back to Braverman's.

Whistling "Highland Laddie," Neal opened the door to the restaurant. Sarah stood in the foyer balancing a stack of three large styrofoam cups with plastic lids, topped by a pile of paper napkins and three plastic spoons. "Welcome back," she said. "As soon as I got back from the restroom, dinner was served."

"This, my dear Sarah, is only the appetizer," he said. Neal took a spoon and his cup of clam chowder from her, then inclined his head and upper body in an Old World half-bow. "Well, my lady," he said, with a glint in his eye, gesturing toward the door, "all is well, and all manner of thing shall be well."

"I hope you're right about that," she said. "Your mood has certainly improved."

"Indeed."

"And are you going to tell me why?"

"Oh, yes." Neal opened the door for her. "In the chariot, on the way home."

CHAPTER 36

Magic

"*M*oonlight Sonata*," said Barbara.
"Made in England in the late thirties, with Paderewski playing himself. His airplane has trouble and lands in rural Sweden. He is taken into the home of a wealthy matron whose innocent young granddaughter has fallen in love with a clever, handsome gigolo. During the film, Paderewski plays a Chopin Polonaise, his own Minuet, and the first movement of Beethoven's *Moonlight Sonata.*"

Barbara shook her head, "You're much too clever, Murray. I was always a dedicated cinema-goer, even when I had to enjoy it alone after Ian came back blinded from the war. I thought I had seen a lot of films, but the scope of your knowledge is amazing. I never thought you'd guess that one."

"Hard to stump an agent who worked in Los Angeles for over forty years."

It was eight-forty and they were having after-dinner coffee in Sarah's living room. Bitsy and Owen were sitting on the rug in front of the fireplace, building houses out of playing cards, knocking them down, and then starting over. Owen worked his way through a slice of blackberry pie topped by a melting, lopsided dollop of vanilla ice cream. Bitsy, a much faster worker, was almost finished with her second helping.

The telephone rang and Murray leapt to answer it. He listened briefly, spoke a few words, and then hung up. "That was Sarah," he announced. "The vet thinks Mazie's pelvis may be fractured, and she could have internal injuries. He is going to take x-rays and call Sarah later. He may have to operate, but he doesn't know for sure yet. Anyway, there's nothing more they can do, so Sarah said she and Neal will be back in about forty minutes. They stopped to get some take-out clam chowder just in case I ate all the food here at home." Murray sighed theatrically and added, "My grandniece knows me too well."

Bitsy and Barbara laughed.

"By the time they come back it will be well after nine, and the wee lad is already rubbing his eyes," said Barbara.

"I'm not tired. Grandma," Owen protested, punctuating his sentence with a gaping yawn.

"I can certainly see that," said Barbara. She leaned toward Murray and said, "I'd like to take him home and put him to bed. I think it's too late for our discussion, and Sarah and Neal will be too tired tonight."

"I could drive you and Owen home," suggested Bitsy.

"Why, thank you."

"No," said Murray. "Bitsy, take the rest of the evening off. I'll drive them home. And here," he said, handing her two twenties. "Take a friend to the movies."

"Thanks, Mr. Appleman, I will, but I don't think I'll go see *Moonlight Sonata*." Bitsy grinned, then gulped down the remainder of her pie and ice cream, and left, wishing them all a cheerful goodnight.

Murray wrote a brief note for Sarah and Neal, and taped it to the refrigerator door. "All right," he said, "let's go." Then he escorted Barbara and Owen out to his car.

"Wow, this is a big car, Uncle Murray," Owen remarked from the cavernous backseat of the 1979 Lincoln.

"Yes, indeed, as big as a dinosaur, and almost as old. Like me," Murray said.

"Well, it's a grand old dinosaur," Barbara remarked, smiling, "just like its owner."

Murray's smile was luminous.

When they arrived at the MacGregor home, Barbara seemed surprised when Murray announced that he would stay until Neal came home. "Oh," she said, "in that case, would you like something to drink before I go upstairs and put the wee one to bed?"

"No, thank you. I'll just wait down here in the parlor for you."

Murray ruffled Owen's hair. "Goodnight, boychik."

"Goodnight, Uncle Murray. That was some good pie and ice cream, wasn't it?"

"Yes, it was."

"Do you think Mazie will be okay? She's my favorite dog."

Murray bent down impulsively and gave the small boy a hug. "Don't you worry about Mazie, Owen. She's going to be fine. Now go on to bed."

When Barbara returned, she joined Murray on the sofa in the parlor. "I think Owen fell asleep before I left the room," she laughed. "I'm sorry we didn't get to have our discussion tonight. Neal is very worried about the situation in this house, but with all the uproar about the dog, perhaps it was best to postpone our talk."

"Well, tomorrow is Sunday, and since no one is working, maybe we can all get together again. Sarah and I discovered some interesting information this past week."

"Did you really? What is it?"

"Well, I'll tell you what I found," answered Murray, "and Sarah can tell you what she discovered later."

"By the way," said Barbara, "I was disappointed that I didn't have the chance to talk with your grandniece tonight. She is lovely, and I know that Neal thinks she's a wonderful girl. Has she ever been married?"

"Not yet. She's never married, but she fell in love with a violinist in New York, a professional schmuck, who left her for another woman and broke her heart. She's not even dated anyone since then, and that was three years ago."

"Well, my grandson hasn't fared much better. His wife has led him a merry dance for a long time, and now she's left him."

"Has she?" Murray interrupted. "I didn't know. Hmph. Well, that changes things, doesn't it?"

"Quite. And in my opinion, she did him a favor. They were a mismatch from the start. He is so honorable and loyal that if she hadn't left him, he would have gone on in misery for years. Now that she wants a divorce, he'll have a chance for happiness with a good woman."

Murray laid his forefinger against his nose and glanced sideways at Barbara, "I happen to know a good woman."

"My thought exactly." Barbara's smile was conspiratorial, "Let's say no more and hope it will all work out."

Barbara suddenly cocked her head, listening. "Do you hear something, Murray? What's that noise?"

"There's your answer," Murray replied.

Sparker dashed down the stairs, skidded around the corner, scrabbling for traction with all four paws, and finding purchase, raced down the hall toward the kitchen.

"Is that normal for her?" asked Murray.

Barbara shrugged, "*Normal* is not a word I associate with cats. Sparker is a lively creature, a good mouser. Who knows? Maybe she was after one of the little devils or playing her own game."

She smiled, "What about a cognac and then you can tell me what information you discovered this week?"

"Sounds good to me," said Murray.

After Barbara returned with the drinks, they settled back on the sofa and tasted the cognac. Then Murray prompted Barbara, "Now you know my theory about music being the key to this whole situation, don't you?"

"Aye."

"Well, this is what I found out." Murray described all the information he had gleaned about music from ancient times to the present while Barbara listened raptly. "So you see," he finished grandly, "all the traditions agree, Hindu, Jewish, Christian, and twentieth-century science, too, that music is one of the most powerful organizing and creative forces in the cosmos."

"And?"

Murray rolled his eyes toward the ceiling and blew out a rush of air. "Oh, hell," he exclaimed in an exasperated voice, "I knew you were going to ask that question. And that's as far as I've got. I still don't know what to do."

Barbara smiled and sipped her drink. "Well, I have thought long and hard about Ian's experiences." She swirled the liquid in her glass a moment, and then gazed at Murray. "Putting it all together with what you told me tonight, I have an idea. Shall I tell it?"

"Absolutely."

"You won't laugh?"

"Never."

Barbara leaned toward Murray, and in a low voice, as quietly and tensely as a spy leaking information to a foreign agent, she explained her idea. Then she sat back and waited, watching for his reaction.

Murray pursed his lips, mulling it over.

"What do you think?" asked Barbara.

"It's so simple, and yet—"

A muffled bang from upstairs cut off Murray's reply.

Barbara started and Murray put his drink down. "What the hell was that?" he asked.

"I don't know," said Barbara, rising from the sofa, "but the wee lad is up there alone—we'd better go and find out at once."

"Owen."

His eyes fluttered open. Someone called his name.

"Owen."

Everything was dark, and for a moment he didn't know where he was. Something pressed down on his foot. He lifted his head and saw Sparker curled in a ball on top of the covers. Then he realized he was at home in his own bed.

"Owen." There it was again, the soft voice in the distance.

"Owen, come here."

He sat up abruptly. It was Tod's voice, far away. Owen rubbed the sleep out of his eyes, threw off the covers, and stood up. Sparker jumped onto the floor, stretched, and meowed. "Shhh," Owen whispered, shushing the cat, "We have to be quiet, if we're going to play with Tod, so Daddy doesn't know." He opened the door carefully and stepped out into the hall. The cat followed him, rubbing against his ankles and bare feet He could hear the sound of voices from downstairs. Uncle Murray said something and then Grandma laughed and answered.

"Up here, Owen."

He tiptoed to the landing and looked up.

"Hello, sleepyhead."

"Hi, Tod."

Tod sat in the shadows at the top of the stairs, holding something between his cupped hands.

"What've you got?"

"It's a fairy creature."

"Can I see it?"

"Yes, come up here."

Sparker huddled on the landing while Owen held onto the railing and climbed the dark staircase. When he reached the top, Owen sat beside Tod.

"Watch this," Tod said, elevating his hands. Light flickered between his fingers and cupped palms. He opened his hands. A tiny globe of brilliant silver light, the size of a marble, hovered just above his palms.

"Dance!" he commanded.

The light flew up to the ceiling and whirled so fast that it looked like a silver crown. Then it darted down the staircase, bobbing and turning in a tightening spiral. Sparker watched it, fascinated, her eyes following every motion. It flew at her head, and she hissed and spat, then bolted away downstairs.

"Find Owen," Tod said.

The light flew up the stairs and began to circle Owen's head.

Owen laughed. "Does it have a name?"

"Its name is a secret, but you can call it Jinn," Tod answered. "It will do work for me if I command it.

"Open the door!"

The light whisked over to the study door and the padlock popped open, rattled a moment, and then lifted up and fell on the floor. The study door slowly opened.

Owen laughed in delight. "How did it do that?"

Tod shrugged, "I don't know. It just has certain powers."

"What else can it do?"

"Turn on the lamp," Tod said.

The light disappeared into the room and then the lamp by the window inside the study clicked on.

Tod stood up and entered the study. Owen stood up, too, but hung back on the threshold. He was not supposed to go into the study.

"Now make the books dance."

The tiny silver globe disappeared under the bottom row of books, and suddenly the books began to rise and fall as though a wave ran under them. Their pages flapped, rattled, and whirred as they rippled on the shelf.

"It's like a magic wand," Owen said, watching the rows of books zip up and down, until every book on every shelf had danced.

"Open the window," Tod ordered. The lower half of the window flew up with a bang.

"Make the chair float!" The leather armchair lifted up and began to float about six inches off the floor. It traveled across the room to the doorway, hovering right in front of Owen.

Owen jiggled his feet and clapped his hands. "It's magic, Tod. Do some more."

Tod hopped up into the chair, clapped his hands, and said "Float and spin."

The chair traveled around the room, revolving slowly in a counterclockwise direction. With a thump, it landed back in its original place.

"Want a ride?" Tod asked.

"Yes!" shouted Owen. He ran across the room and leaped into the chair.

CHAPTER 37

The Unjust and the Faithful

"This is delicious," Sarah told Neal. "It's the best clam chowder I ever had."

"So you see, you can trust me," he replied. He kept one hand on the steering wheel and drank his chowder directly out of the styrofoam cup. They were on their way back to Sarah's house.

"Yes, on important matters like ranking clam chowder."

Neal looked at Sarah. "A saucy remark like that tells me you're feeling a lot better."

Sarah laughed and licked her spoon, "I am."

"Well, you know," Neal added, "if you can trust someone in small matters, you can trust them in large ones, too."

"Is that so?"

"Yes, indeed, and so is the reverse. *He that is faithful in that which is least is faithful also in much: and he that is unjust in the least is unjust also in much.* The gospel according to Luke."

"And your point?"

"My point is about reading the signs concerning the unjust and the faithful. Let's begin with the unjust. When you said that Vicky's boyfriend looked mean, I remembered something else you said earlier. You asked what kind of person would run over a dog on purpose. It clicked: Jim Nordquist would. He's mean, drunk, belligerent, and immoral. He's committing adultery with my wife, who, by the way, moved out two weeks ago. He was the perfect candidate for the crime.

"So I followed them outside, and guess what?"

Sarah's spoon halted in midair, halfway between the cup and her open mouth, "What?"

"They drove off in that old Ford, the white pickup truck."

She put her spoon back in the cup without eating any chowder, "I saw a man and a woman in the truck that hit Mazie."

"And I saw a dent on that truck's front right fender."

"He hit her on that side."

"Got a pen and paper?"

"I think so." Sarah held the clam chowder with one hand and rummaged in her purse with the other.

"I memorized the license number."

When Sarah was ready, he recited the number and she wrote it down. "Thank you, Neal." She put the pen and the scrap of paper back in her purse, and then looked out the window into darkness. "You know, I'm sorry about your wife and Jim Nordquist; I'm sorry we ran into them together tonight."

"Well, it was a shock to see her with another man, but Vicky has been distant for months, and I've known for some time that she was having an affair."

"Well, I didn't know until recently." Sarah continued, "Weeks ago, they came into the bookshop together. I didn't like him then. He was rude and condescending; he tossed the money at me and ignored me when I spoke to him." She turned toward Neal, "By the way, do you remember when Uncle Murr asked about the airline your grandmother traveled, because Northwest had just put one of their pilots on probation for flying under the influence?"

"Yes."

"I'll bet anything that Nordquist was the pilot."

"Probably so. The airline is making him pay for his professional sins, and I intend to take care of the rest. I'll make him pay all your vet bills, Sarah."

"Do you think we can prove he did it?"

"We can damn well try," Neal's tone was cheerful.

They were silent for a while as Sarah sipped her tea, and Neal drove on through the night. Five minutes later, they rounded a curve and saw the flashing rotator lights of a police car in the distance. The cruiser was parked on the right shoulder of the road.

"He's pulled someone over," Sarah said. "And here comes another cop from Coveland." They heard the siren and saw the flashing lights coming toward them.

As they neared the scene, Neal slowed the Jeep and indulged in a little rubbernecking. When they came abreast of the flashing lights, Sarah inhaled sharply and her mouth fell open. "Look at that!" she exclaimed.

Neal waited until he was completely past the scene before slapping the steering wheel and whooping with glee, "Perfect! They caught the rotten bastard."

"Why do you think they stopped him?" Sarah asked, turning in her seat to look back as the second police car arrived and Jim Nordquist climbed out of the cab of the white pickup truck.

"Someone tipped off the Stone Harbor police that a drunk male driving an older model white Ford pickup truck with a certain license number had earlier hit a dog on Beach Road and left the scene."

Sarah's smile was radiant. She pointed at Neal, "You?"

"Me."

"Thank you, Neal. He deserves to be caught and punished."

"So much for the unjust," Neal said, smiling with a gleam in his eye. "Now it's time for the faithful."

"The part about he that is faithful in small things being also faithful in large?"

"Yes."

"Why are you speeding up, Neal?"

"I want to get back to your place as soon as possible."

"Hungry?"

"In a manner of speaking," Neal answered. "Anyway, I want to tell you a little more about myself and my marriage; that is, if you want to hear it."

"Yes, I do, but what were you going to say about the faithful?"

"Patience, Sarah." Neal grinned at her, "Give a guy a chance to explain. For starters, Vicky and I have been living in the same house, but for most of this year, we have not lived as husband and wife. Vicky's unhappiness began when she got pregnant almost immediately after we were married. She never really accepted the responsibilities of being a mother. She had a pretty illusion that our life together would be an unending honeymoon-slash-vacation. When life didn't pan out that way, and when she grew increasingly dissatisfied about my less-than-prestigious job and salary, she turned away from me. In her mind, she was the princess whose prince became a frog. I couldn't please her, although I tried. That's partly why I bought the house." Neal sighed and ran a hand through his hair. "And frankly, I think this affair she's having is just her way of escaping into another illusion. Anyway, we struggled unhappily together almost from the first. We were a terrible mismatch. Except for Owen, we had very little in common."

Neal turned the Jeep onto Harlech Road. "Vicky and I are going to get a divorce, Sarah. In my mind—and tonight really seals it—the marriage is over except for the legal formalities.

"Vicky told me she wants custody of Owen, but I intend to fight her on that, and I think I stand a good chance of winning, since she walked out and has no job." Neal turned into Sarah's driveway, parked, and switched off the motor. He turned in his seat to face Sarah. "That's a long prelude, but my point is that through it all, I remained a faithful husband, even though I knew I had married the wrong person."

Neal smoothed his mustache and said, "You told me how badly Danny Levinson treated you, how he betrayed you with another woman."

Sarah turned her head away abruptly, and Neal hurried on, "I know he destroyed your trust in men, Sarah. But I am not like that. I am a man you can trust."

She looked at him, "What are you saying, Neal?"

He unbuckled his seatbelt and handed Sarah her keys, "Let's discuss it inside, all right?"

Neal noticed the trembling of Sarah's fingers as she unlocked her front door.

"Murray's Lincoln and Bitsy's car are gone," she said. "I guess they all left. It's late." They walked through the living room into the kitchen, where Sarah saw the note taped to the refrigerator. "Uncle Murr took Owen and Barbara back to your house, so Owen could go to bed."

"I'm glad they decided to take him home."

"Well, you're hungry, aren't you?" Sarah asked, chewing on her lower lip. "Shall I take out some food?" Her dark blue eyes were shadowed by two plum-colored half-moons, track marks of strain and fatigue.

He didn't want food. He wanted to hold her, to touch her, to trace the delicate hollows and ridges of her face. He wanted to taste her lips again, but he knew he had to wait for her to come to him. She was beautiful and fragile and afraid.

"Food in a minute," Neal replied, "but first, to return to our discussion in the Jeep. Consider this, Sarah—if I was faithful to a woman who didn't love me, don't you think I would be faithful to one who did?"

"Well, yes."

"All right, you asked me if I was hungry," Neal said.

"Yes," Sarah agreed, raising her eyebrows, a little nonplussed by Neal's change of direction.

"Do you want an honest answer?"

Sarah smiled, "Always."

"Well, I am hungry, but the only food I want is a kiss from a woman who loves me as I love her."

Sarah's smile faded. She stood very still with her eyes locked on Neal's.

"Are you that woman, Sarah?"

She dropped her glance, and Neal thought his heart would plummet through the floor. Suspended in a globe of fear—fear that he had pressed the issue too soon—he endured an excruciating silence.

Sarah lifted her head, "Do you want a truthful and direct answer?"

Neal's stomach tightened, but he nodded. "Always."

Sarah lifted her hands to Neal's face and drew him down to her. She kissed him long and hard, the way a woman kisses her man when he is about to go off to war. Afterwards, she pulled away and said, "There's your answer."

Laughing in relief, Neal said, "Then I have no more questions." He enfolded her in his arms and stroked her hair. "Where you are, Sarah, is the center of the world for me. I wish I had met you years ago." He kissed her, and then added, "But when this is all over, if you'll have me, I intend to love you as you deserved to be loved."

He kissed her again in a moment that seemed to expand and intersect with eternity.

Earthly time resumed with the ringing of the telephone. Sarah answered it reluctantly. "Dr. Ruderian! How is she?" Sarah beckoned Neal and held the receiver so that he too could hear the veterinarian speak.

"The x-rays show that Mazie has a fractured pelvis. The good news is that I don't think she'll need surgery. It will take six to eight weeks, but Mazie will mend on her own. You're going to have to confine her somewhat, though. And fortunately she just urinated."

"That's fortunate?"

"Yes, because it means her bladder is intact. The other great danger was that it was ruptured."

"Oh, thank God, and thank you, Dr. Ruderian. When can I take her home?"

"Tomorrow's Sunday and we're closed, but call on Monday morning and we'll see how she is then."

Sarah's eyes were alight as she replaced the receiver, "Mazie's gonna be okay!"

Neal countered, "And Nordquist the bastard is gonna pay!"

She took his hands in hers and they whirled around in the kitchen in an improvised dance. Neal laughed and exclaimed, "The Highland Fling!" He broke away, singing his own accompaniment and high-stepping through the dance while Sarah clapped time through gales of laughter. They were still laughing and gulping air when the phone rang a second time.

"Sarah, is Neal there?" Murray spoke urgently in a strained tone.

"Yes."

"Let me speak to him."

Sarah frowned, puzzled by his peremptory manner. "It's Uncle Murr," she said, handing the receiver to Neal.

"Murray?"

Sarah watched as Murray's words erased Neal's smile and drained the blood from his face. When Neal spoke, his voice shook, "I'm on my way," he said, grim-faced.

"I've got to go home," he told Sarah, "Owen's hurt."

Before she could speak, he ran for the door. "I'm coming with you," she shouted, and raced after him.

CHAPTER 38

The Gloves Come Off

"What happened?" Sarah asked, as Neal roared through the Mustang's five gears in twenty seconds.

"Owen fell from the third floor window—the study window."

Sarah gasped, "Oh, my God."

"As far as Murray can tell, by some miracle, he seems to be okay, although he has a swollen knot on the left side of his head near his temple, and he bit the inside of his cheek. Thank God he's young and limber, and I haven't mowed lately. The grass is deep on that side of the house."

"How did it happen?"

Neal shook his head, "Don't know yet. Murray said he and Grandma saw it happen and they'd try to explain later. The main thing right now is to get there and make sure he's okay. God only knows he could have all kinds of internal injuries."

In less than five minutes, Neal's Mustang bounced and rattled over the long, uneven dirt driveway. He pulled into the space beside Murray's Lincoln, slammed on the brakes, cut the ignition, and threw open his door. Sarah, too, was out of the car in an instant. They hurried through the kitchen into the parlor. There they found Barbara in a corner of the sofa with her arm around Owen, who was dressed in pajamas and covered in a blanket. Murray stood by the fireplace.

Neal, trying to control his fear, knelt on the floor in front of the boy and spoke quietly so as not to frighten his son. "Hey, Owen," he said, "How are you?" Neal gently touched the swollen lump just above Owen's left temple. "That's quite a goose egg you've got there."

"I have a bad, bad headache, Daddy."

"I gave him some children's aspirin," Barbara said.

"But why does my head hurt so much?"

"Why, laddie," Barbara looked at Owen in surprise, "we were just talking about it. You fell and bumped your head, remember?"

"I did?"

"Yes, you were playing up in the study and the window was open and you fell."

"I don't remember, Grandma."

"Owen, do you remember going over to Sarah's house tonight with me and Grandma?" Neal asked.

Owen shook his head, "No, Daddy." He looked bewildered.

Murray said, "You ate blackberry pie with ice cream, and you and Bitsy made card houses in the living room."

"I don't remember," Owen said, his eyes filling with tears.

Neal took his hand, "It's okay if you don't remember. I think it will come back to you later."

Barbara, eyes riveted on Neal, mouthed a single word. "Concussion."

Neal nodded. His stomach felt like a knotted steel cable. "You've had a hard fall and bumped your head, Owen," he said, "so I think the best thing now is to go to the hospital to have a doctor check you."

Owen looked at Barbara, "Grandma, will you and Uncle Murray and Sarah come, too?"

"Well, of course we will," Barbara answered.

"Let's go," said Neal.

Barbara held Owen in her lap in the passenger seat of Neal's Mustang, and Murray and Sarah followed in the Lincoln. It was a short ride to Coveland Hospital, but a long wait in the emergency room. After a preliminary exam of simple neurological tests, Dr. Worden, tall, young, bespectacled, and toothpick thin, told them, "Memory loss is fairly common with concussions. I've scheduled a CAT scan for Owen, and after that, we'll know if he can go home tonight, or if we should keep him here. When they're ready for the scan, they'll call you. In the meantime, Owen can rest in this room." He led them to a small room, still in the emergency area, and Owen climbed into the bed.

"Good thing I've got my pajamas on," Owen remarked.

"Don't let him go to sleep," was Dr. Worden's parting warning.

Neal stood next to Murray in the cramped space. "I'm anxious to hear the whole story," he said.

"I'll sit with Owen," Barbara offered, "if the three of you want to talk outside in the hall."

Murray, Neal, and Sarah formed a tight, tense group in the hall just outside Owen's room, "Murray, what the hell happened?" Neal asked, his voice cracking with strain.

Murray, speaking softly, recounted the sequence of events. "Barbara put Owen to bed as soon as we got back to your house, Neal. When she came back down to the parlor, we chatted for a while before two things disturbed us. First, the cat came tearing down the stairs and ran into the kitchen. We didn't think too much about it. But soon after, from upstairs, we heard a kind of muffled bang. That's when we both became alarmed."

Murray ran his palm over his head from forehead to nape. "We hurried upstairs to Owen's room, and found the bed empty. We checked the bathroom, but Owen wasn't there either. Then we heard voices and laughter. At first I thought you and Sarah had come in from Stone Harbor, so I walked about halfway down the stairs to check. When I didn't see anyone, I called your names, but of course there was no answer. Then I knew the voices had come from the third floor."

Murray wiped sweat from his brow. "I can't tell you how frightened I was when Barbara and I rushed up the staircase to the third floor. The padlock lay on the floor, and the study door hung open. The light was on in the room. Owen sat in the armchair, and—and . . ." Murray's voice trailed off.

Neal, eyes intense under knitted brows, prompted Murray, "And?"

"Neal, the damn chair hovered six inches off the floor and revolved like a carnival ride."

"Was Owen scared?" Sarah asked.

"No, he was delighted. He kept saying, 'Make it go faster, Tod, faster.' But there was no one else in the room." Murray quickly shook his head and corrected himself, "No, no, I should say there was no one else we could *see* in the room. But I tell you there was a presence. Something was there in the study. It was as though Barbara and I stood on the threshold watching a magic show orchestrated by an invisible magician. It made the hair on my neck stand up." He shook his head again.

"Then the chair started to whirl faster and faster and travel in an ellipse," Murray described a large oval in the air with his right arm and index finger. "Barbara and I were so stunned at first, we were speechless. Then she nudged me and pointed to the window. It was open as wide as it could go.

"Barbara asked Owen to hop down and come out of the room, but when she did, the chair began to bob and spin faster and higher, and Owen grew frightened. As the chair whirled faster, he drew his legs up into the seat and pressed himself back, holding on to the chair arms for dear life. The chair kept coming closer and closer to the walls of the room and the open window. The only solution, I thought, was to grab Owen and lift him out of the chair. When I stepped into the study, an icy chill enveloped me and almost stopped me in my tracks. I tried to grab the chair, but it bobbed and spun just out of my reach. With every second its speed increased, and on the last go-round, it struck me and knocked me to the floor."

"Oh, Uncle Murr, are you all right?"

Murray waved off Sarah's concerns with a hand in the air. "Bruised knees only. The thing that hurts me the most is that by that time, Owen was screaming, 'Stop it, Tod, stop it! Help me, Uncle Murray!' And I could not." Murray took a deep breath, squeezed his eyes shut and shook his head. "I have never felt so impotent in my entire life."

"What then?" asked Neal.

"The chair sailed straight at the window. The seat hit the windowsill, stopping the chair, but Owen pitched forward, out into the darkness.

Barbara screamed and ran downstairs as fast as she could. I got up and looked out the window. Owen lay motionless, face down in the grass. And suddenly, the presence in the room was gone.

"I hobbled down the stairs and took the blanket from Owen's bed. By the time I got outside, Barbara was with him, kneeling on the ground. Thankfully, he was breathing, but his mouth was full of grass, dirt, and blood. He was moaning, and we didn't know whether to move him or not. Barbara asked him if he could get up. He rolled over, put his hands on his head and wailed. Then he sat up on his own power. I figured his back was okay, so I helped him stand. He couldn't walk on his own, though. His knees gave way. Barbara and I supported him, and we slowly made it back into the house.

"Then Barbara cleaned his face and mouth. That was when we realized the blood was from the inside of his cheek, where he had bitten himself on impact. As soon as we put the blanket around him, and sat him down on the sofa, I called you."

"Neal," asked Sarah, "who is Tod?"

"I thought he was Owen's imaginary playmate. Grandma heard Owen talking to someone in the living room one day, and when she questioned him about it, Owen told her he was playing with Tod. The first time Owen mentioned him to me was the day I found him running headlong for the edge of the bluff. I stopped him just in time. Owen insisted that he was chasing after Tod. They were looking for Tod's dog, he said, and they thought it had run down on the beach. I just dismissed it as Owen's overactive imagination. Now, tonight, this episode in the study." Neal smoothed his mustache. "Well, it appears that Tod—"

"Is the Erlking," supplied Sarah. "The Erlking manifested in a form that would appeal to Owen." She put her hand on Neal's arm, "In the Schubert song, you remember the Erlking entices the child," she reminded him. "He speaks softly and coaxes the boy to come with him. He promises all sorts of pleasures, but in the end, he reveals his true nature."

"Makes sense to me," said Murray. "That is exactly what happened tonight. It started out as a game for Owen and then it turned ugly. I didn't see anyone other than Owen in that room, but what I felt was the icy presence of pure malice."

"You know," Sarah added, "the German word for death is spelled t-o-d." She pronounced it like the English word *tote*, with a long o sound, "*Tod*."

"Death," Neal said, with a barely perceptible nod of his head. "My son's playmate was Death. Owen insisted that Tod was real, and I didn't believe him. Thanks to Tod, Owen almost fell off the cliff, and just this past week, while he played with Tod, Owen started a fire on the porch that could have gone out of control. Tod—the Erlking—toying with my son's life all this time, right under my nose, and I didn't even know it." Neal closed his eyes and rubbed his face with one hand.

"Owen could have died tonight. If this is only a concussion, we are really lucky." He smoothed his mustache and the corners of his mouth turned down, "What I know for sure, is that I am going to get that goddamned vile spirit out of my house."

"Excuse me, sir." A nurse pushing an empty wheelchair approached Neal, "are you Mr. MacGregor?"

"Yes."

"We're ready for Owen's CAT scan."

When she guided the wheelchair into Owen's room, Barbara lifted her head, and Owen sat up in bed. Smiling at Owen, the nurse gestured at the wheelchair. "Ready for a ride, young man?"

CHAPTER 39

Messages

Forty-five minutes later, Neal paced the hall outside of Owen's temporary room in the emergency area, while the radiologist read the boy's CAT scan and consulted with Dr. Worden. Murray and Sarah had gone in search of tea and coffee, while Barbara sat in the room with Owen.

At last the gaunt Dr. Worden returned and informed him that there was no bleeding in the brain. "To be on the safe side, however," he told Neal, "I think we'd better keep Owen here overnight for observation. We'll check him into the hospital and have a room for him shortly."

By the time Owen was tucked into his hospital bed, it was almost midnight. Thirty seconds after his head struck the pillow, he slept, taking slow, rhythmic breaths. His head was turned to one side and the bruised lump rose in stark contrast above his pale left temple like a volcano on a plain.

Neal, Barbara, Murray, and Sarah stood at the foot of the bed. "I'm going to stay the night with Owen," declared Barbara.

"Grandma, you should go home and rest."

"By the look of you, Neal, you're the one who needs the rest. You've been from one emergency to the other tonight, but there's nothing more to do here. Owen's safe now. I came from Scotland to help you, and help you I will. You need to eat and rest yourself.

"And if you don't mind my saying so, so do you, lass." Barbara turned her bright brown eyes on Sarah.

Sarah smiled, and said, "Oh, as long as Owen and Mazie are okay, so am I, although I am hungry. Clam chowder will only go so far."

"It won't be too comfortable here, Grandma."

"You forget that I am no stranger to hospitals. I was a sister—a nurse as you Yanks call it. That wall seat makes a single bed, and I'll get sheets and a blanket from the staff. But I will ask you one favor, Neal. If it's not too much trouble, will you fetch my dressing gown and my toothbrush and toiletries from your place? Oh, and the book on my bedside table."

"Of course," Neal said.

"I'm staying, too," Murray announced. "I couldn't help Owen when he needed me, but at least I'll be here in case there's anything at all I can do during the night."

"Now don't go blaming yourself, Murray Appleman." Barbara said. "You tried to help him, and that was bravery indeed. I was rooted to the floor with fear. There was not a mortal man that could have helped Owen in that study. We should all be thankful that the good Lord saw fit to preserve the child's life." Barbara clasped the small gold Celtic cross she wore at her throat. "And if you ask me, we're going to need more help where that came from."

"Uncle Murr, it was a brave thing you did. I'm so proud of you." Sarah took his arm. "But the only place for you to sit is that uncomfortable chair in the corner. You won't be able to sleep."

"Ah, hell, at my age," Murray grinned, "who needs sleep?"

"Well, I'll go pick up your things, Grandma. I should be back in a half hour or so."

"Why don't you get something to eat before you come back?" suggested Barbara. After you've had a chance to eat and catch your breath, there's something I want to discuss with you."

"Can't we discuss it now?"

"Later, after you've eaten."

"Neal, I'm coming with you," Sarah said. "I don't want you to go back to your house alone. And after we get your grandmother's things, we could have dinner at my house. I've got a ton of food."

"Let me qualify that statement," Murray interjected. "Since I ate at Sarah's tonight, we now have to say there *was* a ton of food."

"You see, Neal," said Sarah, "we'd better drive there fast before he has a chance to return."

"Sarah, I would rather you stayed here. Besides, I think I'll be quite safe," Neal said. "The Erlking is not after me. It's Owen he wants." Neal's eyes rested on his sleeping son.

"Well, then," Sarah replied, "if there's no danger, you won't mind if I come along."

Neal's smile was lopsided, "You're a persistent one." He took her hand, "All right, then, come with me."

As they left, Neal glimpsed Murray's glad smile and thumbs-up sign to Barbara.

The lights still burned at Neal's house, since in the rush to the hospital earlier, no one had turned them off. As Neal and Sarah collected Barbara's dressing gown, toiletries, and the book from her bedside table, Sarah asked, "Who's that?" She pointed to the calico cat in the doorway.

"Oh, that's Sparker, Owen's cat." Neal placed Barbara's things in a small canvas bag that he brought down to the kitchen.

"Ready to go?" Sarah asked.

Neal set the bag on the table. "Not yet. Before I leave tonight, Sarah, I've got to go up to the study. I have to see the place where it happened."

Her eyes widened, "Oh."

"But I want you to stay down here in the kitchen."

"You keep trying to get rid of me," Sarah said. "I hope this is not a pattern."

Neal kissed her impulsively. "You know I just want you to be safe. Now that I've found you, not even the supernatural world can take you from me."

"Good," she said, "A smile, a kiss, and a promise. Now would I let a man like you go?" Sarah asked. "Not on your life. I'm coming with you."

Neal laughed, "Okay, let's go."

Hand-in-hand, they ascended the staircase. At the study door, they paused and surveyed the scene. The window was wide open, and a river of cold air flowed into the room. The leather armchair faced the window where it had dropped, about six inches from the wall. Across the room, the books stood in place, and on the near wall, the roll-top desk, the lamps, and the computer were all undisturbed. "What's that whirring sound?" Sarah asked.

Neal looked at her, "Do you mean the sound of the wind?"

"No," Sarah said, and pointed, "you must have left the computer on. I hear the fan."

"What the hell?" Neal exclaimed. He walked into the room with Sarah on his heels, and faced the computer. "This shouldn't be on," he said. The screen saver floated soundlessly across the monitor. When he touched the mouse, a disembodied voice announced, "You've got mail." He clicked the mail icon, and typed in his password. "Two messages," Neal said. He clicked the first one and the four-word message in a huge font filled the screen, ***NEXT TIME HE'LL DIE.***

Sarah inhaled sharply and her hand flew to her mouth.

Neal's face flushed and he pivoted to face the center of the room, "You son-of-a-bitch," he growled, "there won't *be* a next time." He marched to the window and slammed it shut. *"There will not be a next time!"* he shouted.

"Neal," Sarah urged, "calm yourself—your reaction is probably just what he wants." She walked to him, took his hand in hers, and placed one hand on his chest as if by doing so she could quiet his heart. It seemed to have a calming effect; Neal closed his eyes and drank in several deep breaths.

"Maybe we should check the other message," Sarah suggested.

Returning to the computer, Neal clicked the mouse and the second message appeared on the screen:

Dear Mr. MacGregor,

I know this is late, (but just by one day). Please accept my interview with my Great Uncle George Mallory who was a journalist in England after WWII. He covered the trial of an SS officer accused of war crimes. Please have mercy on me and give me credit.

Your groveling student,
Jack Baird

"Is Jack related to Bitsy?" Sarah asked.

"He's her first cousin, one of the myriad Baird clan." Neal opened the attachment and began to skim through it.

MASSACRE AT LE PARADIS

Jack Baird: I am interviewing Mr. George Mallory, my great uncle on my mother's side, who was a reporter with the Norfolk News in England for many years. Mr. Mallory, what was your most interesting assignment in your career as a reporter?

George Mallory: In October, 1948, I went to Hamburg to cover the trial of an accused war criminal, Lieutenant-Colonel Heinrich Fritzinger of the Totenkopf SS.

"Fritzinger," Sarah pointed at the name on the screen. "The name of the people who built this house."

"Yes, Gunter Fritzinger built the house, and he had a son named Heinrich," Neal said. "Very interesting, indeed." He clicked the print icon. "I'm going to print it and take it to your house. I don't want to stay here any longer."

As soon as the last page of Jack Baird's interview emerged from the printer, Neal gathered up the entire copy and shut down the computer. "Let's go, Sarah." Before he turned out the light, he announced to the room and its invisible resident, "I'm going now, but like MacArthur, I shall return."

The moment they stepped over the threshold, the door slammed shut behind them. Sarah squealed and jumped involuntarily. She put her hand to her chest, "Looks like your challenge was answered."

"So be it," said Neal. Without another word, he took Sarah's hand, and together they flew down the stairs and out of the house.

CHAPTER 40

Massacres

As soon as they arrived at Sarah's house, she went about the business of preparing a hot meal. "You see, Neal," she explained as she took the salmon and a container of peas from the refrigerator, "my family theory, with Murray being the prime exponent, is that food cures all ills." She quickly took out plates, forks, and knives while she reheated the fish and peas in the microwave. Neal took the salad and blackberry pie out of the refrigerator and set the table. They ate rapidly with little conversation, both a little dazed and disoriented by fatigue, emotional strain, and the lateness of the hour. After dinner, Sarah brewed a pot of coffee. She filled two mugs and they took those into the living room, where they sat side by side on the sofa.

"Feeling better?" asked Sarah, sipping the hot, strong drink. "I am."

"Yes, thank you for dinner. Your family theory is correct: food helps. I'm beginning to feel human again." Neal sipped his coffee and draped one arm around Sarah's shoulders. "Would you mind if I glanced through Jack Baird's interview?"

"No, let's read it together. I'm very curious about this Heinrich Fritzinger."

"So am I," said Neal, picking up the copy of the interview he had printed. "Did Murray tell you about the visions I had of the boy Heinrich who grew up in my house?"

"Yes, the blonde boy who streaked the wall with his bloody hands."

"Exactly. And he became so dissatisfied with America that he emigrated to Germany in the twenties. Let's see what George Mallory has to say about Lieutenant-Colonel Heinrich Fritzinger of the *Totenkopf SS*." Neal held the paper so that Sarah could see it, too, and they began to read Jack's interview of his great uncle.

JB: First of all, why were they called the Totenkopf SS?

GM: The German word Tod means death and kopf is head. Death's Head. Their emblem was a skull and bones. They also ran concentration camps such as Dachau in Germany.

JB: What was Fritzinger's crime?

GM: On the night of May 26-27, 1940, the 1st Battalion, SS Totenkopf 2nd Infantry Regiment was part of a German attack against the British Expeditionary Force. During the night, the Germans crossed the La Bassee Canal and met heavy resistance from the 2nd Battalion of the Royal Norfolk Regiment and the Royal Scots who held the French villages of Riez du Vinage, Le Cornet Malo, and Le Paradis. Le Paradis was the Battalion Headquarters.

"Oh!" Sarah looked up from her reading, "Neal."
He waved her off, too intent to be interrupted.

The Germans first took the village of Le Cornet Malo and left it burning with the dead scattered in the fields. Then they attacked Le Paradis. Near the village, about 100 members of the 2nd Royal Norfolk, exhausted and much depleted from earlier fighting, barricaded themselves in a farmhouse. The farmhouse was surrounded by a company of the Totenkopf SS under Heinrich Fritzinger's command. By 11:30 a.m., the Norfolks were isolated and had to fend for themselves. The British soldiers in the house fought fiercely for nearly an hour with rifle and machine gun fire, killing and wounding a number of Fritzinger's men. Eventually, though, they ran out of ammunition and decided that further resistance was in vain.

They agreed among themselves to surrender. They showed a white flag and marched out unarmed with their hands over their heads, expecting to be taken as prisoners of war. The SS marched them across the road into a barnyard, kicking the British and striking them with rifle butts in the process. As a number of SS soldiers gathered to watch, the 100 prisoners were placed against the barn wall. Fritzinger gave the order to fire and the men were cut down in a crossfire between two heavy machine guns. It was later ascertained from the spent cartridges that the gunners fired over 200 rounds into the heap of bodies. Finally, all the shrieks of the wounded and all movement ceased. Then Fritzinger ordered a squad of his men to fix bayonets, and they moved among the bodies, stabbing or using pistols to shoot anyone who showed the faintest sign of life.

This went on for some time, until Fritzinger was satisfied that every British soldier was dead. Then his company moved out.

Sarah tried again, tugging Neal's sleeve, "Neal, I wanted to tell you—"
"Just a minute, Sarah. Let me finish reading."

JB: *Well, if all the soldiers died, how did the British authorities find out about the massacre?*

GM: *Miraculously, two men survived, Privates Albert Pooley and William O'Callaghan. Though they were badly wounded, they feigned death convincingly enough to fool the Germans. After the SS company left, they crawled out from under the heap of their dead comrades and hid in a pigsty for three days, eating raw potatoes and drinking water from puddles. A Frenchwoman discovered them and risked her life to aid them. Later they had to give themselves up to the Germans, but they were both well-cared for. Pooley, who had been the more seriously wounded, was repatriated to England in 1943, while O'Callaghan remained a POW in Germany until 1945.*

After the war, Pooley had a desire to avenge his murdered comrades. It was the testimony of Pooley and O'Callaghan that resulted in Fritzinger's trial by a British military tribunal at Altona, near Hamburg, in 1948.

JB: *Why did it take until 1948 before Fritzinger came to trial?*

GM: *A very good question. Pooley first reported the massacre in 1943 at his convalescent camp in England, but the authorities didn't believe him. After the war, in 1946, Pooley visited Le Paradis, and on his return to England, the War Crimes Investigation Unit began its inquiries.*

Pooley and O'Callaghan made sworn statements at Kensington Gardens in London and successfully identified suspects in separate identity parades.

JB: What's an identity parade?

GM: I believe you call it a line-up. Anyway, later Fritzinger was found and brought to London for examination.

JB: What do you know about Fritzinger, I mean about his background?

GM: At the examination, he said he was born in Munich in 1907, and attended grammar and secondary school there. Thereafter, until 1933, he held jobs as a laborer, errand boy, and clerk. He joined the Waffen SS in 1934. At the beginning of the war, he was assigned to Dachau when the SS Totenkopf Division was formed.

JB: Can you describe the trial?

GM: Yes. The trial took place in mid-October, 1948. Fritzinger pleaded not guilty. Usually, the beginning examinations of the accused are tedious, but a surprise moment occurred when the prosecution presented evidence that Fritzinger had lied about his background. It was his father, not he, who had been born in Munich. Fritzinger's country of origin was the United States, coincidentally the state of Washington, your home state. He had moved to Munich in 1928, to the home of a cousin of his father's, and from there on, the rest of his story was true.

JB: Why did he lie about his background?

GM: It became clear that he was fanatical about being Aryan. Like a convert, he wanted to be more German than the native Germans, and he was ashamed that he had not been born on German soil. It was, of course, very foolish, and gave the court reason to doubt other claims he made. For instance, he told the court that the British soldiers had used dum-dum ammunition and misused a flag of truce.

JB: Did they?

GM: Very doubtful. In any event, the judge ruled that had the British done that, the Germans should have conducted a proper legal trial. No such trial took place, and Fritzinger murdered the British on the spot. Thus, he did commit a crime. Fritzinger even denied that he had been present and so could not have given the order to open fire. The prosecution brought in the Frenchwoman,

Madame Castel, who had discovered and aided Pooley and O'Callaghan. She identified Fritzinger as the man who was looking for British prisoners, and she stated that he had also threatened her.

JB: *What was the court's verdict?*

GM: *Fritzinger was declared guilty and sentenced to death by hanging. The sentence was carried out in January of 1949.*

Neal finished reading and slapped the paper with the back of his hand. "Lieutenant-Colonel Heinrich Fritzinger has to be the boy who grew up in my house! And secondly, George Mallory's account verifies one of the visions my grandfather saw."

Sarah's voice was excited, "Exactly. That's what I wanted to say. I read about what happened at Le Paradis in one book this week and in another book I found information about the other massacre. *Both* of your grandfather's visions actually took place. Let me get my notes, and I'll tell you more."

She disappeared into her spare bedroom and brought back a single piece of paper. Consulting her notes, she told Neal, "On May twenty-eighth, one day after the Le Paradis massacre, eighty men of the 2nd Royal Warwickshire Regiment, the Cheshire Regiment, and the Royal Artillery were taken prisoner by a Battalion of SS, Leibstandarte Adolf Hitler, near the town of Wormhoudt. In that case, the prisoners were marched into a large barn. The SS lobbed in stick grenades. The British soldiers died in agony as the shrapnel ripped through their bodies. Those who could walk were taken outside and shot with automatic weapons. Then the SS went back into the barn and finished off those who were still alive.

"Incredibly, fifteen men survived, but surrendered later to other German units and served out the war as POW's. But unfortunately, after the war, none of the survivors could identify any of the SS soldiers involved, so their comrades were never avenged."

"So Grandfather's visions were true." Neal's voice was soft. "You know, I called the history project *Links*, expecting that the students would find links to themselves, that history would come alive for them. I didn't expect to find a direct link to my life."

"But you did."

"Yes. With his second sight, Grandfather saw the massacres at Wormhoudt and Le Paradis. He saw Heinrich Fritzinger order the murder of those British soldiers, and what's more, he saw what no one else could see—the black-shrouded being standing at Fritzinger's side, delighting in the cruelty and murder."

Neal shook his head, like a dazed and weary prize-fighter, "And now to find out that Fritzinger grew up in the very house where I live."

"Good heavens," Sarah said, "maybe that's where the whole thing started."

"What do you mean?"

"Maybe Heinrich was the Erlking's first victim. Maybe the evil spirit invaded his mind when he was a boy—from all accounts, a very unhappy boy—and that's what eventually led to the massacre."

"That's possible. The Erlking stood beside him during the murder of all those men."

"But why do you think the Erlking wounded your grandfather?"

"I've thought about that often, and the only answer I have is that in my grandfather's eyes, he stood revealed. As the Bible says, *For every one that does evil hates the light, neither comes to the light lest his deeds should be reproved.*"

"And because Ian saw him for what he was, the Erlking punished him?"

"Him and his line, from father to son. Ian to Peter, and through me, to Owen." Neal sighed heavily, "And somehow, I've got to end it, and break this hold he has on my family."

"Yes," Sarah agreed, "but the question is how."

"The question of the hour. We were supposed to have our council of war tonight, when all hell broke loose," Neal said.

Sarah set her mug of coffee on the table and picked up a glossy-covered magazine and two books that lay there, a small, slim blue one and a thick green volume. "Well, what Murray was going to discuss is right here. He found some interesting passages in this book *Orpheus*," she tapped the thin, blue book, "and this volume from *The Golden Bough*, and there's a fascinating article in the journal he subscribes to, *Intersections*. Here, take a look," she said.

Neal read the passages Murray had marked in the books, and then the article from the journal, taking his time. Sarah poured them both more coffee and leaned back in the corner of the sofa, watching him while he read.

"I've not read these particular passages before," said Neal, finally, "but I am familiar with the ancient Greek concept of music as one of the basic organizing and mathematical principles of this world. The Greeks saw the world as a manifestation of perfect order—symmetry, number, and proportion, all proceeding from a primal cause that must be in itself perfect symmetry and order. To them, the musical scale and its ratios represented the mathematical structure of creation, in both man and the cosmos. They saw those relationships not as allegories, but as fundamental realities. And it seems to me that Jenny's and Chladni's work, in effect, demonstrates those principles visually."

"Yes," said Sarah, "It was pretty amazing to actually see the organizing principle in music, how sound moved sand from disorder to order. Jenny's photographs of the geometric patterns music generated are fascinating."

"But how does that apply to the problem of the Erlking?"

Sarah shrugged, "I wish I knew, Neal. We keep running into a stone wall down that road, don't we? But now that you've seen what Uncle Murr considered important, and you know about the two massacres, maybe we should go back to the hospital and discuss it all."

"Yes, maybe the four of us can come up with a plan of action. But before we leave the house, I have something important to say." Neal took her hands in his. "Thank you, Sarah."

"For what?"

"For everything you provided tonight." Neal smiled, "First, as Murray would say, for dinner, secondly for your research, and last, but far from least for being so damned beautiful." He released her hands, sat back, and smoothed his mustache. "But I'm afraid there is something sadly lacking." He sighed and shook his head.

Sarah wrinkled her brow, "Really? What?"

"Kisses, woman, kisses!" he shouted. "What about some kiss—"

First of all, she didn't let him finish the sentence, secondly, she knocked him flat on his back, and last, but not least, it was five minutes before she let him come up for air.

CHAPTER 41

The Power of One

"This is the only room I found unoccupied," Murray explained. "I certainly didn't want to have this discussion at Owen's bedside or out in the hall." Murray and Barbara sat next to Neal and Sarah on a wooden pew in the middle of the small hospital chapel. The light was subdued and the air in the chapel was cold. Sarah kept her jacket on, and Barbara slipped on a cardigan and nervously fingered the book Neal had brought her. A single candle in a clear glass holder, suspended from the ceiling on a chain, burned brightly near the altar.

Murray was not convinced that this was the time and place for their meeting. "Don't you think, Neal, that it would be wise to postpone our discussion until tomorrow, when everyone is more rested and clear-headed?"

"No, I don't, Murray. I've got to bring my son home tomorrow, and I'm not going to bring him to a house where his life is endangered. Tonight, when we picked up Grandma's things from the house, there was a message on the computer, saying, 'Next time he'll die,' a direct threat to Owen from the Erlking. There can't be a next time, Murray. I've got to take some kind of action tonight to destroy that creature."

"I see," said Murray.

"I know it's late," Neal continued, "and everyone is tired, but we can talk together for a few minutes and maybe figure out a solution. By the way, Murray, Sarah showed me the information on music you researched this week." Neal turned to Barbara, "Did you know about that, Grandma?"

"Yes, Murray told me about it tonight before Owen got hurt."

"And Sarah found written accounts of the two massacres Grandfather saw in his visions." Neal addressed Barbara again, "He was not deluded, Grandma. Those massacres actually took place in late May of 1940."

Barbara laced her fingers together. "I lived with Ian and his story for over fifty years," she said, "and I believed him from the first."

Neal reached over and touched her arm for a moment. "I know you did, Grandma." Then he continued, "The other significant message tonight was an e-mail from my student Jack Baird. He sent his interview for the school history project, and it involves Heinrich Fritzinger, the son of the man who built my house." Then Neal told Barbara and Murrray the details about Lieutenant-Colonel Heinrich Fritzinger's career with the Totenkopf SS in Germany, and his role in the massacre at Le Paradis.

When he finished, Neal added, "So we have all these bits and pieces of information, but how do we put them together and form a plan of action? What do we do?"

For a moment his question dangled in the silence. Then Neal gazed at Barbara, "As you said, Grandma, you have lived with the knowledge of the Erlking longer than any of us. What do you think?"

"Well, this is what I wanted to discuss with you, Neal. Murray said something that gave me an idea. Remember, the night he came over for dinner, he talked about the power of music for war, in Joshua's case at the Battle of Jericho, and for healing, when David calmed Saul? And he said to consider what happened on the beach at Dunkirk when the Erlking returned and almost overpowered your grandfather. Just a phrase of music by the supernatural piper dispelled the evil spirit."

Barbara's brown eyes flashed, "You are a piper, Neal. The instrument you play goes by the name of the Great War Pipes. The music of the pipes frightened the Germans and gave the Scottish soldiers the courage to charge into enemy fire. What if you stand in the center of the study, in the lair of the Erlking, so to speak, and play the pipes? Maybe you can banish the evil spirit."

In spite of himself, Neal laughed. "I'm sorry, Grandma, but that seems ridiculous." Barbara looked at him calmly, her dark eyes unwavering.

"You're serious, aren't you?"

"Yes I am. If the atmosphere of the room is disordered or diseased, powerful music, played with good intent may be able to restore order. Play the pipes in the study—the sound in a small room will be overwhelming, irresistible."

Sarah broke in, "Neal, you yourself said tonight that the Greeks believed that the same principles and ratios found in the musical scale are the basis for the creation of the cosmos. If music can create order out of chaos and restore physical health and sanity, then that holds true in the Jewish Temple, in Pythagoras' school, in Jenny's experiments, and in the study in your house. Otherwise all that you read was pure bunk."

She stopped and her blue eyes blazed at him, "I don't believe it's bunk, and neither do you, I hope."

Barbara added, "And by the way, Murray came to the same conclusion as I."

"Did you?" said Neal, turning his gaze on Murray.

"Yes, I did. Barbara and I talked about your playing the pipes to banish this creature," Murray replied. "I know you think it sounds simplistic, but consider this—when you played at Coveland House, you quoted an old soldier who spoke of the transforming, miraculous music of the pipes, how its power roused the men's courage and made them defiant in the face of death. And when I listened to you play, in my bones and my blood, I could feel that. There's a power and call in the sound of the pipes. Music is a mighty force and the pipes are a stirring instrument, powerful and irresistible. Once before, the Erlking could not withstand them."

"True," Neal said, "but the piper was supernatural. I, clearly, am not. Against a powerful demon like that, what can one man do?"

Barbara took a deep breath and then expelled it. She spoke slowly, choosing her words carefully, "I think that with faith, courage, and a method, a man can defeat what appears to be an unconquerable foe. Look at history, lad, your subject." She tapped the book she held in her lap. "The man of my generation who did just that was Winston Churchill. When everything was at its darkest and Britain stood besieged and alone, his speeches inspired the British people and the free world, and changed the course of history."

"If there was ever need for inspiration, this is it," Neal remarked.

Barbara opened the book. "This is from Churchill's first speech over BBC radio as Prime Minister, on May 19, 1940. Holland had already fallen to the Germans, and the French military commanders had resigned themselves to defeat. The British Expeditionary Force, of which your grandfather Ian was a part, was about to withdraw toward Dunkirk. In this speech, Churchill tried to hearten the French and prepare the British for what was to come." She read:

> Our task is not only to win the battle—but to win the war. After this battle in France abates its force, there will come the battle for our Island—for all that Britain is, and all that Britain means. That will be the struggle. In that supreme emergency we shall not hesitate to take every step, even the most drastic, to call forth from our people the last ounce and the last inch of effort of which they are capable. The interests of property, the hours of labor, are nothing compared with the struggle of life and honor, for right and freedom, to which we have vowed ourselves.
>
> Side by side, unaided except by their kith and kin in the great Dominions and by the wide empires which rest beneath their shield—side by side, the British and French peoples have advanced to rescue not only Europe but mankind from the foulest and most soul-destroying tyranny which has ever darkened and stained the pages of history. Behind them—behind us—behind the Armies and Fleets of Britain and France—gather a group of shattered States and bludgeoned races: the Czechs, the Poles, the Norwegians, the Danes, the Dutch, the Belgians—upon all of whom the long night of barbarism will descend, unbroken even by a star of hope, unless we conquer, as conquer we must; as conquer we shall.
>
> Today is Trinity Sunday. Centuries ago words were written to be a call and a spur to the faithful servants of Truth and Justice: "Arm yourselves, and be ye men of valour, and be in readiness for the conflict; for it is better for us to perish in battle than to look upon the outrage of our nation and our altar. As the Will of God is in Heaven, even so let it be."

Barbara lifted her head, "Then on the fourth of June, 1940, after Dunkirk, in a speech he delivered to the House of Commons, Churchill described the battle that had taken place in France, and what Ian and all the men at Dunkirk endured:

The enemy attacked on all sides with great strength and fierceness, and their main power, the power of their far more numerous Air Force, was thrown into the battle or else concentrated upon Dunkirk and the beaches. Pressing in upon the narrow exit, both from the east and from the west, the enemy began to fire with cannon upon the beaches by which alone the shipping could approach or depart. They sowed magnetic mines in the channels and seas; they sent repeated waves of hostile aircraft, sometimes more than a hundred strong in one formation, to cast their bombs upon the single pier that remained, and upon the sand dunes upon which the troops had their eyes for shelter. Their U-boats, one of which was sunk, and their motor launches took their toll of the vast traffic which now began. For four or five days an intense struggle reigned.

"And he goes on to describe the battle. I skip now to the end of the speech, where he gives his vision, his encouragement, his determination and hope to the people."

Of course, Neal knew the speech before Barbara read it. But perhaps there was something in the lateness of the hour and the still, charged atmosphere of the chapel, for when Neal closed his eyes and listened, the power, spirit, and authority of the speech made the hair rise on the back of his neck, as though the words unlocked time, and he was there, in the presence of the speaker, the first time they were uttered.

I have, myself, full confidence that if all do their duty, if nothing is neglected, and if the best arrangements are made, as they are being made, we shall prove ourselves once again able to defend our Island home, to ride out the storm of war, and to outlive the menace of tyranny, if necessary for years, if necessary alone. At any rate, that is what we are going to try to do. That is the resolve of His Majesty's Government—every man of them. That is the will of Parliament and the nation. The British Empire and the French Republic, linked together in their cause and in their need, will defend to the death their native soil, aiding each other like good comrades to the utmost of their strength. Even though large tracts of Europe and many old and famous States have fallen or may fall into the grip of the Gestapo and all the odious apparatus of Nazi rule, we shall not flag or fail. We shall go on to the end, we shall fight in France, we shall fight on the seas and oceans, we shall fight with growing confidence and growing strength in the air, we shall defend our Island, whatever the cost may be, we shall fight on the beaches, we shall fight on the landing grounds, we shall fight in the fields and in the streets, we shall fight in the hills; we shall never surrender, and even if, which I do not for a moment believe, this Island or a large part of it were subjugated and starving, then our Empire beyond the seas, armed and guarded by the British Fleet, would carry on the struggle, until, in God's good time, the New World, with all its power and might, steps forth to the rescue and the liberation of the Old.

Barbara finished reading, and there was complete silence in the chapel.

When Neal opened his eyes, Barbara said, "Those are words that turned the course of history. We're at war here and now, against an invisible enemy, but wherever and whenever war is fought, the principles and the stakes are the same. The Germans were a powerful, deadly foe. They had already overwhelmed the Continent. They seemed invincible, yet by a simple means—these speeches, and those that followed—in the face of defeat, Churchill gave the people the spirit to resist, and the faith to believe in victory. And we all know it was the Germans who fell."

Sarah spoke up, "It was only a stone that slew Goliath."

"True," Barbara said, and sat back in the pew. "Well, lad, you knew I'd have my say. That's why I came over from Scotland."

"Thank you, Grandma," Neal smiled. He put his hands on his knees and bowed his head. Everyone was silent. At last Neal lifted his head and said, "Well, it's worth a try."

"Good lad," said Barbara.

"And one more word about Dunkirk," Murray said. "At the beginning of the rescue operation, they hoped to evacuate 45,000 men. Did you know, in the end, they brought home over 338,000 Allied troops?" He ran a hand over his hairless scalp, "Remember, Neal, not only does music have the power to banish evil spirits, but like a wordless prayer, it may also summon help. If you make the effort, Heaven itself may come to your aid."

"I hope you're right, Murray." He slapped his knees, "Time to go and see.

"Thank you for your words of encouragement, and for staying the night with Owen. Sarah, will you drive me to my house—and don't even think I'd let you stay there with me. You're going to take my Mustang and drive home."

"Yes, sir," Sarah said.

Barbara took something out of the pocket of her cardigan. "Take this with you," she said, handing Neal a small object wrapped in a handkerchief.

"What is it?"

"Never mind now," she said. "Unwrap it when you get home. And give your old Grandma a kiss."

Neal bent down and kissed small, white-haired Barbara. She hugged him with all her might. When she released him, he said, "Grandma, with that grip, you could come out of retirement as a professional wrestler."

Barbara smiled and slapped him on the back. "You see, there's strength in this family. Now go and do your part. Play strong—make Ian proud."

"I will, Grandma," he said, and then he and Sarah left the chapel.

When they had gone, Barbara asked Murray if he would return to Owen's room and sit with him for a while.

"Of course," said Murray. "What are you going to do?"

"I want a few minutes alone here in the chapel," answered Barbara. "You know, Murray, the Erlking wounded my husband grievously and ruined my son Peter's life. Now the bloody creature threatens Neal and Owen. And tonight may be Neal's only chance to end all the suffering. If my grandson must fight the bloody creature, I intend to go down on my knees, all night if need be, to get him some heavenly help."

Murray nodded. "Prayer is all that's left us, isn't it?" Then he smiled, "You're a helluva woman, Barbara MacGregor. I'm honored to know you, and I'm very glad you're on our side." He touched her cheek with his hand. "Well, however long it takes, I'll be waiting for you."

CHAPTER 42

Night and Fog

"Heaven is crowned tonight," Neal said, looking up at the brilliantly jeweled lights set in the dark dome above them. Sarah, driving him home, agreed. "It's a magnificent night, and I'm convinced it will have a magnificent ending," she said. But the truth was that her confidence in the outcome was riddled with misgivings. She had encouraged Neal to confront the Erlking, but now as that moment drew closer, she grew more and more apprehensive.

"Well, let's hope I'm the last one standing," Neal replied in a low voice.

He spoke no more after that, keeping his thoughts to himself. Sarah was quiet as well, wrestling in silence with her fears for Neal's safety.

In only a few minutes, Sarah turned into Neal's driveway. "Oh, my God," she said, "I can't see the house."

"Stop the car," Neal said. Sarah braked to a halt, just off the road. The house was obscured by a grayish-white, roiling fog. About twenty feet in front of them, they could see the wall of mist, twisting and writhing in the glare of the headlights.

"This is like that eerie fog Mazie and I encountered the day I first heard you play the pipes."

"I remember," said Neal. "It made me as uneasy then as it does now." He turned to Sarah, and spoke with an edge, "Drive home now, Sarah. I want you far away from this place. Promise me you'll do that. I've got enough to think about without being worried about your safety."

"What if—"

Neal cut her off, "No what if's. Promise me you'll go home."

"All right," Sarah said, as her heart sank, "I promise. But I'll be waiting to hear from you."

For Sarah, their parting was a moment charged with intensity—electric as the atmosphere before a thunderstorm. She held onto his hand when he opened the door to get out. He turned toward her and the interior lamp shone on his thick, wavy red hair, creating points of gold. Deep lines scored his broad forehead and dug trenches from the roots of his nose to the corners of his mouth. His brown eyes were dark pools where, like a seer, she tried to read the future, and could not.

Neal leaned over and kissed her, holding her face between his hands. "You are a beauty, my love, inside and out. Now go, so you'll be safe, Sarah."

Love and fear conspired to tie her vocal cords in knots. Unable to utter a reply, she nodded in farewell. He got out of the car and watched while she pulled away.

It took all of Sarah's will and self-control to leave Neal standing alone in the darkness. But she had promised and she had to keep her word. As she turned onto the road for home, a thousand fears beset her. Stomach knotted, she gripped the steering wheel with white-knuckled hands. For all their brave talk in the hospital, it was Neal alone who had to walk into that house and face the fury. Sarah bit her lip until she broke the skin.

She had loved him from afar the first time she saw him, that day on the beach when she had heard him playing the pipes. When he walked into the travel shop and she had mistaken him for Hamilton Deel, he had seemed to materialize out of thin air, an attractive man in a kilt with the warmest, kindest eyes she'd ever seen. She'd been so surprised and transfixed by him that for a moment she had forgotten where she was.

When he kissed her on the beach, she had responded so absolutely that she could not even remember the kisses as kisses. A white fire had exploded behind her eyes, filling her with heat and light. Her whole body had tingled. She had known afterwards that they could never just be friends; it would be torturous to be near him and never be able to touch him again.

Then, tonight, she had been dumbstruck when he told her that he was getting a divorce. After he reassured her that she could trust him, she had begun to tremble. It had shaken her to the core. But the moment she chose to trust him, when she kissed him, was one of liberation, a dream realized. She had soared for a few brief moments to the pinnacle of hope and joy. Because of that, she now had to endure the pit of fear; she might very well lose him.

She turned into her driveway and got out of the car. She was home; she had kept her promise. Sarah unlocked the dark house, and hurried into her bedroom. She changed into jeans, a turtleneck and a sweatshirt. She drew on her hiking boots over thick white socks. In the closet she found her anorak and a knit cap. She retrieved her flashlight from a kitchen drawer, donned the anorak, and slipped the flashlight into a pocket. She turned off the lights in the house, let herself out the front door and locked it behind her. She put on the knit cap in the chill air, and set off walking rapidly down Harlech Road toward the beach.

Neal had told her to drive home, and she had, but he'd said nothing about returning. She couldn't take his place and do what he had to do, but she could damn well be as near him as possible if he needed help.

She flicked on the flashlight when she got to the top of the bluff above the beach. The wind that buffeted her was cold, but colder still was the stone of fear in her stomach. She carefully descended the steep, sandy path to the beach, and then picked her way through the driftwood logs to the sandy part of the shore. The strong smell of the sea and the noise of the breakers comforted her a little. This was her haven, but she had never come here alone at night without Mazie.

She kept the beam of the flashlight on the ground ahead of her and hurried up the beach toward the point. Thank God the tide was out, otherwise the water would have made this way impassable. When she rounded the point, she saw the fogbank about fifty yards ahead of her.

Before she entered the strange mist, Sarah stopped for a moment and looked up at the clear night sky. Out here, away from any lights, the stars were brilliant, myriad. "Heaven is crowned tonight," Neal had said. With her eyes on the jewels of the sky, Sarah, in hope and fear, prayed with all her heart, willing High Heaven to hear and respond, "Protect him, O Lord, and give him the strength and help he needs in this hour."

Sarah walked to the bluff face, having decided to keep it within touching distance of her right arm. When she reached Neal's property, even if she was blinded by the fog, she would easily find the wooden staircase that connected his lawn to the beach. She gathered her courage, fastened the anorak tightly around her throat and stepped forward into the mist.

The icy gray cloud swallowed her; its clammy touch made Sarah's skin crawl. She passed into a ghostly, veiled world where the wind died and the sound of the sea was muffled. She made slow progress, clambering and sometimes stumbling over logs made damp and slippery by the mist. She felt as though she moved in slow motion, like a snail through a petrified forest, in a dream, where all her actions took on unreality. She felt remote and vulnerable, imprisoned alone in a bizarre, nebulous place where at any moment she could be ambushed by evil itself, hooded and cloaked.

After several minutes, Sarah stopped for a moment to catch her breath. She sat on a log and shone the flashlight on her watch. From the time she had changed clothes and left her house, twenty-five minutes had passed. The fog was still a thick, wet blanket, impenetrable and disorienting. She had no idea how far she had to go to reach the staircase.

"Well, I'm not making any progress this way," she muttered to herself. She stood up and felt for the face of the bluff. It was a relief to feel the damp, sandy earth under her fingers, a contact with something real and solid. She resumed her slow, torturous trek to the muffled funeral drum accompaniment of the sea.

After another ten minutes, Sarah became aware of a different sound. She stopped and strained her ears, listening. No, nothing. She stepped over another log and heard it again. She stopped and listened. Faint music— the sound of bagpipes. Sarah smiled. Her heart picked up its rhythm and her hopes soared. As long as he played, he had to be unharmed. She knew she had to be very close to the staircase now.

The music of the bagpipes ebbed and flowed, now softer, now louder. It was a strange tune, rising and rising on itself, not one she had heard before. It lifted her spirits, buried as she was in the stifling fog. Somehow it made it easier to breathe and gave her courage at the same time. Sarah stayed very still, closing her eyes and focusing all her concentration on her sense of hearing.

Something brushed against her leg and Sarah cried out, stiff with fear. When she played the flashlight beam in a tight circle around her, the light was reflected back in two feral eyes. Then the two eyes blinked, and Sarah laughed with relief. She bent down and called in a soft voice, "Here, kitty."

Tail high and dignity intact, Sparker came into the small circle of light. "Hey, girl," said Sarah, "what are you doing out on a night like this?" She crouched with one knee on the sand and stroked the cat's long, silky fur. Sarah laid the flashlight down for a moment, picked up the small calico cat and hugged her, burying her face in the warm, soft fur. It was a tremendous comfort to touch another living being.

"Listen," Sarah said to Sparker, "you can hear—"

Sarah, still holding the cat, stood up. The sound of the bagpipes had ceased.

CHAPTER 43

The Power of Darkness

With a heavy heart, Neal watched Sarah drive away. It might be the last time he would see her. His grandfather Ian had faced the demon, unaware of its power, but it was Neal's lot to confront the Erlking in its lair, fully conscious of his peril. Would he survive blind or mute or deaf, or would the demon simply destroy him and then have its way with Owen? Well, no matter the outcome, the task still loomed ahead. Comfortless and alone, he did what he had to do: he turned and walked into the fog to face his fear.

The mist was cold, thick, and clammy, chilling him immediately. It had the quality of a living being. As the fog closed over him, he became disoriented and suffered a moment of claustrophobic panic, as frantic as if he was trapped in the belly of a beast. He had to stop and calm his breathing. "Slow, deep breaths," he told himself. He focused his mind on his breathing and gradually regained his equilibrium. Looking at the ground, he had enough visibility to see one of the dirt tracks of the driveway. "Follow that, one step at a time," he said aloud, glad even for the sound of his own voice.

After what seemed an eon of small, shuffling steps in the disorienting mist, he finally found the house and the kitchen door. He entered the house with a great sense of relief. This time, all was dark. He snapped on the kitchen light and the bulb flashed and burned out. "Hell," he swore in the darkness. Something rubbed against his leg, and Neal started.

He heard mewing and immediately relaxed. "Oh," Neal said, "Sparker." Laughing at himself, he bent down and petted the purring cat. "I'll bet you're hungry, aren't you? We forgot you in all the uproar." When he found her bowl, it was empty. Neal told her, "Hold on, I'll feed you." He filled her bowl and then set it outside. "If all hell breaks loose in the house, at least you'll be safe out here, Sparker. Run for the woods." He stroked her silky fur. Let one innocent be unharmed, he thought, thinking of Owen, and the injured Mazie. Whatever it was that inhabited the study was powerful and malevolent, and he was about to challenge it. Anything could happen.

After he fed Sparker, he went upstairs to his bedroom, showered, and shaved. Outside, the monstrous fog rolled in in greater density from the sea, surrounding the house, blinding the windows, and deadening all outside sounds. Neal dressed slowly, carefully, putting on a long-sleeved white cotton shirt and a black tie, his kilt of MacGregor tartan, the wide black belt, his thick woolen knee socks, black wingtips, and finally, the black leather sporran. He faced himself in the mirror, combed his hair, and adjusted his tie. He put on his black jacket, drew a deep breath, and said to his reflection, "Courage, man. You'll either get rid of this thing or die trying."

He suddenly remembered the little object his grandmother had given him. He fished it out of his pants pocket and unwrapped it. Inside the handkerchief in a folded piece of paper was the small gold Celtic cross and chain she always wore. He noticed handwriting on the paper, a note from his grandmother. *Neal: Play the tune from Ian's journal.* Why, of course, he thought. If ever there was a time to play it, this was it.

Sitting on the edge of the bed, he held the cross in the palm of his right hand. As he lifted the cross closer to the lamp, its warm gold seemed to give out its own light. He turned it over and saw there were words inscribed on the back. On the vertical axis he read the words, *To guide*, and on the horizontal, *To protect*.

He tightened his fist around the cross, closed his eyes and prayed, "Strengthen me, O Lord, and let Your virtue and power fill this house through the music of the pipes. Let the light dwell here, so the darkness can have no place. Amen." Then he fastened the cross around his neck.

While night and fog held the house in a chill grip, Neal took out his pipes and tuned the drones. Then he walked to the foot of the stairs, inflated the bag, and began the attack. The sound of the drones startled the air, and the stirring sound of "Scotland the Brave" preceded Neal as he slowly mounted the stairs. The polished wood glowed and the white walls gleamed, clean and inviting.

Who would ever suspect that this handsome old house harbored a being so ancient and so malignant? As he played, Neal wondered if the Erlking knew his intent, that he was mounting the stairs to force a confrontation. But why wouldn't the creature know? The Erlking had played his hand and lost the last round. He had deceived Owen and Neal by pretending to be Tod, Owen's playmate, but that ruse wouldn't work any longer. With that cover blown, there really was nothing left, Neal thought, except confrontation, and they both knew it.

It was when he reached the landing that all the lights in the house went out. He stopped there, still playing, and let his eyes slowly adjust to the darkness. The sound of the pipes was huge and heartening in the small space. The old wood creaked under his feet as Neal continued slowly up the staircase, repeating "Scotland the Brave." A wave of cold air flowed over him, issuing from the presence that awaited him in the tower room. It felt as though every step brought him closer and closer to the ice-bound heart of darkness. Enclosed in the chill air, he ascended the dark staircase with grim determination. Time slowed for him; every second seemed to expand into minutes.

At the top of the stairs, Neal halted just outside the open study door. He faced the room, marking time with his feet, and played "High Road to Gairloch." The reedy, incisive sound of the pipes filled the space and gave him courage in the darkness. He played through the tune twice, seeing in his mind's eye the battalions of Scottish soldiers who had gone into battle in all the wars that ever were, led by the stirring sound of the Great War Pipes. Readying himself for an onslaught from the demon and steeling himself against his own fear, he played "A Man's a Man for a' That," and then he strode into the study.

It was like stepping into a charnel house filled with rotting corpses. The stench of putrefaction was nauseating, overpowering. Fighting a terrible reflex to gag, Neal kept playing. Every breath he took was loathsome, and he broke out into a sweat in spite of the chill. It took everything in his power to stop himself from bolting. The only thing he could do was to pace a circular, clockwise path in the center of the room. As salty drops of sweat rolled down the sides of his face, he set his mind upon the skirling music, forcing down his nausea, never allowing his fingers to falter.

When Neal thought he could not draw one more breath of the putrid air, the lights suddenly came on, causing him to blink furiously. The foul odor dissipated as though it had never been. There was a pause in which the room seemed normal—neither hot nor cold, and Neal sensed no presence. But he was not deceived; he knew he hadn't scared the demon away. No, the creature waited like a snake, coiled, watching, tensed to strike.

Well, time for the next move, Neal judged. He came to the end of "A Man's a Man for a' That," and began to play Ian's strange tune from Dunkirk. Somehow, with the rising of the tune, his spirits rose; his task seemed lighter, and he regained strength, as though the tune had magic in it. At the same time that it cheered Neal immensely, the music provoked a powerful reaction from his foe.

Without warning, great, deafening booms came from the walls and floor, as though an angry giant pounded on the house. The floor shook and the walls vibrated visibly like the head of a bass drum when it is struck. The window flew up with a bang, allowing wind from the sea to roar in, and the room convulsed. Furniture slid across the floor, impelled by an invisible fury. Neal dodged the leather armchair as it hurtled past, slamming into the wall behind him. Continuing to play the tune, he ducked as the Chinese table lamp flew at his head, and then, missing its target, shattered, even as it broke the glass in the window. The books jumped and jiggled on the shelves, animated in a demonic frenzy. Some of them vibrated out and fell onto the floor where they continued to jitter and twitch. The drapes flew out almost horizontally, flapping and popping in the gale-like wind.

Neal played on in the tempest, still struggling to pace in the screaming wind, stepping over debris and books that jerked and skittered around his ankles. He was alarmed, and yet curiously heartened by the increasing furor. It meant that there was a potency in the music, something that had power to agitate and rouse the Erlking. *Writhe in agony, you damned snake*, he thought, growing more confident.

It was when he began the tune again that he thought his eyes deceived him. He saw the roll-top desk lift itself five feet off the floor and begin to spin, slowly at first, then blindingly fast, like a top, until it was a brown blur. Without warning, the heavy desk rocketed through the air directly at him. He threw up his right arm to protect his head and he heard the bones in his forearm snap on impact, as the weight of the desk knocked him down. He cracked his head on the wood floor, and the desk landed on top of his chest.

Before he passed into unconsciousness, he saw, towering over him, the wraithlike, shadow-molded Erlking, eyes glittering black, toxic with hatred. The last thing he heard was its voice, mocking and contemptuous, "The brave Scot falls—no better than swine shit." His laughter was soft and nickering. "What pleasure I shall take with your delightful boy."

CHAPTER 44

The Wind from the Sea

Overcome by sudden dread when the strange tune ceased abruptly, Sarah felt a powerful impulse to hide. Cradling Sparker against her chest, she dropped to her knees and crouched in the narrow end of a V-shaped space between two large driftwood logs. She shivered, chilled more by fear than the cold, unnatural mist. Even the cat seemed subdued and acquiescent, huddling still and watchful against Sarah's chest.

Whether it was due to her state of fear or not, the fog seemed to Sarah to have taken on a gelatinous quality, thick and oppressive, as if she could drown in it. It pressed in on her from every side, blinding, choking, alien, silencing all sound. Even the murmur of the sea was stifled. The only thing audible to Sarah was the pounding of her heart and the rasp of her own breath—harsh, rapid rhythms, hammering insistently.

Close to panic, and needing some small measure of comfort, Sarah closed her eyes and pressed her face into Sparker's fur, grateful for the presence and living warmth of the cat. Never in her life had Sarah felt so diminished, small and insignificant, and yet at the same time conspicuous, like prey in the eyes of a predator. Blind as a fluttering moth caught in a giant spider's web, she could not see the spider, but she knew it lurked nearby. There was an Intelligence in the fog, something aware that she was trapped and frightened. As surely as the web issued from the spider, Sarah was certain that the unnatural fog emanated from a dark

Intelligence, the Erlking. And Neal stood even now at the epicenter of it all, confronting that presence, in the same room with it.

Thinking of Neal's peril, Sarah immediately felt ashamed. She had come to help him, to play backup if he needed her, and now, after the music stopped, she was sure he did. Sudden anger moved her. She had not come this far through darkness and danger to crouch on the beach, a quivering mess, cowering in fear when the man she loved stood alone against such a foe. She had to rise, climb the staircase, and enter the house in order to help Neal. She tried not to think about what she might encounter in the tower room. Her only mission was to go to Neal's side.

"One step at a time," she advised herself. "Down you go, Sparker." Sarah released the cat, whispering, "God protect us all," and rose to her feet, trembling but resolved. She climbed over the log and ran her hand against the face of the bluff, inching along blindly until her arm bumped into the wooden railing of the staircase that led up to Neal's lawn. Gripping the railing with one white-knuckled hand, she mounted the first step and stopped, lifting her head. There was movement in the fog around her, a swirling of the mist that presaged a change. A change for good or bad? She didn't know, but she sensed a shift in the air. There was a faint stirring above her and she hesitated, her breath and pulse quickening.

Well, no matter what, she had to help Neal. She bit her lower lip and forced herself to climb even though her legs were heavy and she found herself curiously drained of energy. The stairs seemed endless, and in the mist she couldn't tell how far she had to go. As she climbed higher, she noticed the mist seemed thinner and there was a slight breeze. She became aware of a rhythmic sound—the waves breaking on the shore. Oh, thank God, she could hear the sound of the sea again. The fog was losing its power.

The air on her face and hands seemed faster-moving with every step upward. To rest for a moment and reconnoiter, Sarah stopped and looked up. The wind was stronger where she stood, and it had torn the mist to tatters. Above her there were clear patches of sky and she could see the stars. She was so relieved that she almost cried. The top of the bluff was clearly in sight. She saw that she was about halfway up the staircase. As she began to climb again with new energy, she noticed that the wind speed increased dramatically, dispersing the mist around her.

Once the mist was gone, the wind took its place as a dominating presence. Sarah guessed the gusts coming off the sea might be forty miles an hour. The powerful cold blasts buffeted Sarah and frightened her. The sudden gale seemed as unnatural as the fog, but she preferred the clean, stinging wind to the foul, stifling mist. When she looked out at the strait, she was not surprised by the roughness of the surf. Trails of spume flew off the tops of the churning, white-capped waves. Sarah noticed a faint high-pitched sound in the wind that seemed to crescendo with every passing second. As she turned up her collar, the roaring sound of the wind grew, and there was something else, something like voices in the wind, a high, crying call. Sarah froze and the hair rose on the back of her neck.

The sound was otherworldly, wild and strange. If there were words in the high singing, they were unintelligible to her. Sarah stood transfixed, her face to the sea. Her impression was that something approached from seaward, something powerful, borne on the wind. The sound grew in power and she could not tell its source, but it surrounded her and she was aware of nothing else. The wind was sound and the sound was the wind. Although she was afraid, her fear was more awe than fright. There was a cleanness, a purity in the high singing that heartened Sarah and humbled her at the same time. Feeling exposed and vulnerable on the staircase, halfway between the top of the bluff and the beach, she dropped to her knees and hugged one of the wooden supports.

The high, keening sound grew so powerful that the entire staircase vibrated. The wooden support trembled in her hands, and the structure shook. Sarah closed her eyes and held on for dear life, hoping she wouldn't be shaken off or blown away. When she thought she couldn't stand it another moment, when the structure, strained to the limit, pulsed in waves of kinetic energy, throbbing like an engine, a thunderclap boomed out of nowhere. Sarah cried out, recoiling in surprise, and at the same instant she heard a terrible wailing cry, like a great, half-human animal in extremis, a howl that rose sharply in pitch and then faded away.

Sarah gasped and clapped her hands over her ears, wishing she could shut out all memory of the ghastly sound, for as well as pain and distress, it contained appalling rage. Eyes squeezed shut, hands pressed to her head, recoiling from the dreadful cry, she crouched on the staircase, unconsciously rocking from side to side. She swayed, retreating to a safe place within herself, for how long she later could not recall. When she allowed herself to open her eyes, she saw that the sea was calm, and the wind had ceased.

Feeling something push against her leg, Sarah looked down and saw Sparker. She immediately scooped up the cat and held the warm, small body against her cheek, breathing in the cat's earthy, homely smell. "Oh, Sparker, you survived all that, too."

And what about Neal? The thought galvanized her. Sarah, still holding the cat, rose and ran up the stairs to the top of the bluff, where she stopped for a moment. The house looked abandoned, dark and silent, with no sign of life. Her heart sank. Oh, God, let him be all right, she prayed. The cat sprang out of her arms and bolted toward the kitchen door, as Sarah, following suit, sprinted close behind.

CHAPTER 45

Of Pipers

When he awoke, he had no idea how long he'd lain unconscious. The room was in shambles, but all was still. His pipes lay sprawled on the floor, a few feet away. Once again the air was icy. He had lost: the Erlking was still there; he could feel its presence. It had mocked him and nearly killed him. The pain in his arm was terrible, but the pain in his heart was worse, because he knew he'd gambled and failed. He really was swine shit. He had fought in vain and now Owen's life was forfeit. He wondered why he was still alive. The demon probably wanted him alive, because it knew that Neal would rather be dead than endure the torment and agony of Owen's suffering.

It was difficult to breathe with the weight of the desk on his chest. Using his good arm, Neal pushed against the desk, moving it a little, and making it easier to draw breath. Why was that music, a weird variation on Ian's Dunkirk tune running through his head?

And why in God's name had he thought he could defeat such a powerful, supernatural opponent? He was no hero. And now he was weaponless; he had played his one card and lost. Helpless though he was, he did not fear for himself. He agonized over Owen. What cruelties awaited his son at the hands of the Erlking? Neal knew the demon would show no mercy.

He shook his head as if he could push the torturous thoughts away. He squeezed his eyes shut—God, the mind was a quirky thing. Why now, in the midst of his mental and physical pain did he hear that tune again, faint but persistent? It grew in strength with every passing second. He suddenly realized it was not his imagination—he heard the pipes playing. He strained to hear the music over the sound of the wind. There was another tune now, something he didn't recognize. And it wasn't a lone piper; it was the sound of many pipers.

Gripped by excitement, and ignoring the pain in his swollen, mangled arm, Neal used his good arm to push the desk off his body. He crawled to the window where his bagpipes lay sprawled on the floor, took hold of them, and stood up. What he saw took his breath away.

The fog had lifted, and the night was clear. In the bright starlight he could see the waves breaking on the rocky shore. There, striding above the sea, as on an invisible plane, level with the top of the bluff, and playing grandly, was a host of pipers—a thousand or more in proud columns—some kilted, some wearing the battle-dress of other times and places. After a moment, he recognized their uniforms. They were the men his grandfather had told him about, the fallen pipers of the Great War, from the Battle of the Somme, Regina Ridge, and those from the Second War, from El Alamein, Tunis, Burma, and Dunkirk. The Black Watch, the Argyll Highlanders, the Queen's Own Camerons, the Gordon Highlanders. The proud, brave men who had walked into enemy fire armed only with their pipes and their courage.

Neal was stunned. Somehow, he had summoned the past. And the past was present, playing on that invisible plane in defiance of death and time. Their playing was as powerful as if the sea had transformed its depths into music, a music that, as the pipers approached, swelled like the tide, vast and irresistible.

Leading them, at the forefront, was a tall, shining form whose hair and face and body seemed to be light itself. Neal's knees grew weak. He knew it was the piper his grandfather had tried to describe. No wonder Ian had failed in the attempt, for who could put into words the power and the majesty of the being or the grandeur of the music?

It was a music that was strange and yet known somehow, elemental and complex, as though it made audible the link between the chord at the center of existence and the chord at the heart of man. It was akin to earthly music, and yet transcended it the way a Beethoven symphony surpassed the tinkling of a wind chime. Surely, Neal thought, this was the music in which atoms aligned themselves; the crooked was made straight, the incomplete made whole; wounds were healed and sorrows ended. He suddenly understood what Ian had tried to explain, that this music, once heard, forever changed the hearer.

As Neal listened to the music, he became aware of an opposing sound, a low, dull roar in the room behind him. He turned from the window and saw that the Erlking had taken a new form: a dark cloud swirled in the room, spinning and churning counterclockwise like a tornado. The cloud crackled and rumbled with energy, gaining strength and speed, leeching brightness and vitality from its surroundings. As the light in the study dimmed, the air grew oppressive, heavy and thick, with a sharp, metallic smell. As the spinning accelerated, the low roar swelled, rising to an earsplitting shriek. Neal crouched beside the desk and covered his head with his good arm in the screaming wind.

The walls began to moan, flexing in toward the center of the room, and Neal's ears ached as the air pressure dropped. Broken glass, debris, and books slid across the floor, sucked into the churning vortex; the drapes popped off their rod and disappeared into the cloud. When the chaos grew so great that he was certain the room would implode, the vortex burst out of the house with a terrible wailing sound, taking part of the wall with it. It stormed onto the plane above the sea, enveloping the pipers.

Neal struggled to his feet, still holding his pipes in his left hand. His heart was in his throat, because he knew that everything hinged on this confrontation. Fear threatened to overwhelm him. If the shining piper and his host were overcome, what hope would be left him?

In a moment of clarity, he realized it must have been the same for the people of France, Holland, Belgium, and all the occupied countries fifty-five years ago when the Nazi power had enmeshed the world in torture and death. How their hopes must have rested on the Allied troops, even as they feared the evil at the heart of the Nazi cruelty. And now, once again, that evil went forth to attack another force, the pipers, symbol of all that was gallant and good in the world.

The shriek of the vortex was so strong that Neal could not hear the pipers. He could not even see them. He strained forward, all his senses taut. There was a blinding flash, like the detonation of a bomb, then a deafening report and a concussion that flattened him. White-hot pain shot through his arm and his head struck the floor again.

After a moment, lying there bruised and battered, with excruciating pain in his right arm, Neal laughed. He laughed until he cried, because he heard the pipes, triumphant, enduring. Order and life reigned over chaos and death—for sure, forever. He knew it, without a doubt.

When he raised himself on one knee and looked out, he saw that the black cloud was gone; the Erlking was banished. The pipers were playing an indescribable music, wild and free, martial and triumphant. It gave him chills and raised the hair on his neck. He wondered if he was hearing the music his grandfather heard, the music his grandfather now played. For surely, Neal thought, playing there in the midst of the host, clear-eyed and proud, was brave young Ian MacGregor.

Neal breathed deeply and slowly as the breeze ruffled his hair. He could smell the clean, salt breath of the sea. Gripping the windowsill with his left hand, he slowly and painfully pulled himself to his feet. Gazing out at the pipers, he lifted his own pipes high above his head in salute. "Thank you," he murmured. His son, his life, had been given back to him. Owen was safe; the threat was gone and there was no more fear. His heart swelled and then he could not see, for the sea invaded his eyes and poured its salt down his cheeks. He squeezed his eyes shut and shook away the tears. When he opened his eyes, the piper host was gone.

Neal blinked and then he noticed movement at the edge of the bluff. A small white figure scampered across the lawn toward the house. He smiled in delight—Sparker, too, was all right. Then, to his everlasting surprise, another figure emerged over the edge of the bluff, following after the cat in a dead run.

He couldn't believe it. "Sarah!" he shouted. "I'm here," he called, "Up here." He stood at the opening of the ruined wall, and she saw him.

"Neal!" She stopped in her tracks and covered her mouth with her hands "Oh, thank God, you're all right!" she cried. "I'm coming up."

"No, stay there, I'm coming down."

Of course she met him on the second floor.

"Don't you ever follow directions, Sarah?" He kissed her eyes and mouth.

She was so excited that she spewed her words at a speed and pitch that rivaled an auctioneer's delivery. "Well, I promised to drive home, and I did. But you didn't say anything about coming back, so I walked here on the beach through that deadly fog, and then a powerful wind came off the sea and out of nowhere, a mighty thunderclap—"

Sarah stopped her fevered rattling and searched Neal's eyes. "It's gone, isn't it?" Her voice was low and calm. "The Erlking is gone."

"Yes. Forever."

Holding his gaze, she said, "Neal, did you know this is the night of May twenty-seventh, and now after midnight, the twenty-eighth—the anniversary of the two massacres in 1940?"

"So it is—what perfect justice."

"And thank God, Owen, Mazie, everyone is going to be all right." She threw her arms around him and squeezed.

"*Ow!* Sarah, my arm."

"Oh, heavens," Sarah said, at last taking her eyes from his face, "you're hurt."

"My arm is broken."

"Neal, what happened up there in the study?"

"Well, Sarah, I'll tell you, Grandma, and Murray the story, when we get to the hospital. And after that," he winced at the pain in his arm, and smiled ruefully, "maybe Owen and I can share a room."

"Here," she said, "let me take the pipes. I'll help you down the stairs and we'll call an ambulance. Put your good arm around my shoulder, Neal. Lean on me."

Neal's eyes shone, "I hope to, dear heart, for a long time to come."

One Year Later

"**C**'mon, Owen," Neal urged, "put your jacket on and let's go, or we'll be late for the wedding!"

Owen stood at the open window of his room, surveying the lawn. It was a magnificent May morning. The sea was a chest of emeralds, sapphires, and fiery diamonds, sparkling in the brilliant sun. On the lawn, the wedding guests sat on folding chairs facing the garlanded canopy where the rabbi and minister stood. To the left of the chairs, tables of food and drink waited under a blue and white-striped pavilion that guyed easily in the light breeze. Seagulls glided over the scene, and the air through the open window was laden with the smell of salt and the sea, mingled with the odor of freshly mown grass.

But it was the music that held Owen's attention. Sarah's friends, The Musicians of Brooklyn, played a cheerful piece, and Owen hummed along. "I know that one, Daddy. It's Mozart, isn't it?"

"Right," Neal said, helping his son into the jacket of his new navy blue suit. "The name of the piece is *Eine kleine Nachtmusik.*" Neal smoothed Owen's hair and then his own, and checked his tie, kilt and sporran in the mirror.

"What does that mean?"

"It's German and it means *A Little Night Music.*"

"Well why are they playing it during the day?"

Neal looked at his watch. They were already five minutes late. "Owen, if we don't go now, Grandma and Murray will get married without us. Come on, and I'll explain about the music later." Neal grabbed his bagpipes with one hand, and Owen's hand with the other, and they hustled down the stairs and out the kitchen door.

Neal took his place to the right of the canopy. As soon as the Mozart ended, he played the processional. Sarah, wearing a pale blue dress that fell loosely from the bodice, carried a single white rose. Her gentian eyes sparkled at Neal as she walked up the aisle. Owen came next, bearing the rings, his silky red hair ruffled by the breeze. Neal played another tune, and Barbara, small and slim, brown eyes and white curly hair shining, came dressed in a white gown on Murray's arm. In later years, when Neal described the wedding to his younger children, he always said, "And Grandpa Murray was so happy that he shone." There was a light about them both, Neal thought, as he took his place as Murray's best man and his wife stood beside Barbara as matron of honor.

After the ceremony, Neal stood with an arm around Sarah's thickening waist and greeted the guests, twenty-five per cent of whom were Bairds. Bitsy, on summer break from Columbia, ebullient as ever, was there talking, laughing, and eating with her cousin Jack, her parents, and assorted siblings, nephews and nieces. Yoshiko added a dash of ethnic flavor to the mix with her pale yellow kimono, the color of her husband Ingemar's hair. Cheerful Peggy Williams, Neal's real estate agent, gestured at the house, talking about it with her son Bill, who was home from the sea. And Ellie Lawndale, Neal's colleague from the high school, knelt on the lawn to pet Sparker, the cat she had given the MacGregors years ago.

In the background stood the house, the three-storey blue Victorian with white trim, perfectly restored to its former beauty, repaired on the outside, and healed on the inside. Neal looked with pride and affection at his home. Exorcised of its ghosts, its demon, and its atmosphere of gloom and depression, with Sarah as its mistress, it truly was his home, his center, a place of serenity where a bright future waited.

A key part of that future, a seven-year-old boy, red hair shining in the sun, skipped across the lawn to the pavilion. Neal watched Owen fill his plate, then disappear underneath the long cloth that skirted the food table. Curious as to what his son was up to, he strolled over to the food pavilion. He parted a flap where two tablecloths came together, and saw his son and Mazie sitting on the grass in their cozy hideaway, dining together on turkey, roast beef, and grilled salmon. Mazie was very polite, waiting patiently for each morsel Owen offered. Owen saved the wedding cake, nuts and mints for himself. It got a little crowded when Sparker joined them and sniffed at the empty plate. "Hold on," Owen told her, "The salmon is really good. I'll go get you some. Wait here." She did.

Owen's exit from under the table led him between his father's black wingtips and white woolen knee socks.

"Ah, there's my fine boy," Neal said and picked him up. "Having a good time?"

"Yep. Daddy, are we going over to Sarah's old house—I mean Grandma and Grandpa's after this?"

"Yes, for a little while. We'll pick up their luggage and take them to the airport for their trip to Scotland."

"When are they coming back?"

"They're going to spend the summer at Grandma's house in Edinburgh, and they'll come back in October and spend the rest of the year until next summer at Sarah's old house, which Murray bought."

"Good," Owen said, and then squirmed, "Let me down. Daddy, Sparker and Mazie are hungry."

"Are they?"

Owen pointed beneath the table, "They're under there. Take a look, Daddy."

Neal knelt down and peeked under the cloth, and there they were, the red-blonde Nova Scotia Duck Tolling Retriever panting beside the gooseberry-eyed calico cat. Neal, laughing, dropped the cloth. "Fill up that plate, Owen, you've got two hungry customers waiting."

"Daddy," Owen said, putting a large chunk of grilled salmon on his plate, "You never told me why."

"Why what?"

"Why did they play *A Little Night Music* during the day?"

"Oh, well, Mozart may have written it for a party that happened at night, but that doesn't mean that's the only time it can be played. People like it so much, they play it in the daytime, too."

"What's the one they're playing now?"

Neal smiled, "That's a great piece. It's also by Mozart. It's actually a song he wrote for a soprano voice. It's a funny sort of song because it only has one word that is repeated over and over."

"What word?"

Neal surveyed the scene, the place he loved and the people he loved with all his heart. He saw Sarah, beautiful with child, embracing his grandmother Barbara, as Murray stood by, glowing with joy. Over it all was the music, Mozart's exultant melody and harmonies, conceived, then imagined—not successively, but all at once—whole and complete in the composer's mind, and only then committed to paper, written note by note.

Creation is like that, thought Neal, a song in the mind of God: what was, what is, and what shall be, existing simultaneously, whole, complete, and perfect, played out note by note, a music so intricate and majestic that its temporary dissonances could only be part of an astonishing, profound, all-encompassing harmony.

Owen repeated his question, "What's the one word in the song, Daddy?"

Neal looked into the innocent, earnest brown eyes of his son. Owen, Sarah, Barbara, Murray, they were well; they were safe, and Neal's heart rejoiced. "The word, my son, which describes this day: *Alleluia*."

Notes and Acknowledgements

The massacres at Le Paradis and Wormhoudt, the war crimes tribunal, and all the participants were real events and people, except for the character Heinrich Fritzinger, who replaced the actual commanding SS officer at Le Paradis, Fritz Knochlein. Stephen Stratford's website, "British Military and Criminal History in the period 1900 to 1999," was a great resource for the trial information.

In Chapter 33, the direct quotes come from pp.127-128 of G. R. S. Mead's book *Orpheus,* and from p. 54 of *Adonis, Attis, Osiris,* by Sir James George Frazer. I read about Amphion's myth and other accounts of the power of music to lift heavy stones in Joscelyn Godwin's *Harmonies of Heaven and Earth.* The specific measurements in the account of Tibetan monks levitating stones came from David Pratt's website, "Gravity and Antigravity."

Much of the information about pipers came from Patrick King and Grahame Wickings' stirring two-part film, *Instrument of War: Ladies from Hell* and *Call to the Blood.* The rest came from observing my son Nicholas, who has played the bagpipes for the past fifteen years.

Thanks to Christine Moore, Music Librarian and String Instructor, Prairie View A&M University and David Bynog, Assistant Head of Acquisitions, Fondren Library, Rice University, for their cheerful and generous help with images and copyright information. Thanks to Martin Jakob Gander and Felix Kwok, Université de Genève, for their help with the Chladni figures and their article about the Chladni figures and the collapse of the Tacoma Bridge. Thanks to Jeff Volk for pointing out my inaccuracies concerning Hans Jenny's work. Special thanks to Liliane Licata of *AT Verlag* for her helpfulness and Christiaan Stuten for clarifying how the images were produced on the tonoscope.

Finally, this novel owes its life to Robert R. Ward, editor of *Bellowing Ark* Literary Journal and Bellowing Ark Press. Without his advice and encouragement, the novel would not exist. He published an earlier version (*The Elf King*) as a serial in *Bellowing Ark,* 2004-2005.

References

Burckhardt, Titus. *Alchemy: Science of the Cosmos, Science of the Soul.* Baltimore, Maryland: Penguin Books, Inc., 1967.

Chladni, Ernst F. F. *Entdeckungen über die Theorie des Klanges.* Leipzig: Weibmanns, Erben und Reich, 1787.

Davis, Henry. "Henry Davis Cartographic Images." www.henrydavis.com/MAPS/EMwebpages/226.html.

Frazer, Sir James George. *Adonis, Attis, Osiris:* Vol. 5, *The Golden Bough: A Study in Magic and Religion.* London: Macmillan, 1914.

Godwin, Joscelyn. *Harmonies of Heaven and Earth.* Vermont: Inner Traditions International, 1987.

Jenny, Hans. *Cymatics: A Study of Wave Phenomena and Vibration.* © 2001 MACROmedia Publishing, Eliot, ME, USA. wwwcymaticsource.com. Used by Permission.

King, Patrick and Wickings, Grahame. *Instrument of War: Ladies from Hell and Call to the Blood,* film in two parts, 2000.

Mead, G. R. S. *Orpheus.* New York: Barnes & Noble, 1896.

Pratt, David. "Gravity and Antigravity." http://davidpratt.info/gravity.htm

Stratford, Stephen. "British Military and Criminal History in the period 1900 to 1999." www.stephen-stratford.co.uk/pooleys_revenge.htm.

Author Bio

Wendy Isaac Bergin, a cradle Episcopalian and Louisiana native, is Associate Professor of Music at Prairie View A&M University and principal flutist of Houston's Opera in the Heights. Her paternal forbears include farmers, a Syrian Orthodox priest or two, and a pistol-packin' great grandmother. Included in her maternal line, amongst lumberjacks and teachers in the Pacific Northwest, is at least one red-haired piper who hailed from Edinburgh.

AUG -- 2014

CPSIA information can be obtained at www.ICGtesting.com
Printed in the USA
LVOW13s1705080714

393411LV00005B/1232/P